LARGE PRINT - MOS

REUNION AT MOSSY CREEK

To Edith O.K.
from
fond memories!

REUNION AT MOSSY CREEK

Why not?

To Edith

Good Luck!

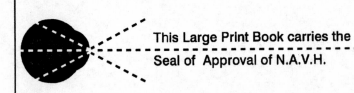

This Large Print Book carries the
Seal of Approval of N.A.V.H.

REUNION AT MOSSY CREEK

SURE! ☺.K.

A COLLECTIVE NOVEL BY
DEBORAH SMITH, SANDRA CHASTAIN,
DEBRA DIXON, VIRGINIA ELLIS,
NANCY KNIGHT, MARTHA SHIELDS,
CAROLYN MCSPARREN,
DEE STERLING, CARMEN GREEN,
AND SHARON SALA

O.K. **THORNDIKE PRESS** *thats enough!*
An imprint of Thomson Gale, a part of The Thomson Corporation

THOMSON
✶™
GALE

Detroit • New York • San Francisco • New Haven, Conn. • Waterville, Maine • London

THOMSON

GALE

Copyright © 2002 BelleBooks, Inc.
Mossy Creek Map: Dino Fritz.
Mossy Creek Series #2.
Thomson Gale is part of The Thomson Corporation.
Thomson and Star Logo and Thorndike are trademarks and Gale is a registered trademark used herein under license.

Thorndike Press® Large Print Clean Reads.
The text of this Large Print edition is unabridged.
Other aspects of the book may vary from the original edition.
Set in 16 pt. Plantin.

LIBRARY OF CONGRESS CATALOGING-IN-PUBLICATION DATA

Reunion at Mossy Creek / by Deborah Smith . . . [et al.].
   p. cm. — (Mossy Creek series ; #2)
ISBN-13: 978-0-7862-9518-0 (hardcover : alk. paper)
ISBN-10: 0-7862-9518-X (hardcover : alk. paper)
1. Large type books. I. Smith, Deborah, 1955–
PS3600.A1R48 2007
813'.6—dc22   2007003194

Published in 2007 by arrangement with BelleBooks, Inc.

Printed in the United States of America on permanent paper
10 9 8 7 6 5 4 3 2

REUNION AT MOSSY CREEK

MOSSY CREEK
POP. 1700 EST. 1839

1. CHINA BERRY
2. LOOKOVER
3. YONDER
4. BIGELOW
5. BAILEY MILL
6. TOWN HALL
7. O'DAYS PUB
8. GOLDILOCK'S SALON
9. DAN Mc.NEIL'S FIX IT
10. MAGNOLIA MANOR
11. THE NAKED BEAN
12. BEECHUM'S BAKERY
13. BLACKSHEAR'S VET.
14. HAMILTON'S DEPT. STORE
15. CANDLE FACTORY
16. HAMILTON HOUSE INN
17. BALL FIELD
18. POLICE STATION
19. HAMILTON FARM

WELCOME TO MOSSY CREEK
"AIN'T GOIN NOWHERE
—AND—
DON'T WANT TO"

W. MOSSY CREE

PINE ST.

SPRUCE ST.

MOSSY CREEK

TRAILHEAD R

N

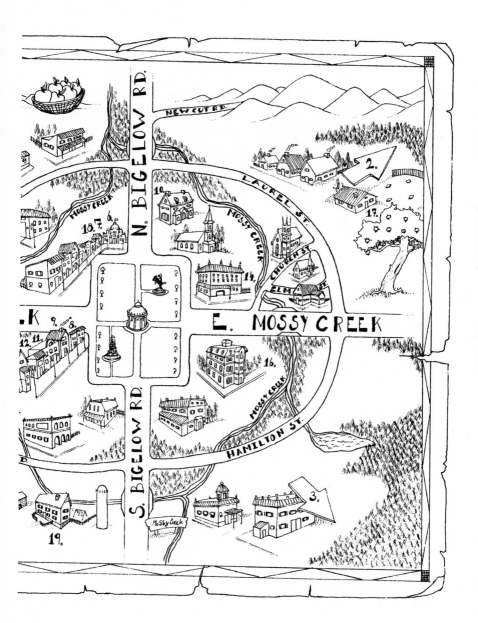

REUNION AT MOSSY CREEK

ABOUT MOSSY CREEK AND ITS AUTHORS

Welcome back to Mossy Creek!

We're so pleased to hear from readers who love our wise, warm, wonderful Southern village. This time, we invite you to enjoy the voices of some new writers who adore Mossy Creek as much as we do. They're all enthusiastic members of the "Mossy Creek Storytelling Club," with one goal in mind — to share a funny, thoughtful, and uplifting view of life in the little town we'd all like to call home.

Joining us for Reunion At Mossy Creek are five acclaimed authors whose tales are sure to win your hearts. Martha Shields is both an award-winning novelist and a new partner in BelleBooks. Sharon Sala is a *USA Today* and *New York Times* best-selling author of 42 books. Carmen Green, Carolyn McSparren, and Dee Sterling are all well-known and respected authors with

9

nearly two-dozen published novels between them. As an added treat we want you to meet Bubba Rice, the alter ego of down-home Tennessee chef, Wayne Dixon. Starting with Reunion At Mossy Creek, Wayne, aka Bubba Rice, will be sharing a few of his favorite recipes — and his own smile-inducing philosophy of life and food — with readers.

We're thrilled to introduce those new citizens of Mossy Creek, and we're sure you'll enjoy the love, laughter, and wisdom they have to offer along with those of the characters you've already come to know.

Thank you all for your tremendous support and enthusiasm. The Mossy Creek series has been received with enthusiasm beyond our fondest hopes. We owe it all to you the readers, booksellers, and librarians who have taken our town into your lives and made it your own.

A special thanks to Fred Rawlinson and Laura Austin for all their support, help and brushstrokes. We also want to thank our copyeditor, Maureen Hardegree, for keeping track of the many details of life in Mossy Creek, our friend and author Dee Sterling for her excellent editorial help, and our friend Anne Bishop for her wise, witty advice.

To: Lady Victoria Salter Stanhope,
Cornwall, England
From: Katie Bell
Mossy Creek, Georgia, *and*
Dear Vick: *thats enough!*

"Katie Bell," I ask myself as we start a year that will end with the biggest school reunion in Mossy Creek history, "do you need to write about the Ten-Cent Gypsy the town got from an anonymous troublemaker on New Year's Eve, or do you need to write about the reunion, or do you need to write about what people are *really* discussing: Are we finally going to learn who burned down Mossy Creek High School twenty years ago?" *O.K. YES*

Well, all three. Because the return of the Ten-Cent Gypsy, the reunion, and the fire are part of the same mystery.

The fire has become as much a part of

11

our town's heritage as the pioneer feud between Mossy Creek and Bigelow nearly 150 years ago, when — as you and I know, Vick — Isabella Salter disappeared after jilting her Bigelow fiancé and married Richard Stanhope, an Englishman who was here to work as a land surveyor. I figure it was my duty to help you solve the Salter/Stanhope mystery, and it's my duty to solve this new mystery, too.

Since nobody confessed to the fire twenty years ago, and it doesn't look as if anyone's going to step forward to confess sending the gypsy on New Year's Eve, I've decided to send out some surveys and see if I can get Creekites to reveal what they know. Of course, I have to be sly about it so I won't scare off the culprits, so I'm focusing on some innocent-sounding reunion questions.

See, I just *know* Creekites will wander off on tangents and tell stories about other things going on in their lives to try and distract me, because Creekites love a good story over telling the painful truth. But I'm going to ask them, anyway. Even if they don't answer, it'll get them talking. To show what a good sport I am, I'll tell them I intend to answer the survey, too. But I'm only sharing my real answers with *you*, Vick. Do you honestly think I'd let my whole town know all about *me*, the gossip queen? No way.

The first survey question is, *What do reunions mean to me?*

Do I answer that question honestly? Do I say that until I went to work for Sue Ora Salter Bigelow here at the newspaper I believed I was a nobody with nothing to make me special?

The Bigelow High School annual called me the Perkiest Student in the Senior Class. But *perky* can also mean *annoying,* a pain in the neck. When Sue Ora Salter Bigelow hired me, she gave me permission to be *really* perky. So I'm perky and important. People come to me. They want the inside information on what's going on in Mossy Creek. As for the reunion, do I want to go? You bet I do. I want all those out-of-towners who don't know how important I've become to find out that I'm a local celebrity — not that I'm in the least conceited about that.

When I look at the vacant lot where Mossy Creek High stood until the mysterious fire twenty years ago, I think,

What a waste. People get attached to a place and its past, but Creekites pay homage more than most. That isn't a bad thing; it's more of a promise. We don't destroy you because you are no longer of use. We wrap you in memories and keep you here.

Next question: *Do I have a hurtful, public humiliation in my past?*

All right, I was jilted on the night of the senior prom at Bigelow High — everyone knows us Creekite kids had a rough time attending Bigelow after Mossy Creek High burned down. I say it doesn't matter any more. But it does.

On to question three: *What was the one thing that happened to you in high school that made you what you are today?*

Well, I've already confessed. Being stood up for that prom. I decided then that I'd find a way to make the world notice me. Being the business manager and gossip columnist for the paper may be a small thing in the scheme of things but it gives me prestige. And guess what — I finally figured out that the power I have heals more than my own wounds. There are a lot of people in the world like me, and I can slant the news any way I choose, to help them out.

14

If I can just solve the fire, reunion, and New Year's Eve mystery of the Ten-Cent Gypsy, I can help the whole town and maybe win a Pulitzer Prize. Hey, stranger things happen all the time . . . in Mossy Creek.

Read on, Vick, and you'll see what I mean. O.K. SURE

RAINEY

THE TEN-CENT GYPSY

Maybe beauty is only skin deep, but our memories of childhood can't always be made pretty and pink.

Reunions. Lor'. Nothing but trouble. Everyone in Mossy Creek was excited about the next fall's big celebration except me. I knew the truth. The secret of who caused the fire. And that secret would tangle my town's memories and sorrows worse than a cheap perm.

The mysterious gift Mossy Creek got on New Year's Eve haunted my dreams at night, driving out fond favorites where I'm doing Wynona Judd's hair backstage at the Grammy awards and Hank Williams, Junior, walks into the dressing room to introduce me to Elvis. Young Elvis, not Las Vegas Elvis.

No more good dreams like that, no. In the weeks since New Year's, the 'gift' had been all people could talk about in Mossy Creek, and all my nightmares were filled with it. Mayor Ida ordered the thing set inside the lobby of city hall. "The gift," Mayor Ida announced, "was sent to us as a taunt. It belongs to the town, and the town has to deal with it." Mayor Ida dares people to come forward and confess what they know about the night Mossy Creek High School burned to the ground twenty years ago. I agree with the mayor's plan in principle. That night represented one of the darkest unsolved mysteries of our town's history, and, some would say, the darkest secrets of our own hearts.

Including mine.

Early this morning, I bundled up in my favorite pink ski jacket and my pink jeans and set out to look the past square in its dark, plastic eyes. Thirty-four years old and scared of a fake fortuneteller. Lor', the embarrassment. I put on pink blush and pink lipstick and even did my nails pink. Pink is a happy color, and though people often think I'm just a good ol' girl with tacky taste, I considered myself a sophisticated *pink* good ol' girl. With tacky *pink* taste.

I trudged up Main Street on that cold January morning, blowing frosty breaths and keeping my head down. I even waved off Jayne Reynolds at The Naked Bean when she appeared in the coffee shop doorway and held out my favorite pink mug full of latte. I just shook my head. Jayne looked at me kind of funny. Everyone was looking at me kind of funny since I'd blurted out that "I only mixed the perm, I didn't put it on her," comment at the New Year's Eve party, when we opened the crate and saw the Gypsy inside.

For the past two weeks, I'd laughed off the moment and told everyone I was just drunk on Irish Ringers, a hot whiskey-and-cranberry drink Michael Conners invented at the pub. But no one has forgotten what I said.

"Are you feeling all right?" Jayne called out, wrapping her pregnant self in one of Ingrid Beechum's baby blankets. "You look pale, Rainey."

Pale? I whipped out my compact and added a dab more pink powder to each cheek. Lor', even my pinkness was failing me.

"I'm not pale," I called. "I'm chilly."

I made myself keep walking. Mossy Creek Town Hall loomed ahead of me like a temple of doom, though it was the friendliest government building you can imagine, with a lot of natural stonework and warm oak timbers. The Mossy Creek Garden Club kept up the front terrace, so even in the cold dead of winter there was a neat bed of pinebark mulch around the big mountain laurels and a few dozen pansy seedlings poking their tough green leaves out from under dwarf azaleas that would bloom a soft watermelon color in springtime. I brushed a hand over one of those bare azaleas for courage just before I opened the lobby door. I thought of all the good intentions Mother Nature hides inside a plain wood stem. I tried to think of my innocence that way, too.

No sooner had the glass door swung shut behind me than I saw the object of my misery. It sat in the middle of the lobby, which is ordinarily a sweet and inviting place. Creekites go into the lobby of town hall to read the community bulletin boards. Not to be confronted with the guilty mistakes of their pasts.

I stopped like a squirrel trapped in front of an oncoming truck. Just stopped, my heart pounding in my throat the same way it did that night at the Hamilton House Inn, when Dan MacNeil opened the crate.

The Ten-Cent Gypsy looked back at me.

She hadn't had an easy life, wherever she'd been stored over the past twenty years. Her metal carnival booth was all dented up and a little rusted. The gypsy herself stared back at me through a windowless opening in the booth's top half. I told myself she was still just a mannequin, not even a full-length mannequin, because her waist disappeared in an apron of ratty, fake-red silk bunched up on a rusty metal shelf. Her paint was old, and her plastic face needed a good makeover. Fuzzy-curly black synthetic hair hung in tangles from beneath a dusty scarf tied around her forehead. Somebody had spilled something greasy on her puffy red blouse, and half the beads in her flashy arm bracelets were missing. She was also missing a forefinger on her card hand, and she needed a manicure.

"You don't scare me," I lied loudly. "Just you do your job and provoke somebody to tell the truth about that fire, so me and Hank Blackshear and Rob Walker can finally clear our consciences. *We didn't cause the fire.*" I paused, feeling sick at my stomach with doubts that had gnawed at me for twenty years. "And even if we did, we didn't mean to. You hear?" She stared back like the silent dead. My eyes went to the little slot below the window. The instructions were still simple:

Put in 10 cents and pull the lever.
If you dare.

"You're all brag and bad eye shadow. Haven't got a single card left in your system, I bet."

I jabbed a dime into the slot, grabbed the rusty lever on the booth's right side, and jerked it down. The mechanical innards whirred and clicked, and suddenly the gypsy's dusty card hand began to rise. I took a step back. The gypsy's stiff arm went up and up until the hand with its missing forefinger was pointing right at me, or sort of, anyway, considering the pointing finger was busted off. It was like she was shaking her fist at me, instead. I looked at the slot in the hand's palm, and, Lor'! A little card popped out.

I couldn't move. I didn't want to touch that card. Finally, I thrust out a hand and snatched the card by my fingertips.

THE TRUTH MUST BE TOLD.

I jammed the card in my pocket then made myself walk out of the building with a calm face. My knees were weak. I trembled. When I got back to my salon, I locked the door and sat stiffly in one of my styling chairs. In the mirrors parading down one faux-pink-marble wall, I saw my scared and guilty and sad face from a dozen angles.

21

It was going to be a long year in Mossy Creek, with a lot of nail-biting and second-guessing and gossiping and maneuvering for answers to a question that had haunted us for twenty years. Who had burned down Mossy Creek High School?

I still didn't have the courage to admit what I knew about *that.*

KATIE BELL

MY DETECTIVE WORK BEGINS TO PAY OFF

Rainey came to me with her survey answers, but to tell you the truth, they weren't worth reading — she'd just written a lot of cute little pleasantries that weren't the least bit revealing. So I said, casually, "I heard you went to see the Ten-Cent Gypsy. Sandy Crane spotted you coming out of town hall with one of the cards in your hand. Anything interesting on it?"

And Rainey jumped. Aha.

Rainey's the kind of woman who's never quite gotten past things that happened to her as a kid, so she rushes back to her childhood friends when she's upset. I could go into specifics, but I won't, other than to mention that I'm one of the few people who know she's been in love with Rob Walker, the mayor's son, for over twenty years.

"I didn't get any card from the Gypsy," she lied. "Sandy's mistaken."

"Oh, well, I was just curious." I filed her

little lie for future consideration. "It'll be interesting to see how that gypsy provokes people's attitudes around here. The effect's already noticeable, you know."

"How do you mean?" she asked in a nervous voice.

"The examination of personal secrets and truths has begun. You'll see. Roots are coming to the surface."

Rainey touched her hair as if calculating her next dye job. "Not mine."

I smiled. Everyone has to take care of his or her roots, and sometimes that means burying them too deep for the world to touch.

On that terrible night in Mossy Creek twenty years ago, I watched the fire destroy my alma mater and cried like everyone else in town.

Did you know that the Miss Mossy Creek Pageant was discontinued the year after the school burned? The only contest left for our girls was the Miss Bigelow County Pageant. The last holder of the Miss Mossy Creek title was LuLynn Lipscomb, now married and known as LuLynn McClure. Her nineteen-year-old daughter, Josie, competed gallantly in last year's Miss Bigelow pageant, trying to uphold her family's honor and Mossy Creek's, too. Poor Josie. I don't think napkin arranging qualifies as a talent, even in Mossy Creek.

But that's an observation I'll just keep to myself.

JOSIE

THE EYE OF THE BEHOLDER

It's always the quiet girls who are up to something secret and shocking. But what do you do when you've fallen in love, and everybody needs to know it?

I saw Katie Bell's survey in the paper. I even wrote out some answers. I just never sent them in. Nobody would've expected me to, anyway, if they'd thought about it. I'm not expected to do anything well. Not anymore. But here are my answers.

What do reunions mean to you?

Reunions? I guess Katie Bell means *family* reunions. I only graduated from Bigelow High School two years ago, so my class certainly wouldn't have had a reunion yet.

I think I'd better not answer that question. It'd hurt Daddy's feelings for sure. The McClure family reunion, held at a state park just north of Mossy Creek every year, has always been pure torture for me. The Mc-Clure relatives feel sorry for poor, plain little

Josie. They think I don't hear them talk while I'm helping Mama set out the food, but I do. I don't like going to reunions. I wish I never had to go to another one.

When you look at the empty spot where the high school stood, what person comes to mind, and why?

Mama, of course. She's told me the story of how the homecoming queen crown was stolen from her so many times, I know it by heart. Mama was about to be crowned queen of Mossy Creek High when the school mascot, a ram — which in my opinion is just a fancy name for a boy sheep — shot out of the stands with sparklers tied to its wool. That sheep left a path of mayhem and destruction that's affected Mossy Creek to this very day.

What is the most hurtful and publicly humiliating thing that ever happened to you in high school?

That one's easy to answer. It was when Derk Bigelow asked me to the Christmas dance my junior year at Bigelow High, and I stupidly believed he meant it. He'd just broken up with his girlfriend, Marjorie Tutmeir, after all, and even though Derk is from the richest family in Bigelow County — he's a second cousin of Governor Ham Bigelow — he's not the cutest puppy in the litter, if

27

you know what I mean.

Mama proudly bought me the most beautiful green velvet dress in Miss Martin's Boutique in Mossy Creek. I would rather have kept my business to myself, but of course Mama had to brag to everyone that I needed the dress because I was going to the Christmas dance with a Bigelow — though I have to admit I secretly enjoyed their reactions. They were shocked that Josie McClure, of all people, could manage such a feat. A girl they considered such a wallflower that surely I must've taken root by then. Unfortunately, that publicity meant that everyone in Mossy Creek found out about my ultimate humiliation as well.

The night of the dance, I waited at the double doors of the high school gym like Derk had suggested since he didn't want to drive all the way up into the mountainous northern end of Bigelow County at night to get me. I noticed other kids staring at me, some snickering together, but they'd always done that if I happened to show up at an extracurricular school function, which was as rare an occurrence as roses in January.

When Derk showed up at seven on the dot, Marjorie was on his arm. He hadn't broken up with her at all. Turns out I was the victim of a bet he'd made with a couple of other boys, members of the cruel Fang and Claw Society, no doubt. Would I be stupid enough to dress up and wait for him at the gym door?

I was. Derk made his buddies pay him right there in front of me.

If I'd only known then that Derk was a Scorpio-Rat . . . and what that means. After Derk, I started studying astrology so I could recognize people when I saw them coming. Astrology is just another of my peculiar interests. I guess it doesn't matter now, but I never went to another school event after that.

What is the one thing that happened to you in high school that made you the person you are today?

That's an easy one, too. My tenth grade Home Ec class. That was where I discovered the zen of decorating.

I fold napkins.

Like me, that's more special than it sounds.

When you live in the mountains, you grow up hearing tales of Bigfoot. Any mountains. From California to Maine, from Ohio to Georgia, Bigfoot or Sasquatch has made an appearance. I'd long suspected he was made up by mothers who used the legend to keep their children from wandering the steep terrain and getting lost.

Once I realized that Bigfoot was simply the Appalachian version of the boogie man, and that the biggest dangers I faced in the wooded coves were black bears and the elements, I was out the door of my parents' house and climbing the ridges up Mount Colchik to my playground, my freedom, my sanctuary. Colchik made a wild green hummock against the northern horizon of Mossy Creek. Up on Colchik, I was queen.

When I began studying feng shui — led to it by an article about the Eastern philosophy of decorating in an issue of *Martha Stewart Living* — I learned that mountains are really sleeping dragons, and the peaks, the humps of their backs. Not only is dragon's breath the best *chi* — or energy — there is, but Snakes and Dragons get along extremely well. That's important because I'm a Snake, astrologically speaking. Blending the Western and Eastern astrologies — which I always do — I'm a Cancer-Snake. A shy, secretive, home-loving recluse. A wallflower, in other words, though I prefer to think of myself more as a mountain laurel, perhaps, that blooms high up on the cold slopes, mostly unseen.

But I knew before I'd ever heard about

feng shui, or even astrology, for that matter, that there was no danger for me in my mountains. Every time I disappeared into the primal forests, I felt as if my friend the Dragon were folding safe, warm arms around me. I feared neither black bears — which I occasionally spotted — or Bigfoot, whom I never saw.

Until . . .

I began seeing the footprints last spring, just before the dreaded Miss Bigelow Contest, which Mama forced me to enter. I needed the Dragon's strength quite a bit then and visited Mount Colchik every day. The sun's warmth had penetrated the thick hardwood foliage enough by May to keep the earth thawed.

The first footprint was in the mud beside the pool beneath a waterfall so deep in the mountains it had no name as far as I knew. I swam in the pool during the summer months. I passed the footprint off as a freak incident. Animal tracks falling together in a familiar pattern. Sort of like seeing shapes in the clouds.

By the time I found the fifth print several months later, I suspected some children were playing pranks. My pool was several hours hike from the nearest road or farm, and I'd never seen anyone else — child or grownup — wandering my mountain. Still, I'd found the pool when I was ten years old. Other children could've found it, too.

The possibility depressed me. Not that children might be clowning around. Children did those kinds of things. But I felt as if my privacy had been violated. Colchik was *my* mountain. This was *my* pool. I didn't want to share my space with anyone. The possibility of a real Bigfoot existing never occurred to me, not in any serious way. How many humans had bare footprints that measured close to eighteen inches?

None of the explanations frightened me, and none could keep me from finding solace in my mountains. Especially after the Miss Bigelow Contest when Mama railed night and day about me losing. The forest was the only place I felt welcome, the only place I felt part of the world around me. Nature didn't care where you placed in any kind of contest. It treated you with the same nonchalance with which it treated every other creature. Mama, however, was another matter.

As I've said, Mama was Mossy Creek High School's last homecoming queen . . . but she was never crowned. The high school burned down that night, dooming Mama's glorious reign. She's never gotten over it.

So for the last nineteen years she's been trying to make me into the beauty queen she never got to be.

There's only one problem. Me. Wallflowers get crowned only in fairy tales.

Mama, however, didn't find it easy to face reality. She groomed me for the Miss Bigelow Pageant from the day I was born, though I cringed every time she mentioned it. She was determined that her daughter would be queen of the entire county, and she dedicated her life to this end. I had every kind of grooming, etiquette, and dancing lesson she could find within a day's drive. She was constantly telling me how to walk, how to stand, how to wave, how to smile. Nothing I did was ever good enough. It certainly wasn't good enough to win the Miss Bigelow crown. When I came in dead last, the entire reason for Mama's existence fell in like a house of cards. She blamed me, of course. She'd done her part.

I was the one who wouldn't do mine.

Mama began sipping Daddy's best whiskey. Mama hated winter, hated the cold weather that was coming. She made me feel like she hated *me,* too. I'd never felt so depressed. Never felt so ugly, so totally worthless. So I escaped up on Colchik even more. That's where I finally met Bigfoot.

I sat on the edge of the pool under Josie Falls — as I'd named them — and pondered what to do. I didn't want to go back home — ever. Why should I? I was a grown woman. Nineteen years old. Graduated from high school. Mama didn't want me. Every time she looked at me, she started crying, cursing, or drinking. On the other hand, I couldn't leave home because I had no way to support myself. No skills beyond textbook Martha Stewart decorating, and decorating jobs required at least some college education. I'd checked the Internet on the library computer.

As I stared into water so clear I could see trout swimming six feet down, so cold it formed a crust of ice around the edges at night, the water seemed to whisper to me, inviting me in. *You're needed here, Josie. The mountain loves you. Stay here and stop fighting your loneliness.*

The falls had never lied to me, so I listened, even though I knew I was depressed and should back away. As the afternoon began to wane, I became convinced the whispers were right. I wanted to merge with my mountains, to melt into the tears that spewed from its side.

I rose stiffly, my muscles cramped from

inactivity and the cold rock I sat on. Slowly, I undressed. I'd always swum nude, though never in weather cold enough to hurt me. I'd never been embarrassed or ashamed of my nakedness here. I was down to my underwear when out the corner of my eyes, I saw movement in a shrub nearby. Looking up — way up — I saw a man's face.

I turned to run. My feet caught in the clothes I'd just removed. With a cry, my arms flailing for support, I fell into the ice-cold water. Needles stabbed into every part of my body, disorienting me so much I couldn't tell which way was up. I tried to surface but sank like a lead doll. I couldn't move. I couldn't feel my hands or feet.

Then the world turned black.

The next thing I knew, I awoke to blessed warmth. *Maybe this is a dream,* I murmured. I sighed and snuggled into my blanket co-coon.

"Did you say something?"

The deep voice directly above me made my eyes spring open. A mountain of a man leaned over me. The biggest, longest-bearded man I'd ever seen. His large hand probed my face. "You're not running a fever, thank God. Can you hear me? Do you understand what I'm saying?" His voice

35

rumbled more than spoke, so deep it came from his belly instead of his throat. A dark red, puckered scar covered his forehead and left eye. There was probably more to it, but that's all I could see above his beard.

"Are you an angel?" I asked.

His eyes narrowed. "Very funny."

He certainly didn't look like the traditional representation of an angel, but since I'd studied feng shui and the philosophies it was based on, my spiritual path had meandered along many nontraditional trails. "I'm not trying to be funny," I whispered. "Am I alive?"

"Of course you're alive." He straightened. His head seemed to brush the raw plank ceiling of his cabin. "Though it's a miracle. If I hadn't fished you out when I did. . . ." He heaved a sigh and moved away from the bed.

I rolled over in my cocoon of warm blankets so my gaze could follow him. Three strides of his long legs took him clear across to the other side of the room to a stone fireplace. A roaring fire blazed in the natural stone hearth under a black cauldron suspended from an iron bar running across the top. He stirred whatever simmered in the pot. It smelled wonderful.

"You saved me?" My mind felt as if it, too,

were wrapped in a cocoon.

"Somebody had to."

"Where am I?"

"My cabin."

"I mean where is *that,* in relation to Josie Falls?"

He straightened from the hearth. "Josie Falls?"

"I named them. Do they have a name already?"

"Not that I know of."

"Then I officially name them Josie Falls."

"What made you decide to take a swim today? You haven't been in the pool since early September."

"How do you know that?" But the idea that he'd been watching me didn't alarm me. Rather, it felt . . . warm . . . intriguing.

"Well, I'm not a stalker. When people start dropping their clothes by a pool, I assume they're about to go swimming. I don't stay around to watch."

"Who are you?" I tried to sit up, but weakness and the tight cocoon hampered me. He stepped over and easily lifted me against the bed's rough headboard. His head really did almost touch the ceiling, and his shoulders were as wide as a century-old hemlock. "Gracious, you're big."

He shoved both hands back through his

thick black hair. "Good thing. A smaller man would never have been able to carry you two miles over rough terrain."

I leaned over to look at his feet. "Ohmigosh. You're the Bigfoot!"

He growled something and turned back to the hearth. I didn't know then that he'd been called the awful name ever since he'd grown into his size twenty-two shoes.

"I've seen footprints ever since April."

He scooped some of the cauldron's contents into a bowl. "Who are you?" I repeated. "Why are you living way up here alone?"

After pouring something from a brown bottle into a tin cup, he brought that and the bowl over to the bed. Looking from them to me, he finally sat down and lifted the spoon to my mouth.

I turned my head away. "I want answers."

"Eat. You put your body through a traumatic shock and you need nourishment."

I was alone with a mountain of a mountain man who spoke like a college professor. Whoever he was, even hidden behind the beard he was clearly no backwoodsman — and a good deal older than me. As a shy wallflower, I should've been frightened out of my wits, but somehow I knew he would never hurt me. My astrological instincts, you might say. Emboldened by my certainty, I glared at him. "Not until you tell me who you are." I struggled to free my arms from the blankets. "Let me out of this thing."

He sighed, put down the bowl, and loosened the coverings enough for me to fight my arms free. As I did, the blankets fell to my waist, and I looked down to see nothing but my thermal undershirt.

I yanked the blankets up. I wasn't feeling *that* bold.

Hot blood stung my cheeks.

He coughed and stood up. Yanking open a chest of drawers, he grabbed a flannel shirt and tossed it on the bed. "Awfully big, but you can wear it."

Once he retreated to the other side of the cabin to stare into the fire, I let the blanket drop and quickly donned his shirt. The soft, thick material swallowed me, suffusing my brain with an unknown yet primordial and familiar scent — the musky warmth of a man. Rattled by my perception, I folded back the sleeve cuffs four times so I could find my hands, then fastened every button except the collar. Finally, I announced, "I'm decent."

He returned to the bed, picked up the bowl and once again lifted the spoon to my mouth. "Eat, and I'll tell you who I am."

I opened my mouth.

He slipped the spoon inside. "My name is Harold Rutherford. I bought this place two summers ago."

I swallowed the thick flavorful stew. "This is delicious."

"Thank you."

"Why?"

His lips, half-hidden by his beard, curved upward. "Why is it delicious?"

He had a sense of humor. I fell half in love with him at that moment. "No. Why did you move so far up into the mountains?"

He hesitated, then deliberately turned his scarred face toward the fire. "To hide."

"Those scars look like burns. Were you burned?" I reached out a hand. "When?"

At my first touch, he stood abruptly, upsetting the tin cup still sitting on the bed. I caught the cup before it could spill, then licked the drops that sloshed onto my fingers. "Whiskey. You're a real mountain man, I guess. From what I hear, they use whiskey to treat everything."

"I thought it might warm you up."

"You accomplished that without whiskey." I couldn't believe the huskiness of my voice. It sounded almost . . . sultry. Me. Josie Mc-Clure.

He must've heard it, too, because he

turned back to me. "Josie . . ."

"You know my name." It didn't surprise me.

The fire popped, drawing his attention. It took a moment before he looked at me again. "Look under the pillow beside you."

I reached under the feather pillow to find my navy blue sweater.

"You left it beside the falls about a month ago."

I didn't have to look at the tag to know my name was written there in indelible ink. Mama couldn't get over the fact that I wasn't in grade school anymore. "I remember. It grew warm that day, and I took it off before I waded in the pool. I was halfway home before I realized I'd forgotten it. Since it was so late, I decided to come back for it the next day. When it wasn't there, I figured some animal had stolen it to pad his den." I grinned. "I was right."

He was not amused.

I dropped my gaze to the sweater in my hands. "Were you . . . watching me that day?"

He seemed to struggle with himself, then finally said, "Yes."

"I see." I lifted the sweater to my nose and inhaled. It smelled faintly like me, but mostly like warm wool, and mountains . . .

and Harry. I smiled. Harry. What an appropriate name. I didn't feel the least bit bad about shortening his name without his permission. Then I shivered, realizing I was already able to recognize his scent.

"What in the world are you thinking?" he asked.

"That you smell good."

He hesitated, then said firmly, "Stop joking."

"No joke." I swung my legs over the side of the bed and stood. The tail of his shirt fell to my knees.

He took half a step toward me. "You need to stay in —"

"No."

He watched, seemingly mesmerized, as I walked over to him. I wobbled the slightest bit, more from shyness than weakness. I'd never done anything so bold in my life, never approached a man without something to serve him in my hands. But instinct told me Harry wasn't going to come to me . . . and I had an overwhelming need to touch him.

He flinched as I reached up, but he didn't move away.

I ran my fingers across his forehead. "You're just like me."

"What?" He shook his head. "No. You're

beautiful."

Tears stung my eyes. "No one has ever said that to me."

"I can't believe . . ."

"You feel like a freak, don't you?" My harsh words made him blink, but I kept going. "You think no one wants you, so you hide high in the mountains."

"I'm doing the world a kindness, believe me. Children have actually run away when they've seen me. My four-year-old niece screamed . . ." His voice choked.

"I have the opposite effect. People look right through me. I blend into the walls." Hesitantly, I rested my hands on his broad chest. "So we *are* just alike. I'm your mirror image."

"No, we're not just alike," he said. "You won't eat, and I will."

"Try me."

We settled on opposite sides of a rough-planked table, which he told me he'd made. He'd fashioned everything in the cabin from wood he'd cut in the forest around him.

We talked the night through. There was no pretense, none of the silly games that men and women play as they get to know each other. Because we already knew each other's darkest secrets, all that remained was catching up on our lives until now. We

43

did that with avid interest. I was not at all surprised when I discovered that my Harry was a Dragon. A Taurus-Dragon. Might and bite married together in two earth elements.

Although he was living like one, technically Harry hadn't made a career out of being a hermit. A Ph.D. in environmental botany had earned him a grant from the University of Georgia to study the effect of acid rain on the indigenous plants of the Appalachian Mountains. He lived up there alone in the mountains above Mossy Creek because he believed he didn't fit in anywhere else. From the time he was old enough to notice, Harry had been taller and smarter than everyone around him. He was six-two by the time he graduated from high school at sixteen, and had reached his full six-foot-eight by twenty-three when he'd earned his doctorate. A serious house fire at twenty-seven had left him badly burned. He'd spent nearly a year in the hospital, then three years being scarred inwardly by people's reactions to his appearance. Now he lived on Mount Colchik.

The next morning, Harry gave me my dry clothes and walked me down the mountain. He stopped a good mile from the edge of our farm, adamantly refusing to return to civilization. There, amid the falling leaves of a maple, he took me in his arms and kissed me.

When he drew back, we stared into each other's eyes. It felt wrong leaving him. "If you won't come down, I will go up."

"You're too young," he said, as if trying to convince himself. "You don't need to spend time with an old man."

I rolled my eyes. "Thirty-two is hardly old. Besides, I've found you now, and I'm not going to let you go."

I ran the rest of the way home. When I opened the door, I found my mother in hysterics.

"Where have you been?" she demanded.

"In a dragon's lair," I said, and nothing else.

Our relationship changed that day. She no longer intimidated me or made me desperately want to explain myself. I realized later that I didn't just *awaken* in Harry's cabin on that January day.

I'd been reborn.

I trekked up to the top of Colchik almost daily for the next two weeks, to visit Harry. I quickly found out why I'd never seen him all those months he watched me. He was stealthy as a mountain lion. I would walk into the forest and suddenly he would be

45

walking beside me, or he would scoop me into his arms, or a sprig of holly would appear in front of my face, held by a large, callused hand.

I wanted him desperately, but he was determined that we keep our distance. He'd given up the world, and I would have to as well, if I admitted I'd fallen in love with him. At that point in my life, I would've given up everything to be with him. He made me feel special and beautiful and sexy — me, Josie the wallflower who finished dead last in the Miss Bigelow Beauty Contest — and I loved him with every cell in my body. But as winter wrapped a firm grip around the mountains, my life began to change even more.

It was as if change begat more change.

Yet Harry wouldn't come down from the mountain, wouldn't venture into my world. At the same time, my world began to expand as if the change in me showed.

I entered The Naked Bean coffee shop on Main Street and ordered a cup of amaretto-flavored cocoa and two shortbread cookies, then settled into a seat at a far corner table.

I'd nibbled halfway through one of the cookies, closing my eyes to savor the rich buttery taste, when the scrape of a chair made them pop open. Jayne smiled at me a little sadly as she sat down carefully. I barely knew her — she was new to town — but I'd heard all about her and her tragic story. Her husband had died of leukemia. Right after the funeral, she'd learned she was pregnant. Mired in grief and searching for comfort, she'd moved to Mossy Creek from Atlanta with nothing but her savings, her cat, Emma, and her unborn baby. She patted her large, pregnant stomach and began to ask questions . . . about me.

No one except Harry had ever showed an interest in what I did — mainly because I didn't do anything — so I was leery at first. I've watched people for a long time, however, so I recognize false interest when I see it. Jayne's was sincere.

"I hear you have a talent for decorating," she said.

"I . . . only fold napkins."

"Now, really? That's fascinating."

She mentioned how badly The Naked Bean needed a professional touch and asked how Martha Stewart would redecorate. I gave her a few suggestions — and I have to admit they weren't all Martha's. Jayne particularly liked one of mine. I suggested hanging the works of local artists on one wall.

"That's great," Jayne said. "Not only would it be something for people to talk about, it'd be a reason for them to visit the shop."

"I'm sure some of the local artists would love to use one of your walls as a gallery to sell their work." I got up enthusiastically and began measuring her front windows with the span of my arms. "I can picture blue toile curtains on these windows, and over there in that corner, a whitewashed antique cupboard full of tea cups, and a delicate little white lamp on a tiny shelf in that corner, and . . ." I stopped, embarrassed.

Her eyes sparkled. "You're hired."

"What?"

"How soon can you have a re-decorating plan outlined for me?"

The door chimes jingled. She got up to meet her neighbor, Ingrid Beechum, who entered carrying a carrot cake from her bakery. I sat there with my mouth open.

Someone would actually hire me to decorate? I would do it for free, and I told Jayne so when she returned to the table.

"No, you won't," she insisted. "You'll never be a professional until you charge money."

And so I did. Not much, mind you. Just

enough to satisfy her.

When I finally climbed Colchik a few days later, I saw Harry when I was still thirty yards away — which should've been my first clue something was wrong. I never saw Harry until he wanted me to see him.

He picked me up as I ran into his arms. "Where have you been? I was so worried."

"Don't squeeze so hard," I said. "I can't breathe."

He set me on the ground and pushed the hair off my face with trembling hands. "I thought something horrible had happened to you."

"My dearest Harry. Something *wonderful* happened."

I told him about my work for Jayne in vivid detail as we walked the mountain. I didn't notice until we reached Josie Falls that misery had settled in his dark eyes.

I stopped. "Why aren't you happy for me?"

"I *am* happy. It's just that you're finding your place in the world. Down the mountain — in Mossy Creek. I envy you. But it tells me you don't belong up here. With me."

I stood back from him and said simply, "There will never be a single moment in my life when I don't want you."

He touched my face very gently. "Stay tonight, Josie."

I didn't know what to do or say. I wanted him so much, but I was afraid I'd never go back down the mountain if I let myself fall more in love, and I owed him the truth. I bowed my head. "Swee Purla is a famous decorator down in Bigelow. She saw the work I did at The Naked Bean and offered me a job as her assistant. She did some mean things to an assistant named Geena Quill last year, but I've heard she's trying to be nicer to her employees, now."

He didn't move a muscle, didn't say a word.

I took a deep breath of cold mountain air. "I accepted."

"So you've come to say goodbye?"

"Of course not. It's just a part-time job. I'll only be working when she needs extra help. I'm sorry I haven't been to see you, I just got so involved in the project, and before I knew it, five days had passed. I've never had an opportunity like this, and I probably never will again. I have to see it through. I have to see if I'm any good at it. If I don't, I'll wonder all my life."

He stepped back. "It feels good to be appreciated, to be accepted. I know."

"Mossy Creek would accept you if you'd come down off this mountain. People are herd animals. We're meant to live together, not like hermits."

"Then live with me." His deep voice held a thin edge of pleading. "Decorate my cabin. Keep me from being a hermit."

"We'd just be *two* hermits, then." I took one of his hands and held it against my cheek. "Come to town and live with *me*, Harry. We could have a house at the edge of the forest. You wouldn't have to socialize often. The people in Mossy Creek are all a little weird themselves, anyway, so they would never say anything to —"

He grabbed my hand and began dragging me toward his cabin.

"What are you doing?"

"I'm going to show you exactly what they'd have to accept."

When we reached his cabin, he dug a mirror and razor out of his chest. He hung a small mirror on a nail in the wall, dipped soap in hot water from the cauldron he kept over coals, and shaved off his beard. After he wiped off the last trace of soap, he hesitated, then turned to me.

The burn scars curved around his face, half red, half white, crudely forming the shape of the classic symbol for yin and yang.

My eyes wide with wonder, I edged closer to him and ran my fingers along the scars, whispering reverently, "You've been kissed by the Dragon."

"A fire-breathing dragon." But his ire was uncertain now, as if he didn't know how to react to my reaction.

"Yin and yang represent perfect balance — dark and light, positive and negative, male and female. Opposites working together to create a balanced whole. Mirror images." I smiled. "Like us. Oh, Harry, you're the most beautiful man I've ever seen. I love who you are — here . . ." I placed a hand over his heart. ". . . And here." I put my other hand on his cheek. "Now I know why I developed a sudden interest in studying Eastern philosophy. I was getting ready for you."

"Josie . . ." His hands circled my wrists.

I met his gaze squarely. "I have to take this job, Harry."

He nodded. "I know."

"The only way you and I can spend more time together is for you to come down off this mountain."

His eyes were bleak. "I've been there, done that. It wasn't fun."

"But I wasn't there." When he was silent, I knew. "Then there's nothing else to say, is there?"

He searched my eyes. "Is this goodbye?"

"No. I don't know. Yes. You want me to

give up the world." Tears blinded me. "I want to share it with you. You don't know how long I've waited."

"Yeah, I do. That's why I won't stop you."

"Josie, do you *ever* stop folding napkins?"

Startled by the wry voice, I looked up to see Katie Bell standing on the other side of the refreshment table. I'd already decorated the table, making it ready for the desserts everyone brought to sweeten the Presbyterian Church's annual Valentine's Sweetheart Bingo.

"No, ma'am," I said.

Though Katie Bell's words were sharp, she didn't intend them to be mean. She was a Taurus-Tiger, after all. They pounced on everything. That's why she was such a good journalist, and certainly why her gossip column was a must-read for everyone in Mossy Creek.

"Practicing your talent for next year's Miss Bigelow Contest?"

I tucked the tail on a napkin whooping crane into its spine and set it alongside the dragon I'd made first. Dragons always came first. "No. My beauty pageant days are over. Now I only make my napkin animals for the good of mankind."

"Have you told your Mama you're not

making another run for the crown?"

"Yes, ma'am." I picked up another napkin, wishing Swee Purla had allowed me to spend the extra little bit for deluxe napkins. They had so much more body than these cheap bulk things.

Katie Bell let her gaze wander around the fellowship hall of the Presbyterian Church. "I'm the first one to arrive?"

"Yes, ma'am." Then I added, "You always are."

The smile Katie Bell turned on me reminded me of a cat that had created some trouble I didn't know about yet. "It's the reporter in me. Got to get a jump on things, you know."

"Like riflin' through the bingo cards until you find your lucky one?"

The surprise in Katie Bell's eyes was gratifying, but it lasted only a second before she chuckled. "I've always had the feeling you aren't what you seem. What's with the wallflower act you've been maintaining over the years? Surely your Mama — of all people — has told you that shy girls don't get husbands."

"Like *you*, Katie Bell?"

She guffawed. "Shy is one thing nobody's ever accused *me* of being." She studied me shrewdly. "You stand back, taking it all in, don't you? You've got good observation skills. Are you planning on stealing my job as gossip columnist?"

To hide my smile, I lowered my eyes and began transforming a red napkin covered with tiny white hearts into a butterfly. "No, I'll stick to decorating."

"Uh huh." Losing interest when she couldn't get a rise out of me, her attention returned to the room. "The bingo cards are under the sign-in table like they always are, I suppose?"

"Yes, ma'am."

She padded off. Katie Bell always moved stealthily, like the tiger she was.

I returned to my napkin folding. People made fun of it, especially since it was the only talent I could come up with when Mama forced me into entering the Miss Bigelow Contest. Few considered it the art form it was, close kin to origami. I took a mundane, functional napkin and transformed it into something magical — all with a Martha Stewart swash.

My heart twisted. Harry kept a collection of my napkin animals on his mantle.

I glanced up to see if Katie Bell noticed the misery I couldn't keep off my face, but the Reverend Hollingsworth had come in with the cash box. He had Katie Bell's attention and was about to have the money for her lucky bingo cards. He was followed by a trail of church ladies and townspeople, wandering in the crepe-draped door in twos and threes. Most toted Tupperware containers or covered dishes filled with goodies, which they brought to the table where I worked. I interrupted my napkin folding so I could sort the dishes — all of them desserts — into Sweet, Very Sweet, and Melt-Your-Teeth Sweet.

When the table was half-full, Eustene Oscar set down a plate of divinity candy, then smiled. "Hey, Josie. Your Mama here tonight?"

"No, Mrs. Oscar. She wasn't feeling up to it."

Mrs. Oscar's unnaturally bright red hair — Rainey Ann Cecil's salon work, no doubt — glowed in the fluorescent lights. "She's been feeling poorly for several months now, hasn't she, dear?"

"Yes, Mrs. Oscar. Since last spring."

"Since the Miss Bigelow Contest." The no-bones statement came from the no-nonsense mayor of Mossy Creek, Ida Hamilton Walker. She nailed me with a kind but penetrating smile. "Isn't that right, Josie?"

"Yes, ma'am." I placed Mrs. Oscar's candy next to the carob-dipped strawberries Maggie Hart sent over by way of her boyfriend, Tag Garner.

The mayor went on, "When Josie didn't win, her mother couldn't decide whether to murder the judge or go into a decline. Since the deciding judge was our very own Amos Royden, I was able to convince her that a decline is so much more elegant for a Southern lady than wearing a tacky orange prison uniform."

"Mama hates orange," I agreed.

Mayor Ida laughed. Sagittarius-Dragons always enjoyed a good joke. "I do believe you've grown up, Miss Josie McClure. A year ago you wouldn't say boo to me. Was it dealing with all those beauty contestants, or working for Swee Purla?"

If our mayor only knew.

Luckily, I didn't have to answer because my attention was stolen by Jayne, who came in pulling the bright red wagon Ingrid Beechum had given her. Strapped into the wagon was an industrial-sized cooler of spiced tea, a winter specialty at The Naked Bean. And her pregnant!

I excused myself and hurried over.

"No, just one set," she said to the Reverend as he tried to sell her bingo cards. "I doubt I'll be paying much attention to them, anyway. Just trying to help the cause."

"Did you haul that wagon all the way from The Naked Bean?" I asked.

Jayne smiled. "Who else was going to haul it?"

"I could have helped you bring it here."

"I'm fine." She placed her change in her purse. "It's only a block."

"I'll take care of it from now on. Please. I insist." I grabbed the wagon's handle. Suddenly I noticed the eerie quiet and that everyone standing within earshot was staring at us. I froze, only now realizing what I'd done. I'd forgotten all about my wallflower persona. My cheeks stung with heat.

"We'd better get the tea to the refreshment table." Jayne's comment saved me. She cleared a path, and I followed in her wake.

As I gathered strength to haul the cooler onto the table, my hands were pushed out of the way.

"We'll get that, Josie," Amos Royden said. Mossy Creek's police chief and his pal, lawyer Mac Campbell, lifted the cooler easily.

Chief Royden was in his late thirties, tall and good-looking. He usually made me feel so shy I could barely breathe.

His friend Mac leaned near me and whispered dramatically, "Any chance your mother sent along one of her chess pies for the chief?"

Chief Royden looked as if he wanted to kill Mac.

I coughed and pointed at the Very Sweet section of the dessert table. As much as Chief Royden loved Mama's chess pie, the three she'd brought to him prior to the beauty contest hadn't made him vote for me. Thank goodness. You had to respect a man who couldn't be bribed.

I whispered to the chief. "I have another one in a cooler outside. If you want it, I'll put it in your squad car right now."

Chief Royden kept scowling at his friend, who kept grinning. "No, thanks, Josie. I'm a little busy planning how to arrest someone on a Smirking In Public charge."

He winked at me as he walked away. Jayne and I spent the next few moments arranging desserts. I was slicing Mrs. Beechum's famous Italian Creme Cake using Martha Stewart's method for optimum servings when I felt Jayne's elbow in my side. I looked up to see Oscar Oscar, the double-named grandson of Eustene Oscar.

Oscar stood on the other side of the Melt-Your-Teeth desserts, looking nervous and shy. "Hey, Josie."

"Hello, Oscar. Do you want a piece of

Mrs. Beechum's cake? Won't cost you a dime, tonight."

"No. I mean. . . ." I swear he was shuffling his feet. "Sure. That'd be cool."

I used Mama's silver cake knife to place a piece on one of the red paper plates with a huge white heart in the middle. "There you go. Good luck."

But he didn't go.

"Oh, ah . . . thanks." His face turned a shade close to Chinese red. "I was wondering if you had a date to Cupid's Cotillion."

If Cupid himself had shot me with an arrow at that moment, I doubt I would've felt it. "Me? You're asking me to the Cotillion?"

He grinned. "I sure am."

"Why?"

"I don't know. Because I want to, I guess. I'm movin' to Tennessee to work in my cousin's hardware store."

I planted my hands on my hips. Neither he nor any other boy in Bigelow County had ever acknowledged my existence. Now he wanted to take me out on Valentine's Day? "I don't think so."

Oscar frowned. "You already got a date or something?"

I opened my mouth to tell him hotly that my date waited for me on Colchik Mountain — the misguided love of my life, in fact, who could snap his scrawny neck like a wishbone — when Jayne answered for me. "No, she doesn't."

I gaped at her.

She ignored me.

Oscar's confused face cleared. "I'll pick you up at seven, then."

"Pick her up at The Naked Bean, Oscar," Jayne told him. "It'll be closer for you, anyway, than driving out to the other side of Bailey Mill."

That's just what I needed, another man who wouldn't see me to and from my door. I crossed my arms over my chest. "I'll think about it."

"See you Saturday." Oscar grinned, and with a bite of Italian Creme Cake, he walked away.

I glared at Jayne.

She smiled. "You're an angel. Men are starting to notice you. I'd like to help."

"Oscar's not a man. He's a boy. And I'm not an angel. I'm a snake."

Jayne laughed. "He'll be good practice for real dating later, then."

I blurted without thinking, "You don't understand. I don't want anything to do with him! He isn't Harry!"

"Most guys aren't, at his age. He'll probably get hairier as he gets older."

I stood there, grateful she'd misunderstood, stunned by my near revelation of Harry's existence, and just plain miserable about my situation with him. "I don't have a dress to wear to that stupid dance."

"I've got several that will fit you! I'm certainly not using them right now. All right?"

Suddenly all of the euphoria I'd been feeling because Swee Purla had given me the sole responsibility for decorating the church hall vanished. I couldn't get out of going to Cupid's Cotillion with Oscar without telling everyone why.

What was Harry going to say? Would he care?

And why should I care what he'd say when he'd made it clear he wouldn't come down off his lonely, remote mountain to take me himself?

"You're gorgeous!" Jayne exclaimed.

I stared into the full-length mirror in her apartment above The Naked Bean. It was close to seven, the "Oscar" hour. Not exactly the witching hour, but it's how I'd been thinking of it. "Don't go overboard."

Although I had to admit she was right. I could scarcely believe it was me staring at myself. The deep red velvet of the long-sleeved, knee-length dress complimented my auburn hair, and the form-fitting stretch velvet hugged curves I never knew I had.

"Shut up, Josie McClure. You might as well admit it, because everyone at the dance is going to be telling you how beautiful you look."

I yanked up the plunging neckline. "Mama would have a fit."

Jayne yanked it back down. "It's perfect, just the right spot for the corsage he's bringing."

"How do you know what he's bringing?"

She wasn't a bit contrite. "He asked me what to get, and I told him."

"Since you're so hot for all this, maybe you should go to the Cotillion with him."

"I'm manning the refreshment table."

"That's what I've done for —"

The doorbell rang.

"There he is," she said brightly.

Panic and misery rose in my throat, threatening to choke me. "I don't want to go."

"One day you'll thank me," Jayne repeated for the umpteenth time as she headed for the door.

"Yeah. On the day rhododendrons bloom in December."

Oscar's reaction was everything Jayne had

hoped for. Any customers who might've
been in the shop below — if all shops in
Mossy Creek hadn't closed early today —
would've heard a loud thump when Oscar's
jaw hit the floor. "Josie? Is that really you?"

"No, Oscar, it's the wicked witch of the
west." I was in no mood for compliments
from him.

"Hush, Josie, and say 'thank you.' " Jayne
said with a meaningful glare. "Give me the
flowers, Oscar, and I'll pin them on."

Oscar handed her the plastic box. "Gawd-
almighty, Josie. You're purtier than a ten
pound trout."

"Sheer poetry, considering the source," I
murmured so only Jayne could hear.

She stood right in front of me and had
just pulled a wicked faux-pearl tipped pin
from the corsage. She held it up with a
threatening glare.

I rolled my eyes. "Thank you, Oscar."

Jayne and Oscar continued to gush all over
me as Jayne pinned the lovely corsage of
baby's breath and two red roses at my
bosom. Five minutes later, Oscar escorted
me to his car.

"Why ain't you never dressed like this
before, Josie? It wouldn't a taken me so long
to ask you out."

He opened the passenger door to his

decade-old Chevy truck, and I did a little glaring of my own. "If you're thinking of trying anything funny tonight, Oscar Oscar, you can put that thought right out of your head. Cause if you do, I'll slap you so hard you'll think a grizzly's got a hold of you."

"Ain't no grizzlies in these mountains, Josie," he said patiently. "Them suckers is out west."

All the way to the Moose Lodge, I got a monologue on the bears native to the Appalachians. He'd missed my point entirely. I don't know why I was surprised. At least his talking kept me from having to talk.

Jayne's prediction proved correct. Everyone who came within speaking distance of me raved about my sudden transformation. My dance card — Mossy Creek still kept the tradition — was filled before Joe Biddly and His String Quartet began to play. The "strings" being a lead guitar, a steel guitar, a dulcimer, and a fiddle. The sweetest request was from eight-year-old Timmy Williams for the second waltz. As my date, Oscar had the first dance and the last one. It irked him that he couldn't have more, but I didn't mind one bit.

I was the belle of the ball and should've loved every minute of it. The only man who'd ever asked me to dance at the Cotillion was my Daddy. At nineteen, I'd become a permanent fixture at the refreshment table where my napkin folding never failed to be a hit with the ten and under crowd.

But I didn't love it. The only reason the evening didn't drag by like a fox with a dead bear was my discovery that I loved to dance. Mama had forced dancing lessons on me at an early age, of course, but I hated them because I was always the last girl chosen as a partner. Tonight I swung around the room with every man who asked me. If one of my penciled-in partners wanted to sit one out, all I had to do was turn around to find another willing set of arms and legs. It didn't matter to me who I danced with, as long as my feet kept moving.

I saved the seventh dance for Daddy, who beamed at me as he led me onto the floor. "You're purtier than a wild mountain rose. Your Mama's already making plans for next year's Miss Bigelow Contest. She claims she understands her mistake now. She should'a dressed you in red."

With a frown, I glanced at Mama, who held court with a bevy of her cronies. She looked happier than I'd seen her since before last year's contest. Her purpose for living had been revived . . . or so she thought.

"Daddy, I'm not going to enter that contest ever again."

"Ah, honey, you know what it means to your Mama."

"I don't care, Daddy, I . . ." My words died away when I noticed the hush that had fallen over the room. Everyone stared at the door, so naturally I turned to see what had captured their rapt attention.

Harry filled the doorway. *My* Harry.

I nearly fainted. The only thing that saved me was Daddy's hand on my arm.

"Who is it, honey? Do you know that man?"

Harry's gaze locked on to mine. The expression I saw in his black eyes brought blood back to my brain and purpose to my heart.

"Yes, Daddy. I do." I tried to pull away from Daddy's hand, but he held on.

His worried gaze studied the massive man who completely blocked the doorway. "He looks dangerous, honey."

I smiled indulgently. "Not my Harry."

"*Your* Harry?"

I reached up on tiptoe and kissed his cheek. "Yes, Daddy. *My* Harry."

Daddy let me go, and I began weaving my way through the crowd. When people noticed me moving toward Harry, they slowly parted, their whispering echoed my father's fear. I was ten yards away before I had a clear path to Harry. I wanted to run and throw myself into his arms. If nothing else, to show Mossy Creek they had nothing to fear from my gentle giant. Instead, I made myself stop.

Dressed in a dark gray pinstriped suit that fit him like a bird fits into its feathers, Harry had a new haircut and a clean-shaven face. The yin curve of his scar stood out starkly against the yang. He'd come clean shaven on purpose, I knew, to test the mettle of Mossy Creek. I hoped my fellow citizens lived up to my boasts.

But now Mossy Creekites were the last thing on Harry's mind. The way he looked at me meant more to me than all the compliments I'd received all evening.

"You're beautiful," he said simply.

A collective sigh went up from the crowd.

It startled him, and he glanced around. He lifted his chin, as if wanting to give them a better view.

"You look pretty spiffy yourself." I searched his face in wonder. "I can't believe you're here."

His dark eyes were intense, and saw only me. "Just because I have a Ph.D. doesn't mean I'm stupid. I know when I've fallen in love with the most wonderful woman in the world." He lifted his huge, meaty hands. "And since this was the only way I can have you, here I am." He bowed slightly at the waist. "May I have the next dance?"

Another sigh, accompanied this time by hushed chatter . . . which died away after a few seconds, so avid was everyone to hear what we said next.

I tore my dance card into little pieces. I threw them into the air like confetti and walked to his side. I proudly slipped my arm through his and turned to the crowd. "Everyone, I'm very pleased to introduce Dr. Harold Rutherford, my fiancé. Harry, this is the entire population of Mossy Creek."

My announcement set the room buzzing again. To one side, Mama cried out, then succumbed to the fainting spell I'd fended off earlier. The cronies around her caught her.

"I told you." Harry looked down at me. Panic hid in the depths of his eyes, just behind a thin veneer of determination.

"I can't believe you're not halfway out the door by now."

He straightened. "Once I make up my mind to do something, I see it through, come hell or high water."

"My sweet, stubborn Taurus-Dragon." I

smiled and patted his arm. I wanted to tell him that these people weren't staring at him because of his face, but because he was a stranger . . . and a huge one at that. But I couldn't be absolutely certain. Mossy Creek had to show him.

"Hey, Josie," Jamie Green shouted from the back of the crowd. "Is this that feller I been delivering mail to up on Colchik Mountain?"

"You mean the one who's mail you've been reading?" Harry shouted back.

The crowd tittered, and it felt as if the entire room heaved a relieved sigh.

Both of us felt a tug on Harry's jacket, and we glanced down to see eight-year-old Ida Walker, Mayor Walker's granddaughter.

"Are you the Bigfoot?" she asked breathlessly.

Harry stiffened, but I knew Little Ida was far from horrified.

"He wears a size twenty-two shoe, Ida," I said. "Is that a big enough foot for you?"

Little Ida thrust her dance card at Harry. "Will you dance with me, Mr. Rutherford?"

"*Doctor* Rutherford, Ida. That's what Ph.D. means." Mayor Ida stepped forward and offered her hand to Harry. "Let me be the first to welcome you to Mossy Creek, Dr. Rutherford. Congratulations. You've raised the average IQ of Mossy Creek by ten points."

Harry's hand swallowed Mayor Ida's whole. "I don't know about that . . ."

The mayor pumped his hand energetically. "I hope we'll see you at town meetings, now that you're marrying into the community. We can always use a level head at city hall."

"You mean a level head like the one that shoots up welcome signs?" Harry asked. "I've heard a lot about Mossy Creek."

"Well, bless me, we've got a live one here. You're going to be an interesting addition to our little town, no doubt about that."

I squeezed Harry's arm, and he glanced down at me.

I grinned. "I told you Mossy Creekites wouldn't run screaming."

Harry smiled. "You can throw my words back into my face all you want. I finally feel like I've come home."

"You once told me that your arms are my home. Well, mine are yours." I wrapped my arms around him. "Welcome home."

Mayor Hamilton raised her glass of red punch. "I'd like to pose a toast to the King and Queen of this year's Cotillion. To Josie and Harry. Mossy Creek's very own Beauty and her Bigfoot."

RAINEY

HOMECOMING DAY, 1981, PART ONE: WHEN THE ELEPHANT CAME TO TOWN

Life — and homecomings — are always about big, stomping choices. You have to lead, follow, or get out of the elephant's way.

I was twelve years old that autumn day when Mossy Creek High burned down. Until then I had a few simple, urgent goals in life: To stay as cute as whipped cream, to be the most famous curly-haired beautician in the history of Mossy Creek, and to make Robbie Walker's heart pound as hard when he looked at me as mine pounded whenever I looked at him. His mother wasn't mayor then, but even so, she was Ida Hamilton Walker. So Robbie was the rich son of Mossy Creek's most powerful woman.

And, well, I was Rainey Ann Cecil. Might as well have been Rainey Ann Nobody. I tried so hard to win Robbie's admiration and impress the whole rest of the world, too. In vain. Vanity was my downfall.

"Don't you let me catch you in that makeup counter this morning, Rainey Ann," Mama ordered. Goldilocks was her shop then, and had been Grandma Cecil's before that, and would be mine, someday. "Aw, Mama, just lemme wear a little pink lipstick. For a perk-me-up."

"I'll perk you up with the flat of my rat-tail comb, Lady Fingers. You ain't goin' around Mossy Creek lookin' like you're growed up and on the prowl for trouble. Now out. *Out.* I got customers."

A whole bunch of antsy ladies filled the shop that morning, all glaring at me, with good reason. It was the Saturday of Homecoming, and all the mamas in town wanted to look good for the big football game and the high school homecoming dance afterward. Who said chaperones couldn't kick up their heels along with the teenagers?

About that time, I heard a rapping at the shop's glass doors. There stood Robbie Walker and Hank Blackshear, peering in at me like I was a serious fish in a funny bowl. Robbie slouched, pretending to be a bad character, his hands shoved in his jeans' pockets. He had taken to wearing an old leather aviator jacket that had belonged to his daddy, Jeb. It swallowed him.

He was tall for twelve, with dark hair and

a strong, thoughtful face, though in the past year, since his daddy had died, he looked mad and sorrowful most of the time. His mama, Miss Ida, was still grieving so bad she barely set a foot outside the big house out at Hamilton Farm. But Robbie had taken to roaming, and everybody in town was trying to rein him in. A heartsick twelve-year-old kid could count on that kind of help in Mossy Creek. Plus all the girls had crushes on Robbie and wanted to make him smile again. I know I did.

As for Hank Blackshear, he was just a skinny little third grader who grinned a lot and didn't have much to say except to critters, which he loved. His daddy was the town vet, and Hank seemed to know that someday he'd take over that legacy, just like I'd take over my mama's. Hank was sweet and friendly and acted like a pet puppy around me and Robbie. It makes no sense to explain how the three of us got to be good friends, since Hank was four years younger than me and Robbie, and I was a girl with intentions on Robbie — not that he noticed. Hormones and teenage smugness hadn't set in yet, so we all got along.

Robbie crooked a finger at me, then pointed in the general direction of the high school. *Elephant,* he mouthed.

I swung around toward Mama. "The elephant's here! The carnival's started! See you later, Mama!"

She sighed with relief and waved a hot curler at me. "Don't eat too much junk food. Be back by lunchtime. Here." She scooped a handful of change from her tip jar.

"If it was me going, I wouldn't get within a mile of a nasty elephant," grumbled Wanda Halfacre, Mama's assistant. The Halfacres lived out in the wilds of Chinaberry Mountain, and they were Cherokee Indian. Wanda had inky black hair cut in a shag and a tiny gold feather charm in one ear lobe. She wore only cotton shirts and tie-dyed jeans, leather sandals — even in toe-freezin' cold weather — and turquoise Indian jewelry. She took herbal pills and said she was all natural. "It's not right, an elephant in these mountains," Wanda went on, and pursed her cherry-red mouth. "Not natural." She squirted some more perm solution on a lady's hair.

If Wanda set Mama to thinking, I might be forbidden to go. "I like odd critters," I announced quickly. "Odd critters and odd people that are so ugly you can't hardly look away and so you want to fix 'em up to look prettier."

75

Every woman in the shop stared at me. "Like, uh, elephants," I tried to amend. My voice trailed off.

Mama looked at me as if she could, right then, snip me off at the roots.

"Bye," I yelped. I hurried outside, pulling a pink jacket over my embroidered pink sweater and fake-designer jeans, hugging a macrame purse full of Mama's tip money to my side. I glared down at Hank, who chortled like a third-grade monkey, then up at Robbie, who bit back a wicked, pre-teenage smile.

I punched both boys on their shoulders. "Shut up. Let's go see the elephant."

When you're twelve-years-old, life seems simple. That was the last day it ever would be.

Mossy Creek High School was small and old and beautiful, and we all loved it. The next year Robbie and I would enter the eighth grade there, and we talked about our plans all the time. Our parents and grandparents and great-grandparents had gone to the high school. The school building dated back to the turn of the century, about when town hall and the jail were built, too.

All three had the same look — solid and friendly, made of big blocks of mountain stone with curved red-brick arches over the doors and the windows. The school's main doors were a good fifteen feet tall. The floors were made of wide chestnut boards from before the blight wiped out all the big chestnuts in the mountains, and the inside walls were topped with fancy, curlicued cornices, like some kind of Greek temple. The state board of education had started making dark noises about the school needing upgrades on its pipes and electricity. But we knew who was really behind the complaints. Bigelowans.

"Those people down at the county seat in Bigelow won't rest until they snatch our high school into the craw of great big modern Bigelow County High," Wanda Halfacre always said. "They just can't stomach the fact that we've got a naturally superior way of life up here."

She was right about that. Hank, Robbie and I strolled along the grassy shoulder of East Mossy Creek Road, admiring the autumn trees and breathing in pure, cool air like a perfume. We had the confidence of kids who knew they'd one day graduate into the adult world as Mossy Creek High School Fighting Rams, continuing all our town's best traditions.

The school was an easy, ten-minute walk

down East Mossy Creek through a fringe of hemlock forest outside town, past the graveled lane to the town swimming hole and over a strong wooden bridge that crossed Mossy Creek's right fork. Then the forest opened up into a broad, flat clearing with Mount Colchik in the background and the brightest blue sky overhead, and there stood Mossy Creek High. Big laurels and rhododendron shrubs and huge beech trees framed the old school. It was as wholesome as a fresh-fluffed bouffant.

The traveling carnival had set up in the big front parking lot and beneath the long metal awning of the drop-off bus lane. I whistled happily at the sight of the carnival's whirring ferris wheel, clanking roller coasters, and gaudy game booths, all glowing with neon lights in the cool sunshine of that Saturday morning. The scent of grilling hamburgers and the hot, sizzling oil of funnel cakes wafted from concession stands, and old-fashioned carnival music, like a whacked-out steam calliope, blared from speakers somewhere. Cars and pickup trucks were parked all over, and several hundred Mossy Creekites were already crowding into the area.

"This is what heaven is like," I said.

Hank screeched like a thrilled barn owl

and nodded his agreement. But Robbie slowed to a walk and glared at me. "Don't say that. It's not heaven if my dad isn't here. Ask my mother. She's like me. We know there's no heaven, anymore."

"Robbie, I'm sorry," I whispered.

His face went grim, and he looked away from our sympathy, then walked on. We sighed and followed him.

When the three of us rounded a hedge of tall laurel we stared at the scene in front of us and halted. Out on the school's side lawn sat a big, life-sized concrete statue of a ram with his head down and his big, curling horns poised to slam into somebody. Nowadays he'd be judged violent and accused of promoting bad attitudes. Back then, we just thought he symbolized the pure truth: Mossy Creek's slogan was "Ain't goin' no where, and don't want to."

I'll butt anybody who tries to change that, the ram seemed to say.

"Look," Robbie said suddenly.

Hank chirped like an upset squirrel. I gasped.

Every year for homecoming the senior class painted GO MOSSY CREEK RAMS BEAT BIGELOW WILDCATS on the statue's side in green-and-white letters — our school colors. But this year, someone had snuck up during the night and painted some words about Mossy Creek I won't repeat. The ram was R-Rated, at least.

A crowd of adults hunkered around the big statue, pointing angrily at the words and talking loudly about catching the Bigelow kids who'd written them. I saw Chief Battle Royden shaking his head while the school principal, Mr. Doolittle, wrung his hands and said, "Look for fingerprints, Chief."

Just as we finished absorbing the whole eyeful of obscene anti-Mossy Creek slogans, a group of red-faced daddies flung a big blue tarp over the ram, and the school janitor spotted us. "The show's over, you three," called big, burly Lock MacNeil. "Pull in your eyeballs and keep movin'."

We ducked back behind the laurel then headed for the carnival area, sputtering. Of course the dirty words were the work of fat-cat Bigelow Wildcats.

"Snotty Bigelowans," Robbie said.

"Nasty Bigelowans," I agreed. "Writing all that crap for little kids to see." Irony and me weren't on a first-name basis, yet.

Hank just looked at the tarp-covered ram, and growled.

A sign said the elephant's name was Rose. She was, well, yeah, an elephant. Smelled like one, looked like one, not much more to the description than that. She blinked slowly in the cool November sunshine, her skinny, gray, elephant tail switching a little. She wore a wide, red-leather harness around her neck and middle, with little bells on it. Hank walked right up to her, and she seemed to smile at him. He sure had a way with animals. Rose wrapped her long, snuffling trunk around his upstretched hand and shifted her feet like a dog glad to see him. Her bells tinkled. Her owner, a little-bitty old man in a clown suit but not wearing any clown makeup, which made him look kind of weird, had chained her by one ankle to the bumper of his camper.

ROSE THE AMAZING WILD EL-EPHANT, was painted on the camper's white siding in big, overstuffed red letters.

"She looks about as wild as a dead possum in the middle of the road," Robbie commented.

"Hush, she's pretty." I stared up at Rose. She was as tall as the school's big front doors. I'd never seen anything big enough to make those doors look small, but Rose did it.

She looked happy enough with her life. She stood in a deep bed of straw, slurped from a galvanized wash tub full of fresh water, and patiently let a steady stream of kids feed her peanuts. "One dollar gets you a bag of peanuts for the wild pachyderm," her owner sang out, as he reached up with a pole to scratch Rose between the eyes. "Two dollars gets you a photograph of yourself sittin' on the *back* of the wild pachyderm."

I swiftly fished two bucks in quarters from my macrame purse. "I'm gonna sit on the back of the wild pack-a-perm," I declared.

Five minutes later, I was viewing the world from Rose's broad shoulders. I clung to a leather handhold on her harness and grinned weakly down at Robbie and Hank. "Y'all get in the picture, too," I ordered. "And if I fall off, y'all catch me."

So they stepped close to Rose the elephant and posed solemnly, while a crowd of kids watched in awe. The half-made-up clown took our picture with an instant-snapshot camera. When I climbed down, the boys and I studied the photograph while it developed.

First we were shadows, and then we were real. We looked cocky and brave. All the other kids were jealous.

"We're the Three Musketeers," I said.

Robbie smiled a little. "The Three Musketeers with their noble pack-a-perm."

It was a great moment. We weren't afraid of the elephant at all.

Let me tell you, we should have been.

There was an ill buzz in the Creekites at the carnival; people were getting all worked up. "You know who I think wrote that filth on the statue?" I heard one mama say to another. "That Fang and Paw Club down at Bigelow High."

"Fang and Claw," the other mama corrected. "Fang and Claw *Society*. But the Fang and Claw died out years ago. Bigelow High got rid of it."

"Mayrene, did your folks raise you to be an idiot? It's a *secret* club. Always has been. Going all the way back to World War II. Secret. Rich boys pullin' nasty pranks. In *secret*."

Mayrene put her hands on her hips. "Betty, I know more about the Fang and Claw Society than you'll ever know, you fool. My Judith Bea dated a Bigelow boy, and he said you can tell who's in the society because they wear a fang and claw necklace. And he said nobody wears one, anymore."

"*Because they wear 'em in secret.* And don't call me a fool!"

"Look, don't you call *me* an idiot!"

"It's idiots like you that make us an easy target for Bigelowans!"

"It's fools like you who believe in secret

boys' clubs!"

The mamas lurched toward each other. Their families got between 'em before any fisticuffs or hair-pulling could commence, then led them away in opposite directions. A big crowd of folks stood there gape-mouthed, watching. We didn't see many mama-brawls in Mossy Creek.

"Lordawmighty," I said under my breath. "Everybody's goin' crazy."

Robbie stood in weighty silence, gazing into the sink-a-basket-and-win-a-basketball booth. Hank was tossing nickels inside a booth full of little goldfish bowls complete with fish. If he landed a nickel in a bowl, he got a fish. A goldfish was the only kind of pet he didn't have at home. I wiped a wisp of cotton candy off my jacket and looked around curiously, hoping to hear more adults squabbling in the crowd.

Robbie shook his head. "That lady was right. Creekites are always an easy target for Bigelowans."

"Aw, that's just because we aren't sly as snakes, like them. That's what my grandma says."

"We've got to show everybody Creekites can fight back."

"How?"

"I don't know. I'll think of something."

I nodded.

I should have left the carnival and dragged the boys with me. But I didn't.

So our fate was sealed.

To: Lady Victoria Salter Stanhope
From: Katie Bell

Dear Vick:
After the fire, we found elephant foot-prints all around the school, but no elephant. Rock Bottoms, our local brick mason — father of Mutt, Boo, and Sandy — made a large plaster cast of the elephant's tracks. It was displayed at the post office for a year or so, like a wanted poster. Finally, Chief Royden donated it to *Ripley's Believe It Or Not* museum down in Florida. Least that's what he said. I think he just couldn't stand the thought of the unsolved crime, anymore. Or the embarrassment.

Not many police chiefs couldn't find an *elephant*.

You could say his boy, Amos, has been looking ever since.

Katie

Amos

What is it about an unmarried man that makes everyone determined to see him tied up and accounted for by some woman? Or is it just that no one can resist a little romantic blarney on St. Patrick's Day?

I had to smile at Katie Bell's indomitable spirit. Only an optimist would send out a survey asking for our deepest, darkest memories and expect us to return it to the town gossip columnist. It was certainly a clever way to stockpile column material for the next year. It would certainly be interesting reading. If anyone sent anything in. That wasn't happening. At least not in my case. I admired Katie for trying to create this pamphlet of memories and sharing, but I didn't think I'd be contributing. I knew better than to volunteer incriminating information.

Not that I had anything to do with the

high school fire. Not me. I was holding down the bench for the football team. Coach always seemed worried about the possibility of the wind carrying it off, so he made sure I anchored it. I've always wondered if a seat in the bleachers would have been any less frustrating. I practiced like a maniac. Ran more laps, lifted more weights, waded my way through a labyrinth of tires, and took more practice hits than any other defensive end we'd ever had. I'd done every bit of it because I'd been too young to know that adults often leave words out of axioms.

When adults say, "If you work hard enough, you can be anything you want," they really mean — "If you work hard enough, you can be *almost* anything you want."

The secret Katie would like and I won't voice is that when I look at the grass grown almost-over the old high school's foundation, I see the loss of innocence. A million years ago when I was sixteen, I truly believed that if I kept showing up for practice . . . if I kept saying, "Yes, sir, Coach, I'm ready!" . . . if I held that bench down long enough, I was going to get in the game. I'd have my chance to save the day and make the play. Before that high school burned down, I was going to be a hero. Battle was going clap me on the back and drag me into one of those too-proud-to-be-distant father-son hugs and say, "Damn, I'm proud of you!"

All I had to do was work hard. That's what they kept telling me.

And still do.

But the high school burned, and I discovered that if you work hard enough, you can hang on until the Bigelow High School coach makes his last cut of senior try-outs. If you work hard enough, you can earn the coach's respect and one of those silent hand-on-the-shoulder squeezes as he gives you the bad news, but working hard wasn't enough to earn a spot on the team. Not on a team with the talent Bigelow had when they absorbed the Mossy Creek Rams.

When I look at where the high school used to be, I see one of those classic unfinished moments that defined my relationship with Battle. Sometimes you can't have what you want. Sometimes what you want isn't something you can control. You pick yourself up. You learn. You realize that the experience is as important as the goal. If I hadn't tried, if I hadn't worked hard enough, I wouldn't even have been sitting the bench. If I hadn't been sitting the bench, I wouldn't have had a front row seat when the lights went out in

Georgia.

But I'm not sharing that with Katie Bell.

I'm not stupid, and as adorable as she is . . . she is the town gossip columnist.

I'm not the only one around here who's reluctant to talk about himself. Every man, woman and child in Mossy Creek imagines they have a secret. Some — a very small percentage of them — do manage to keep the embarrassing and damaging snippets of their lives tucked safely away in a bureau drawer, jewelry chest or their own mind. But for the majority of Mossy Creek, the notion of privacy is a figment of their imagination. An illusion.

In Mossy Creek, it's a hard fact of life that "Latin" *and* "Privacy" are dead languages. No one speaks Latin, and no one understands Privacy.

If I didn't think Ida'd take aim — possibly at me — I'd put up a sign at the edge of town as a warning: "Check your privacy at the door. Or we'll check it for you."

What's my point?

I miss the subtle nuances of big city social behavior. I miss taking out my garbage without an audience. I miss going to the grocery in my favorite, almost-disintegrated Eagles' "Hell Freezes Over" t-shirt from ten years ago without Ida Hamilton Walker raising an eyebrow and inquiring as to whether my salary is adequate. When I was a cop down in Atlanta, women never questioned my Eagles shirt.

And on a morning like St. Patrick's Day, when March is finally looking more and more like spring, I miss sitting in a doctor's waiting room with complete strangers. Why? Strangers aren't likely to tell thirty of my closest friends that Doc Champion's nurse leaned over the office counter and bellowed, "Amos! Doc's running behind. Said he doesn't need to check you again if the cream is clearing up that nasty rash."

One of life's great mysteries is how gentle, reassuring Thelma Proctor — a tiny, blue-haired nurse who gives a shot like an angel, can open her mouth and belt out words like a carnival barker pitching his voice to be heard the length of the midway. Another great mystery is how she can say all those words, at what seems like the top of her lungs, and still not communicate the essential facts.

It's not so much what she says; it's what she leaves out. Sometimes the addition of two little words would make a world of difference.

Like poison ivy. As in — "That nasty

poison ivy rash."

Or your leg. "He doesn't need to check your *leg* again."

Makes all the difference. Trust me.

When those particular words are left out of a sentence, you'd really rather be in a room filled with strangers you'll never see again. Strangers who know their place, who know the rules and speak the language of Privacy. Strangers who pretend to read their magazines. Strangers who rarely ever snicker and who never give advice on how smart fellows could avoid poison ivy in the dead of winter. Talk about freak bad luck.

It happened this way: Sandy Crane dragged me into retracing a mountain trail where Rose the elephant was last seen twenty years ago. "Maybe we can get a feel for what direction she was taking," Sandy said. "You know. Like was she was going south for the winter."

"I don't think elephants head for Miami Beach."

Sandy didn't speak to me for quite a while, after that.

On the way back to town, we stopped by Zeke Abercrombie's place to check a report that neighborhood kids had lobbed a base-ball through one of his greenhouse windows. Jotting notes for my report, I sat down on a bench in the middle of Zeke's jungle of orchids and cacti and mysterious escaped ground covers. Seemed like a good place to pull off my boot and figure out how something hard had worked its way under my foot.

Sandy yipped. "Better not sit on that bench, Chief. That looks like poison ivy at the base. Nobody's got the heart to tell Mr. Abercrombie his eyes are going. He thinks it's a sprig of pepperonia."

"Not in the middle of winter. Not poison ivy. Not even in a greenhouse." I pulled a small plant up by the roots, and examined a leaf between my fingers. "Couldn't be." I tossed it away and then pulled up my pants leg to check on the boot situation. Bad luck, that. Because it was indeed poison ivy in the middle of winter in a greenhouse, and I'd just smeared it all over my leg.

"Sorry, Chief," Sandy said when I made a doctor's appointment. "I told you not to sit on that bench."

Sandy's no different from other Creekites. They love to give advice. At the drop of a hat. Your hat, their hat, anyone's hat. Give them an excuse, and they're happy to sort things out for you. Creekites believe you want their opinion and have merely forgotten to ask for it. God knows they've volunteered opinions on everything from the size of the tires on the department's new Jeep to the lack of good quality bran in the breakfast cereals I buy.

Hey, everyone has a weakness. Superman has kryptonite; mine happens to be multi-colored cereals coated in sugar, and especially ones chock full of magically delicious marshmallows. What's not to like? You pour. It's sweet. You eat.

Mossy Creek doesn't see it that way. They live to comment. It's the comment capital of the world. Nothing is sacred when an opportunity to dispense advice presents itself. I was even given advice on how to leave town quietly after judging last year's disasterous Miss Bigelow County contest. Not everyone understood why my vote didn't go to one of the Mossy Creek girls. Especially since everyone in town had taken the time to give me explicit advice on the subject. I'm just glad Josie McClure has found true love and sworn off future contests. One more year of her mother's chess-pie bribes and I'd need a cholesterol check.

And, of course, everyone is quick to point out that I really should stop arresting the mayor. Although I'm at a loss to understand why or how it's my fault when Ida decides to break the law. I'm also at a loss to understand why I like Mossy Creek. And I do.

Most of the time.

Except maybe today.

Especially not today when Thelma is broadcasting my personal medical history to everyone in the waiting room and focusing every pair of eyes on me. On me and my nasty rash.

All the previous advice I'd received from well-meaning citizens paled in comparison to what was about to be unleashed on me. I'm not ashamed to say that the thought of facing a barrage of helpful suggestions for curing my rash terrified me. Believe me, after hearing Thelma's announcement, everyone in the waiting room was poised and ready. They had scooted right to the edges of their fake-flame-stitched upholstered chairs so — just as soon as I answered — they could bounce up and begin dispensing advice.

Or, God help me . . . compare rash stories.

Silence swelled around me, becoming positively pregnant with anticipation. Even Betty Halfacre, Wanda's sister, stopped sorting and winding the needlework threads that had absorbed her from the moment she'd planted her square solid body in the chair beside me. She wasn't a woman who wasted time or words, although she muttered in Cherokee from time to time. Nor did she let her attention stray from the job at hand. That quality of focus was the main reason Ingrid Beechum had hired Betty. It was the reason they got on so well when most people didn't last long working for Ingrid. But even Betty looked up to find out how the nasty rash was coming along and what my answer would be.

I had no choice. I did what any moderately intelligent law enforcement officer would do. I gritted my teeth and falsified my report.

"Yes." I was careful to pronounce each word clearly, if not as loudly as Thelma. "The poison ivy rash is practically gone from my leg. You can cancel my appointment. I need to head back to the office anyway."

The disappointed sigh was actually audible. The subtle undercurrent of anticipation fled the room like a frustrated leprechaun who'd been denied the promised pot of gold or an Irishman denied a pint of brew on St. Paddy's Day. Everyone resettled in his or her chair to await the next victim.

Without so much as a blink, Betty returned her attention to sorting the tangle of color in her lap. And right on cue, the insidious pulse of itchy-awareness below my knee blossomed into an insistent tingling and then threatened to errupt into a full-blown riot of itch-mania. I gritted my teeth, nodded a curt goodbye to Thelma and got the hell out of Dodge before I gave in to the growing urge to scratch wildly at the traitorous patch of skin.

The door snapped shut behind me. I took a deep breath, refused to scratch, and decided that from now on someone else would be in charge of any law enforcement event that included poisonous vines. This wasn't my first embarrassing brush with the laws of nature. The summer before, I'd been covered with poison ivy from my right knee to ankle, leading to my moratorium on rescue operations for kittens-trapped-under-rickety-wooden-porches. The kitten hadn't really been trapped, but little Melanie Myerson had been terrified enough that a big fat silent tear spilled onto her cheek as she tugged me toward the empty house next to hers. She and her mom lived on the old part of Laurel Street. Some of those houses are fast earning the name "fixer-upper."

I had no idea what I was getting into when she waved frantically at the jeep as I drove by on patrol, but when a little tyke like that waves you down, you hit the brakes pronto.

The story and the tear spilled out before I'd even gotten the door open all the way. Two minutes later, I was belly-crawling under a porch, making come-here-kitty noises at Fluffy Anne — who was supremely unimpressed — and then inching back out with kitten in tow. I'm pretty sure wiggling out from under the porch did the poison ivy damage when my right pant leg ripped on a nail. Just above the protection of my boot.

All three of us learned a lesson that day. Melanie learned that tears are a great motivator of men. Fluffy Anne learned that playing hard to get makes humans do stupid things. I learned I still didn't know poison ivy from pansies. I also learned that the hero always gets the girl. Melanie plans to marry me just as soon as she's allowed to cross the street by herself.

She'll have to get in line. Lately I'm getting more than my fair share of charming ladies tossed in my path. What bothers me about the situation is not the ladies themselves, but that I don't seem to have a choice in the matter. Every dinner invitation is an ambush with Cousin Eva, Sister Susan or Aunt Tess jumping out of the closet to yell, "Surprise! I'm your blind date!" I've been so busy fending off the matchmakers, I haven't had much time to look up the few old flames and high school heartbreakers that I ought to be looking up. Coming back to live in Mossy Creek had certainly been more than I bargained for.

When I blew through the door of The Naked Bean, I realized my feet had taken me from the doctor's office to the coffee shop. I knew why. I wanted some privacy, and there was none to be had at the police station. My small office does have a door — not that Sandy Crane seems to notice. My dispatcher-clerk has never quite grasped the idea of knock-and-wait. She guards my office like a tigress . . . except from herself.

When I hired her, with no prior experience to speak of, she was so grateful she decided I hung the moon and all but swore fealty on the spot. If I'd had a sword, I would have had to knight her. One of these days, she'll realize I'm getting the best end of the bargain. Until then, the tiny offices we call the station, the job . . . that's her prized territory. Including me. It never occurs to her that as much as I respect the job she does, sometimes I wish she'd do it a little less intensely.

So, I stood in the Naked Bean, feeling a lot like someone running away from home, but not quite understanding why I'd run here. To this specific and very public place.

Jayne Reynolds looked up at the sound of the tinkling bell, obviously surprised to see me in the middle of the afternoon. Probably surprised to see anyone. Coffee shops don't do a booming business on St. Patrick's Day. Wanna-be Irishmen aren't looking for a cup of Joe. They're looking to raise a pint. Or three. Michael Conners at O'Days would be doing most of the beverage service in Mossy Creek today.

The surprise at having a customer didn't last long. Jayne just nodded toward my table and turned around to fix my order. That's when it hit me. Like a paving brick to the back of the head.

I'd become a regular. Not only did I have a "usual"; I had a table for God's sake. The one farthest from the door, in the corner where I could lean my head against the wall and close my eyes for a moment.

But it wasn't the comfortable corner and rich coffee that drew me to the shop today. Or even the pretty-but-pregnant widow. Somehow, without my realizing it, The Naked Bean had become a brief refuge from being the "chief." The place wasn't like Mama's All You Can Eat Café with its family-style jumble of conversation and no-one-eats-alone philosophy. Jayne seemed to understand I needed a place to sit without being on display or kept company. She accepted that sometimes I liked being a customer and not one of the family.

She gave others coffee and conversation, but she just gave me coffee and that crooked, half-sad smile she had. That suited me fine. She never interrupted my thoughts to see if I wanted a refill, but the minute I needed one she seemed to materialize.

As she fussed with the tools of her trade, I decided she probably understood me because she understood a little bit about how it felt to be watched all the time. To carry a town's expectations on your shoulders. In an odd way, her pregnancy had become town property. The town wanted her to be happy, to be over the sadness of losing her husband, to find her bearings and her life here in Mossy Creek.

Yep, Jayne and I shared a thing or two about expectations. I closed my eyes and leaned my head back. I was expected to be my father, to follow in his footsteps as Chief, to look the other way sometimes, and to settle down with a nice Mossy Creek girl. Lord knows I have no objection to finding the right woman, but the right woman always seems to be unavailable. Or my job sends her running for the hills. Can't blame a woman for that objection. You're never truly off-duty in a small town.

For me that's especially true. I'm still struggling with the job on a daily basis. I probably get involved in more calls than I should. If I've heard it once, I've heard it a million times — "Ol' Battle Royden wouldn't have done it that way." At least I don't hear it as often as I used to. I'm proud of that change, but I'm still feeling my way. I know it, and the town knows it.

I'm not Battle — never will be — but I do finally understand that Battle had a strange sort of logic about him, about how he applied the law. Still, for someone like me, who likes life in easy-to-read shades of black and white, there are too many gray areas in a small town. I'll never be as comfortable with those grays as Battle was. It'll take me longer to let go of the things that get hold of me, to stop silently second-guessing my decisions.

Like whether or not I should have followed up this morning on what I thought I saw in Violet Martin's yard when I checked her place. She was off visiting one of the granddaughters. When I heard she'd be gone, offering to keep an eye on her house seemed like a good idea. Heck, it even seemed like the sort of thing that Battle would have done.

I made the offer before I knew I'd be landing on the horns of a dilemma worthy of a ten-point buck.

This morning I checked her windows. I jiggled her doors. I gave the grounds a once-over. But I didn't actually stare through the glass door of her sunroom to determine if what looked like scruffy tomato plants in big clay pots were actually weeds. *Weed,* to be precise. Marijuana. Acapulco Gold. Truth be told, I'm not sure I want to know. The woman has glaucoma, and judging from the cornucopia of medications on her kitchen window shelf, she probably suffers more than her fair share of nausea.

A year ago, without question, I would have stared long and hard to be certain. Today, I'm having a hard time getting all worked up over the thought of 704 year-old Violet Martin quietly breaking the law by baking Mary Jane brownies to settle her stomach. Today, the line between right and wrong has grown a little fuzzy, and it's not likely to get any clearer.

I'd give anything for this job to magically transform into something nice and tidy and simple. But it won't. Today, I finally realized the quiet burdens of choice that Battle chose to carry around with him every day.

My father embraced what I'm only beginning to understand. Knowing the people you protect guarantees hard choices. You see them every day. You know their hearts, their secrets, their troubles. When you know all of that, everything changes. The black-and-white world begins to fade to gray. Empathy pushes you in new directions. When I first became a cop in Atlanta, Battle gave me some advice. I dismissed it as self-important mumbo-jumbo, verbal slight-of-hand, which conveniently justified his habit of looking the other way all too often.

"Find the balance, boy. Don't be looking so hard for the letter of the law that you miss the right thing." After a year in Mossy Creek, I've decided that maybe his advice wasn't mumbo-jumbo, but I haven't yet had the guts to adopt it as a philosophy, either.

To cloud matters further, my empathy kicked in with a vengeance this morning. Given a choice, I'll take a groin pull over a bout with nausea any day. Which means I understand Violet's need to quell queasiness. There were no beer guzzling competitions in my college days. No legendary frat parties in which I drank everyone under the table. Truth is . . . I can't hold my liquor. I guess I should actually say, I can't hold on to my liquor.

Some people have glass jaws. I have something of a glass stomach. That's one of the secrets Mossy Creekites haven't ferreted out yet. God help me when they do. They won't be content just to know this embarrassing tidbit. They'll want to know exactly which drink is one too many for my stomach. Two beers? Three? A couple of scotches? They'll marvel and puzzle over why a big strapping man like me can't toss back his fair share of home-brewed. One or two of the older folks will lament the sad loss of mountain-stock sturdiness in the younger generation.

But that wouldn't be the worst of it.

Oh, no. Sandy would run the betting pool just as efficiently as she ran everything else. Holiday parties would be a misery as people watched to see how much and what the chief drank. Until someone won the pool, I'd have every hostess in Mossy Creek offering me a beer — several beers — before dinner, during dinner and after dinner. I'd run out of polite excuses for refusing unless I admitted I tended to toss my cookies after two stiff drinks or three beers.

The temperance ladies would pounce on this as proof that the chief frowned on spirits, which I don't — taken in moderation. And the softball team would split their uniforms laughing. An epitaph suggested itself — Amos Royden . . . damned good catcher but hurls his liquor like a girl.

A clunk on The Naked Bean's café table forced my eyes open. Jayne slid a gigantic bowl-sized cup toward me and tucked a chunk of ponytail-escaping, brown hair back behind her ear. My surprise at the size of the cup must have showed in my eyes.

She laughed. "My treat. I made it a double today."

"Nice call. What are you? Pyschic?"

Some of the tiredness that seemed to haunt her eyes disappeared for a moment. "No. Just my keen powers of observation."

"That obvious, huh?"

"One look at your bad mood and Bob would have emptied his nervous little chihuahua bladder. Twice." She whispered as if Ingrid Beechum's incontinent dog might appear outside her door at any moment.

I felt the corner of my mouth quirk in a smile as she left me alone. Without ever asking me why I'd been frowning.

Another place, another time, I could have fallen hard for Ms. Jayne Reynolds. This wasn't the time for her or the place for me. At least not yet, not in the fish bowl that was Mossy Creek. Trying to sort through the pieces of the twenty-year-old high school fire was enough of a challenge for me at the moment. I was on the trail of a mystery that included a lost elephant, not a temptress. Of course I was about the only one in town who listened when I said I didn't have time for romance.

I know the words came out of my mouth; I heard myself say them. More than once. But I might as well have been speaking Latin. I've never seen a town more convinced that its chief should find a nice girl and settle down. Pronto.

Only Ida Walker and Jayne Reynolds had refrained from introducing me to someone "special." More's the pity, because those were the only two women of my acquaintance who had a clue about what might interest me.

The bell over the door jangled. Mac Campbell walked in, head down and making a beeline for the counter. Must've been a bad morning at the courthouse. Mac hated to lose. Rarely did. If figuring out how to cut the corner off a circle could make the difference in winning or losing a case, Mac would figure out how to do the impossible.

I waved him over as soon as he'd collected his order from Jayne. Even without a kilt and bagpipes, he looks the role of big, brawny Scotsman. Until he opens his mouth and proclaims himself a Southern Son with his accent. We're both Southern Sons of

Mossy Creek legends. His dad was the judge; mine the chief. I think we were five years old when Mac beat me to a pulp the first time. I wasn't stupid. I figured if you couldn't beat 'em, you'd better join 'em.

He's been a friend ever since.

Neither of us ended up where we thought we'd be or what we thought we'd be. Neither of us could wait to leave Mossy Creek behind. He was going to be a rock star, and I was going to be anything but a cop. Fate had a good laugh at those plans and jerked us back in line.

Mac had long ago come to grips with his rebellious demons, graduated law school, snagged a wonderful woman, and found some sort of balance in his life. To my knowledge, he never regretted the road not taken. Or the guitar solos not written. But then his father was still alive; they spoke. Mine was dead, and I had his job.

The espresso claimed Mac's complete attention for a gulp or two. When he looked up, the bad morning in court was washed away with the caffeine. "You're just the man I need. Patty said to drag you to dinner if I found you. Consider yourself found. Now, what's got you looking so thoughtful?"

"Sewing circles."

His brows drew together as he banged

the heel of his hand against one ear the way you'd whack a television to improve bad reception. "Patty's right. I can't hear anymore. Did you just say sewing circles?"

"Patty's wrong. You can hear, but you don't listen. Sewing circles." I warmed to my topic. I don't know why I hadn't asked him before. He'd know. "Sewing circles. What is it about a single man that sets sewing circles to twittering and planning his future? Why is everyone trying to fix me up?"

Mac snorted and turned a sly look on me. I remembered why I didn't like my best friend very much and why I hadn't mentioned this before. He wiggled his eyebrows and enlightened me. "Sewing circles are twittering because — and I'm quoting Patty here — Amos Royden is one long tall collection of mysterious he-man parts."

I stared at him, horrified. Or gratified. Or both. But he hadn't answered the question. Not really. "I am not the only single, employed, reasonable looking, thirty-something man in town. So, why me? Why all the attention and women stopping by with food? I understood why they were on my doorstep with bribes before the pageant, but the attention didn't stop afterward. The players just changed. Why is everyone so interested?"

"You sure you want to know?"

His question intimated that I ought not to pursue the answer. Of course his question also guaranteed I wouldn't let the subject drop.

"Enlighten me." I leaned back, braced by the wall.

"Three reasons." Holding up a finger, he said, "One. You're tall, dark, and brooding. You've got baggage. Women can't resist a man with baggage or mystery. There's all that time in Atlanta that no one knows anything about. That's like a red flag to a lot of women. It's the dark secret. Love of a good woman and all that."

A second finger joined the first. "Two. Your preoccupation with the job might as well be a sign you carry around that says, 'Betcha can't catch me.' They think you're playing hard-to-get, and that's turned it into a competition with you as the prize. They all want in the game because they all think they have a shot. I mean you like women whether you mean to or not. It's the damnedest thing. Tall, short, skinny, fat, older. You appreciate women and forget to hide it."

"What's wrong with that?"

"Nothing except that it tends to make the rest of us look bad and makes you look like you're looking." He paused as if asking for permission to continue.

I shut up, and he lifted a third finger. "Three. They're afraid you'll fall into the wrong hands."

I started laughing, but sobered quickly enough when I realized Mac hadn't cracked a smile. He was serious. "Mac, that's the stupidest thing I've ever heard. I'm not some top secret report on Area 51's UFO encounter. How on earth am I going to fall into the wrong hands. And whose hands would the wrong hands be?"

He gave me one of those pitying looks that friends give you when you're being naïve, but as he opened his mouth, the doorbell jingled again.

Loralee Atwater bounced in. She took only two fluid bounces toward Jayne before swiveling in our direction like a bird dog on point. Loralee's a recently divorced tennis mom who lives in one of the new developments on Lookover Mountain. Her ex-husband was a Bigelow banker. Big friends with John Bigelow, Sue Ora Salter's husband and a former lawyer, now president of the Bank of Bigelow County. Loralee's husband got the safe; Loralee got the money. Most of which she spends in Bigelow, not Mossy Creek. Her interior decorator is Swee Purla. Swee bought a Porche with the commission from Loralee's post-divorce, house-redecorating mania.

Loralee wouldn't be caught dead in something less trendy than The Naked Bean. She takes a tennis lesson down at the Bigelow Country Club every Friday and has two pre-teen hellions in private school. Today was Friday, and she had one of those swirly tennis skirts on. Perky and physically adorable do not begin to describe her. The woman does actually bounce, but anyone who has spent any quality time with Loralee knows that appearances are deceiving. She's Tigger-with-teeth. As soon as she smiles, you know it's time to check your ammo. It's a self-preservation instinct.

"Well, hello, Amos." She smiled. I was glad I had reinforcements with me already. She didn't take her eyes off me as she added, "Mac."

Mac had handled her divorce. He doesn't discuss clients. Doesn't have to. You can see it in his eyes. He didn't like Loralee. Mac's a little touchy about folks who use kids as weapons in divorce proceedings. Especially in Loralee's case. Everyone — Sandy was my actual source — knew she wouldn't take the kids unless they came with plenty of money. Parenting interferes with an active social life.

"You boys takin' a break?" She'd have pulled over a chair and joined us if Mac hadn't gotten up.

"Not anymore. I've got appointments."

I followed his lead and checked my watch. "I've got a committee meeting for the big grammar school reunion this fall, and I should probably get in a couple more hours of catching criminals and stopping crime before I go home for the day."

She affected a little pout of disappointment. "Oh, darn. I did want to talk to you about the boys. We aren't actually Mossy Creek citizens, but I thought you might help me figure out how to keep them out of trouble this summer." Then she brightened as if an idea just occurred to her. "But, you know, dinner would be better. Why not tonight, if you're just going home after work? You can come by my place, and you won't have to cook."

I bought myself a few extra seconds by pulling some bills from my wallet to toss on the table. Loralee had managed to smother her invitation under a blanket of fake parental concern. Fortunately, I knew she didn't give a flip how much trouble those boys caused this summer. As I turned back to her, inspiration struck.

"Can't." I managed not to sound relieved. "Patty'd kill me."

"Patty?"

"Mac's wife."

He chimed in. "Tiny woman. Mean as a snake if he doesn't show up at least once a month for inspection. Tonight's the night. She's gone to a lot of trouble for tonight."

When he finally shut up, he looked mighty pleased about something. Warning sirens should have sounded then, but I was too focused on escaping any future Loralee invitations.

"Tell you what," I offered. "Come down to the station anytime. Bring the boys with you. We'll talk. I'll see what I can do."

My walkie-talkie crackled and beeped. I pulled it off the belt and keyed the switch. "Go ahead."

Good ol' Sandy. She's an employee you can count on in a tight spot. "Chief, I need to talk to you about a dead moose. Over."

"On my way. Out." I slipped the walkie-talkie back on the belt, shrugged as if it were an emergency, and headed for the door in one motion. I'm sure Sandy was staring at the equipment back at the office wondering why I hadn't at least asked her where she'd gotten a dead moose. We don't have moose in Georgia. But I didn't really care at the moment.

Mac followed, and once outside he fell into step with me. His office was on the way to the station. He didn't wait long before commenting. "Moose?"

"I haven't a clue, and I don't care."

"Coward."

"That would be correct. Would it also be correct if I assumed that Loralee is who or what they mean by the 'wrong hands.' "

"Yep."

"They actually think I'm that stupid?"

"Sometimes Battle was."

"I'm not Battle."

"They're beginning to figure it out. Give 'em time." He split off toward his office door. "Six-thirty. Don't be late."

"I never am."

Sandy always has my messages ready as soon as I walk in. That doesn't mean I'm allowed to actually read them. She held them up and then impaled them neatly on the message spindle.

"Nothing important, Chief. Just complaints about the St. Paddy's parade tonight. Some folks are afraid that it'll be too rowdy."

"Parade?" That got my attention. "I hesitate to ask, but when in hell did we get a parade? Did I miss a meeting?"

She grinned. "This morning. Bigelow's having one. So we have to, too."

Of course. I should have known that it was Bigelow's fault. Creekites tended to over-react since that damned mechanical gypsy arrived and stirred up talk about the mystery of the high school fire. Just seeing it had fanned the flames — pardon the pun — of the old rivalries. Besting Bigelow was no longer a charming town hobby; it was becoming a town mission.

Leaning closer, Sandy got that gleeful look she wore sometimes when she was about to divulge good information. "Dwight Truman wasn't real happy about the parade. Told Michael he couldn't have a parade without a permit, which it was too late to get from you. Mostly because Dwight's mad at 'Father Mike' for getting new insurance quotes. Dwight had to drop his rates or lose the business. Anyway, Miss Ida got wind of it — the permit power play — and waltzed into the insurance agency pronto. She walked right into Dwight's office, right past the secretary, and gave him that look. You know the one?"

I nodded, chewing on my cheek to suppress a grin. I did, indeed, know that look.

Ida was far more dangerous than some bouncy little Tigger-with-teeth. When she smiled, you didn't bother to check your ammo. It was too late. I definitely enjoyed that smile. As long as it wasn't directed at me. "I'm guessing a permit was produced?"

"Yep. Most of the people calling us calmed down when we told them that Bigelow was making a big deal out of their parade. And I reminded them that the force would be on hand to manage the rabble rousers."

"How many of those are we expecting?"

"Michael said he thinks maybe about forty. Unless they cancel bingo. That'd be another ten or so. It's just from General Hamilton's statue to the pub. No drinking in the park and only green, non-alcoholic punch on the sidewalk outside the pub. Mutt says he doesn't figure most of the crowd will stay for the charity costume karaoke party in the pub."

Costume karaoke party at the pub? For charity? I didn't ask. I figured the answer would just make my head hurt, so I concentrated on the original problem. The parade.

A couple of officers could handle forty plus the bingo crowd. I wouldn't have to disappoint Patty. What Mac said about presenting myself for inspection was mostly true. Patty doesn't have siblings either, so she'd appointed herself to the role of big sister.

I looked at Sandy for a minute. "Think you're ready for crowd control and traffic?"

"Absolutely, Chief!" She snapped to attention without actually saluting. "I'm ready. Folks think of me as part of the force. I know they'll listen to me if I ask them to quiet down or pick up their litter. The parade's only a couple of blocks long. From General Hamilton's statue to the pub and —"

"Whoa! You got the job. You don't have to convince me. Mutt's on duty tonight. He'll show you the ropes. But take off now so I don't have to pay you overtime."

"Right!" She pulled her purse out of the file cabinet. "That'll give me some time to work on Rose the elephant."

"Wait a minute," I said, as she raised the counter section that served as the entry to the clerical area of our little station. "No one's leaving here until you explain about the dead moose and update me on the elephant investigation. I'm not going back out in the woods to retrace twenty-year-old elephant trails."

She stopped, counter top not quite settled back into place. "Oh, yeah." She let go; the counter clunked as it fell the rest of the way.

Facing me, she strangled her purse straps with both hands. "I'll do it all on my own time, Chief. I swear."

"The moose or the elephant?"

"Both. They're the same thing."

"Not really."

Grinning, she admitted, "Well, no. Of course not. What I mean is that the dead moose is what made me think of the elephant."

"The elephant I understand. I'm drawing a blank on the moose." I slung my hands on my hips and did my best impression of a chief-waiting-for-a-coherent-answer.

"No one ever found the elephant because I think they were afraid to ask questions. Because they didn't want to deal with what would happen if they found out who cut her chain. She didn't just pull free and bolt inside the school, Chief. Somebody cut her chain and *shooed* her. Maybe that somebody didn't count on her causing a fire. So that somebody had a vested interest in getting her out of town." Sandy made her pronouncement with a sage nod and a knowing wink. "See, me and Jess were having dinner with Sue Ora last night, and she and Jess started talking about writing. She's a big role model for him, you know, and he's not just saying that because she's his boss at the newspaper. Anyway, they were talking. Metaphors or similes or allegory or something. I just kind of smile and nod when they get into the technical stuff about writing. I don't want to interrupt them."

"Sort of like me not wanting to interrupt you, so you'll get straight to the point of what a dead moose has to do with any of this?"

"Exactly."

Sometimes hints don't work with Sandy.

"Sue Ora was talking about some issue the council didn't want to address being a dead moose and just laying there on the table. Only nobody wants to be the one to point out that they've got a dead moose. They'd all just rather pretend that it isn't there. That way, nobody has to be the bad guy. If anything is going to get done, Sue Ora says someone is going to have be brave enough to call that dead moose a dead moose and get it off the table. See, they've got to deal with it before it stinks up the place."

"You weren't, by any chance, paying any attention to the specific political issue Sue Ora was talking about?"

"Not really. My brain just kept buzzing me, telling me I was supposed to see a connection somehow." She looked up at me, clearly expecting me to have grasped the obvious.

I hadn't. She gave me a hint.

"Pink. . . ."

"Elephant in the corner," I finished. "The dead moose is just like the pink elephant in the corner everyone is too polite to mention. That made you think of the carnival elephant and wonder if the reason it was never found was because Battle and everyone else in town ignored it as the least of their worries at the time. Or because sometimes it's best to let sleeping elephants lie rather than stir up a nest of pachyderms."

"Doesn't that make sense? How could the town honestly lose an elephant? Even up here in the mountains where there're lots of places to hide one? Whether it was for pity or profit or to get rid of evidence, *somebody* helped that elephant escape from Mossy Creek. No offense to your daddy, but if he'd canvassed the mountains around here with an eye out for the elephant's accomplice, the elephant might have been *found.* I'm going to get the truth. Somebody knows something. Whoever sent that mechanical gypsy *wants* us to figure it out."

If anyone could find a twenty-year-old elephant in a haystack, with an accomplice, my money was on Sandy.

■ ■ ■ ■

Mac and Patty have a modest house on Elm. You'd expect something a little more upscale of a successful lawyer, but Mac never cared much for status and Patty cares even less. I suspect they both know they'll eventually inherit the old homeplace from the judge, and they're bright enough to realize they'll need every penny they can lay their hands on to maintain it. Hundred-year-old houses that haven't had more than a new coat of paint in fifty years are trouble waiting to bankrupt you.

I don't envy Mac all that work. Patty might not care about status, but she does care about restoring things. If you stand still long enough, she's liable to slap a coat of paint on you and stencil your forehead. She's forever finding 'visionary pieces' at flea markets and garage sales. That tendency of hers explains why she appointed herself my "sister." I suspect that I'm a visionary piece to Patty.

For all her love of restored antiques, she's not a fussy woman. The house has that lived-in and rumpled designer look that Mac calls "shabby *chick*" just to irritate her. Personally, I can't figure out why you should have to work so hard to make new things look like you've owned them for a hundred years. Or why it's chic to be shabby. But I won't deny it's a comfortable place. A place where a man can put his feet on the coffee table and not get yelled at.

A place where children could run wild. Or at least dogs. Patty can't have children, so while they're waiting for the wheels of adoption to turn, they raise Labradors instead of toddlers. Loud Labradors. The woofing and wailing began as soon as I slammed my car door.

Patty and the dogs met me on the porch. I'm not sure who looked more excited — Patty or the dogs, Butler and Maddie.

Butler's about eighty pounds of black Lab puppy in a three-year-old body. His name has nothing to do with being the Rhett Butler of handsome retrievers and everything to do with his status as a suspect in all manner of mayhem, mystery, and chaos during the first year of his life. When in doubt as to which dog had taken the contents of the kitchen garbage and decorated the living room, it was safe to assume that "the Butler did it."

Maddie, a seven-year-old creamy yellow Lab, was positioned behind Butler. Her tail thumped noisily against the door jamb. She looks like a law-abiding angel, but technically she should be hauled away to doggie-jail. She breaks the leash law every time her "parents" take her for an evening walk. To be fair, she does have a leash clipped to her collar; there just isn't anyone at the end of it. She walks herself, carrying the folded leash in her mouth as carefully as a well-trained field dog carries a dove. In a town where pets are expected to be as eccentric as their owners and where Bob The Incontinent Chihuahua made big news when he nearly became snack food for a hawk, Maddie stands out as a class act.

"Heyya, guys!" I supplied rib-thumps all around and then gave Patty a hug as we all squeezed through the door in a clump.

She thumped my ribs in return and said, "You haven't been eating."

"I've been running more. Running and freezing and hoping the weather'll keep warming up."

"Good! I'm glad to hear you don't have any objection to things heating up."

I let my arm fall and turned around to squint my eyes at her. Something told me I wasn't going to like this. "Why?"

"Because I've got a surprise." She grinned and pushed past me into the living room. "Look who's here! Don't you remember?

Bitsy Cameron!"

I plastered a smile on my face and whispered just loud enough for Patty to hear. "Et tu, Paté?"

Stephanie Heather Cameron.

Bitsy to her friends.

The unattainable golden girl of my youth. Princess of the doomed homecoming court on the night of the fire. Fledgling cheerleader. She didn't flirt all the time. Only when she was awake. And she didn't date underclassmen. Only seniors, which meant I never had a chance with Bitsy. Not until I was a senior at Bigelow High, and by then she was dating Bigelow college men exclusively.

"Amos." The smile was still dazzling. "How long has it been?"

I'm not sure who I had in mind when I thought of finding time to look up heartbreakers and heartthrobs from high school, but Bitsy fit neatly into both those categories. For all of ten seconds, the years rolled back, and I could remember being that lanky tongue-tied teenager carrying around a hopeless crush. But only for ten seconds. Then my brain kicked in, and I remembered that I had it on excellent authority that I was one long, tall collection of mysterious he-man parts.

So, I smiled back down at her. "Way too long. How's life been treating you?"

She grinned and did a little pirouette. "How does it look like it's been treating me?"

Patty piped up. "A lot better than the rest of us. Now stop showing off and get your toned tush in here for dinner. I just heard Mac come in the back door with the steaks."

For a moment Bitsy tried to look offended, but that's nearly impossible to do when someone calls your tush toned. So she fell in line and marched in to dinner with the rest of us. When I pinned Mac with a stare over the table, he had the decency to look apologetic. He'd known exactly what I was walking into tonight and hadn't warned me. Fortunately since the betrayal involved practically plopping Bitsy Cameron in my lap, I was feeling charitable. I forgave him.

That was a mistake.

I should have left the jury out a bit longer on Bitsy. The problem created when you're reunited with the object of a teenage crush is that you aren't a teenager anymore. Life has a way of changing most of us. Except Bitsy. She still believed the world revolved around her. Somehow that particular trait seemed cute when I was in high school. The fake little pout was cute back then, too.

Times change. I changed. I found I didn't like the pout Bitsy managed right before she began to complain.

"Oh, Patty, you won't mind throwing the dogs out will you? I just don't think I can eat a bite with them staring at me like that. They look so . . . well, wild." She gave a delicate shudder that managed to convey all kinds of insults to Patty's four-legged children. "I guess it's all that hunting."

Mac snorted. "Hunting? That'll be the day. The only bird they ever managed to find was last year's Christmas turkey."

I had to smile. "Yeah . . . too bad it was before you carved it. Did Maddie's wish ever come true?"

The rigid set of Patty's mouth began to soften as she relaxed at our teasing, but I could see Bitsy didn't get the joke. I explained. "Wishbone. They each grabbed a side of the turkey and pulled."

"How . . . cute."

"They are that. But don't worry about 'em tonight. As long as you don't baste yourself in Patty's orange-honey glaze, you should be safe enough from the Holiday Bandits."

Bitsy didn't look convinced and pulled her chair as close to mine as possible. The rest of the dinner just went down hill from there. We discovered that the steak would have been much better if Patty had done something called an 'expresso rub' before Mac grilled them. Bitsy was appalled that we were so backward that we weren't familiar with this nouveau cuisine technique.

When she used my forearm to demonstrate the rubbing technique, I thought Mac was going to choke on sirloin. Patty looked uncomfortable, and I decided reunions definitely weren't all they were cracked up to be. The idea of a reunion is often much more fun than the reality. A lot more fun.

Bitsy informed us that she'd taken her maiden name back after the second divorce to symbolically reclaim her sense of identity that had been stifled during her marriages. What I found interesting was that she didn't give up any of the married surnames in the process. She is officially, Bitsy Cameron Ashworth Tanner Cameron. No hyphens. I haven't a clue how she manages to sign all of that on her checks, but I figure it looks impressive on the letterhead of her gallery in Atlanta. She sells fine art to fine folks. Of course she refers to them as the 'best people.' Emphasis on best.

Seems good ol' Governor Ham Bigelow even bought his art from her. She was a big contributor to his campaign since he was part Hamilton, after all, and she owed at least that much loyalty to Mossy Creek. She lowered her voice dramatically to proclaim the man "perfectly dreamy."

I sent Mac more than one you-will-pay-for-this looks across the table. His expression implied that he already was — dinner with Bitsy was an obstacle course for his Southern hospitality. Mac disliked frivolous people, hated class distinctions, and had no qualms about thumping anyone who hurt Patty's feelings.

Except he couldn't thump a woman.

After torturous minutes of listening to Bitsy's European buying trips, it looked like she might be winding down. "But I'm boring you. What do you care about Europe? Y'all stay close to home. Why, I'm surprised Patty doesn't already have a gaggle of babies to run around after. Oh! And aren't those bronze marathon runners of Tag's just magnificent? Imagine! Finding a sculptor of Tag's caliber has just been the surprise of my visit. Who knew Daddy's having that heart attack would turn out to be such good luck?"

Mac couldn't take it anymore. "Amos, don't you and Bitsy need to be going?"

Since I hadn't brought Bitsy, I didn't see how *we* needed to be going anywhere. I gave him a purposely blank look. "Not really.

Sandy's covering the parade."

"But surely you and Bitsy will want to go down to the pub? How would it look if the police chief didn't turn out for charity? What would Father Mike think?"

"A charity event?" Bitsy perked up and rested her beautifully manicured nails on my arm.

"Not your kind of party." I warned Mac with a look and warned Bitsy with information. "It's a St. Paddy's Day karaoke costume party. Father Mike — Michael Conners — is giving two dollars to our Parks and Recreation Fund for every costumed customer and every song."

She immediately lost interest until Mac prodded. "Yeah, you gotta wear green. Too bad you can't get into your old cheerleading outfit. Weren't the old high school's colors green and white? That'd be a blast from the past. An instant costume."

Patty bit her lip. I bit my tongue. And Bitsy bit the bait. She was extremely proud of her legs and her toned tush. Mac knew exactly what he was doing, because she squared her shoulders, ready for battle. "I'll have you know that I can certainly still fit in that outfit!"

"Really? But surely not good enough to wear it in public!"

I kicked Mac. Hard. I was doomed, but it made me feel better. Made him wince, and the expression on his face made Bitsy think he was wincing at a mental picture of her in her cheerleading outfit.

"Really," Bitsy huffed. "In fact, I'll show you. Come on, Amos. We'll run by Daddy's and meet them at the pub."

"Right." I agreed because I had no other choice. But if I was going to suffer then Mac was going to suffer right along with me. "We'll all go! Mac's kilt is a green plaid isn't it, Patty?"

"I believe it is."

"Okay then! We'll meet you there." I pushed my chair back. "Make sure he brings the bagpipes, Patty."

She was grinning. Mac was not. Served him right.

If it weren't for Bitsy, the rest of the evening might have been fun. How often do you see a man perform *Yellow Submarine* on bag-pipes? Mac was a huge hit. In between requests, he did his best to get rid of Bitsy, but since each of his attempts involved my having to go off alone with Bitsy, I wasn't agreeable.

First he dragged out old stories in which my "manliness" figured prominently. Bitsy couldn't have gotten any closer to me if you'd painted her on. Then he spun the yarn about our local Bigfoot and suggested that only lovers in the woods ever saw this creature. Even though Josie McClure seemed to have located the Bigfoot and even convinced him to show up for the Valentine's Day dance.

Gosh, Mac wondered aloud, why didn't *we* (Bitsy and I) go see if Bigfoot was out tonight? Bitsy was all ashiver and atwitter to check it out. I lied about being on call and kicked Mac again.

Next he convinced Bitsy to sing a painfully horrific karaoke version of that song about liking a man with slow hands. I looked everywhere but at Bitsy, who was definitely singing to me. By the time Bitsy sashayed off the makeshift stage and snuggled up to me again, I didn't bother to stop her running her stocking foot up inside my pants leg. Bitsy always got what she wanted, and apparently she wanted poison ivy on the bottom of her foot.

But when she put her hand on my thigh, I shot up from the chair like a six-year-old volunteering to open birthday presents. "Time for me to sing and do my bit for charity!"

Ida Walker and Del Jackson came in just

in time to catch my warm-up and drive home a truth I'd been trying to ignore. I fiddled with the microphone stand for a moment before I admitted to myself that I didn't much like Jackson. Something about the retired military colonel grated on my nerves, made me bristle. Tonight I figured out why.

I didn't like Jackson because Ida flowed into the room at his side.

She might be in her fifties, but the woman didn't look that much older than me. She wore a simple gypsy outfit. This was not a woman you'd confuse with the rusty carnival-game gypsy sitting in the foyer of the town hall. Nope. Ida was warm, sensual flesh-and-blood. The long green skirt that cinched in at her waist undulated around her body like a living thing when she moved. Her shoulders slid in and out of view as the classic gypsy shirt slipped off one shoulder and then the other when she waved and returned greetings. Gold earring hoops dangled. It wasn't so much a costume as a transformation. Ida looked like the genuine article, right down to the unruly auburn hair. I wasn't put off by the dramatic gray streaks at her temples. Racing stripes.

She smiled with honest enjoyment at the scene around her, melting into the experience, listening. On the other hand, my unintended date called attention to herself by executing a cheerleading move parody and screaming, "Go Amos!" I looked at Bitsy and then at Ida. The contrast couldn't be ignored. Or my reaction to it. I didn't want a Bitsy. I wanted an Ida.

That's when Jackson stepped in front of her, meeting my gaze and cocking an eyebrow. My one moment of unguarded emotion had been caught on tape, Jackson-wise. His grim expression said *Back off before you get any serious ideas.*

Too late, my man. Too late. The gypsy's out of the bottle.

Then Ida pulled his arm, and they threaded their way through the crowd to a table. I finished my song — now I can't even remember what it was — and decided the night hadn't been a total loss after all. I'd discovered there was the proverbial dead moose on the table between Del Jackson and me. What we were going to do about it was anyone's guess. But at least we'd stopped pretending it wasn't there.

What Del didn't know was that I'd had plenty of practice sitting on the bench, waiting for my turn, and wanting things that just weren't practical. Life is a lot like high school football. If you expect a front row seat, you better show up every day, ready to play.

And don't forget that the home team always has the advantage.

From: Ida Hamilton Walker
To: Katie Bell

CONFIDENTIAL
Katie Bell, if you publish even *one* more hint of gossip about that scene at O'Day's, I swear I'll use you for target practice. Even if you *are* my favorite third cousin once removed. Even if you *do* keep me up on certain facts about our citizenry that I, as a concerned mayor, obviously need to know.

But as for that incident at O'Day's: I am grown woman and often accused of not acting my age, especially in regards to the opposite sex. So what. Good for me. I encourage no one to act her age. His age. A politcally correct age. Whatever.

I am still a fine, tall, sensual specimen of a New South Southern woman, as any man over the age of puberty will tell you. I wear my jeans tight and listen to my music loud and occasionally put on a low-cut, braless t-shirt under my business suits. People forget sometimes that I founded the *Women Are Not Girls* feminist club at the University of Georgia when I was a business major there in 1964, or that I swore I'd play the field the way men do — until Jeb Walker sidelined me, and I happily let him. Like all the women in my Hamilton lineage, I expect to remain extraordinarily lithe and alluring well into the eighties. My eighties, that is. Allure, of course, is all about attitude.

Power to the Allure, Baby.

But as you well know, I stopped my heart's clock the year Jeb died. How he died is not something I can bear to discuss, even now, but all that's important is that he died young and dearly loved by me and Rob. Our marriage has held me in suspended animation all these years since. Of *course* I don't age normally. I've become timeless, remembering Jeb.

So, regarding this rumor of feelings between Amos Royden and myself, well, *yes,* I'm aware of the subtle tension between him and me, the sassiness of our interchanges, the unspoken but urgent longing. Not that there has ever been any hint of disgrace between us, or even any open admiration that might be misunderstood. We have some sweet and very noble history, but that's no one's business but ours. You'll never pry the details out of him or me, so don't bother trying.

While he is older than my Rob and I may be a shameless flirt and a gentleman's woman — that is, in the sense that there are 'ladies' men,' I am a woman who blatantly attracts and enjoys modern gentlemen — but I am not the kind of woman who hires and then seduces her own town's young police chief. Nor am I the kind of woman who cheats on an established relationship. Thus, Del Jackson's trust is safe with me.

I hope I've settled the issue. Thank you. Remember what I said about target practice.

From: Katie Bell
To: Lady Victoria Salter

Dear Vick:

Sorry to be so long in answering, but I've been keeping a low profile since a little tiff occurred between me and the mayor. No big deal, just something I'm not comfortable discussing unless I'm wearing a shotgun-proof vest. Anyway . . .

Forget our discussion of the Ten-Cent Gypsy, the fire, and the reunion plans this week. Jayne Reynolds had her baby on Monday. Her water broke the other afternoon while she was pouring a cup of chamomile tea for Adele Clearwater at The Naked Bean. Old Miss Adele, who has become a big supporter of Jayne's, shrieked so loud that Jayne's cat, Emma, went tearing out onto the sidewalk, collided with Ingrid Beechum's infamous Chihuahua, Bob, and rolled him like a rat in a bag. Bob took off at a dead run for the town square but Emma caught him under the spring azaleas. All anyone heard after that was her growling and him yelping. Suddenly Emma burst out of the azaleas with pink blossoms scattered on her fur and a look on her calico face like something stank and the something was *her.* She raced back to the coffee shop, leaving moist pawprints on the sidewalk.

Because Bob had peed all over her.

Anyway . . . Jayne yelled out the door for Ingrid Beechum, and Ingrid came running. Ingrid and Amos got Jayne into Amos's patrol car, and Amos drove her down to Bigelow County Hospital. A good twenty or thirty Creekites followed right away to stand vigil for Jayne, since she's a young widow and has no family in the county. Ingrid, always a tough and take-charge woman, stayed with her in the birthing room. Ingrid will never have a grandchild of her own. She counted on Jayne's baby to be a good substitute.

The end result? Matthew Reynolds, Junior. A healthy, dark-haired boy. Seven pounds, eight ounces. Ingrid, crying like a grandmother, held him up to a window of the birthing room so we could all see him.

Jayne sent a message that made the rest of us cry, too. "He's been born a Creekite," she said. "So now he has a whole town for a family."

We take people to our hearts quickly. It's a testament to the magic of this town that we still feel that way. We endured a lot of strangers in Mossy Creek right after the high school fire — and not happily, I have to admit. Nobody liked the investigators from the state crime lab and the reporters from the Atlanta newspapers and TV stations. The investigators treated us like ignorant small town hicks, and the reporters made sure the rest of the world thought so, too. Zeke Abercrombie was so upset his blood pressure went sky high, and Dr. Champion ordered him not to serve as mayor again. That's when Ida stepped in. She ran for the office, she won, and she vowed to check out every newcomer in town from then on. I couldn't agree more.

That's why, even now, we don't let newcomers keep to themselves. We don't like mysteries, even little ones. We have a saying about strangers: *Throw 'em in the Creek quick, and see if they float.*

It's kinder than it sounds.

Read on and see what I mean.

PEGGY

THE P-PATCH

Life's not just about what you plant, but
what you harvest.

I'd always loathed gardening, in part because gardening loathed *me*. That saying
about 'if at first you don't succeed, try, try
again,' is idiotic. If you don't succeed at
something, then for pity's sake drop it and
take up something you're good at. With that
said, I have to tell you that none of what
happened after I moved to Mossy Creek was
my fault.

It was the zinnias'.

I tore every one of them right out of the
ground and threw them into the trash.

But I suppose this story really starts with
Ben. Ben Caldwell, my husband. He convinced me to retire early as a professor of
English at the University of Tennessee
when he retired from his law firm in Knoxville. Then he moved us down here to
Mossy Creek, Georgia so we could be close

to our married daughter, Marilee. We hadn't lived close to her since she went away to college, and Ben was determined to reunite the family in case there should be grandchildren.

Ben actually longed to get his hands on the acre and a half of derelict garden that came with our grand old house on a side street off the square in Mossy Creek. The previous owner, Astrid Oglivie, was apparently a legend among the local gardeners until she developed cataracts at ninety-three. By the time she went peacefully to meet her Maker at ninety-six and we bought the house, the untended garden reminded me of the impenetrable thicket that surrounded Sleeping Beauty's bower.

Ben had ambitious plans to make the garden a showplace again. Unfortunately, the first time he dragged me into the back yard, I nearly tripped over a copperhead snake the length of a football goal post. My relationship with the garden was all downhill from there. It's taken women millennia to drag themselves up off their knees. Why should I grovel in the mud in the blazing sun while blood-sucking creatures attack the back of my neck and my skin goes leathery? I'm in that age group where I'm turning leathery enough, already.

I was delighted to leave Ben to the outdoors while I stayed indoors in the new central air conditioning reading the latest murder mysteries and chatting with my university friends on-line. Ben was completely happy. He loved puttering around outside, and cleaned out most of the encroaching jungle right away. He kept running inside to tell me about his new discoveries. There was even a small 'secret garden' at the back of the property, hidden behind mossy stone walls. I took his word for it.

Then six months after we moved in, he keeled over dead in the zinnias. I haven't forgiven him for that, yet. I still get angry when I see gray-haired couples tottering hand in hand down Mossy Creek's main drag. That was supposed to be *us* a few years hence. In my mind, the garden killed him. So you can see I am not well-disposed to green-growing things.

Or, I *wasn't.*

Sooner or later I knew I'd get up the gumption to put the house on the market and move back to Tennessee. Preferably to a high-rise condominium within walking distance of a mall. In the nearly nine months since Ben's death, I hadn't been able to overcome my inertia.

Marilee swore I was clinically depressed.

Well, heck, yes, I was depressed! In a little over a year, I'd lost my job, my city life, and my husband. But I wasn't *clinically* depressed. Just garden-variety, if you'll excuse the allusion. If Marilee hadn't brought in the mail when she came to see me, if she hadn't seen the *Mossy Creek Garden Club* return address on their invitation to me, none of it would have happened. So in a sense it's her fault. I would have declined the invitation politely and gone back to the latest true-crime police novel on my nightstand.

But Marilee, who is unfortunately a status-conscious Bigelow by marriage, screamed so loud when she saw the invitation that my Maine coon cat, Dashiell, leapt to the top of the nearest bookcase and hissed at us. "Mother, you have to go to that tea! The garden club is the smallest, most exclusive club in Mossy Creek! My Claude would kill to be a member."

"Since I've heard that you have to be female, over fifty, and definitely not a Bigelow to be invited, I don't think he's got a snowball's chance in hell."

"Please, mother, say you'll go. Since Daddy died all you've done is sit in this house with that wicked cat and read books." She waved a hand at the bookshelves that were double and triple-shelved with paper-backs. "One of these days I'll find you buried under a pile of books with one frail hand scrabbling feebly at the carpet."

"My hands are not frail, thank you very much. Your father and I should never have allowed you to audition for the Playmakers at the University of North Carolina, Mari-lee. You've over-dramatized ever since."

"Say you'll go to that tea, mother. Swear!"

I knew I'd never get rid of her otherwise, so I swore. Garden club indeed. Those exclusive old ladies would take one look at me, shout 'unclean' at the tops of their voices, and kick me out.

The party was at Ida Hamilton Walker's. Ida Walker is mayor of Mossy Creek and just barely eligible, age-wise, to join the club. Looks-wise, she could be forty, tops. A good-looking forty, too. I knew she lived just outside town at the Hamilton family's showplace farm, in a large, Victorian home full of inherited antiques, but I'd never been invited there, before. I expected to be grilled about my theories on rutabagas by Mayor Walker and a crowd of superbly svelte crones sporting perfectly coiffed hair, fake fingernails, and a combined carat weight of diamonds that would sink the Titanic. All drinking *oolong* out of *Lowestoft* cups.

And wearing ultra-suede, lots of it. I have a friend who swears ultra-suede rots the post-menopausal brain.

When Ida's housekeeper, June McEvers, ushered me into the library, instead I found half a dozen women in Wranglers and chinos knocking back mimosas with their Nikes propped on stacks of gardening magazines atop Ida's antique butler's table. I felt overdressed in the black blazer and skirt I'd dredged out of the back of my closet for the occasion. I even had on panti-hose and pumps with heels.

I was introduced all around to women with names that meant almost nothing to me. I've never been good at names, even though there were only five of them, not counting my hostess. I knew the mayor, of course, and had met a couple of the others casually at Mossy Creek's Mt. Gilead Methodist Church, but I felt certain none of their names would stick, especially since I never expected to be asked to another meeting.

They shoved a mimosa into my hand and proceeded to try to get me drunk as a skunk.

While I was fending off a giddy urge to hiccup, the aged elf next to me, Mimsy, put a nearly transparent paw on my arm and whispered, "We want you to join our club, dear. We like the way you drink. But lose the pumps, all right?"

Okay, I thought, *while I can still walk, I'd better disabuse these ladies of any hope that I could be an asset to them.* "You ladies really don't want me in your club. I swear."

That brought a flurry of disclaimers. I held up a hand — I still saw only one, thank God — and said, "Look, you're wonderful people, and I've enjoyed this 'tea' thoroughly. But you are about to clasp a viper to your bosom. I'm no gardener. I can even kill *philodendron.*"

Gasps. *Nothing* can kill philodendron.

"You remember Nathaniel Hawthorne's story about the princess whose father kept her in a poison garden?" I went on. "Then one day she got out, and every plant she touched died? You are looking at Rappaccini's great-great-great-whatever granddaughter. I am come as a *blight* upon your land." As a former English professor, I tend to talk flowery when I get smashed, which I do about once every twenty years.

"But dear, anybody can garden!" Mimsy said.

"That's like saying anyone can cook or ride a horse or do quantum physics. It ain't necessarily so. My *husband* was the gardener. If you've driven by and seen our place looking half-way decent, it's because Ben did a bunch of work before he died, and my daughter and son-in-law have tried to keep the lawn mowed and the shrubs cut back since then. Frankly, I haven't had the heart."

"Don't worry. We'll help you." This from a large woman wearing a Hawaiian shirt. She looked like a small tropical island after a typhoon.

"I don't want to be helped. I want to sit indoors with my cat and read mysteries."

"And get old and shriveled and just wait to die?" Mimsy added helpfully.

After a moment of dull dignity, I gave up and nodded.

I saw Ida's fingers begin to drum on the candle table by her chair. I heard concerted sighs. I saw an exchange of looks that could only be called 'speaking.'

That's when I should have tossed my empty mimosa glass at them and run for cover.

"We're staging an intervention on your behalf," Ida said, leaning toward me and motioning for a tiny lady near Mimsy to refill my tumbler. "We need you. Mossy Creek needs you. Your garden needs you. Surely that makes a difference."

"Not to my *ability*."

The tiny lady actually began to stroke my hand, much the way I stroke Dashiell when he's annoyed at me. "We always counted on dear Astrid," she said. "At least until she got so blind she couldn't tell an ageratum from a hydrangea."

Titters all around. Apparently ageratum and hydrangeas look different to the trained eye.

"We can't afford to lose just because she died and sold you the house."

"Lose? Lose what?"

"The contest, dear. The gardening contest against the Bigelow Garden Club."

Oh, boy.

One of the first discoveries I made about Mossy Creek is that it is locked in an eternal competition with its neighbor at the south end of the county. This includes Bigelows — the family — and Bigelow — the well-to-do small city — and Bigelow — the county, which includes the town of Mossy Creek. The feud is complicated by the fact that the governor of Georgia, Hamilton Bigelow, is Ida's nephew by way of being the only son of Ida's estranged sister, Ardaleen Hamilton Bigelow. Ida despises Ardaleen for family reasons going back to their girlhood, and the feeling is mutual. Ardaleen hates, loathes and abominates anything and everything to do with Ida and Mossy Creek. She thinks her sister and the entire town is out to destroy the life, happiness, and possible presidential candidacy of her pampered, arrogant son, Hamilton.

Which, in all fairness, it pretty much is.

"You see," Ida said, relaxing into her wing chair, certain that she had me corralled between Mimsy and the Brunhilde in the Hawaiian shirt, "This year, as part of the reunion festivities, we're having a contest between the gardens of Bigelow and Mossy Creek. It's an uneven contest, of course. Their garden club has almost twenty members, while we have six — *seven* with you, Peggy."

I started to say something, but she shushed me. "It's not a straight 'Yard of the Month' sort of thing. That would be too simple. The contest is judged by neutral officials of the state garden society. This is a very elaborate contest in which each category acrues points. The town with the most points wins."

"Then you've already lost," I said.

"No, we haven't."

"And we *won't*," Brunhilde chimed in. I got the feeling she was threatening me.

"We all specialize in different sorts of things," said Ida. "We know we can count

151

on Eleanor over there to win the rose division. She's bred three roses that are named after her. Nobody can touch her roses. She's safe points."

Which one was Eleanor? Oh, right. Eleanor Abercrombie. She was the tall, thin one with the dyed black hair in a bun at the back of her neck. She appeared to be sleeping and was snoring quietly. She looked like a cross between a librarian and an aging Hell's Angel. She grew roses?

"Mimsy's herb garden is pretty much a shoo-in, too."

Mimsy bridled happily. "I have fourteen different varieties of basil."

Brunhilde sighed. "But after that we hit the problem areas." Brunhilde, whose real name, I finally remembered, was Erma Something-or-other, went on, "My spring garden is to die for, but since the contest is going to be judged in June, the only way to judge the spring gardens is by pictures. Jess Crane over at the *Mossy Creek Gazette* heard that witch Helen Overbury from Bigelow hired an actual TV production team to videotape her garden with music. A couple of Polaroids won't do it."

Ida threw up both hands. "So we'll do our own video production complete with fancy camera work and a mixed chorus, if we have to. I'll speak to Bert Lyman over at WMOS about it. You know? He's turned his barn into a small television studio. He's producing shows for local-access cable. He'll help us."

Everyone looked eager and nodded.

"Elton John still keeps an apartment in Atlanta," Brunhilde said. "I know his personal florist. I bet we could talk Elton into narrating our tape."

These women were beginning to scare me.

"The 'Formal Garden' points are bound to go to Eustene Oscar," Ida continued. "That's another guaranteed winner for us."

Brunhilde looked at me. "Eustene's not here today. Had to visit her mother at Magnolia Manor. But trust me, Eustene has hard-to-beat topiary boxwoods imported from England before the Revolutionary War."

"And the design was copied from Capability Brown," Mimsy said with pride. Apparently I was supposed to recognize the name. She picked up on my blank stare. "He was a famous garden designer in the eighteenth century in England."

"Oh."

"But Eustene's nearly eighty. With her arthritis, the topiary is getting really hard for her to trim, even with help. Last year the elephant looked more like a rhinoceros with a sinus condition." A spatter of conversation commenced regarding the elephant as a symbol of Mossy Creek's unsolved school mystery, and how Eustene vowed to keep the elephant topiary going until the twenty-year-old mystery was resolved — something involving a carnival elephant named Rose — but by that point, I just sat there in a kind of stupor, thinking about Eustene and her mama.

Eustene was nearly eighty? How old was Mama?

Brunhilde turned to me again. "But the most points go to the Top All-Around Garden. That's the problem. We *never* win the top-all-arounder."

"As it stands, Ardaleen Bigelow is bound to win," Mimsy said. "She cheats. I'm sorry, Ida, but it's true. Your sister cheats."

"I hope to shout," agreed Ida, unoffended.

"I beg your pardon?" I mumbled.

"She cheats," Mimsy repeated with a sneer. "That nitwitted son of hers, *Governor* Ham Bigelow, pardoned a landscape designer from Atlanta a couple of years ago just so he could come up to Bigelow and design Ardaleen's garden."

"Disgraceful," Brunhilde-Erma snorted.

"That man only served four years for cutting off his wife's head with a hedge trimmer."

I stared at her, dazed. "Can you *do* that with a hedge trimmer?"

"Ardaleen does not know her liriope from her acuba, but then, she doesn't have to. She's got half the trustees from the county jail working in the yard at her mansion three days a week."

"Is that legal?"

Everybody laughed.

"Since when does my nephew care about what's legal?" Ida said. "He uses the trustees to do the yard work at the state house and the governor's mansion. All above-board, on that count. But obviously, he considers his boyhood home in Bigelow to be like a second White House is to the President."

"So long as her son is governor, nobody's going to be able to win the Top All-Around Garden category but Ardaleen."

"When the prize should go to Ida," Brunhilde-Erma said. "Ida has a *beautiful* summer garden — color coordinated and everything. And she does all the crucial upkeep herself, except for bribing the Mossy Creek Boy Scout Troop to weed —"

Ida coughed. "I bought them a few camping tents. Hardly a bribe."

I took a deep sip of my mimosa. "So where do I come in? That is, *if* I were willing to entertain this madness for a minute?"

"The only category that's up for grabs in the competition is Most Unusual Garden. *That's* where you come in."

"Most Unusual Garden. As in *dead?* Would *that* win? Or maybe *Best Weeds?* Or how about *Most Likely To Harbor Giant, Venomous Snakes?*"

"We're serious," Erma said. I wasn't certain she could be anything else. "You have the perfect space for a showcase — that darling little walled garden down at the bottom of your back lawn."

"Huh? Ben hadn't gotten to that when he died. I've never even opened the gate. It's got to be a *jungle* in there. What was it originally?"

"A Shakespearean garden," Mimsy said. She sniffed and ran her fingers under her eyes to wipe away the tears without smearing her mascara. "Dear Astrid was so like you. She was an English teacher, and she loved to read. She only chose plants that were mentioned in Shakespeare — either the plays or the sonnets. It was a perfect little garden, and it could be perfect, again. Look, Peggy, we've got all spring to clean up your garden and replant. By the time the contest happens, you'll be ready with far and away the most unusual selections of any gardener in Bigelow County. You'll certainly beat that stupid bunch of bonsai trees in Geraldine Matthews back yard down in Bigelow."

"And your walled garden is quite a small area," Ida said. "Not too much for a new gardener like yourself to handle, in terms of maintenance." She pointed to the up-to-now silent member of the group. "Valerie is a professional landscaper. She can help lay out the beds and plan what goes where."

I set my mimosa down. Took the situation by the horns. The roots. Something. "How is using a professional landscaper different from Ham pardoning a hedge-trimmer killer? Wouldn't this be cheating, too? Besides, why doesn't Valerie do her own most unusual garden?"

Valerie, who didn't look nearly old enough to be a member, shrugged her silk-shirted shoulders at me. "Professionals can't enter. But I *can* advise an amateur. I just can't enter one of my own gardens."

Everyone looked at me hopefully, and waited.

I must admit the idea of a Shakespearean garden intrigued me. All that stuff that Ophelia wandered around sticking in people's faces before she jumped in the river. Rue? Rosemary? I'd have to go home and start reading. What *was* rue anyway?

Whoa! Halt! Stop! Ben had died in the zinnias. I wasn't going to encourage my yard to kill anyone else. Had these women drugged the mimosas with something that sapped both my good sense and my will to resist? I had to get out of there before I committed myself. Or needed committing.

I stood up. "I'll let you know." My knees wobbled. I had no business driving down Ida's driveway, much less up South Bigelow to Mossy Creek. "Uh, Ida, is there anybody sober enough to drive me home?"

Ida smiled. "I hope to shout."

Her housekeeper poured me into the passenger seat of Ida's favorite car, a silver, '58 Corvette convertible. "Where's James Dean?" I slurred to Ida, as June slid into the driver's seat. "Thanks for the party. Marilee will drive me back to get my car as soon as I sober up." And after I recovered from what was probably going to be a horrendous hangover. I suddenly remembered why I never drink.

"We'll be over to assess the walled garden Wednesday afternoon," Ida said and waved with calm satisfaction as June drove me out of the yard.

I groaned and let my head fall back against the seat. Oh, God, what had I gotten myself into?

The next morning I fortified myself with caffeinated Diet Coke, Excedrin and cheese toast, then dragged out my Shakespeare compendium and began to take notes.

By ten o'clock, I was bored out of my mind. It had been at least thirty years since I'd read all the plays. I vowed to re-read *A Midsummer Night's Dream,* at least, because the Mossy Creek Theatrical Guild planned a midsummer production of it and Anna Rose, the director, had asked me to give a little talk to the actors about the play's history. But as for the rest . . . I could probably make it through them again — well most of them. I wasn't certain about *Titus Andronicus.* But I would never in a million years be able to plough through those whiny sonnets.

I threw the book — the *Rockwell Kent* edition, so it weighed about ten pounds — across the living room. Dashiell snarled at me. "The hell with it," I said and picked up an old Agatha Christie I hadn't read in four or five years.

After lunch, I felt so guilty I put on my heavy rubber boots and walked down the back yard to Miss Astrid's walled garden. They weren't walls, really, just wrought iron fences covered in so much ivy they looked solid. I think I strained a trapezius muscle forcing the rusted iron gate open enough to slip inside.

What a sorry sight! Thank God the early-April day was too cool for the copperheads to be out of hibernation yet, because the tangle of dead shrubs and fallen tree branches were perfect hiding places. Around all four sides were raised beds that had once contained flowers, but now they held only winter-wilted weeds and dead things. Hopeless, lonely things, like me.

In a brick square at the center of the garden, beneath a small tree of some kind, sat a rusty iron table and four elaborate iron chairs. They all needed a good cleaning and a couple of coats of Rustoleum, but they were still pretty and had obviously been fine at one time.

I sank into one of the chairs. "Boy, talk about T. S. Eliot's *Wasteland.* Great place to kill a victim in a murder mystery. You could hang the object of your deadly affections from the tree over the table, or feed the poor soul some poisonous mushrooms . . ."

People in mysteries were always being bumped off by poisons plucked from their flowerbeds. I knew from my reading that you could distill digitalis from Foxglove, but I'd never actually seen a foxglove and had no idea what one looked like. Or deadly Nightshade either, for that matter. Were poisonous plants easy to grow? Were they pretty?

I hadn't a clue.

I came home from the Mossy Creek Library that afternoon with a backpack full of gardening books and books on poison plants courtesy of Hannah, the head librarian. Turned out that Foxglove was a pretty, spikey whitish-pinkish-maroon-flowered thing, and that deadly Nightshade had purply blue flowers that would look good in a bride's bouquet. The books so engrossed me that I didn't hear the telephone ring until the answering machine picked it up.

"Mother?" Marilee's voice. "If you're there, pick up. We want to hear all about the garden club party."

As I lifted the receiver, I thought for the first time since moving to Mossy Creek, My daughter married a Bigelow. She is a member of the enemy camp.

So I told her I'd had a wonderful time and would probably never go back. Hah. Let her pass *that* on to Claude to be passed on to the rest of the Bigelows.

Actually, Claude Bigelow was a nice young lawyer. A little stiff, but charming. The trouble with Bigelows — the family — I'd decided, was that even when they were obnoxious — like Ham and Ardaleen — they were often successful and smart and hard to resist. Mossy Creek's own die-hard Creekite newspaper publisher, Sue Ora Salter Bigelow, couldn't bear to divorce John Bigelow, the good-looking, thirty-eight-year-old president of the Bank of Bigelow County. They slept together but didn't live together. They were raising a well-adjusted teenage son, Will Bigelow, but pretended they weren't a family.

Mixed marriages between Creekites and Bigelowans never ran smoothly.

Ben and I had just thanked our stars that Marilee hadn't married an itinerant actor from her college infatuation with the theater. When we'd met staid, dependable Claude Bigelow, we were thrilled at his pedigree and assumed she'd loosen him up. Unfortunately, instead he tightened *her*.

"Here, Claude wants to speak to you," my daughter said.

I closed my eyes.

"Good evening, Mother Caldwell," Claude said cheerfully. "Marilee is extremely worried about your being alone in that house all the time. You know you'll always have a place with us down here in the city. Just say the word. We'd be happy to sign you up for bridge at the club and origami lessons at the senior center. My Aunt Ardaleen would love to introduce you to her circle of friends. None of them are readers, but —"

"The word is *No,* Claude, but thanks for the offer." I'd as soon move into the lion habitat at Zoo Atlanta.

He lowered his voice to a whisper. "Listen, Mother Caldwell, I know Marilee is encouraging you to join the Mossy Creek Garden Club, but trust me, those Creekite women are eccentric and socially unpredictable."

I made a solemn vow to deck my son-in-law the next time he called me Mother Caldwell. Right after I told him goodbye, I phoned Ida Hamilton Walker.

"Okay," I said. "I'm in. But you may not like what I want to do."

Ida laughed.

The amazing thing was that my fellow *gardeneers* of the Mossy Creek Garden Club not only loved my idea, they agreed to pitch in with things I hadn't even known were available.

Eleanor of the Roses said, "Now, many of

the plants you need grow wild or volunteer. First we have to *find* them, then we have to *transplant* them, and finally we have to coax them to *live* in captivity. It won't be easy, but at least this early in the spring most of them should still be dormant."

"Mushrooms will be harder," said the eighty-five-year-old Eustene, back from seeing Mama at the nursing home. "They get downright ill-tempered if you try to make them grow where they don't want to. They like shade and lots of wet dung."

"A bunch of the plants, like the lilies of the valley, we can just order from the plant catalogs," said Mimsy. "And I can let you have some of my iris and daffodils."

"For pity's sake, Mimsy! Iris and jonquils will be dead as doornails by late June," said Erma.

"Oh. You're right, dear." She perked up. "Then how about a castor tree to shade the patio and some cannas? And Oleander? They'll all look lovely against trumpet vine and English ivy growing up the wall. Oooh, Dutchman's britches! We have to have some of *that.*"

About seven that night we ordered pizza and ate it on my veranda with sweaters pulled around our shoulders. At eleven Mimsy and Eustene were the last to leave.

As Eustene started out the door, I asked, "This may sound rude, but just how old *is* your Mama?"

She laughed and waved her hand. "About the same age as dirt." She leaned over close to my ear. "I'm her baby. She married young."

My first day alone pulling grass and dead things in the walled garden, I came close to chucking it all until Valerie showed up with a half-dozen mystery book tapes from the library.

"You do have a Walkman, don't you?" she asked.

"I use it when I walk on the treadmill." I hadn't been on the treadmill in months and had no idea where the tiny tape player was, but I wasn't about to admit that to Valerie the Trim Valkyrie.

"It's the only solution," she said. "Working alone like this when it's chilly and dreary gets old fast. To be followed by working alone when it's so hot you can't draw an easy breath."

"When is it fun?"

"Maybe two days a year. But those days are worth the effort."

Working alone wasn't so bad with a mystery tape playing in my ear. Not that I was alone that much. Seventy-six-year-old

Mimsy — the aged elf — and sixty-four-year-old Erma made me their project. It didn't surprise me that Erma was strong, but Louetta could work us both under the table. Little by little, the bones of the walled garden emerged — naked, of course, but that was better than overgrown. Eustene dragged me out to the secluded corner of Ida's dairy-cow pastures to dig up wild versions of the plants I needed and show me how to cosset them properly once I got them home.

"Eustene," I said as I followed her — twenty years my senior — up a grassy hill with a canvas sack full of plants over one shoulder, "starting next week, you can visit me *and* your mama at the nursing home."

I went to bed most nights so achy I prayed for a nice friendly tornado to keep me indoors, and considered buying liniment by the case.

Whenever Claude and Marilee would drop by, or when Claude sent his Bigelowan yard man to cut my grass, I'd lock the wrought-iron door on the garden and sit on the back steps reading until I was alone again.

"I'm glad you didn't join the Creekites' garden club," Claude said. "Those women only cause trouble."

I nodded innocently.

One day, I heard Marilee's horn in the driveway. I barely had enough time to shut the garden gate on Eleanor and Erma and get myself up the hill to meet her.

"Mother, you're huffing and puffing." She put her arm around me. "Are you having heart problems? Are your ankles swelling? Why on earth are you so dirty? And what on earth is that smell?"

It was well-rotted goat manure for the mushrooms, but I wasn't about to tell her that. It wasn't so much that I didn't trust her as that I knew she'd tell Claude, and everybody would sit around their Bigelow dining tables and laugh at me.

There'd be plenty of time for laughter when the state garden society judge arrived.

When we weren't working on my garden, the *gardeneers* and I worked on the other members' gardens. I discovered there were little wheeled carts to keep me off my knees and gloves to protect my hands. I refused to adopt Mimsy's old-fashioned sunbonnet, but I did buy a big straw hat at the Wal-Mart in Bigelow. The stack of unread mysteries beside my chair grew daily. Dashiell took to sitting on them and lashing his tail at me.

One morning at seven, Ida called me.

"Get to Eleanor's. Pronto!"

I drove up to find I was the last member to arrive. "Who died?" I said as I got out of my Land Rover.

Eleanor began to keen.

God, somebody really *had* died.

Ida, who was dressed in an elegant blue dress-suit and had been on her way down to Atlanta for a statewide mayors' conference, took my arm and whispered. "Root gall. Come on. This is serious."

I already knew that roses had to be sprayed for aphids, watered just so, planted just so, and fed just so. Now I discovered that the real horror for rose growers was root gall — some kind of rot that not only ate the roots of infected roses but poisoned the soil around them. Infected roses had to be dug up and burned. Then the soil around them had to be disposed of as though it were loaded with Strontium 90.

Eleanor was no help. She sat on the ground and wept. "They did this!" she wailed. "Those Bigelow devils! I'll give them *tent caterpillars!*"

There were only three rose bushes with gall, but that was a disaster because one of them was a brand new variety, Mrs. Ida Hamilton Walker, that Eleanor planned to unveil in Ida's honor during the contest.

"The roses are really so near to being blue you have to look real close to see the purple." She wept. "One of the big rose wholesalers has already offered me a fortune for the budwood."

"Is that the only one?" I asked, staring at a sickly-looking rose bush.

Eleanor sniffed. "I have three more in the greenhouse, but they're so much smaller, they'll never catch up in time."

"All we can do is try," Erma said and flexed her meaty biceps. "Now, where do you want us to bury this dirt?"

"In my heart," Eleanor moaned.

The next crisis came a month later. Again, Ida's morning call: "Get to Mimsy's. Pronto."

Eleanor had wept about her roses, but Mimsy *fumed* about her herbs. "A pig! Would you believe it? It's ten miles to the nearest pig farm. You can't tell me that some of those juvenile delinquents from Bigelow didn't tote a blasted porcine assault weapon over here in the middle of the night and turn it loose in my thyme! You know they say the evil Fang and Claw Society is still in existence. Stupid high school fraternity pranks! Should call it the Snout and Hambone Society."

"What pig? Where?" I asked stupidly.

Mimsy turned on me. I backed up a step at her expression. "That animal is somewhere between here and Bigelow dragging the weight of four loads of rock salt in its fat rear end."

"You shot a *pig?*"

"If I could have found the box of buckshot, we'd be eating barbecue."

"Have you called the police?"

"The chief says without the pig we don't have any evidence. Let me tell you, if his daddy were still alive we'd be heading for Bigelow to do a little pork roast by now. Battle Royden didn't need 'evidence.' He could *smell* a Bigelowan pig prank a mile away. Just because he couldn't ever find that carnival elephant . . ." She trailed off into irate muttering.

I sighed. Police chief Amos Royden is a conscientious — some would say too conscientious — young lawman, unlike his legendary father. Amos is a stickler for real evidence as opposed to gut feeling, which was all Mimsy had to offer.

"Ooh, that man!" Erma said, revving up, again. "Ida, sometimes I think you ought to fire him."

"Don't be silly," Ida said and quickly changed the subject. "Now, let's see what we can do to repair the damage. And we'd better set up some electric wire around the garden so this won't happen again. I'll call Dan MacNeil at the Fix-It Shop."

Sitting on Mimsy's back porch that evening drinking iced tea, we agreed that we might very well be hearing the opening salvos of a war we'd have to fight alone. A war no man could enter. A war of gardeners. Women gardeners. Earth Mothers. We were all widows with the exception of Eleanor, and she wasn't the save-me-you-big-brawny-man-you type. So I bought a heavy padlock for my garden gate and considered strewing broken glass around the outside, but was afraid I'd hurt one of the neighborhood cats. Ida bribed the Boy Scouts to take turns camping at her place every night. Erma swore she was such a light sleeper that she'd hear any intruder before he did any damage and "damage him, first, just like Mimsy did with the pig." We believed her. Eleanor demanded that we mount a counter-attack on Bigelow roses, but we managed to restrain her.

It was a thorny time.

One morning I picked up the phone expecting another 'pronto' summons, but Ida said, "Ardaleen's forced her own handpicked judge down our throats. He's a retired botanist from the University of Tennessee. Thought you might know him. Name's Carlyle something. Dr. Carlyle something."

"Carlyle Payton? Lord, yes, I know him. Not well, but for a long time. Science doesn't mix much with the humanities."

"What's he like?"

"Pleasant. Competent."

"Bribable?"

"I wouldn't think so. He's got plenty of money. He has a good reputation. Actually, he's very attractive — or was the last time I saw him. You know the type — tweedy with patches, gray beard, lots of gray hair. Shorter than I am and a little tubby, but an all around good guy."

"I wonder what my sister's got up her sleeve, then?"

"I can't imagine, but what . . . what are you asking me to do about it?"

"Use your feminine wiles on Dr. Payton."

I sat down. "Let me see if I can remember where they are," I said finally.

The day of the contest, I was a nervous wreck. Carlyle Payton was staying in the best hotel in Bigelow but arrived in Mossy Creek leading an entourage of Bigelowans and driving a beat-up pick-up truck with a few clods of dirt in the bed.

Because the judging locations were widely separated from one another, the competition started with opening ceremonies and coffee at the Mossy Creek First Baptist Church community hall. Then we all sat down to look at the tapes of the now-defunct spring gardens. Bigelow drew the short straw and went first.

When the opening trumpets of *Also Spracht Zarathustra* — the theme from the famed science fiction movie *2001* — hit us from all sides, I nearly fell out of my chair. The production was so far over the top that I expected Moses to part the Red Sea and reveal a field of multi-colored irises in the background. I was sitting right behind Carlyle. I could see his shoulders shake. He was laughing.

In contrast, the tape of Erma's spring garden, produced by WMOS Media, Inc. courtesy of Bert Lyman and his studio/barn, was a model of restraint. The soundtrack ran the gamut from Mozart to Beethoven to Bruce Springsteen, but never seemed intrusive. Erma's garden looked spectacular. Bert's wife, known only to WMOS listeners as *Honey, My Board Operator,* served as the unpaid cameraman. Honey certainly deserved a raise.

Carlyle's shoulders did not shake. Once he even leaned forward to get a better look.

Then we adjourned to drive down to Bigelow and view the Bigelow roses.

Ida was right. Even with three bushes missing, Eleanor's roses were a shoo-in.

Ditto our Formal Garden. And this time Eustene's topiary elephant really did look like an elephant, because we brought in outside help. Rainey Ann Cecil had come over from Goldilocks Hair, Nail, and Tanning Salon to trim the pachyderm — though she'd looked more than a little squeamish when the mayor asked her to do it. There was a story there, but I didn't know what, yet. At any rate, Rainey's salon-styled hedge elephant was a winner for us.

That left the Most Unusual Garden and the Best All-Around to be judged. Carlyle made notes, but kept them in his pocket. I was dying to see what he'd written, but picking pockets isn't one of my skills. He'd greeted me like an old friend — I was — but he'd been carried off by Ardaleen, who kept a tight rein on him and looked at me with suspicion.

I have to admit the Bigelow Bonsai Garden was pretty tough competition in the Unusual Category. I felt like a giant stomping through one of those miniature landscapes they build for model trains. I was terrified to put my foot down for fear I'd stomp on some five-hundred-year old miniature peach tree.

Then it was my turn. We all drove back up to Mossy Creek. I'd been up since four a.m. sweeping and dusting and tidying. Not indoors. Outdoors. I couldn't breathe, and I fumbled so badly with the latch on the walled garden that Ida had to step in and open the gate for me. I stood aside while Carlyle, the Bigelowans, the Creekite gardeners, and assorted spectators filed in.

"I don't see what's so unusual about this," Bigelowan Helen Overbury whispered. "Looks messy to me."

"Just an old wild flower garden," said Ardaleen, *sotto voce*. "Anybody can do that."

Carlyle said nothing but walked along the paths beside the raised beds, staring at each flower and vine. In the far corner, he started to laugh.

I have never been so mortified. I wanted to run back to the house and hide. He turned around, found me in the crowd, and began to applaud. "Peggy, you are something else! I can't think of another soul who'd create a garden like this."

The Bigelowans began to mutter suspiciously. He pointed. "Well, for pity's sake, people, where are your eyes? Lily-of-the-valley, English ivy, snow-on-the-mountain, trumpet vine. . . . How on earth did you manage to train that rebel onto the wall?"

"So what?" Helen Overbury said under her breath.

"And the foxgloves are some of the finest I've ever seen." He walked around the four sides of the garden and called out the names of the plants as he passed them. Now the Bigelowans were really miffed because they still hadn't gotten his point.

"You've even got mushrooms," he crowed. "Amanita *Phalloides* and Amanita *Virosa* both. Darn near impossible to cultivate." At last he came up to me, bowed, and said, "Signora Rappaccini, I salute you."

Then Bigelowan Geraldine Matthews yelped, "My God, those are *death angel* mushrooms! And look over there — deadly nightshade. Oleander, and a catalpa tree! Castor beans! And Hemlock! My lord, everything *in* here is poison!"

Ardaleen whispered, "She's crazy! She's trying to kill us all!"

The way all those Bigelow women tried to squeeze through the garden gate, you'd have thought I was waiting with a bubbling cauldron to pour hemlock down their throats.

"Well, I never," said Mimsy.

"All I wanted was to grow something I really wanted to know about," I said nervously.

"And you did an admirable job," Carlyle told me. "I'd very much like to bring a couple of my colleagues here to see this. May I?"

"Sure. Although I may be locked up in the loony bin by the time you come."

"Nonsense. Well, ladies, time to follow the stampede to Ardaleen's to view her entry for Best All-Around garden."

The Mossy Creek Garden Club arrived in Eleanor's minivan and Ida's Corvette just behind Carlyle in his truck. The Bigelowans were waiting on the sidewalk before Ardaleen's mansion. Ardaleen stood in the center with her hands on her hips.

"Before we go any further, I demand that Peggy Caldwell be disqualified for Most Unusual Garden," she said the moment Carlyle reached her.

"Now wait just a minute, Siseroo," Ida snapped.

Siseroo. You don't call the governor's mother Siseroo. Ida and Ardaleen traded murderous looks. "That garden of hers is an abomination," Ardaleen said. "It should be destroyed. It's a public nuisance. It's *dangerous*." She pivoted toward Carlyle. "It should be disqualified."

Carlyle smiled sweetly. "Now, Ardaleen, I don't think you want to start this kind of controversy. Peggy keeps the garden gate shut. Besides, if you want to destroy poisonous plants, you're going to have to start with those azaleas of yours."

"What?"

"And the iris and the cannas over there in the corner under the window."

"They're not poisonous!" Helen Overbury cried.

"Oh yes, they are," Carlyle told her. "Actually, nearly every flowering plant and many of the non-flowering are quite toxic. Maybe they won't kill you, but they'll sure make you wish you'd died."

"Don't be ridiculous, Carlyle," Ardaleen snapped. "Nobody eats azaleas."

He winked at me. "That's my point, Ardaleen. Nobody eats wild hemlock either — not man, nor beast. Not even cows."

"Too bad pigs won't try it," Mimsy interjected.

"Everything in Peggy's garden grows wild in half the pastures around here. The plants that don't are grown in plenty of gardens simply for their beauty. No disqualification. So come on, Ardaleen, calm down and give me the tour of *your* pretty, poisonous flowers."

He hooked her hand under his arm and walked away. She was trapped. She had to follow, and where she went, there followed her courtiers. Over her shoulder, Ardaleen threw me a look that would peel paint. Then she stared at Carlyle. "Carlyle, I had no idea you were on a first name basis with Mrs. Caldwell."

"Dr. Caldwell, actually," I said. But I didn't say it loud enough for Ardaleen to hear.

I felt Erma's heavy hand on my shoulder. "If anybody says to hit her, I'll do it. I can make it count."

I tried to keep from grinding my teeth as we trailed through Ardaleen's garden. Beside me, Ida looked grim. "We're dead," she announced. "The convicts have this place looking spectacular. The borders look like they've been edged leaf-by-leaf with switchblades."

"Keep the faith," Mimsy said. "Pray for a miracle."

We walked under the shade of hundred year old oaks and admired the shade plants under them. Then we rounded the far corner of the mansion. Suddenly we stepped into full sunlight, and ahead blazed the most beautiful red-orange flowers I'd ever seen.

I think we all gasped. They were darned near fluorescent. Stems nearly three feet tall, and flowers the size of small dinner plates. Unbeatable.

"Oh, well," I said. "Better luck next year."

Carlyle stopped so quickly that Ardaleen nearly tripped into him. He dropped her hand and walked up to the bed. It was large — by far the biggest concentration of one sort of flower in the garden. Why not? They were the prettiest flowers of them all.

Carlyle came back to Ardaleen, took her hand and sighed.

She simpered. "Aren't they wonderful? I saved them for last."

"Now, listen to me very carefully. I'm afraid there *is* going to be a disqualification this year after all."

"Good, you've come to your senses."

"Not Peggy's poison patch. This garden. Yours."

"What?"

We were all stunned.

"And I think you had better call your yard man right this minute and tell him to pull up these plants as quietly as possible, put them carefully into leaf bags and bury them in the nearest landfill. The governor's public relations people will have a fit, otherwise. It just looks too odd."

"No! I will not destroy this flower bed." She glared at me, and at Ida. "What's behind this? What kind of joke? Ida, I'll speak with you in private, you traitorous —"

"I'm not the traitor in our family," Ida said evenly. "And if you did your own gardening instead of conniving to get the taxpayers of this state to do it for you, you might learn something about plants. Including which ones are on the rules' list for automatic disqualification."

"What in the world are you talking about?"

"I'm talking about your drug stash, Siseroo."

"My *what?*"

Carlyle shook his head. "In the future, you need to pay a little closer attention to those trustees from the prison who work for you. They must have had a good laugh." He touched a brilliant red flower. *"These are opium poppies."*

In the midst of the gasps — Bigelowans — and stifled laughter — Creekites — that followed, Erma leaned close to me and whispered, "They could harvest enough raw

181

opium from those plants to zonk the entire prison out for a month."

About that time, Ardaleen fainted.

So Mossy Creek won the contest by default.

De fault of de poppies, that is.

I do not know why Ardaleen Hamilton Bigelow blames me for what happened. I swear I didn't call the Atlanta newspapers to alert them to the poppy patches at the governor's boyhood home.

Nor did I call the national news services. Or CNN.

I think Ida did.

Last week, Carlyle phoned to ask if he could take me to dinner. His drive down from Knoxville will take a good four hours, so I guess he really is serious about me. I feel like a teenager going on her first date. He's no beauty, but he's a sweet man and we know all the same people. And many of the same poisonous plants. Then Marilee told me she was four months pregnant. She went for a sonogram. It's a girl. Claude is ecstatic. So am I. I'll have a Bigelowan granddaughter. Oh, well. I may even let Claude call me Mother Caldwell.

Now I can never go back to Tennessee to buy that hi-rise condo. I'm the only hope for my grandchild. Otherwise, she'll be raised as stuffy as her parents. I won't let that happen, even if I have to kidnap her and raise her myself in Mossy Creek.

The garden club is looking for a bunch of new members to fill in the spaces that are likely to occur in the near future. Considering all the publicity we've gotten in addition to this reunion year bringing some old-timers back to town, it shouldn't be too difficult. The club has broadened its horizons. Heck, if they could turn me into a gardener, they can turn anybody into one.

I've bought a kitten for Dashiell. He was getting terribly lonely. I only have time to read to him at night.

I'm still angry at Ben for dying on me. But every day I come closer to forgiving him. After all, if he had to die, at least he had the good sense to do it in Mossy Creek, bless him.

I may even plant zinnias. He'd want it that way.

To: Lady Victoria Salter Stanhope
From: Katie Bell

Dear Vick:

You have to understand how much the high school fire changed our town's future. Let me give you an example: Dwight Truman, our Chamber president, is a prissy, ambitious weasel, but he's *our* prissy, ambitious weasel, so, more often than not, he does what's best for Mossy Creek. Some say that includes sucking up to Governor Bigelow a little *too* sincerely, but I'll give Dwight the benefit of the doubt on that.

Anyhow . . . twenty years ago, Dwight was a rookie teacher at Mossy Creek High, but he sold insurance on the side and already had big dreams of owning his own business *and* being a politician. He ran for state senate that year, and he had a good chance of winning. The Creekites were behind him full force, not because he was beloved, but because no Creekite wanted the opposing candidate to win.

That candidate? Ham Bigelow. Our future governor and sort-of hometown son — to refresh your memory, his mother, Ardaleen, is a Hamilton. Ham was running for state senate, too. The Bigelowans predicted the start of Ham's fame as a politician. All he had to do was win his first race. But all Dwight had to do to beat Ham was keep the faith among Creekites and take care of the ram.

Samson, the high school mascot, that is.

Dwight was in charge of shepherding Samson to and from the homecoming game that year. It was a major duty, not assigned lightly, since the Bigelow students had a tradition of trying to kidnap our mascot. Every teacher vied for the honor of guarding Samson. Dwight bragged that with him in charge Samson would be safer than a wool rug in moth balls. Suffice to say, Dwight was wrong. What happened to Samson that night and the resulting fire ruined Dwight's political support, and we've been stuck with Ham ever since. Even worse, we lost some of our good-hearted trust and began eyeing one another suspiciously.

There were whispers that Millicent Hart knew who caused the high school fire. She had a reputation even then for stealing little bits of information along with dimestore knicknacks. Chief Royden questioned her, and *WSB Channel 2 News* down in Atlanta even taped an interview with her as if she were a serious suspect — during which she stole the cameraman's wallet, but that's another story. Millicent never confessed a thing. I wouldn't be surprised, though, if she didn't finger the culprit or culprits one day.

In the meantime, Millicent is a menace to nobody but her own daughter's stubborn heart.

Katie

MAGGIE

MOVING DAY

Mothers, boyfriends, and movie stars.
Can't live with them, can't live without
them. In a year of reunions, some people
know it's finally time to come home. And
some people know it's finally
time to leave.

Since I'm widely regarded as Mossy Creek's
only real hippie — or the closest semblance
thereof — I have to uphold my generation's
let-it-all-hang-out reputation and answer
Katie Bell's survey. No problemo. Seems
like all I've done since starting a middle-
aged romance with an ex-pro football player
turned punk-haired sculptor is indulge
public curiosity. Hey, when you were raised
by a mother whose main hobby was stealing
from everyone else in town, you get used to
thinking up quick answers to personal questions.

So here goes. I'm baring my soul to Katie
Bell and her readers.

What do reunions mean to me? I love reunions — most of the time. Who *doesn't* love visiting with old friends and family? Except maybe for recently, I've really looked forward to every kind of reunion in Mossy Creek. But now, with all this emphasis on the year the high school burned down during homecoming, I find myself hesitant, even reluctant, to participate. It's as though the mystery of that awful night *shouldn't* be solved.

Our town's rivalry with Bigleow is part of who we are as Creekites. If someone from Bigelow High caused the fire at Mossy Creek High, do we really want to know? After all, the fire happened so long ago. But that event, that single event, still focuses our animosity toward the whole town of Bigelow. We're convinced the Bigelowans stole a part of our heritage that night.

Those of us who graduated from Mossy Creek High really resent that our grand old traditions went up in flames. The wooly dignity of our ram mascot — and the silly devotion that seeing him on the sidelines of football games engendered — was a warm memory for many of us. We'd sit in the bleachers on chilly fall evenings cheering the Mossy Creek Rams on to victory or consoling each other in defeat. But we never lost the camaraderie that bound us together. We were a family, a diverse family, devoted to a single purpose.

I long for those carefree days when life didn't press in on you. A time when mothers were mothers and daughters were daughters, and there was no mixing of the two roles. Now, the roles are reversing. And, in some respects, I see my life blurring into a nothingness that suddenly looms before me. I feel a bit of panic at the changes being forced on me.

Does that empty spot where the high school stood bother me? Oh, yes, in more ways than I can explain. But, I guess the greatest feeling I experience when I look at that open, grassy lot with the blue-green mountains framing it, is fear of life, itself. On the outside, things look pretty much the same unless you look closely, but the changes are there on the inside. What was fresh and pink and pretty is soon charred and fragile. Everything that was understood to be a solid, unchangeable fact soon alters, shifting the foundation of my soul.

What is the most hurtful and publicly humiliating thing that ever happened to me in high school? The day my steady boyfriend, Allen Singleton, the lead guitarist of the Chinaberry Charmers, broke up with me in front of the entire student body. He actually *raced* onto the stage during a pep rally and proposed to Bonnie Hamilton. My heart froze in that moment. My life changed. And my soul stilled itself into a vague shadow of the lifeforce that had resided there before that moment.

That, also, would be the one thing that influenced me most and shaped me into the person I am today. A loner struggling to trust love.

"Sex. That's what you need, Maggie. Good ol' lusty sex and lots of it. Which you can't enjoy with me sleeping in the same house."

"Mother!"

My mother, Millicent Hart, had never uttered anything like that — or even close to it — in all my fifty-one years. The closest we'd come to a mother-daughter talk about sex was, "Don't do it."

"You need to be able to sleep with your manfriend in this house," my eighty-year-old mother said as calmly as discussing the weather.

"Why are you talking about this?"

"If you don't want to have sex with Tag by now, I can't help you. But I can move out of this house so you won't feel shy about inviting Tag to spend the night."

"You're not going, and that's final."

"I'd like to see you stop me. I've got my dentures in. I'll bite you."

"Mother, just listen to reason. You're not old enough for Magnolia Manor."

She snorted.

I tossed my hands. "All right, you *are* old enough. But you're too young at heart."

"Magnolia Manor is a nice place."

"Of course it is, but that's no reason for a perfectly healthy woman to pack up and move there. A nursing home is for people who are sick or who don't have anybody to take care of them. Not people like you, people who just want to be cantankerous."

"I'm not being cantankerous. This time, I'm going."

I watched helplessly as my mother packed the last of her pristine white underwear into the suitcase she'd used only infrequently over the past few years. She wasn't one to travel very far from home. "Mother, you know you don't like sleeping in strange places."

"I'll adjust. Maybe I should stop by Hamilton's this afternoon and pick out some new furniture."

I knew better than to allow her to go on her own. Her idea of shopping usually consisted of picking out a few items and leaving without remembering to pay for them. She stole things whether she needed them or not. I thought she'd reformed in the past year, but then she backslid. She swiped Bob the Chihuahua's water dish from outside Beecham's Bakery. Ingrid had a hissy fit when that happened. I do believe she'd rather Mother stole half the bakery's bank account than anything to do with that dog. Especially after nearly losing Bob to a hawk.

There's usually no rhyme or reason to what Mother takes, but occasionally I find little motifs. Like last year, before her temporary retirement as the town klepto-maniac. She was stealing gifts to go in my hope chest. Little did I know she was also plotting to throw me into Tag's arms. I have her to thank for adding romance to my life. Tag Garner and I have been dating for almost a year. He's an amazing man in many ways — even if he does have a funky blue streak in his hair.

Now, in her misguided effort to force Tag and me into living together, she was steal-ing . . . away. I blinked hard. "Please, Mother, let's just think about this."

"My mind is made up." She sat on the edge of her flower-print four-poster bed and looked at me. "You and Tag need to be alone. You don't need an old lady hanging around watching every move you make. For pity's sake, you can't even chase each other around in the nude if I'm still here."

The image of that brought a smile to my face, and I choked back a laugh. "In the first place, we're not ready to move in together. In the second —"

"Do you think I'm blind as well as old?" She rose, adjusted her blousy print t-shirt and white Bermuda shorts, and crossed her arms. "I've often thought that you've never gotten married because of some silly sense of responsibility for me. In fact, I know it. Well, that responsibility is gone. As of now. You're on your own."

I heard the door chimes downstairs in my shop, and I knew I'd lost the battle. In the time it would take me to wait on a customer, Mother would slip downstairs and out a back door, suitcase in hand. "Please, please, don't do this."

"You can't hide behind me anymore, Maggie. It's time you started to live your life instead of just observing from backstage. This man means too much to you. I'm not going to be the reason you chase this one away." She hugged me and held me close for just a minute. "Go help your customer. I'll be here when you get back."

There was nothing I could do but obey. Without another word, I left her bedroom and headed for the curved staircase that led from our living quarters down to Moonheart's Natural Living, my fragrant little shop of handmade soaps, teas, potpourri, and various other wonderful items.

One loud bark told me exactly who had arrived. Tag and his newly acquired dog, Giselle. The sound of claws scratching on the staircase preceded the gleeful bark when the mixed-breed Briard raced up to meet me. "Hello, pretty girl, what are you doing here so early?"

Tag's deep voice followed. "Magster, are you up there?"

Magster. One of Tag's many pet names for me. The little flutter in my heart urged me to hurry down the stairs. Mother was right about one thing. Tag and I were close — very close.

"Coming," I called. We met on the landing. He took me in his arms and kissed me. "Well, well, I'll take a greeting like that any day."

"What's my fragrant little vixen been up to this morning?"

"Dealing with Mother."

He held me back at arm's length and studied my face. "Doesn't look like she gave

you a black eye. Did she bite you somewhere?"

Mother was a notorious biter. She'd bit-
ten Tag when they met.

"No such thing," came Mother's scolding
voice with more than a bit of humor marking its tone. She leaned over the railing of
the upstairs landing, watching us.

"Careful, Mother. I don't want you to
fall."

She pointed to the suitcase beside her feet,
then at Tag. "I presume you're here to give
me a ride in that fancy sports car of yours. I
called you more than an hour ago."

"Sure. Where do you want to go?"

"The Magnolia Manor Nursing Home."
She walked carefully down the stairs to
stand beside us. "I'm checking in today, and
Maggie flatly refused to take me. So, either
you do it or I walk over there in the summer heat. I'd hate to have a heat stroke and
die. Maggie would never forgive herself."

Tag glanced from Mother to me. "Is this a
joke?"

"Yes."

"No, the time has come for me to get out
of y'all's way so the two of you can chase
—"

"Mother!"

"Magnolia Manor has a few assisted liv-

195

ing apartments, and I've rented one for myself. Maggie has made excuses for me nearly all her life . . . what with my, well, with my *hobby* of borrowing things from people. It isn't fair for her to spend the *rest* of her life looking after an old lady with itchy fingers."

Tag looked as if he was trying to figure out what exactly was going on in the Hart household and how he should respond to it.

Tears burned again behind my tightly squinched eyelids. "Mother, you know I don't want you to do this."

"I know, dear, but you don't have much choice in the matter, so get used to the idea." She sighed. "I'm my own person. You're not my legal guardian, so unless you're prepared to take me to court and declare me incompetent, I'm on my way."

"Miss Millicent," Tag said patiently, using the title all ladies of a certain age demanded in Mossy Creek society, "Neither Maggie nor I want you to move. This is your home. You belong here."

In that moment, I realized how wonderful he really was. He meant every word of what he said. "Mother, please, listen to Tag. If something's wrong, we can work it out."

"Something wrong? My dear, what could it possibly be?" She walked on down the stairs and then looked back at us. "Tag, is the top down on your convertible? I feel like having the wind whip through my perm."

"Well, Miss Millicent, the top's down, but Giselle pretty much takes up the whole front seat. I didn't know that you —"

"We'll share. It's time Giselle and I got better acquainted, since we'll probably be in-laws soon."

I groaned. "You may have been thinking about this move for some time, but it's a shock to me. Can't you give me a little time to get used to the idea?"

"You're still young enough to be shocked. That's what's important. You'll get used to it pretty fast." She tottered out the front door with Giselle behind her.

Tag kissed me quickly. "What do you want me to do, Mags? I can throw her over my shoulder and bring her back in."

"You're not seriously considering taking her over there, are you?"

"What else can I do? You heard her."

"I *cannot* believe you'd actually drive my mother to the nursing home."

"She'll walk if I don't."

"You've got to persuade her to stay."

Tag shook his head. "Her mind is made up. There's not much I can do at this point."

"There's got to be something."

197

"You just tell me what you want me to do, and I'll do it. Short of kidnapping, that is."

He was entirely right, and I knew it. None of this was his problem. Still, he was providing the means for her to accomplish her little plot. "She's deserting me."

"I wondered what she wanted when she called and asked me to come over this morning."

"She had this all planned out so I wouldn't have any say in the matter. She's up to something else. All this talk about the reunion year, the old school arson mystery — it's rattled her. I know that look. She has a secret. She doesn't want me watching her. That's what this is about. Some kind of secret."

"I'll see if I can find out what's up while I drive her over." He kissed my forehead. "Now, I'd better get out there before she decides to drive herself. See you tonight?"

"Yes," I said as he dashed down the steps.

I watched as he pulled out of my shady yard past blooming flower beds and butterfly bushes filled with life. Mother hugged Giselle with one arm and waved cheerfully. Then she turned to talk to Tag. She was probably telling him how to steer. Look up "back seat driver" in the dictionary, and there's a picture of Millicent Hart. Next she would steal the change out of his ash tray.

I turned and went back in the shop. I'd planned to cut a new batch of soap and make potpourri. Instead, I changed from a sundress into shorts, Nikes, and a t-shirt, and went jogging to clear my mind. I circled the town square a couple of times and ended up near town hall. Suddenly, I couldn't resist and bolted inside to see the old fortune-telling machine. I fished a dime out of my pocket and fed it into the slot. I was greeted by the whirring of the machine as the fortune-teller came to life. A few seconds later, a yellowed card dropped from the slot.

"Romance will come after disillusionment," I read aloud. "Disillusionment. Like I need more of that after this morning. Brother."

I hurried back to my shop and made a glass of iced ginger-peach tea. As I was sitting on the back porch sipping the fragrant brew, the door chimes jingled. I jumped to my feet and rushed to the front.

"Mother? I told you — Oh, I'm sorry. You see, my mother — never mind. It's a long story." A very handsome man stood there looking puzzled at me. He seemed so familiar, but I just couldn't place him. "May I help you?"

"Maggie? Is that really you?" His voice would melt butter.

I gasped. "Beau? Beau Belmont . . . I mean *Belmondo?*"

He nodded.

Mossy Creek's only true movie star had come home.

I sat down and spilled my tea.

Strangely enough, Beau Belmont, whom the world knew as Beau Belmondo, and I had stayed in touch through letters and an occasional phone call. I thought of him as a kid brother, since he was thirteen years younger than me. But I'd hardly expected him to saunter into my shop one morning out of the blue. He hadn't been back to Mossy Creek in twenty years. We read about him all the time and went to his films and watched his interviews on TV. He gave me a quick hug and then looked around. "This is still the most pleasant house in Mossy Creek."

"I thought you were waiting until the reunion in November!"

"Couldn't stand it. Had to come sooner." He shrugged big, handsome shoulders that Julia Roberts had leaned on in his last film. "I could use a glass of your tea."

"Come on." I led him to the back porch. I sat in the swing. I blinked, telling myself this was real.

Beau started to take a seat and then hesitated. "Say, Maggie, my car's out front, and I'd just as soon nobody see it right now. I'm sure Creekites still pay attention to unfamiliar cars parked in their neighbors' yards. Where can I hide it?"

"Hide it? Oh, how about my garage? I don't use that for anything except storage for the gift shop. There's plenty of room."

"Great."

He hurried out to his car while I took the garage key off the rack by the door and met him in the back yard. Beau guided his sleek black Jaguar inside. "How many of these do you have?" I asked.

He shrugged. "I've lost count."

We went back to the swing and sat down. "How is she?" he said.

I put a hand to my heart. This was so romantic. Beau had come back to see Anna Rose Lavender, my best friend. And his high school sweetheart. "She's fine, Beau, just fine. You should let me tell her —"

"No. I'll take my chances." He took a deep gulp of iced tea and changed the subject. "Let's talk about you. I have the *Gazette* mailed to me in Los Angeles." He smiled, showing a dimpled cheek. "The way Katie Bell writes about you and your new boyfriend, you two must be the hottest couple in Mossy Creek."

I nearly choked. "I suppose we are. We're pretty much the nearest thing to a wild romantic duo she can find. It's Tag's blue hair. Folks here just can't get used to the idea that an ex-Falcons linebacker would dye a blue streak in his hair and take up sculpting. You really read the *Gazette* every week?"

"I started subscribing years ago. Just wanted to hear what folks at home were doing."

Anna Rose, he meant.

"Now, it's interesting that you should say that. Folks at home, I mean." I sipped my tea and wondered how I could bring Anna Rose into the conversation again.

"It's funny that no matter where we go we think of the place we grew up as home," Beau said.

"So your huge estate in the Hollywood Hills isn't as appealing as you thought it would be?"

"No. I sold it."

"So where are you going to live?"

Beau put down his mug and looked at me closely. "That depends on what happens with Anna Rose. In the meantime, I need a hiding place. How about here?"

Stay here? Well, why not? "Okay. Mother just moved out, and she left her bedroom furniture."

"Great! I'll get my bags."

Before he could move, I heard the front door chimes. Tag called out, "Hey, Mags, babe, I'm back. You won't believe —"

Tag stopped dead in his tracks when he saw Beau sitting there with me on the swing.

"You have to be Maggie's man," Beau said as if he'd known Tag all his life.

Tag stepped forward, stuck out his hand, and looked a bit puzzled. "Hello. Have we met?"

Beau laughed and rose. He shook Tag's hand heartily. "In a manner of speaking. I'm the customer who bought your Wilderness Battle bronze. The grizzly fighting the cougar. I did it through a broker at Maggie's recommendation. Great work."

"Oh? You look familiar, but I just can't place —"

"I'm totally thoughtless this morning," I blurted, wondering where my manners had gone. If Mother had been here, she'd have scolded me. "Tag, this is Beau Belmondo."

"The movie star?"

"That's me. Pleased to meet you. I used to watch you play."

Tag had met a lot of celebrities in his football playing days, and little impressed him. He was a minor celebrity, himself. He shrugged. "Thanks. What brought you back to Mossy Creek?"

"It's a beautiful little town, almost as quaint as when I left it. 'Ain't goin' nowhere, and don't want to.' " Beau chuckled and crossed his legs. "You know, when I left here, I thought this place would never suit me. I was a dirt poor nobody. I couldn't get away fast enough."

The conversation between the two men flowed over me as I toyed with the idea of calling Anna Rose. She'd kill me if I didn't.

When there was a lapse in the conversation, I said, "Beau, let me call Anna Rose and tell her you're —"

"No, don't call her."

"But this is absurd."

"Let me do it my way." He glanced at Tag and then back at me. "Both of you have got to promise me that you won't tell anybody I'm here. Nobody."

I shot a look at Tag. He had a peculiar expression on his face, and I couldn't tell what he was thinking. "I won't tell anyone, if you don't want me to."

"Thanks. Maggie, can we spend the next few days working on a project of mine? I need some help with a costume."

"A costume?"

"I'll go get the materials." He stood and shook hands with Tag again. "Keep this lady occupied until I get back."

After he left the porch, Tag didn't look happy. "What's he up to?"

"I really can't tell you. I've given him my word."

"You let me drive your mother to the nursing home, but you can't tell me why Mr. Dimples has come back to town and is setting up housekeeping with you?"

"I gave my word." God, how else was I going to keep this from Anna Rose? "It has to do with Anna Rose. That's all I can say." She'd slay me with a sword from her prop shop at the theater if *she* knew *I* knew Beau was in town and didn't tell her. "You know, Anna Rose is directing *A Midsummer Night's Dream* at the Mossy Creek Theater."

"Good. Mr. Dimples is an actor. Let him go sleep at the theater."

"Oh, Tag, he's just come home for a little vacation and doesn't want folks making a nuisance of themselves. He doesn't want Katie Bell to hear. Good Lord, if she heard about it, first thing you know, every paper in the state would mention it and then every TV station. And then we'd be in a fix. It would be worse than leaf season. There'd be a steady stream of cars through here with folks trying to spot Beau."

Tag sighed and shook his head. "I sure as hell don't like the idea of you staying here all alone with him."

"Then you don't trust *me*. Why, Tag Garner, I believe you're jealous of a younger man."

"Damn it, Maggie, I'm not jealous. Why should I be jealous?"

"No reason, but you are. I can see it in your eyes."

I'd never had the pleasure of a guy being jealous over me before. I decided it felt pretty good. Especially, when the guy being jealous was a former pro football player and the guy he was jealous of was America's latest heartthrob.

Tag turned away and crossed his arms as he approached the window. He stared out for a moment. "Are you really going to let Belmondo stay here? Maybe I should offer my place."

"Yes, he's going to stay here. And I resent your implications."

"Now, don't be turning into Scarlet O'Hara on me, Mags. We're going together.

Doesn't that mean anything to you?"

I put my hand on his shoulder. "Of course it does. You know it does. And Beau has nothing to do with *us.*"

That he could even ask such a question really hurt.

"Nothing? My God, Maggie, am I supposed to like it because a strange man — a strange man that ninety-nine percent of women in the world would love to sleep with — is living in the house with you?"

"Come on, Tag. Don't be like this. He's a friend. I used to babysit him. He needs a place to stay."

Tag didn't move. I took my hand off his arm and walked over to the swing to sit down. Too many things — bad things — were happening, all in the same day. Somehow, I had to come to grips with all of this a little at a time. I never would have suspected Tag of jealousy, but here he was just about to burst wide open with a fit of it.

"Don't be like this? Like what?"

"Like . . . like crazy. That's what."

"Oh, so now I'm crazy?" He strode off the porch. "Have a good time with Mr. Heart-throb."

Before I could respond, he was gone through the back flower beds. Brother. Just when you think your life is all laid out

207

before you. Whammo.

Your mother moves out, a movie star moves in, and the man you've fallen in love with tramples your petunias.

In more ways than one.

That afternoon, while Beau was upstairs in Mother's room working on something to do with his "project," the front door chimed.

I hurried into the shop from my workroom and found Anna Rose leaning over the herbal soap display. "Hi ya, Maggie. I just had a question about the press release you're working on for the play . . . What's wrong?"

"Oh, sorry. I thought maybe Tag might . . . Well, that you might be Tag."

"Something wrong in Camelot?"

What could I tell her? I couldn't tell her the truth — that Tag and I had had a fight over her old boyfriend who had just moved into my spare room. "Oh, it's nothing. I'm just a bit antsy. Mother woke up this morning with this bizarre notion to move into the Magnolia Manor. She even called Tag to come and take her over there. And," I continued, unable to stop the flood of frustration pouring forth from my blathering mouth, "Katie Bell dropped by a few minutes ago to warn me that Mother staged this whole thing just so she could move into an assisted living apartment next door to some old Romeo."

Anna Rose hooted. "Did she say who he was?"

"No, and I'd really appreciate some thoughtful sympathy from you instead of a howling laugh."

"I'm sorry, Maggie, honestly, I am. But I have to confess. I can't believe you didn't suspect. Romeo is my Uncle Tyrone."

"Uncle? Your uncle?" I nearly fell over. "Are you serious? After all these years?"

"I couldn't believe it myself. After all the pushing we've done to get them together, they did it themselves. They must figure this is a discreet way for them to live together without saying so."

"Damn! I've got to go over there and talk to her about this."

"Why? What's she done that's so bad?"

"She said she was moving so Tag and I could have some privacy."

"Really?"

"And she said that she thought I needed some 'good old lusty sex.' That's a direct quote. To make matters worse . . . much worse, Tag and I had an argument that started with her and ended with —" I clamped my mouth shut just in time.

"Oooh, that's bad," Anna Rose said with obvious sympathy.

I could always count on her for support, which made me feel even more guilty for keeping secrets. We'd made a pact when we became friends — no secrets. In fact, I'd been the person she went to first when she was pregnant with her daughter, Hermia, who was now at the University of Georgia. Hermia was following in her mother's footsteps — an actress right down to her dramatic toes.

I decided to change the subject. "You know, if Mother wants to live at Magnolia Manor because your uncle is there, I'm glad. I think it will do her good. Maybe it will even keep her from stealing things. Maybe she'll just steal from *him*."

"That would be great." Anna Rose grinned. "Do you see a wedding happening?"

"Do I see a wedding? Anna Rose, I didn't even know why she was moving over to the retirement center. I thought she was mad at me and trying to get even or something."

Anna Rose picked up a freshly packaged bar of soap. "All's well that ends well. Who knows? That smells divine. Isn't honeysuckle your signature soap?"

"Yep, it's Maggie's Heart. The scent is

soothing." I darted a glance at the floor above us. If Anna Rose only knew who was up there . . .

"I need something soothing," Anna Rose said. "My Bottom is flat."

"Wish mine was."

"Be serious. I'm talking about the character, not my rear-end. The play opens in just a couple of weeks."

"So what are you going to do?"

"Where am I going to get a Shakespearean ass at this late date?"

"You should be looking for an actor instead of an ass."

"Most actors *are* asses," she said, laughing, and waved to me as she left the shop.

I heard a soft sound and looked up the staircase.

Beau stood at the top, watching her go with quiet misery and devotion in his eyes.

Life was interesting. Life was hard. Loneliness was something I never really experienced until Tag and I broke up.

I visited Mother daily at Magnolia Manor, but she was rarely home. I rang the doorbell of her tiny, furnished apartment several times, but got no answer.

"Mother, it's me," I called one day. "Let me in, or I'm calling Amos and telling him

I smell a dead body."

She cracked the door and peeked out. I glimpsed her chenille robe. The one with the bunnies on it. "Come back later."

"Don't be ridiculous. Are you sick? Let me in."

"Why don't you meet me down at The Naked Bean in an hour? I need a chance to dress and —"

"It's early afternoon. Why aren't you dressed?" The words were out of my mouth before the answer came to me. Anna Rose's uncle, Tyrone Lavender, must be inside my mother's apartment. They'd been having sex. "Mother! In the middle of the *day?*"

"Shhh, do you want everybody to know?"

"I'd say they'll know soon enough. Are you protecting yourself? What if you get pregnant?"

"Maggie!" It was her turn to be astonished by something I said.

"I'm just kidding. I'll come back some other time."

"I'll meet you for coffee in an hour."

I walked back to my car. Life seemed to be just ducky for Mother. Why was mine falling apart all of a sudden? Tag and I hadn't talked in a week now.

As I drove back toward my house, my big old lonely house, I passed Tag. He and

Giselle were walking down the street past Beecham's Bakery. I waved. He didn't see me as he patted the big, fluffy dog. Her tawny fur rippled in the summer breeze as she marched smartly along beside him. Suddenly, she spotted Bob the Chihuahua drinking out of his bowl outside the bakery.

And the chase was on.

"Giselle!" Tag shouted, trying to grab the leash that had been snatched out of his hands.

I slammed on my brakes, shoved the gearshift into park, and bolted out to try to catch Giselle as she raced past me.

"Giselle, come here, girl!" I shouted, but she didn't even slow down. Poor Bob's little legs were churning beneath him as he ran for his life. They disappeared under the azaleas in the park. I followed.

Tag came loping up behind me, breathing harder than I thought an athlete of his caliber should. "Where are they?"

"I don't know." We stared at the shrubs. "They're here somewhere. They've got to be."

"Giselle! You come here this instant. And don't hurt Bob!"

"They're too quiet. Something's going on. Do you think Giselle killed him?"

I started listening more carefully. Suddenly, I heard little yipping sounds. "Bob! Where are you?"

I followed the sounds, expecting to find a Chihuahua much worse for the wear. I peered between two azaleas and started to laugh.

"What's so funny?" Tag asked, looking over my shoulder.

Bob was trapped between Giselle's front paws. She was licking him on the head. Ingrid Beechum ran up, clutching her throat. "I saw the chase out my window. How badly is he hurt?"

"Brace yourself," Tag deadpanned. "He's being licked to death."

Ingrid groaned in disgust, then pulled Bob out and gathered him in her arms.

He whined, wagged his tiny tail feverishly, and craned his head to look back at Giselle.

Ingrid sighed. "At least he didn't pee on himself. Oh, well . . . spoke too soon. Here he goes."

Holding him out from her body, she carried the Chihuahua back to her bakery. He left a wee trail of Bob wee as they crossed Main Street.

"Come here, girl," Tag called to Giselle. She sauntered from beneath the azaleas, looking forlornly after her tiny, incontinent boyfriend.

I smiled pensively. "True love waits for a second chance."

Tag looked at me. "Do I get a second chance? I'm sorry for everything. I've just been waiting for an excuse to say so. This is it."

"Excuse accepted." We threw our arms around each other and kissed. Once, twice, a half-dozen times. Each kiss lasting longer than the last.

"Maggie! Tag! What are you doing? In public! See, I knew if I moved out, you'd run wild. Good!"

I looked at my mother's beaming face. She peered at us from the other side of the azaleas. "Mother, we're about to make love right out here in the park with the statue of General Hamilton, you, and the chickadees watching. And then we're going back to my house and make love some more. So don't change your mind and move back home. Besides, Beau Belmondo is staying at the house for a while. Sleeping in *your* bed."

Mother hooted. "Beau Belmondo, indeed! Beau Belmondo. Hah! And I expect Mel Gibson's sleeping on the couch. And Sean Connery's bunking in the storage room. Oh, and the Queen of England is coming for tea. All right, I get the point. From now on, I'll mind my own business. And I'm *not* coming home. You can't trick me with jokes about movie stars. I'll be back at my apartment with Tyrone when you're ready to admit Tag's moving in."

She trudged away.

"Well," I said, "I tried to be honest."

"Take her advice. Admit it," Tag said. "I'm moving in."

I smiled. "Smart woman, my mother."

I took my man and his dog home to make friends with the movie star hidden in Mother's bedroom.

To: Lady Victoria Salter Stanhope
From: Katie Bell

Dear Vick:
 I just had to send you this transcript from our local radio station. I tape Bert's morning show to keep up with any potential leads on gossip I've missed. I'm checking out the newcomer Bert mentions. We can't be too careful in a year as strange as this one. This new resident sounds suspicious, to me. That French surname, you know.

A WMOS Welcome
 Good Morning, Mossy Creek! This is Bert Lyman, owner and primetime disc jockey for WMOS, that's W Moss — Big W, Big M, Little "Oss" — the radio voice of greater Mossy Creek. This morning I'm welcoming Mossy Creek Welcome Club President Mal Purla Rhett.
 "Good morning, Bert, I'm heading out today to extend a warm Mossy Creek Reunion Year Welcome to Jasmine Beleau over on Pine Street. I'll be taking her a gift basket from Moonheart's Natural Living and a design consultation certificate from the interior design studios of my sister, Swee Purla, down

217

in Bigelow. Remember, as Swee's motto says, *A classic home tells the world you're truly worthwhile.*"

"Isn't that the truth. Mal, thanks to you and the Welcome Club, Jasmine Beleau will surely settle in smelling like a rose and rooted like a water lily in our Creekite community. For fragrance with a psychic purpose, put your heart into it. Moonheart's, that is. So welcome to Ms. Jasmine Beleau, formerly of New Orleans, Lou-eezy-anna. Do we know any other particulars about Ms. Beleau, Mal?"

"Not yet, but Katie Bell's given her a survey to fill out."

"Well, good. See you next week, Mal."

"Thank you, Bert. Welcoming newcomers is my passion. I always say, 'If you can't say hello, then say goodbye.' "

"Too true, Mal. Now, onto the Bereavement Report. Here's all the news of the dead in greater Mossy Creek. Sponsored by Mossy Creek Funeral Home. Whose motto is, 'If you're dead you'll hear it here, first . . .' "

JASMINE

THE NEW BAD GIRL IN TOWN

Life's tricky when you're used to being an outsider and people suddenly start inviting you in.

Great. I'd set up housekeeping in a town that wanted to know all about me. As if I was going to trust a bunch of small-towners with the truth and nothing but the truth. On the other hand, I wasn't about to stir up trouble by ignoring the local welcome rituals. I didn't want to draw attention to myself by *not* asking for attention. So here's what I wrote for the cheesy survey Katie Bell stuck in my hand one day as I was browsing an antique store on Main Street.

What do reunions mean to me?

Public answer: Reunions are a lovely idea, a way to celebrate a milestone from the past and catch up with old friends. As a new citizen of Mossy Creek, I hope to become a small part of my new hometown's tradition.

Real answer: Not much.

All the people that I cared about in the past are dead or have outlived their usefulness. So, I'm not a reunion kind of girl. As a matter of fact, the past, as far as I'm concerned should stay in the past. Under a rock. I hope I've dashed far enough and fast enough to outrun any possible reunions.

Life for me is about entertaining myself, about planning lunch for today and buying seeds for the garden tomorrow. About living in small normal ways without grand hopes, elegant schemes — or jail time.

What is the most hurtful and publicly humiliating thing that ever happened to me in high school?

Public answer: Oh, that would have to be graduation day when Danny Argenot put a dead crawfish down my back as we stood in line waiting for our diplomas. He slipped it inside my collar and then slapped me on the back to give me the full effect. I had to excuse myself and go to the girls room to get it out. I smelled like dead fish.

Real answer: I never finished high school. Not legally. But I did sort of graduate . . . from a group home.

When you reach seventeen and are able to get into adult trouble, you have to leave. Ready or not. And I had to be ready because I had to look out for my sister, Jade. There was a Danny Argenot, and he did smack me on the back. But, instead of squishing a crawfish, he managed to spring open the safety pin which held my ratty, hand-me-down bra together in the back. The impact drove the sharp part of the pin into my skin, and I had to undress in the bathroom in front of three other girls so the house mother could yank the pin out. The rest of the day, the other kids snickered and asked me why there was blood on the back of my blouse.

Humiliation has its good side. Because of that incident, I swore I would make enough money to have a new bra to wear every day of the week. At the height of my so-called career, I had an entire closet of lingerie created by some of the most expensive designers in the world. I only wore safety pins for the small percentage of my clients who were partial to a little jab here and there.

That was not a fact I intended to share with my new neighbors in Mossy Creek. I believe when I sit down to write my memoirs — and I do intend to get around to putting them on paper — as soon as I lose interest in making new ones, that is — I believe I'll begin with a few simple feminine truths: If there's one thing I've learned, it's that you can start a car with a tube of lipstick.

Now, I'm sure most logical folk wouldn't agree, and you might even think I'm a little cock-eyed to bring it up. But honey, a tube of lipstick in just the right shade and used in just the right manner will get men to start cars for you all day long. Yours, theirs, even ones people leave in those neat little parking spaces on the sides of the road. A tube of lipstick is a downright miracle, or a lifesaver if you're in need of saving and such.

"My daddy doesn't like me wearin' lipstick," Linda Polk said, touching her lips with the blunt tips of her fingers.

We were sitting on my newly-painted porch stairs, watching the occasional car go by and chatting while we waited for her mother to pick her up. The teenager had walked the short distance from "downtown" Mossy Creek to bring me a package I'd accidentally left at her Aunt Effie's fabric store on the square, where she worked after school.

"He says I was born plain, and there's nothin' I can do to change it," Linda continued. "He says my only chance is to find a man with more heart than eyesight, to make up for my shortcomings."

I knew I should stay out of it, being new to town, but men can be such idiots sometimes, and I am living proof they can be taught lessons if the effort is worth it, or that they can be fooled over and over again if I'm too tired to teach. I had to turn a bit on the steps in order to trap Linda's face between my hands.

"How old are you?"

"Fifteen-and-a-half."

Her hair, limp, blondish, and straggling down to her shoulders looked clean at least, but no conditioner, no curl, nothing to help the view. Plain. I studied her dark blue eyes, almost too dark to see blue unless you searched for it, and she simply looked back. "Haven't you ever had a boy tell you you're pretty?"

She thought for a while as I pushed her hair back out of her face and anchored it behind her ears. "No. They've said some things to me, but not that."

I could just bet what things they'd said. Things which could be classified under 'juvenile idiot' in the file. But I wasn't keepin' score anymore. I'd given up the life of my former incarnation and set out on a new path in a new place. The greasy old police chief in New Orleans would probably say I was strikin' out on the straight and narrow — "Hallelujah, *chère!*" Then as he always used to do, he'd punctuate his pronouncement by smacking me on the rump like I was his to handle, and cackle that wheeze his buddies called a laugh. I had to laugh with him then. It was good for business. But I don't have to worry about what men think any more. Never again. I've reached the point where I've accumulated enough money and investments to start a new life, manless and proud of it. Retired at thirty, but then, I'd started young.

I released Linda's face and smoothed my sundress over my knees before hooking my hands around them. She was like most other girls who lacked a pedigree, standing outside an imaginary circle of acceptance and approval, her wistful, everyday face pressed against the impenetrable glass barrier between the haves and have nots. I'd been there, done that.

"Have you ever heard the ancient —" I raised my eyebrows to illuminate the word so she, being a teenager, couldn't lob it back at me like a hand grenade — "saying, *Beauty is as Beauty does?*"

"Huh?"

"I guess it's older than I thought," I mumbled and turned away. Why was I trying to explain anything to this girl? I barely knew her from my occasional visits to the fabric store. I certainly wouldn't recommend the life I'd led to her, but then again, compared to being stuck under the thumb of a father who thought she was plain and . . . "What kind of grades do you make in school?"

"Mostly B's." She looked down at her tennis shoes and wiggled them nervously. "I made a C last semester, and Daddy said that he guessed B's and one C was the best I could do —"

I raised a hand to stop her before she said the dreaded word 'stupid' which almost always came connected to 'plain.' "Are you stupid?"

"What?" She jumped like no one had ever asked her for an opinion before.

"I said, are you stupid?"

She thought for a minute, frowning, then looked me in the eye. "No. I don't think I'm stupid."

"Hallelujah, *chère!*" I tapped her knee in agreement. "That's good, because you're not. It's a start."

"Don't you think I'm plain, Miss Jasmine? You're so beautiful, you must know plain when you see it."

So beautiful. I'd been called that, by rich men, by most men, and a few women as well. Most of the females had been my competition, so I always thought of their flattery as a sort of camouflage, like a Cobra mesmerizing you with his lyrical dance before spitting venom in your eye. The few women who were sincere were . . . not my type. And here I was in Mossy Creek, doing my best to be plain again, letting my hair get to know its natural color for the first time in years, wearing little makeup and going without shoes in the garden when I felt like it. After years of living as a 'luminous' creature of night habits and sleeping away most of the day, I'd been sunburned for the first time in my experience picking blueberries the summer past. A travesty. A Southern 'girl' must take care of her *magnolia* complexion, along with a list of other do's and don'ts that I *don't* care about anymore.

But this girl cared — would probably always care — unless someone like me showed her it was all a power game.

I pulled my gaze from a car passing on the tree lined street, in the town where I'd found what I hoped would be my final home and resting place, and looked at her. There she sat, an open book, giving compliments to me, another plain girl who'd grown into beauty only after winnowing out exactly

226

what beauty really meant. "Thank you," I said, "And no, you're not plain. You *act* plain, that's all."

I was always one for telling the truth . . . except to my men. No use in telling them the truth; it only gave them too much to think about when I intended to do all the thinking for them, anyway.

"What do you mean, act?"

Beauty is as beauty does. "I mean, you can learn to be beautiful."

She made a chuffing sound and looked away, her hopeful expression soured. I could almost hear her father's voice in her head, echoing for all time. "Born plain . . . need to find a man to make up for shortcomings . . . stupid."

"I'm not talking about turning into Britney Spears overnight. To become someone like that, you'd need to start when you're about nine years old and work at it. You'd also need about five hundred thousand dollars or so, but you could do it."

"Five hundred thousand —"

"For stylists, personal trainers, and the right clothes. I know." I smiled to take some of the sting out of my words. "You're poor too, right?"

Tears welled in her eyes, and I felt like the hard businesswoman I'd been. Why had I thought this girl needed to know the truth? The truth can set you free, but sometimes it hurt more than a nice, comfortable lie. I put a buddy-like arm around her shoulders and gave her a good pat. "You can learn to be as pretty as you want to be. All you have to do is want it and work at it."

We heard a car. A woman pulled an old Buick into my driveway. "Linda?" she called out the open window.

"I'm comin'," Linda answered. "That's my mom," she said to me as she pushed to her feet.

"Thanks for delivering my thread and patterns." I stood, casually patting the newel post of my very own, fully paid for, porch.

"You're welcome." She was halfway down the stairs when she stopped and turned. "Do you think you could teach me how to do it? Be pretty, that is? The big reunion's coming up this fall, and there'll be dances . . ." Her voice trailed off. She looked embarrassed and bit her lip.

For longer than I wanted to admit, young girls had looked to me for advice or as the anecdote to their parents' best expectations. And I'd usually helped — some a little, some a lot. My therapist explained about guilt, about my inability to save my own sister, but back then, I thought I had the world and everything in it, figured out. My resume would have read — 'Seen it all.' By the time I learned the error of that assumption, it was too late to save anyone but myself.

I avoided answering Linda's question and waved to her mother. "Hello, Mrs. Polk."

She nodded and raised a hand, but didn't answer. We were strangers, after all, and maybe some Creekites, as they called themselves, weren't quite sure what to make of me. It dawned on me that taking on her timid daughter as a project could remedy the 'stranger' part of the equation. But there would still be the question of friend or foe.

I looked at Linda. "You talk to your mother and bring her here with you, next time. I'll help if she doesn't mind."

She looked hopeful again, then wavered when her mom called her name a second time. Mrs. Polk seemed to be in a hurry.

"I'll try," Linda said and jogged to the car.

That evening I walked to the end of the porch to watch the sun slip behind Mount Colchik, the looming, mother-of-all-mountains west of town. A silver mist hung in the summer air, blurring the edges of the trees and softening the weathered roofs of the houses in the sweetly aged neighborhood. Some of the homes had stood for seventy-five years; some had been built in a rush of prosperity after World War II. They weren't anything like the statuesque variety of New Orleans mansions, but that was fine.

I'd found this place because of a man, of course. After accompanying a very rich, very demanding former client of mine to his mountaintop 'getaway' for a 'business' weekend, I'd headed back to Atlanta in my client's limo. Road construction and a detour had stranded me and the limo driver, by chance, in Mossy Creek. Something about the place — sheltered by bluegreen mountains, surrounded by the creek like a friendly little moat, dotted with pleasant shops and pretty little neighborhoods and sprawling mountain farms — resembled home to me, the home I'd wished I had. The home I would have given Jade, my sister. So, when the charm and the advantages in New Orleans had lost their allure, I'd chased a dream back to Mossy Creek.

I slipped my arms around the porch post and watched Raleigh Yates, an old man who lived across the street, digging post holes along the front edge of his rose-hedged lawn. Raleigh was installing a pristine new picket fence in honor of the festivities around the high school reunion. All my neighbors were cleaning and fixing and painting, although the reunion was still several months away.

"Have to spruce up for the big event," Raleigh explained. "We can't have folks coming home to shabby memories. Why, folks would just feel *lost* if their old hometown didn't look its best."

Lost in Mossy Creek. Impossible. You couldn't get lost in this town if they blindfolded you, spun you around three times, then gave you a shove. Sooner or later, you'd walk into a war monument, a shade tree big enough to live under, or the creek, itself. Mossy Creek's official motto — painted on the Hamilton Farm grain silo beside the main drag into town — says "Ain't goin' no where and don't want to." It ought to add, "So when you're here, you'll always know where you are."

Good. I hadn't come to Mossy Creek to get lost. I'd come here to live in plain sight by the light of day. To garden, to shop, and to take walks, to mow my own lawn and to sweep my own steps, without anyone to please or entertain. To lose my past in my own future.

And to entertain myself. I'd always had that particular talent. Unfortunately, my talent to entertain others became so admired that after awhile, I forgot about myself. People were always comin' to find me — mostly men — to ask, to want, to touch. I'd enjoyed it in the beginning, as we do with all new things. Then when I'd stopped having a good time, I'd turned it to my own advantage, my own enrichment, so to speak. I may not want to repeat a good many of the things I've done, but I don't regret them — with the possible exception of failing Jade. They were choices among the choices each of us make.

Women know all about making hard choices. Men think they do, but they have too much time and usually too much money on their hands to actually have to make and live with one choice — good or bad. At least the men I'd entertained did. They were masters at variety, at doing what they pleased. Some were spoiled, rich, sons of fortune, each perfectly secure in his position in life and willing to convince anyone who'd listen of his own importance. Some were so effortlessly male and beautiful without having to work at it that women would line up and sell their souls to be touched by their elegant hands.

Those men, the 'perfect' ones, in turn usually wanted the women they couldn't have: other men's wives or independent contractors like myself. Now there's a good example of a bad choice.

None of the above could afford or acquire my soul, and that's why they'd flocked to my door. The mystery and image I'd perfected kept them coming back.

I'm not fool enough to think they loved me, but they wanted me and would sink to the level of my choice in most matters to have me, that much I knew. I wasn't kidding about the tube of lipstick.

I laughed to myself as I released the post and turned for the front door. I wondered how these Creekites, these God-fearin', small-town citizens, would react if they had a clue who'd moved into their town. A scarlet woman, the proverbial Jezebel, the woman their mothers warned about and the preachers condemned. Seeing me stepping out of a limo in the French Quarter, draped in a skin-clinging, silk dress which cost more than most of them made in a year, on the arm of a man who owned towns larger than any within a hundred miles of this place, might make them stand back in awe, like watching movie royalty. But seeing me *entertain* that man would convince them a legendary purveyor of original sin had come to life.

I was done with New Orleans, however,

and determined to leave every vestige of the seductress I had created among the Vieux Carre and the tombs of voodoo queens. My siren song had ended.

I had come home to Mossy Creek — an-out-of-the-way, conservative, next-to-nowhere town in hope that it might help redeem my tarnished soul. Either that or burn me at the stake.

It took the better part of two weeks before 'plain' Linda Polk visited me again. By that time, I had nearly forgotten our conversation about beauty, and I was deep into my own sprucing-up-for-the-reunion project of sewing curtains for my living room. I would have made Martha Stewart proud. Not all of my years had been spent in sin and wickedness. Sewing was a talent left over from my youth, when I couldn't afford designer clothes or when I had the picture of a special dress in my mind that couldn't be found in any store. It had been more years than I wanted to admit since I'd had the free time to sew for the pleasure of it. As I stepped over a tape measure, pin cushions and yards of material spread across my Oriental rug, Linda knocked on my door.

"Miss Jasmine?" She put a hand up to

shade her eyes and looked through the screen. I'd propped the outer door open and turned on huge floor fan to draw the scent of summer through the house.

"Hey, Linda."

"Hi, Miss Jasmine." She sounded breathless and more than a little nervous. I'd never get over being called 'Miss Jasmine,' by a teenager or anyone else. Another quaint Mossy Creek custom. "Come on in," I offered and held the door.

As she stepped inside, she saw the curtains in progress and made her way in their direction. "That's the material you had Aunt Effie order from Atlanta, isn't it?"

"Yes, it is. What do you think?"

She gazed from the whimsical, pale-green brocade to the windows where it would be hung and smiled. "It'll be perfect," she said. She glanced around my living room and gasped. "Wow, a real leather couch. Don't see too many of those around here. The mayor has one, I hear. This is so pretty."

"You have good taste. That couch came from New York. It cost over eight thousand dollars."

She clutched her heart and stared at the couch, speechless.

I patted her arm. "Would you like a soft drink or some tea?" I was trying to give her all the time she needed to get to the point of her visit.

"Sure."

I started toward the hallway, and she followed tentatively, taking in her surroundings like an earthling who's been invited on to an alien spaceship. "Is this *you?*" she asked as she stopped near an expensively framed photograph.

"Yes," I answered, but didn't offer an explanation. There had been few mementos of New Orleans I'd loved enough to keep. Most of them were in my bedroom, safely hidden from casual visitors, casual questions. The picture Linda asked about was one of myself with the only two people in the world I'd loved. I'm not sure why I'd hung it in the living room in a special space near the hallway's arch, but I suspected it had to do with wanting to see it each time I moved from room to room. My old life haunting the new.

"Who's that man? He looks like a movie star."

"He's a friend of mine."

She looked at me closely. "A friend?"

"Yes."

"What about the girl?"

"She's my sister." I feigned a shrug. "That picture might as well have been taken a hundred years ago. I hardly remember the details." I'd said less than I could have and more than I should have. I'm not sure why. Perhaps that particular picture would be better off in another place. Before I found myself explaining to the U.P.S. man or the plumber how my frail, half-sister Jade had grown up into an exotic, breathtaking beauty and married the only man I'd ever made the mistake of falling in love with.

I could still hear Tienne's low, affectionate voice . . . *Jasmine and Jade . . . Jasmine and Jade. What am I to do with the two of you?* As if he'd loved us both and couldn't decide.

"Who are those beautiful people with you?" Linda whispered, touching the photograph with awestruck care.

"Enough questions. This way," I motioned her toward the kitchen — neutral ground. There had been little to bring from my former, professionally outfitted kitchen in the apartment I'd owned in New Orlean's ultra-chic Garden District. I'd given most of the fixtures and equipment to my cook — she'd spent more time with the pots, pans and utensils than I had. Now I owned a simple, country kitchen with an antique, cherry wood table, matching chairs and a bench under the window, a collection of blue enamel-ware resting on shelves in the corner, and bonafide lace curtain — as nostalgic and old fashioned as I'd ever wished to be.

Over two glasses of sweet iced tea, Linda and I finally reached the subject she'd come there to discuss. "My mom says she wants to talk to you before —"

"That's fine." I nodded. "She's welcome to hear everything I have to say to you."

"You should know that she doesn't really want me to doll myself up, but she isn't gonna tell my dad until she has to." Linda picked up her glass of tea and took a sip. I couldn't discern what worried her more — her mother, her father, or me.

I, on the other hand, wasn't afraid of anyone. I'd faced too many other, scarier things than a small town chauvinist and his un-emancipated wife. Between my profession and Jade's meteoric fall from grace, I'd seen more human cruelty and frailty than I cared to recall. But, Linda's case of the nerves made me seriously question whether I wanted to get involved in what could rapidly become a family dispute.

I wasn't good at 'family.' And, I had the uneasy feeling I might mar the peace and quiet I'd moved to Mossy Creek to achieve. When it came down to it, this girl's future would most likely fall into place nicely without my help. My own future, judging from what I'd seen happen in the past to me and mine, needed a bit more vigilance. I searched my ambivalence for a final decision.

It's funny how the simplest things can touch a place inside you. As I sat across from my new wanna-be protégée, teetering on the brink of calling the whole thing off, a breeze ruffled the curtains at the window drawing my attention to some flowers I'd haphazardly stuck in a vase. The vase was white, old-fashioned, milk glass. Plain, wholesome, and proud of it. The summers-end flowers were daisies and coreopsis I'd cut from the garden. Yellow and white, ruffled and hard to ignore, they drew the eye like a pretty girl, laughing.

The comparison wasn't lost on me. A plain vase, dressed up with my help, giving me and anyone who happened to notice pleasure and peace. Like a smile from a stranger.

I brought my attention back to the stranger sitting in my kitchen. She'd shown up and called me on my off-hand offer. I'd helped so many others as a business investment. What would it hurt to give one more girl the keys to the kingdom? A little feminine self-esteem could go a long way. If she really wanted my help, then I wouldn't back out.

"I think your mom is right. She knows best how to handle your dad."

Now, Linda looked embarrassed. "She also wants to know how much this is gonna cost."

A not so out-of-line question. I knew what it was like to count pennies instead of fifties. "Well, let's see. I've never hired out as a consultant for a young socialite's debut, before —"

"Debut?" she echoed, wide-eyed. "Young socialite?"

I nodded solemnly. "Uh huh. Hmmm. The cost for my help? Nothing."

Linda's embarrassment fled, and she smiled, looking animated again. "Thanks!"

"You *are* going to have to buy some things, however. You'll need money for a new hair cut, some basic makeup and a few new clothes. Shoes are essential. Here's my first tip — the difference between a good pair of legs and a *great* pair of legs is usually the kind of shoes those feet are wearing."

"I can use the money I make after school working for Aunt Effie. And my mom said she'd help out of her grocery money."

"All right, then." I put out my hand in a business-like manner. "We have a deal. I'll help you as much or as little as you want. Your job is to learn to believe in yourself. You'll have to work at it." Linda grasped my hand, and her dark blue eyes sparkled.

"I'm a good worker. Even my dad says so."

"Believing in yourself is the hardest part. Here's your assignment. First, you have to promise not to call yourself *plain* or repeat anything your father says about you — unless it's good."

She nodded, as if that part was easy.

"I'm serious. In order to reinvent yourself, you have to let go of the past. Each time you catch yourself about to say the 'p' word, stop and change it to something complimentary. Each time your father's frowning face appears in your head, saying that word, force yourself to think of something else. Anything else — a song you love, a person who smiled at you, even a good book you've read. Don't allow anything to derail your transformation, or your brand new, shiny train of self-confidence will end up in a ditch."

I could see her absorbing my words. How much she took them to heart was another question. I didn't have the ability to explain how important self image is to outward beauty. It was a lesson a woman had to learn for herself. I'd learned it the hard way, year by year, man by man. When you go through life depending solely on yourself, you tend to learn your strengths and weaknesses early.

"Okay, now, the next thing is, I want you to go to the drugstore or the bookstore and pick up some magazines. Leaf through them until you see someone with a hairdo you like. Doesn't matter if she's a movie star or a waitress. Find some pictures we can evaluate. When's your next afternoon off from Effie's?"

"Not until Monday," she answered glumly. You'd have thought it was a year away.

I walked across the room to study a wall calendar decorated with photos of roses that I'd hung by the phone. I slipped it off the nail, picked a pen out of a jelly glass, and returned to the table. "Today is Wednesday. Can you and your mom come by on Saturday morning, let's say about ten, so your mom and I can make sure we're in agreement?"

"Yeah."

"Then if your mom gives us the go-ahead on Saturday, you could get your hair done on the Monday afternoon after that?"

"Mom will agree. She just has to," Linda

said urgently.

"She will." I wrote 'hair appointment' on the calendar.

Next, I scrutinized Linda's eyes. "Your hair is the place to start — it's the frame for your face. Once we get it cut and styled, we'll be able to see what makeup to buy. Okay?"

"Okay," Linda said and got to her feet. "I guess I'll see you on Saturday, then." She stood there awkwardly.

"Don't forget what I said about the 'p' word, and the magazines. And about your father."

"I won't," she pledged. She gazed at me as if searching for words. I waited. "Thank you, Miss Jasmine," she said finally. "I want to look great for all the parties and the reunion festival. But more than that, I want to look *new*."

"Don't thank me yet, chère." I put an arm around her shoulders and squeezed. "You're the one who has to do all the work. I'm just the beauty consultant."

On Saturday morning, Linda, a stack of well-thumbed magazines in her arms, and her mother, dressed in a neat but dowdy, at-least-five-years-out-of-style shirtwaist dress, knocked on my door ten minutes before ten. By the obvious energy running through the teenager, a direct contrast to the prim cautiousness of her mother, I could tell we were beyond the 'no' in 'the point of no return.'

I took them through the house to the back porch overlooking the garden and sat them at a cloth-covered table complete with flower arrangement and silver coffee service. As I said before, entertaining had been my business, and I'd been good at it. I intended for them to be comfortable and impressed. That way it would be easier to accomplish Linda's transformation goal with a minimum of anxiety on her part and with less interference from her mother.

After serving them both coffee, I folded my hands in front of me and prepared to present my disclaimer speech. I'd found it better in my dealings with people — men, customers, employees, or political allies — to set the ground rules up front. Many times the ground rule recipients would conveniently, or otherwise, forget what I'd told them, but I had no hesitation about reminding them as the need arose.

"Now, Mrs. Polk, I've promised Linda I would help her improve her image — with your permission. I've had some experience as a . . . beauty consultant, although I'm no longer in the business." Saying that particular sentence tickled my perverse pleasure at the secrets of my past. Mrs. Polk would grab her daughter and run for the door if she'd had any idea of what my version of 'beauty consulting' had been.

I managed to continue with only a slight smile. "As I told Linda, any advice or help I give her is free. I'm not trying to sell her or you anything. I will make recommendations, however, and consider it holding up my part of the bargain to do so. Some of those recommendations will be to purchase items. Whether you and Linda decide to follow my advice is completely up to you. All I ask is that we give this effort at least one meeting a week for four weeks — six if we feel inspired. It takes time to change and then more time to get used to the changes.

"Is that agreeable?"

Mrs. Polk who, as she listened to my words seemed to be hiding behind her coffee cup, cleared her throat, then set down the cup. "What exactly are you gonna do to Linda?"

"I'm going to teach her how to feel beautiful."

"Feel beautiful?" Mrs. Polk frowned. "How do you teach somebody to 'feel' beautiful?"

"By changing the way she looks on the outside until how she feels on the inside catches up." Linda's mother looked doubtful, so I did a little damage control. "We're not going to do anything drastic," I said. "I'm going to evaluate her best assets, then show her how to enhance them."

"We can't afford no nose surgery or —" Her face flushed "— other things like that."

I assumed she might be thinking of breast implants which seemed to be the subject du jour when anyone mentioned improving their 'assets.' "Linda doesn't need any surgery," I said. "Come here, Linda."

Linda obediently rose and moved to stand next to me. I stepped behind her and took her by the shoulders. "She's tall," I said. "That's good. It means she can wear a greater variety of clothing styles. Unfortunately, that probably makes her taller than most of the boys in her class but that'll change soon enough."

I rested my hands on her hips, gathering the folds of the baggy style shirt she wore more often than not. Her waist appeared. "I'd guess she's a size eight, a ten in some things."

"Huge," Linda moaned.

"Just right," I corrected. "Short, tall, fat, skinny — none of that has much to do with beauty."

Linda bowed her head. "But I've got no boobs, and you can't tell me *that* doesn't matter."

"Oh, yes, I can." With Linda's shirt tighter, it was easy to ascertain that her breasts, although not large, were certainly enough material to work with for male approval. Men were silly creatures when it came to breasts, they had trouble telling the real from the artfully enhanced and by the time they found the truth, they usually didn't care.

Linda fidgeted a little under her mother's and my scrutiny, but I didn't let her go.

"You could get her some falsies," Mrs. Polk said.

"Hmmm. It's always been my theory that it's not what you can afford to add on, it's how you present what you were born with. Beauty is an illusion. I'm going to teach Linda how to find her own look and maintain it."

Linda blushed, but her mother nodded.

I released Linda's waist and pulled her hair back away from her face. "All right, my sweet, the first thing we'll do is get you a good haircut. One that works with your bone structure and shows off your eyes. It also has to be one that doesn't take a lot of maintenance." I tugged on Linda's hair playfully, then let it fall forward into place. "The better the cut, the easier the style. Did you find some styles you liked in the magazines?"

"Yeah," Linda answered eagerly. She pulled a stack from a paper bag.

We spent the next hour discussing hair textures, cuts, the pros and cons of highlights versus hair color and by the time they were ready to leave, we'd narrowed the field to one cut with another as a second choice. Mrs. Polk made few comments, either from genuine shyness or, more likely, the willingness to let me hang myself with my opinions. She did, however, say that Linda's father would never allow her to dye her hair a brighter shade of blonde. The haircut in the photo Linda had chosen featured a singer with platinum blonde hair.

I shook my head. "We're not doing any bleaching. We're only changing the cut. I made an appointment at 3:00 on Monday with Rainey Ann Cecil at the Goldilocks salon." The Goldilocks Hair, Nail and Tanning Salon. I'd been assured that Rainey Ann Cecil was the top stylist in Mossy Creek, and no, there was no need to drive twenty minutes south to Bigelow. I also knew that since Linda was too young to drive, it would be better to find someone close to do her hair the way she wanted it.

But with a folksy stylist named Rainey Ann and a shop named Goldilocks, I feared the attack of the big-haired hair-do. If my memory served me correctly, Goldilocks and the Three Bears had not come to a happy ending. That could have been my cynicism showing, however. At this point, my greatest hope was that this Rainey would take an interest in Linda and go all out to help an awkward, duckling of a teenager turn into a swan.

Just like me.

"You want me to do her hair like *that?*" Rainey Ann Cecil said, loudly enough to be heard over the drone of three hair dryers and the conversation about *The Young and The Restless* taking place at the shampoo area.

Suddenly, every ear in the shop seemed to readjust, like antenna, in our direction.

"Her daddy would come in here with a gun if I made this girl look like that, that . . . tattooed punk singer," she said, poking the magazine I held in front of her with a long, pink artificial nail.

"We don't want her hair to look *exactly* like this, Rainey Ann," I said carefully. "Just *cut* this way."

"The name's Rainey, not Rainey Ann."

"Sorry."

Rainey's frown increased, but she took the magazine from my hands and studied it. Then, shaking her head, she handed it back. "That cut won't look right on her," she said emphatically. She spun the chair around. "Here, Linda, sit down. I'll show you how we should fix your hair."

Linda started to obey, but I stopped her. I held the magazine next to Linda's face. "Rainey, don't you see how it's shaped around the eyes? In your professional opinion, wouldn't that be a good frame for Linda's face?" It wouldn't do to order Rainey around. My quick assessment of her shop told me she ran a successful business. And she might be a little on the tacky side, personally, but I'd already noticed a couple of her customers leaving with impressively current hairstyles.

And, the most important part, she was armed with a sharp pair of scissors.

Rainey brought her pink enameled fingers to rest on the hips of her snug pink jeans. "Look. Time is money. You made the appointment. Do you want me to cut her hair, or not?"

I carefully closed the magazine and

handed it to Linda. Every eye in the shop seemed to be on us but I couldn't help that. Even the water faucets in the shampoo area had gone silent. Knowing I was still a stranger in this town, I'd done my best to dress casually and had pulled my own hair back into a non-descript, non-threatening jumble of curls. But, stranger or not, we were paying customers, and I wasn't about to allow a stubborn stylist to change the plans Linda and I had discussed.

"How much is the haircut?" I asked.

"Fifteen dollars with the styling." She leaned close to me and whispered, "Look, I'm not trying to give you a load of grief, but I've got a lot on my mind these days, and the last thing I want is for Linda Polk's daddy to go on a rant because I gave her a sexed-up haircut. I feel sorry for the poor girl just like you do, but if I send her home with a punk-hussy hair-do her daddy will *kill* her."

Her choice of words sent a cold trickle of defense down my spine. "I never realized a hairstyle had anything to do with moral judgments."

"Go tell that to Linda's redneck daddy."

I pulled my wallet from my purse and took out a bill. "Here's a twenty. Keep the change." I turned and captured Linda's arm. "Let's go."

Linda, shocked into confused silence, allowed me to lead her through the shop to the front door. By the time we reached it, Rainey had found her voice. "Lor', if that doesn't put the *ant* in *arrogant*," she said loudly.

The door closed before I had to answer.

"So much for Goldilocks."

"Where are we going now?" Linda asked as I unlocked the car. "To Bigelow?"

"No, I don't think so. Let's stop by my house and make some calls."

Forty minutes later, with Linda's mother's reluctant permission, we were on our way to Atlanta to a stylist named Leon in a shop called "Fresco's." I'd had my hair done there occasionally in the past year but had stopped going after being lectured on my 'lack of attitude.'

"How can you not care that your roots look like corn rows?" Leon had tut-tutted the last time he'd seen me. Instead of insulting me, he'd made me laugh. He'd been scandalized when I'd explained that my hair was in retirement.

"Leon will do the initial cut. Then we'll have to find someone for maintenance," I instructed. "Remember, once you begin this beauty thing, you have to keep it up."

"I will, I promise," Linda said.

Leon descended on Linda's hair like a fairy godmother in full wish-fulfillment mode after a theatrical wink in my direction and a, "You just leave her to me." He pointed out a freshly made pitcher of mimosas near a leather-upholstered bench in the salon's trés-trendy lounge, before sweeping Linda into his mysterious world of high style.

From what I could tell beyond that, Leon never stopped talking.

While sipping a mimosa and thumbing through the latest *W,* I could hear his continuous one-sided conversation punctuated by an occasional "fabulous," or a dramatic gasp followed by a high-pitched peal of laughter.

Mayberry meets South Beach. It made me chuckle just to think about it, and I realized I was actually enjoying myself. Casually meddling in other people's business had been bad for my business in the past. Now that I'd retired, I could do it simply for fun.

Two hours later, Leon waltzed into the lounge looking like the Cheshire Cat . . . with a kitten in tow. He even made me close my eyes before presenting his handiwork. I almost told him not to push it, but I didn't want to spoil Linda's day, so I closed my eyes and waited.

"Okay, now you can look," Leon said.

He was standing in front of Linda holding a lavender nylon smock like a matador waiting for the bull to charge. "Ta, da!" he said and dropped the smock.

It was all I could do not to gasp. Linda, her new 'do' styled within an inch of its life, stared back at me, her expression a mixture of hope and fear.

"It's perfect," I managed. And it was. The deceptively simple cut framed her eyes. He'd even given her the new asymmetrical part that was all the rage in Hollywood. Yet it wasn't a come-hither look. "Leon, you've outdone yourself." I meant that as well. He'd taken it upon himself to layer her hair with highlights and low lights which truly did look 'fabulous.' But, I'd promised her mother we wouldn't do color. And Rainey's warning about Linda's father nagged at me.

Leon bowed slightly before reaching out to ruffle the ends of Linda's hair near her eyes. "I know we didn't talk about color, so I won't charge for the highlights. I just couldn't let this cut go out the door without a little pizazz."

"Do you really like it?" Linda asked, then craned past me to look in the mirror on the wall.

"It looks terrific," I answered, then frowned at my watch. "If we hurry, we have time to stop at Lenox Square and pick up some makeup on our way north to the mountains."

Linda thanked Leon all the way to the front door. To say they'd bonded would be an understatement. The only way he managed to get his hand back from her continuous handshake was to give her a rather clinical peck on her cheek and a little shove. "Go get 'um, girl."

"You're a good man," I said as I handed him a twenty-dollar tip. "Keep being nice, and you might make it to heaven yet."

He hesitated, for a moment going as serious as I'd ever seen him. "No, I'm not a particularly *nice* man," he said, sweeping the bill from my hand. "But I'm a hellava hairdresser!"

"Oui, *cher!*" I concurred.

"See you in six weeks, sweetie," he called to Linda.

We made a brief stop at a *Clinique* counter at the mall, then headed home. During the hour-plus drive, Linda gave me a blow-by-blow-dry description of her first big-city 'styling' experience. Not surprisingly, before meeting Leon and myself, she'd never been asked how she wanted her hair and obviously thought she should share the event. By the second hour of the drive I was beginning to think she'd been possessed by the spirit of Leon — the continuous talker. But, her enthusiasm was a hopeful sign. Just the thing to raise her bargain-basement self-image. How could she possibly be plain when her hair-stylist, Leon, who'd actually met Madonna, claimed she looked smashing?

It was a good start. Hair and a few basic makeup items. We'd had a productive day. My only reservation centered around the niggling worry of what her parents would have to say. Leon or no Leon. The other shoe was poised to fall. So, feeling like I might be sending the lamb to the lions, I dropped Linda off with a smile and a thumbs-up and watched her skip up the sidewalk to her family's front door before I drove away slowly.

Maybe her father would love the change.

Maybe pigs would sprout haloes and wings.

I was glad Leon lived so far from Mossy Creek. It would make him that much harder to find for an irate father. I, on the other hand . . . I'd be easy to find. Although if Mr. Polk thought I'd cower, he'd be badly mistaken. I'd grown up under the thumb of an abusive father, losing patience with him somewhere around the age of seven. After that, he'd never touched me or Jade again. There hadn't been a bully since that I couldn't handle.

I half expected the phone to be ringing when I walked in my front door. When it wasn't, I decided that no news was good news.

It took twenty-four hours for the call to come. And when it did, the call was from Mrs. Polk, not Mister.

"I wanted to talk to you before my husband gets in from work and Linda gets home from school."

"How is she doing?" I asked, hoping Linda's mother would surprise me with the news that everyone loved the 'new' look.

"Well . . . her daddy hit the roof when he saw her hair. He dragged her right down to Goldilocks and told Rainey to dye the highlights and cut the new style out of it."

My heart sank. But that's when Mrs. Polk surprised me.

She laughed. "But Rainey wouldn't touch Linda's hair-do. She told Jimmy right to his face that it was the best cut and highlight job she'd ever seen — better than she herself could have done. And, she'd have no part of ruining it. You have to know Rainey.

Nobody tells her what to do." Mrs. Polk chuckled again.

All right, Rainey! I thought. "Is Linda all right?"

"A little nervous, but she loves how she looks. I've never seen her so excited. She couldn't wait to get to school today. I used to have to wake her up three times every mornin', and she'd still be late. I just want you to know, in case you hear something different, that she'll be at your house on Saturday like you've planned. I'll make sure of it. If you should get a phone call from my . . . uh, my husband, just —"

"Ignore him?" I added helpfully.

"Well . . . yes. I guess that's exactly what I mean. Do the best you can."

"Not a problem. Tell Linda I'll see her Saturday."

On Friday afternoon, I took a walk down to Hamilton's Department Store to order some new curtain rods. On the way back, as I passed the shop and greenhouses of Mossy Creek Hardware and Gardening, a beefy man wearing a tractor cap embroidered with the slogan, *My Way Or The Highway,* stepped off the store's front porch and stared at me. He gave me the evil eye, then spat brown tobacco juice on the gravel of the parking lot.

I'd just met Linda's father. Jimmy Polk was a grading and concrete foreman for a construction company down in Bigelow. I stared at him until he looked away. Then I walked on.

Mr. Jimmy Polk was smarter than I'd thought, because if he'd tried to bully me, he would have gone down in flames right there in front of the hardware store.

On Saturday morning, Linda came through my door dressed in a new pair of embroidered jeans and a cropped white blouse we'd picked up in Atlanta. The jeans fit well, and the blouse short enough to show off her figure, but demurely. I only pressed my luck when I knew I had the advantage. I didn't want my name brought up in the Sunday sermon list of mortal sin and corruption at the Mossy Creek First Baptist Church — and more than that, of course, I didn't want Linda's father to ground her. Linda had been transformed enough for one week.

The shorter length of Leon's haircut had begun to curl up a bit on the ends giving the style a breezy, tossed look that energized her features. And she'd applied a little mascara and barely-there lipgloss. I made my blossoming pet project turn in a circle so I could admire the effect.

"Guess what!" Linda gushed as she dutifully spun around. "A guy in class invited me to the movies next weekend! He's sixteen, and he gets to borrow his grandmother's minivan. We're going to the Bigelow Cineplex. It has stadium seating and a coffee bar."

"Wow," I said. "That's great! Tell me more about the lucky guy."

Linda took both of my hands and squeezed them. "He's from Yonder — Sam Weston. He's a sophomore. I can't believe I did it. I walked right over to him after class on Monday and said hello," she said, flopping down. "Today at lunch, he asked if I'd go to the movies, and I said yes. This is so cool! This being popular stuff is easier than I thought."

"It's very cool," I agreed. Privately, I wondered if things might be proceeding a little too quickly. I'd always been one to distrust the winning-lotto mentality. Most of the important changes and chances in life, especially the glamorous ones, were backed by some form of long, hard work. At this stage, enthusiasm was essential, so it would be my job to ward off any pin-pricks which might deflate this new found balloon of excitement. The parent permission question could be a big one.

"Have you told your mom?" I asked.

"Yes. She's happy for me."

"And your dad?"

"Mama says we'll tell him after Sunday dinner."

Linda's mother seemed destined to surprise me. On the surface, she appeared to be completely cowed by her husband, but I'd underestimated the fact that she also *knew* him. What better time to approach her man about a touchy subject? Any good southern wife worth her biscuits would wait until after he'd heard a Sunday sermon on Christian charity and then eaten a good, home-cooked meal. Maybe I had more in common with Mrs. Polk than I'd originally thought. We both knew how to increase the odds of getting what we wanted from our men. I'd simply had more of a variety of men to work with.

"Your mother is a smart woman."

Linda blinked twice, as though I'd spoken a foreign language, but didn't comment.

"You, however, are still a work in progress. And the most important question at this point is . . . what are you going to wear to the movie?"

We got out the magazines again and

started looking. An hour later we walked down to the square to look in pattern books at Effie's. Since Linda worked there and could get a discount, we'd decided to make a peasant blouse if we could find the right pattern. "Who'd have thought these shirts would come back in style?" I mumbled as we searched.

"When were peasant blouses ever in style?" Linda asked seriously.

I sighed. "Never mind. I feel old."

Effie immediately got in on the spirit of our mission and spent forty-five minutes of her own time helping Linda and I find the right fabric for the flowing, off-one-shoulder blouse Linda had her heart set on. We moved bolts, held up swatches and finally discovered the perfect blue material.

"You'll look like a mermaid in this color," Effie declared.

"And it'll bring out the blue in your eyes," I added.

Measuring and cutting the fabric was nearly a religious experience for the three of us. Linda kept touching the edge as though it might get away before she'd had a chance to show it to anyone. When we got to the cash register, Effie took a pencil from behind her ear and worked up the discount. Then she wrote the total on a small notepad she keeps in her pocket. "Hmmm. Any way I add this, it keeps coming up 'zero.' "

Linda, a wad of dollar bills clutched in her hand, looked up in surprise. "But you don't have to —"

Effie stuffed the notebook back in her apron. "Now, don't argue with me. You're a good girl and a hard worker. You've never asked for a thing. Let's just call this our lay-away system. Besides, it'll be good advertisin' for the store." She patted Linda's hand. "I want to see that blouse on you when it's finished. I bet you'll be right smart lookin'."

We left Effie's fabric store, me walking on the sidewalk, Linda floating along in imaginary clouds beside me. I've always thought one good turn should be followed by another, if possible. And I was enjoying the way the world can come around when one person puts her mind on a goal. A few weeks ago, Linda thought she was plain and stupid. After only a few helping hands, she was beginning to believe otherwise.

"Let's stop at Mama's and have some lunch," I suggested. "I'll buy."

If you thought of Mossy Creek's town square in human terms, the shady park in the middle of the square would be the heart, the pretty little town hall building would be the mind, and Mama's All You Can Eat

Café would be the stomach. Unfortunately, we had to pass by one of the *elbows* on our way to lunch — Goldilocks Hair, Nail and Tanning Salon.

Before we had a chance to make a run for it, Rainey was standing in the doorway, her pink, French tipped nails balanced on her equally pink smock. "Come here, Linda. I want to get another good look at your hair." Rainey smiled at Linda but gave me a hard stare.

Linda glanced nervously in my direction before moving over to the hairdresser to be inspected. I simply crossed my arms and waited.

"You know her daddy nearly had a stroke yellin' at me the other day," Rainey said to me as she parted Linda's hair here and there to examine the layers. "I thought I was gonna have to call Sandy over at the police station to come and wrestle him out of my shop."

"I'm sorry about that. I didn't intend for you to get blamed."

Rainey flicked Linda's hair back into place. "Lor', I don't mind people thinking I did Linda's hair. I meant it when I said I wouldn't change it." She shifted her attention back to Linda. "You come back to me when it needs to be trimmed. I see what you want now. I can take care of it for you."

"Yes, ma'am." Grinning, Linda bounded ahead to get a table for us at Mama's.

Rainey and I traded watchful looks.

"So, you some kind of beauty consultant?" she asked me.

"You could say that, although I'm retired."

"Retired?" She gave me the once over from the tortoiseshell combs holding back my needing-a-trim hair to my casual jeans and sweatshirt. My down-home disguise didn't seem to fool her, as though she could sense a notorious woman when she met up with one. "Retired. All right," she said, drawing the words out.

"A problem?"

"Nope. Listen, whatever you think about me, don't think I'm unfairly judgmental. Lor', there've been plenty of times in my life I'd have liked to get the mercy-end of somebody's opinion." As if she'd said too much, she pressed her pink lips together and frowned. "Well, I just wanted to say you're doing a good job with Linda. Better than I could have done. And Lor', I've tried to get that girl fixed up."

"Thank you. Coming from a professional stylist that's quite a compliment."

"Why don't you come in some time and we'll . . . work on those roots." She peered at the top of my head. "We'll call it, professional courtesy."

I laughed. At least she didn't come right out and insult me as Leon had. "Maybe I will."

I was still chuckling as I walked on. And then it dawned on me.

I'd made my first friend.

Mama's All You Can Eat Café was in the middle of the weekend lunch rush when we arrived.

"Hey Linda. I'll be right with you, hon," the hostess and owner called out as she passed by us with three pieces of chocolate meringue pie balanced in her capable hands. After delivering the pie and stopping to clear the dishes off the only empty table left, she returned, snatched up two menus and motioned. "Y'all follow me."

Now, I'm used to being stared at. I've been the object of intense attention for most of my life. But this was different. Walking through this small, crowded, formica-tabled restaurant full of Creekites felt more intimidating than following the red carpet into a governor's mansion. For one thing, I didn't have my persona, my expensive clothes and extravagant style to announce my lofty place in the world. Secondly, I wasn't in the company of a rich and powerful man people would think twice about crossing.

Strangely enough, suddenly *I* was the protector. I needed to protect Linda from an overdose of attention.

The conversation level wavered table by table as I made my way to the back of the restaurant, where Linda sat. At one booth, four old men nodded and smiled. Across from them, five women, dressed as though they'd just come from a church auxiliary meeting, stopped talking altogether to look at me. Their forks raised in mid-air, they seemed to bristle with curiosity.

The last booth I had to pass made my traitorous heart begin to pound. It's an unfortunate truth that some things we never outgrow. After all the rich and important men I'd charmed, after all the money and power I'd accrued on my own, *the law* still made me nervous. I'm sure it dates back to being a young girl on the street — not wanting to be noticed, or questioned, or helped, or sometimes harassed by the authorities. Just needing to survive.

Two men in the tan trousers and uniform shirts of the Mossy Creek P.D. occupied the booth next to the table Linda had chosen for us. One scrawny bean pole was obviously a young deputy, but the other man, lean and dark-haired and more than a little good-looking despite his somber expression, had to be the police chief. I'd heard about the 'famous' Amos Royden from two of my neighbors, but so far had eluded any direct contact with the heir to Mossy Creek's legacy of inventive police-chiefing. It looked like my luck had run out.

The chief gave me a head to toe evaluation, more professional than judgmental. A sizing-up of my potential to cause trouble in his town, if you will.

I nodded. He nodded back. Most men flirt with me. He didn't. I sat down across from Linda with my back to a lattice screen covered with fake ivy to hide the diner's tea-and-coffee station. At least the people who stared at me would have to take the chance of me staring back.

The phone at the cashier's desk rang, the cook tapped the 'order-up' bell on the ledge of the pass-through window from the kitchen, and the conversation level in the room returned to normal.

Linda beamed at me. "Now *that's* how I want people to notice me when I walk into a room. The way they looked at *you.* Like you were a movie star."

Or a criminal, I thought. "It's all in the attitude."

We'd been served our iced tea and were looking over Linda's blouse pattern when the restaurant's screen door opened with a bang, admitting Jimmy Polk.

"I don't care what you told her!" he yelled.

Mrs. Polk trailed him into the restaurant, pulling hopelessly on his arm.

"Oh, no," Linda said under her breath. She had time to give me one pained, apologetic gaze before her father descended on us like a red-faced human Rottweiler.

"Linda Polk, I've had enough of this defiance! You get up from that table and get yourself home!"

"Jimmy —" Mrs. Polk pleaded. She glanced around with an embarrassed look.

"But, Daddy, I —"

"You heard me!" He jerked her to her feet, knocking the pattern envelope to the floor.

Before I had a good idea of what to do next, I was standing as well. "Take your hands off her."

"What did you say to me, woman?"

Mrs. Polk stepped between me, Linda, and her husband. "Now Jimmy, you leave Miz Beleau alone. And leave Linda alone, too. *Please.* I told her she could go to the movies next week. Look." She retrieved the pattern from the floor and held it up like a shield. "She's making a new blouse and everything."

"You corrupted my baby!" Jimmy Polk shouted, jabbing a finger within six inches of my nose. "I want you to stay away from my baby girl."

"Jimmy, put your hand down." The calm but intractable order came from Amos Royden. Tall and capable and deadly serious, Mossy Creek's young police chief, a former Atlanta cop, faced Jimmy Polk without a glimmer of sympathy.

Although I wasn't afraid of being hurt by mister I'm-bigger-than-you, it was nice to have an even bigger keeper-of-the-peace on my side. Otherwise, I might have had to do something completely outrageous to defend myself like emptying my tea glass over Jimmy Polk's hot head. Instead I offered him an inscrutable, Mona Lisa smile.

I'd dealt with all sorts of tempers in the past and learned the tactical advantages of outer calm. Whether someone wanted to fight over honor, a card game, or 'last call,' the episode invariably took the same basic course. The person who refuses to argue always wins.

I never argued. I cajoled, I illuminated and if all else failed, I ignored. Most men crumbled to one of the three. And if for some reason they didn't, then they found themselves 'put out' so to speak. Ejected from my circle of influence with the efficiency of a Major League umpire after three strikes. *You're outta here!*

But in this case, I was the outsider, cornered in a small town well outside my former circle of influence. I glanced around at the myriad of frowning faces surrounding me and experienced a sinking feeling. Maybe the people in my new hometown might just up and run me out on a rail courtesy of Mr. Jimmy Polk.

"Amos, that woman is corruptin' my girl," Jimmy accused as he wisely lowered his hand.

"Ms. Beleau? I don't think we've met," the chief said as he offered his hand. "I'm Amos Royden." His large hand gripped mine and gave it a firm shake before letting go. "This is one of my officers, Mutt."

"Glad to meet you both."

The chief nodded. "Step back, Ms. Beleau. We'll handle this."

He turned to Jimmy Polk, again. I'd dealt with every sort of police officer from federal agents to state and county, right on down to city and small town 'boys in blue.' One fact always saved me: What I did for a living may or may not have been illegal, but my hide, and my connections, were too expensive to risk damaging. The New Orleans police protected me as diligently as any valuable city asset. Most of them with hope in their hearts that I might express my gratitude in private.

Mossy Creek's police chief didn't know me, didn't want anything from me, and had no reason to protect me, except the best one: I was a citizen of his town, and protecting me was his job. I felt better already — except for the fact that he knew my name without being introduced.

Jimmy continued to bristle. "Amos, this woman is brainwashin' my girl, and I want it stopped." He screwed up his face like he'd smelled something objectionable. "I think she's some kinda pervert."

Mrs. Polk gasped, and Linda blurted, "That's not true!"

"She's makin' Linda into some kind of weirdo."

"Daddy, she is not!" Linda said, close to tears.

Jimmy Polk briefly turned his menacing stare to his daughter, and she sniffed before raising her chin in a tiny show of defiance.

Mrs. Polk slipped an arm around her daughter. "Jimmy, how can you say such a thing? I'm tired of your attitude. Tired, you hear?"

The patrons in the entire restaurant had halted in mid-chew to watch this drama. Even the cook stood poised at the order window so he wouldn't miss a thing.

"Just who do you think you are?" Jimmy ranted at me. "Takin' my girl to Atlanta and gettin' her hair dyed like some, some —"

"Movie star?" I said, helpfully.

"Trashy singer," he finished. "Like that Madonna —"

"Linda isn't trashy. She's a beautiful girl, and I won't allow you to trample her confidence any more."

Jimmy Polk's face went redder, and he sputtered like a bottle of Perrier, shaken, not stirred. Again, he raised a pudgy finger and shook it near my face. "I don't care who you tried to make her look like. You had no business —"

"Jimmy —" the chief interrupted. "Put the finger down, or I'll put it down for you."

"I'm not tryin' to scare her," Jimmy argued, but he lowered his hand once more.

Scared? I would have chuckled if I had less sense and wanted to provoke him. He'd be the one who ended up in jail. That would be like winning the battle and losing the war. Jimmy Polk had already scored with this public airing of his grievance with me. He'd introduced me to the greater part of

Mossy Creeks citizens as the local pervert. I could feel my new, quiet lifestyle slipping back into notoriety. I felt like handing him the Cajun version of 'what-for.' I used cold courtesy instead.

"Mr. Polk. I had your wife's permission to take Linda to Atlanta —"

He made a huffing sound and his face flushed to his hatline. "Mary Beth don't have no more sense than God gave a cow."

Two of the five women sitting at the table closest to Mrs. Polk gasped in outrage. Mrs. Polk squeezed her daughter closer and lowered her eyes.

Her husband snorted. "She had no right givin' any kind of permission without *my* say so." He stared at the chief. "Amos, I want you to tell this *strange woman* —" he spit the words "— to mind her own business and to keep away from my daughter."

"M-i-s-t-e-r Polk," I said firmly. "I find your wife to be both charming and knowledgeable." I met Mrs. Polk's grateful gaze and saw the same two women who'd gasped nod their heads in agreement. "And I beg to differ with you about her right to give permission. Linda is *her* daughter, and she has the right of a mother —"

"Beg to differ? What's she talkin' about, Amos?"

"Miss Beleau isn't from around here," the chief said. "Moved from New Orleans, isn't that right?"

I couldn't tell by the quiet tone of voice if his question was welcome or warning but in any case I felt a hard tug on my past. He knew. I blinked, but held the chief's gaze. A worthy adversary, if it came to that.

"Actually, I'm from a little town outside of Baton Rouge." Truth — I'd been born there. Or dare — not the answer he'd wanted.

One side of his mouth kicked up in a half smile.

We both knew I'd tossed out the question-ender. Revisiting my past with the local chief of police was not on my personal list of good ideas. And doing so in public would be close to the top of my list of personal nightmares.

"And, where's *Mister* Beleau?" Jimmy Polk asked snidely. I suppose he expected my husband to control me.

"There is no 'Mr. Beleau.' In my opinion, Mr. Polk, husbands are a luxury and sometimes more trouble than they're worth, as you seem to be proving to your wife."

The front door to Mama's swung open and in rushed Rainey with her assistant, Wanda Halfacre — her sister, Betty, worked for Ingrid Beechum — one customer with a half-rolled perm, and a small, wiry woman in a tan police uniform and plastic salon smock. Her short, curly hair seemed to be half blonde and half some other color.

"Hey, Mary Beth, hey Linda," the small half-blonde woman said, then turned to the chief. "Chief? Why don't you let me handle this since you and Mutt haven't finished your lunch yet. I know all the particulars. It's a beauty problem. Me and Rainey are on top of it." She pinned Jimmy Polk with an evil look. "Some folks just don't have any table manners."

"Now Sandy —" Jimmy Polk began, and wonder of wonder, the man actually looked worried.

Amos Royden arched a brow, and I swear he almost smiled.

"Jimmy? What exactly is the problem here?" Sandy demanded. "Everybody knows better than to bother the chief while he's at lunch. Do I have to come in here and sit with him to get him some break time? I swear, the chief wouldn't have to swallow anti-acids if idjits wouldn't just —"

"Sandy, why don't you go look for the elephant," the chief said. "And keep an eye out for the moose, too."

Sandy pursed her mouth. "Gotcha, Chief. Sorry."

Jimmy Polk waved his hands. "Isn't anybody listening? Look what this woman did to my girl's hair. And now she's puttin' her up to hang out with boys and make her 'debut' or some such crap this fall at the reunion dance."

Rainey stepped forward. "Jimmy Polk, I told you the other day, and I'm tellin' you again in front of all these good people." She fluttered a hand to indicate the culinary audience, then seemed to notice someone she knew. "Hey, Katie Bell."

Jimmy looked around wildly.

The gossip columnist smiled and raised a tiny tape recorder.

Rainey went on, "It's a woman's God-given right to have her hair done." She turned and gently pulled Linda forward. "Look at this beautiful girl."

Linda looked struck dumb, as though she'd been presented to the Queen.

"I know you're scared about her growin' up, Jimmy, but you can't stop it. Jasmine Beleau here hasn't done anything the rest of us wouldn't have done for Linda — except she did it better."

Mrs. Polk cleared her throat. "I think you should apologize to Miss Beleau, Jimmy."

Several of the restaurant patrons nodded in agreement.

"And as for you callin' me a cow . . . well, you might as well go find yourself a pasture and hope some other *cow* cooks you dinner and gives you a bed to sleep in tonight, because this cow doesn't want to see you for a while."

The five church ladies applauded.

Jimmy Polk looked to Chief Royden one last time for, if not help, then at least a little male commiseration. The chief shook his head and sat down to eat the last bite of his pie.

Jimmy cleared his throat and faced me. "I'm just protectin' my own," he said finally. Not exactly an apology but close enough for this encounter. "Linda's only fifteen, she's still got three years before she can do what she wants. The law says so."

"I'm almost sixteen, daddy," Linda corrected, emboldened by the power of pure righteousness surrounding her. She only flinched slightly when her father looked her way. I wanted to hug her. She'd come a good ways from the 'p' word.

"I'll be watchin' you," he warned.

I knew he really meant he'd be keeping an eye on *me.* As would most of the rest of

Mossy Creek after today's public entertainment.

Jimmy Polk turned and stalked out the door, banging the screen behind him. I only felt slightly better — for Linda's sake. She'd definitely taken my advice to heart about self-confidence, whereas I had completely ignored my own rule about meddling.

Sandy dusted her hands and said, "Well, that's that. I better get back to the salon before my color sets up. Be back at my desk in an hour, Chief. Chief, be sure and drink your milk —"

"Moose," the chief said. Sandy put a hand over her mouth.

"Good work," Rainey said to me.

Then she, Sandy, Wanda Halfacre and their other customer marched out looking as though they couldn't wait to tell the rest of the patrons at Goldilocks.

The chief sighed, stood, and nodded to me. "Welcome to Mossy Creek, Ms. Beleau. Excuse me, now, I think I'll go drink my milk in the privacy of my office."

Welcome, indeed. At least he didn't say, *I'll be watching you,* even though I knew he would.

As I said, when I write my memoirs, someday . . .

My intent to stay out of the limelight had failed. Maybe I was destined to be notorious — my father used to tell me that, and I'd believed him. Mossy Creek had been my clean slate — a place to start over and prove my father wrong. After all, he'd only known the skinny, big-eyed thirteen-year-old I used to be — the girl he controlled as long as he could chisel money out of me and Jade.

I continued to help Linda sew her blouse with her mother's complete approval. But, for the next week or so I stayed close to home. No use tempting fate, as a self-styled psychic named Madam Pearl used to tell me over tarot cards. Fate just might tempt back.

But the next Saturday morning, as I was making coffee for my usual 'beauty consult' meeting with Linda, I opened my door to find that fate had definitely gone overboard, this time.

Linda and her mother stood in front of at least four other women, along with two teenagers who must surely be somebody's daughters. The women were armed with coffeecakes from Beechum's Bakery and gift mugs from The Naked Bean.

I wondered if this might be some unknown ritual peculiar to Mossy Creek. *Yeah, they forced her to eat coffee cake until she waddled out of town.*

On the upside, there were no irate husbands or officers of the law. On the downside, it seemed like I had no choice but to let them in.

Before I could stammer more than good morning, Mrs. Polk spoke up. "Jasmine, these ladies and their daughters need your help. There's the big reunion and dance this fall, and they want to have a beauty consultation." It sounded like a rehearsed speech but she faced me as though she'd been making demands all her life. "Will you help us out?"

"You're a role model," one of the women said.

I started laughing. Jezebel Jasmine in the beauty consulting business. Jezebel Jasmine, a role model. Jezebel Jasmine, a citizen of Mossy Creek, Georgia, with friends who called on her bearing food and good wishes.

And then I hugged them all and said yes.

Jasmine Beleau had found a home.

From: Katie Bell
To: Lady Victoria Salter

Dear Vick:
You asked if Samson, the ram, lived well and happily after the terrible events of the high school fire. Well, yes, he survived the fire and the things that were done to him during the homecoming halftime, but he was never the same.

Some of the other citizens and I visited poor Samson during his recuperation. His singed wool was just starting to grow back, he shifted his sheepish eyes a lot, and any little noise made him jump. We all just stood around him as if in a prayer circle and sobbed. I recall saying to Principal Doolittle, "But surely he'll get over the trauma, in time. He'll be marching in the Christmas parade this winter, right behind Ed Brady in his Santa outfit." Ed would be in the Santa suit, not Samson, that is.

I was wrong. Samson lived on quite a few more years after his fateful duties as The Last Mascot of the Mossy Creek High Rams, but he was never comfortable in public, again. Beauty is only skin deep, but the smell of flaming wool goes straight to the heart. Remember what I said some time ago about our local beauty contestants? And about Mossy Creek welcoming everyone? Yes, but sometimes people have the same problem as Samson with their confidence. And their singed pride.

Katie

Tammy Jo

BEAUTY AND THE BEAST

Sometimes you have to go where you don't feel safe to find out what you fear the most.

They say pride comes before a fall, and looking back, I can see I had plenty of that commodity before fate gave me a big ol' shove. I'd thought I'd hit rock bottom many times.

Most of those times, I was wrong.

But to fully appreciate the impact when I *did* hit, you'd best hear the tale from the start.

I was born a Bigelowan, by the grace of God Almighty, and from the time I was no bigger 'n a minute, I was hailed as the prettiest little thing in Bigelow County — a real comfort to my mama, considering she'd lost my daddy shortly after I was born. My Bigelow relatives looked down on her, saying that Daddy married beneath him. Mama is pure country, and you can tell from the way

I speak that she raised me pure country, too. Everyone else in the Bigelow family speaks what they call Good English. I speak Mama's English, and proudly.

Considering her lowly status in the Bigelow family, Mama took special glee in knowing I was prettier than the other Bigelow girls. My earliest memories have to do with being taught to sing, dance and "smile, Tammy Jo, always smile." I heard it said that Mama spent her last dime to give me lessons. I felt bad about taking that dime from her, and tried real hard to make her investment pay off.

When I grew old enough to sing Elvis's "Blue Suede Shoes" and shimmy across a stage, I won Little Miss Bigelow County *and* Little Miss Dixie. Oh, how Mama's eyes did shine! "Your future's brighter than the sun, Tammy Jo. You do me proud." I felt the warmth of that sun she'd mentioned just a'glowing in my heart. It was no easy task, doing Mama proud.

By and by, my womanly charms developed to their fullest. 36C, to be exact, with just the teensiest bit of surgical help. Mama drove me all the way down to Atlanta to have my colors done by a fashion consultant and my cosmetics picked out by a professional makeup artist. The artist also taught me to apply false eyelashes to "accentuate the brightness of my grass-green eyes."

I was, according to popular decree, the most feared rival in the Miss Bigelow County Pageant during the height of my reign back in the mid 1980s. Only Francine Quinlin from Mossy Creek with her waist-length blonde hair and big blue eyes came even close to measuring up, but my singing and dancing beat her baton twirling by a landslide in the talent category. That made me a vital part of Bigelow's arsenal against our nemesis, Mossy Creek. Everyone in Bigelow loved me for it.

Future Governor Hamilton Bigelow himself — then a state senator and daddy's first cousin twice removed — had a photo taken with me by his side. My, my, the sun fairly blazed within me then!

But two weeks before the pageant, God must have realized how prideful I'd become. Or maybe those lowlife, black-hearted Mossy Creekers — not 'Creekites,' as they like to call themselves, but 'Creekers,' pronounced 'Crackers' by Bigelowans — saw the chance to strike me down. It happened one evening when I was nineteen and had the bad judgment to cross through Mossy Creek territory alone. A tire on my mama's Camaro picked up a nail and blew out on a back road. Having never changed a tire in all my born days, seeing as how there'd always been volunteers to do the chore right quick for me, I had no choice but to trek up to the historic Laslow farmhouse to use a phone.

Out of the evening shadows came a huge, snarling, teeth-baring beast from hell. The thing knocked me down and sank its fangs into me. Wasn't until I woke up in the hospital with a hundred-some stitches in my face and throat that I learned what had attacked me. Tyrone Laslow's rottweiler.

Folks from Bigelow maintain that Tyrone saw clear as day who was traipsing up to his door for help and took the opportunity to handicap Francine Quinlin's chief rival. Tyrone swore it was just a case of a faithful but confused family dog attacking a stranger who was on his land. As if I'd been deliberately trespassing or something! My Bigelow kin, mostly lawyers and bankers, got Tyrone's dog put to sleep and sued Tyrone into bankruptcy so that he lost the farm his family had owned for a hundred years. The Mossy Creekers despised the Bigelows for punishing Tyrone so badly for his dog's misdeed. I think they felt sorry for the dog, too. But if the Creekers had any sympathy for me, I never knew it. And if the lawsuits on my behalf ever netted any money, I never saw a penny of it. Though my Bigelow lawyer seemed pleased.

I was ruined for life. My future as a beauty queen vanished like morning fog on a hot afternoon, what with all the scars puckering my skin from one cheek clear down to my collarbone.

It liked to have broke my mama's heart. She stayed in bed for six weeks and cried every time she saw me.

Neighbors tended to avoid looking at me at all — not only because of the pity I stirred in them, but because I was a living reminder of how Mossy Creek robbed us of our rightful crown in the pageant that year. Any battle lost to the Mossy Creekers brings excruciating pain to the hearts of us Bigelowans.

I thought I'd hit rock bottom.

That's how I came to marry Bunkin Brown, the strong, quiet fella who worked in maintenance at a Bigelow rehab clinic, where I spent so much time. I'd known Bunkin at Bigelow High School. You can't grow up in a small city like Bigelow and not know most of the boys in your own age group. But I'd never paid him any mind until then. I could date the finest and the brightest, and I did.

288

Bunkin wasn't much to look at, didn't star on a varsity team, and his folks didn't belong to the Bigelow Country Club. I did, by virtue of Daddy's kin insisting that Mama and me always have a membership. I might not talk like high society, but thanks to the country club I can play a mean game of tennis and name the ten best white wines that go with fish. Not that those talents do me much good.

Anyhow, after my face was scarred, the other boys stopped coming around. Bunkin was the only person in the world who didn't get a pinch-mouthed expression when he looked at me, or, worse yet, that glow of vindication some of my female visitors tried to hide. And those were Bigelowans. Imagine how Francine Quinlin must've gloated!

Bunkin was my salvation through those dark, dark times. He listened to my woes and said the scars didn't make me any less pretty in his eyes.

Come to find out, he had mighty bad eyesight. But that didn't stop me from marrying him. We moved to Gainesville — a bigger city than Bigelow and a good deal further south toward Atlanta — so he could find a better job, and I could get away from Bigelow, where my deformity seemed bigger than I was. We scraped by to make ends meet, but did well enough. Eventually I gave birth to two fine boys. There was something about being a wife and mother that suited me. Made my heart sing and dance, enough to put Elvis himself to shame.

Guess I was getting prideful again.

Fate slapped me down a second time.

Bunkin fell off the roof of our house while fixing a leak and broke several bones, including his jaw, collarbone and spine. His jaw was wired shut, and he was encased in all manner of casts, the biggest of which he'd have to wear for ten months. My poor sweetheart would be in traction, unable to talk or move, except for one finger on his left hand. And since he couldn't work, we were left with no income and a quickly dwindling savings account.

There was no help for it — we had to move back to Bigelow County. Bunkin's Great Aunt Winnie, the only kin he had left, a sweet old lady living in Magnolia Manor Nursing Home, sold us the house she grew up in, with no down payment required and owner-financing at a very reasonable price.

Problem was, the house wasn't located in the city of Bigelow, but in the town of Mossy Creek. And not on the outskirts, either, but smack dab in the center of the historic district, a stone's throw from the shops on the square.

I was sure I'd hit rock bottom then. I'd be surrounded by my former beauty rivals and all those people who took sides against me after Tyrone Laslow's dog nearly killed me. Mama, who'd kind of given up on me and moved to Atlanta in search of a husband, said she'd pray for us . . . especially for my little boys, who would have it the worst, she said, growing up in Mossy Creek with everyone knowing they were the sons of Tammy Jo Bigelow Brown.

I tried to keep calm last fall when Chip, my nine-year-old, started classes at Mossy Creek Elementary. I chewed my nails and thanked Jesus that at least Toby, my youngest, had a year or so before he'd have to go.

Sure enough, just as I'd expected, Chip was harassed by the other children. One bully actually badgered him into a fight. And when I called the principal, he refused to take proper action, like suspending the troublemaker. Instead, he locked up Chip and the bully in the same small room for detention after school, every day for a week.

I was furious and worried about Chip, and I threatened to sue the bully's parents and the entire school system. My poor, cast-encased Bunkin, strung up in traction in his rented hospital bed, looked as upset by Chip's ordeal as I was, his brow all wrinkled and his mouth crumpled around those wires in his version of a frown.

To make matters worse, my old rival, Francine Quinlin, sashayed past my house every afternoon on her way to lunch from her Aunt Pearl's bookshop, looking as pleased as a pig in sunshine. And why shouldn't she be tickled, flaunting her perfect face, fashionable new haircut and beauty-queen legs, which she made a point of displaying in short-shorts. Francine still looked like a teenage pageant queen, but I looked like I'd been whittled with a dull knife.

With Bunkin out of work I couldn't afford to get my hair professionally cut anymore, and I'd noticed the start of a varicose vein in my right leg. At age 34, I was a has-been in every way, and never felt it more keenly than when Francine strutted her stuff past my house.

I was miserable in Mossy Creek. And lonely inside my own face.

The straw that broke the camel's back, so to speak, was carried into my life by a dog on the property adjoining ours, owned by retired Georgia Tech professor and Mossy Creek town councilman Egg Egbert. The dog was a big, mean, hell-spawn German Shepherd by the name of Killer. The first time I saw him, my youngest boy Toby and I had just come home from Mossy Creek Hardware and Gardening with a new hinge for the back door. No sooner had we stepped out of the car than Killer came charging at us from across Egg Egbert's yard. I snatched Toby up into my arms and ran for dear life. That dog was less than a hair's breadth from sinking his fangs into me when I reached my house and slammed the door.

Trembling so violently I could barely stand, I called Chief Royden at the police station, the Bigelow County Animal Control, and my next-door neighbor, Egg Egbert, Killer's owner. I threatened every one of them with a lawsuit if that dog set foot on my property again.

"Mrs. Brown, that dog's name is a joke," old Professor Egbert insisted. "He's not a killer. He's about a thousand years old, he loves people, and he was just trying to play."

"He attacked me. I know when a dog is attacking. I've got the scars to prove it, Professor." And I hung up the phone.

All right, maybe I was a little hysterical,

but I had good reason. I remembered that Tyrone Laslow said his rottweiler was a friendly family dog, and look what *he* did.

More importantly, I called Bigelow Security Systems, which is owned by one of my cousins in Bigelow, and ordered a high, sturdy steel-mesh fence with sharp barbed wire at the top. I charged it to my credit card and tried not to think about how it would take every penny of our savings to pay it off.

Life, limb and my children had to be my top priorities. I understood now, much clearer than before, that we were under siege in Mossy Creek from both human and canine enemies. Between killer dogs, unsympathetic neighbors, and schoolyard bullies, my children would never make it to adulthood alive unless I took extreme measures.

I explained those measures to Bunkin: I'd have that fence installed around the house, withdraw Chip from Mossy Creek Elementary, and teach the boys at home next year. They'd learn just as much from me as they could from Mossy Creek teachers, except I'd keep them safe.

I'll never forget the look on my poor Bunkin's face when he realized the seriousness of our situation. If he'd been able to cuss, he surely would have. He never has been the type to tolerate a threat against his family.

"You think I'm doing the right thing, don't you, Bunkin?" I asked, needing a little moral support. It was a shame he couldn't talk, or even write, being able to move only one finger. We had a way of conversing, though . . . by means of his finger movement. One crook of the finger meant *yes,* and two crooks meant *no.* The poor ol' sweetheart was so overcome with worry, he repeatedly crooked his finger. *Yes, yes. Yes, yes.*

Chip was happy enough to stay home from school, and Toby was glad for the company, but when they realized they couldn't leave our yard to play — and certainly couldn't let any Mossy Creekers in — they moaned and grumbled about being bored and lonely and having no friends.

"You won't find friends around here," I told them. "You'll have plenty of time to make friends when Daddy gets well and we move away from Mossy Creek." I didn't mention that would take at least two years, seeing as how Bunkin would be in that body cast for another eight months or so, then in therapy for a year after that.

The boys pouted, and Chip asked, "Can we have a dog of our own, then, Mama?

He'll be our friend."

A dog, of all things.

"Absolutely not." Fear shivered through me at the very thought. Every time I stepped outside my kitchen door, I saw Killer looking back at me from a dog run Professor Egbert had installed in his back yard. Killer yipped and wagged his gray-speckled tail, but I wasn't fooled.

"A dog will turn on you in the wink of an eye," I told my boys. "Never forget that, either of you."

Bunkin clearly wanted to back me up on this, as he lay in his rented hospital bed blinking his eyes and wrinkling his forehead, his breath huffing and his throat working. Together, he and I stood fast against the boys' pleading.

Young'uns don't have a lick of sense when it comes to knowing who or what is good for them. As their mother, it was my God-sworn duty to protect them from harm . . . and I meant to do just that.

On Tuesday, a truck from Bigelow Security Systems delivered the steel mesh for our new fence — huge gray bundles of it that covered nearly our whole front yard. By Wednesday, word had spread around town about my plans, and I received phone calls from neighbors, nearby merchants and members of the Mossy Creek Historical Preservation Society.

Even Dwight Truman, president of Mossy Creek's Chamber of Commerce, called to complain. "You can't put that fence up, Miz Brown. It'll look like a prison. You'll ruin the aesthetic value of the shops on the square. Besides, it's against zoning codes. You're in the historical section of town. No changes are allowed without a permit."

"We'll just see about that," I answered. The workmen were scheduled for Monday week to install the fence, and I had no intention of canceling. And just in case anyone got the bright idea of physically interfering with the work, I reminded everyone who called that I wasn't good with a gun, but right handy with knives. I've been known to have deadlier aim than Tell Chesney at his best in the annual dart tournament.

Folks passing by on the sidewalk paid heed to my warnings, I noticed, taking special care to avoid stepping across my property line, but a few of the most rabid historical preservationists and members of the Mossy Creek Social Society picketed on the street in front of the house.

It wasn't an easy time for us. I fought my battles over the phone and yelled at the picketers from our front porch. The boys moped around, fought with each other and generally made nuisances of themselves. Bunkin looked blue-deviled all the time, and refused to talk — or in his case, crook his finger.

Who could blame him for being so upset, when we were besieged by enemies? I vowed to hold them off, to protect my loved ones, like a fortress made of steel.

Maybe I'd become too prideful yet again.

On the Saturday morning before our fence was scheduled to be installed, I woke to find my boys missing. Missing! Both of them! Their beds were vacant, without a single clue as to where they'd gone. Fear gripped me like the jaws of a rottweiler. I swore to God that I'd gladly suffer any attack, bear up under any torture, if He'd only keep my boys safe and send them back to me.

Though I wasn't very good with it, I loaded Bunkin's rifle and set out to find them. I called their names as I searched my yard and the woods beyond, keeping a sharp watch-out for that killer dog — or bears, wildcats, any number of wild beasts that roam old Colchik and the other mountains that surround Mossy Creek. My mind painted frightful scenarios. One was the possibility that the boys had been kidnapped. I tried not to dwell on it, but when a body's surrounded by enemies, it's hard to believe that those enemies had nothing to do with a crisis in the making.

By ten o'clock, I'd worked myself into a pure panic. The neighbors, the picketers and other passersby heard me calling my boys and gathered around my yard, pretending concern and nosing around. I didn't like that worth a damn but couldn't stop to think about it much. I needed help.

I called family members and old-time friends in Bigelow, hoping I could get together a search party, or at least find someone to lend me moral support if I had to go the police.

Guess I'd forgotten how things are among my Bigelow kin — everyone was too busy with their own important lives to bother with a girl who'd failed them long ago. At least, that's how it seemed to me.

"If the boys don't come home soon, call the police," was the best they offered.

Left with little choice, I finally did call for help. Officer Mutt Bottoms and his sister, Sandy Bottoms Crane — I didn't know at the time that she was only the department's dispatcher, not an officer — arrived moments later, both asking questions, jotting down notes, poking about in the boys' bedrooms and insinuating that they had wandered off somewhere of their own volition.

"Boys'll be boys, Tammy Jo," said Sandy Crane. "We've got a lot of kids roaming around the mountains this summer. I started a kind of contest to see if anybody can find the bones of our lost carnival elephant. Your boys are probably off looking for ol' Rose the elephant's remains. Or they're playing with friends."

That only infuriated me. "They don't have friends around here. And if you can't find them, I'll call in the GBI." By that time, I was sure foul play was involved and only federal agents might listen to me. With each tick of the clock, my heart thudded harder and my fears grew more terrifying.

And my house filled up with more intruders. People came in without invitation — people I didn't know, or hadn't seen in years and didn't care to see. Even Francine Quinlin, for God's sake. She, along with the other women, talked on cell phones, asking mothers if they'd seen Chip and Toby, or if their kids might know where they'd gone.

I told them they were wasting their time with that line of questioning, but they kept on anyway. The men milled about, talking among themselves and occasionally muttering into walkie talkies, supposedly forming a search party, although it didn't seem to me that much was getting accomplished.

The conversation level rose to a dull roar in my ears, and everywhere I looked, I saw *Mossy Crackers* — in my house, in my life, *in my way.* I felt cornered by the enemy in my own kitchen. I tried to talk above the ruckus, tried to get their attention, tried to tell them to get out, but no one was listening.

Just as my tension drew to an unbearable pitch, I heard Mutt say into his phone, "I think we might better call in the canine unit, Chief."

Canine unit. That meant *dogs.*

The Crackers were sending dogs after my boys.

I don't remember reaching across my kitchen counter for a knife, or yanking it out of the block, or even taking aim. But somehow, my biggest, sharpest meat cleaver launched from my hand and streaked through a narrow opening in the crowd.

Thwack. Twannnggg.

All conversation stopped. Everyone stared, open-mouthed, not at me, but at the cleaver still quivering in the wall, not two inches from Mutt's head. It had stuck deep into the hardwood trim of the doorjamb, where the handle had nudged the rim of Mutt's hat, setting it slightly askew. He'd gone chalk-white and gaped at me in disbelief.

"Don't you send no dogs after my boys." I barely recognized that low growl of a voice as mine. "Or I'll kill you."

It took another full moment of stunned silence before anyone moved or uttered a word.

To give Mutt credit, he was the first one to gather his wits. "Miz Brown," he said, straightening his hat as he stepped forward, looking dazed, "do you realize you have just assaulted an officer of the law?"

"With a deadly weapon," added Sandy, staring wide-eyed at the deeply imbedded cleaver.

"If I'd been aiming to hit you, I would've."

"Mrs. Brown, you've lost your mind," argued Adele Clearwater, a prune-faced old woman who'd been marching in the Social Society picket line until she joined the invasion of my house. "Sandy. Mutt. Take the woman in hand before she hurts one of us or herself."

It was then, my dear reader, that I truly hit rock bottom. Not because I was staring life imprisonment in the face, or because my boys would probably never return alive, or because Bunkin would be left alone and unattended. No . . . I'd hit rock bottom because of the hatred festering within me. I hated these Mossy Crackers with a black, hot, unholy passion. The ugliness didn't mar only my face, but my very soul. I felt myself losing *me* . . . my inner person. I was turning into a beast. And there was nothing I could do to change it.

The buzz of conversation started again when, lo and behold, Mayor Ida Hamilton Walker stepped out of the crowd and put a hand on my arm. I hadn't even realized Mayor Ida was there, in my home. Of all the Mossy Crackers, she was the one I feared the most — maybe because she always radiated supreme authority that no one seemed anxious to challenge, other than Governor Hamilton Bigelow himself.

"Tammy Jo Bigelow Brown," Mayor Ida said in that royal-edict tone of hers that would give even Ham pause, "if you don't want to be carted off to jail, then you'll do exactly as I say."

I stood there silent as stone, my jaws locked tighter than poor Bunkin's, who lay in his hospital bed in the other room, at the mercy of our enemies. My hatred and fear were too strong too overcome.

"You stay in this kitchen," Ida ordered, "and you bake pecan pies."

It took a moment for the words to sink in. When they did, I blinked. "Ma'am?"

"My granddaughter told me that Chip gave her some homemade pecan pie from his lunch, on his first day of school. I'm assuming you baked that pie."

I hadn't heard a word from Chip about his giving away pie. "Well, of course I baked it. But I don't see what pie has to do with —"

"Consider this a form of community service. The search party will need something to eat when they bring your boys home. You can either bake pecan pies and brew some coffee, or I'll have Mutt escort you right now to jail — or at least to Doctor Champion's office to have you sedated."

It made no sense. Nothing made much sense. I felt as if I'd fallen into some alien dimension from one of my boys' video games. All I knew was, I needed the search party to find Chip and Toby. But I *had* to stand firm. *"There'll be no dogs sent to hunt for my boys."*

"No dogs. You have my word."

I barely saw Ida's face or any of those around me as I turned to find the ingredients for a pecan pie. I blocked out the presence of all the Mossy Crackers and concentrated fiercely on gathering everything

304

needed for the baking process.

It wasn't until my elbow hit into another elbow as I stood chopping pecans that I glanced up and discovered a woman working beside me. Francine Quinlin, of all people. My archrival.

"What are you doing in my kitchen?"

"Making the coffee." She didn't bother sparing me a glance as she measured my coffee into my coffee maker, pretty as you please.

"Who asked you to?"

"Not you, Tammy Jo. You wouldn't ask for water if you were dying in the desert. You're that proud." Her cutting tone made it clear she didn't mean this as a compliment.

"You must be enjoying all this," I hissed, whacking those pecans in half with my knife. Amazingly, Mutt had allowed me to pick up another.

With a muffled curse, Francine slammed down the coffeepot and turned to face me. I pretended not to notice and kept chopping my pecans with a vengeance. "You haven't had a civil word for anybody since you moved to this town. Not even a simple 'hey.' And then you go and order that fence, just to stir up trouble."

I set my knife down and pivoted to glare at her. "I need that fence to protect my family. If it'd been up, my boys would still be here."

"They'd have climbed over it . . . and probably broken their necks doing it, too."

I couldn't help an outraged gasp. "How dare you insinuate that my boys left on their own. Someone stole into this house and took them."

She rolled her eyes in the most insulting manner. "Do you really think you can keep them locked up forever? It's bad enough you're putting up the fence, but to take Chip out of school, too . . . well . . ." She shook her head. "It's not fair to them. You ought not do it."

I wanted to snatch her by the hair of her head and throw her down onto my linoleum. Fortunately, I refrained . . . but just barely. I'd forgotten this about Francine — how she was always handing out advice, like those times when she and I were left backstage alone during our childhood pageants, or waiting outside for our mothers to pick us up from rehearsals, chatting about this or that.

You ought not go to Hollywood when you grow up, Tammy Jo. My mama says Hollywood is wicked. Or, You shouldn't marry a movie star. I heard on Oprah that they get divorced too much.

Oh, but *her* plans were always beyond reproach, or so it seemed — to marry a handsome prince and have lots of children. Daughters, she wanted. We'd both wanted daughters, mostly because we didn't care much for boys at the time, being as young as we were. Why, we'd been so young, we hadn't figured out yet what it meant to be rivals for life's tiara . . . or to be Bigelowan vs. Mossy Cracker . . .

"There's nothing wrong with home-schooling, Francine."

"Maybe not for some people, but your boys need other children."

"I plan to sign 'em up for baseball," I lied.

"After-school activities are not the same as having to work with other kids every day and face the pressures we all had to face — like giving a report in front of the class, or ignoring hurtful taunts, or taking a test while the kid next to you is trying to copy off your paper. How are they gonna learn to cope, Tammy Jo? What happens when they grow up and have a boss who isn't fair, if they've never had an ornery teacher like old Miz Henry?"

Miz Henry. The meanest, orneriest, most unfair teacher at Bigelow High. At least, while we went there, Francine and I. "I'd never wish Miz Henry on my boys."

"My daughter had a meaner teacher than her, and I'm glad. How else will she learn to deal with exasperating people? It's the struggles and humiliations and yes, friendships, whether you approve of them or not, that make children grow strong."

"There's violence in the schools today." She couldn't deny that one.

"There's violence in the streets, too. You want to make your boys afraid to step out of their house?"

"That's your way of looking at things, not mine." And because I couldn't stand to let her walk away unruffled, I just had to finish in my most scathing voice, "Miss Know-It-All Fancy Francie."

She gasped, then pressed closer to me in a non-verbal threat. "Miss Nose-in-the-Air Hammy Tammy."

The linoleum floor was just a'waiting for me to knock her flat, I swear.

"I better start smelling pecan pie soon, ladies," came Ida's stern voice from somewhere behind us. I was mad enough to ignore her.

"How dare you call me 'hammy,' when you're the one prancing around town in short-shorts, wiggling your behind, showing off your *perfect* self." I couldn't help emphasizing that word. She *was* just about perfect, and she knew it. A little older, maybe, but just as pretty as she'd always been. The witch.

Surprisingly, a flash of hurt flickered across her face, and she fell quiet for a minute. In a greatly subdued tone, she finally said, "I hope you don't mean that sarcastically."

I had no idea what she meant, or why she'd gone so still.

Rainey materialized beside me — Rainey, the big-haired, redheaded hairdresser who used to be friendly enough to me in high school, though I'd kept my distance, her being a lowly Mossy Cracker and all. "I'm sure Tammy Jo doesn't know about . . . well . . . you know," she said to Francine, looking uncomfortable.

To me, she whispered, "Francine's had a mastectomy."

A mastectomy. That meant . . . cancer.

I can't describe the feeling that realization gave me. It was like I'd been running along a grassy field, then looked down to find myself about to step off a steep cliff. Cancer. Francine. My breath hitched. My throat constricted. "Is it . . . is it . . . ?"

"The surgeon said he got it all," Rainey confided, "but we don't talk about it much."

For no good reason, a fist closed around

my voice box. "I . . . I didn't know, Francine. I —"

"Oh, shut up, Tammy Jo." She managed a faint smirk. "I might prance around town in short-shorts, but you're no innocent yourself, tending your garden in those tight jeans, drawing all the men's eyes with your perky little butt."

"Perky little butt!" Nothing could have astounded me more. "Me?" I glanced back at my butt as if I hadn't realized it was still attached. It'd been a good fifteen years since any man but Bunkin had noticed my butt. Hadn't it?

"As if you weren't perfectly aware of all the attention you've been drawing from the male shoppers on the square, or the workmen delivering your tacky fence —"

"I'm not smelling that pie yet," Ida cut in, "or that coffee."

Responding to the reprimand, we turned back to our chores. I put the pie together in silence, distracted by my own whirling thoughts and perplexing emotions. The trauma of the day had clearly addled my brain. Why should I give a damn what ailed Francine, or any Mossy Cracker? And why should I be pleased that she thought my butt was perky and little? What mattered were my boys. I spent the next stretch of silence spooning the filling into the pie shell and praying they'd be found unharmed.

I'd barely finished sliding the pie into the oven when Mutt came walking into the house with a boy beneath each arm. One was Chip, all muddied and sunburned, a fishing pole in his hand and a sheepish look in his eyes. The other was not Toby, as I had hoped, but the tall, broad, freckle-faced bully who'd fought with Chip in school. He was just as muddy, sunburned and sheepish looking.

"Dr. Blackshear found these two down by the creek," Mutt said. "Fishing."

"Fishing?" I approached my son in stark disbelief. He'd crept out of our home, against my wishes, to go fishing. With his worst enemy!

Before I could fully digest those incredible facts, though, I had a more pressing issue to address. "Where's Toby?"

"I don't know, Mama. Dr. Blackshear and Officer Bottoms asked the same thing, but Toby should be here, with you. I left him at home, I swear."

"Did he know you were going out?"

"I tried not to wake him, but my fishing pole was in his closet. I told him to go back to sleep, and that he couldn't come along. I thought he listened to me."

The relief I'd felt at seeing Chip now gave way to renewed fear. What red-blooded four-year-old boy who loves fishing as much as Toby does would stay behind while his brother went off to the creek? If Chip had disregarded my rules with such ease, why should Toby hesitate to tag along? 'Course, he couldn't possibly have kept up with the older boys, especially if they'd left before him.

Fear pounded through my veins, my head, my heart. Ignoring the people crowding around me, I hurried to Toby's bedroom, flung open his closet door and looked for his miniature fishing pole. It was, of course, gone.

My baby was alone somewhere on some mountain, in the woods . . . *or in the rain-swollen summer creek.*

Racing through the living room, I ordered Chip to go sit with his father until I came back. I then grabbed my car keys from the hook near the door and headed outside for the old Camaro I'd bought from my mother. If the men hadn't found Toby in the woods, then he'd probably made it all the way to the graveled side road that overlooked the creek. He and I had walked that way a number of times, just to look out over the water. But, God help him, the incline from that road was way too steep for anyone to climb down it.

If he'd tried and fallen . . .

Panic blurred my vision and made my hand shake as I attempted to unlock the driver door of my car.

A hand reached out and took the keys away from me. "Let's take my truck. It's four-wheel-drive." Mayor Ida stalked away with my keys, and I had no choice but to follow. As I slid into the passenger seat of her Land Rover, someone else crowded in next to me, holding a stack of towels, a length of rope and a first-aid kit in her lap. Francine.

I told Ida where I suspected Toby might be, and she set out for that lonely stretch of back road. She also talked into her cell phone, telling Mutt where we were headed. We didn't say much. I kept a careful lookout along the way, combing the woods with my eyes as we passed by . . . praying, praying . . . squeezing the hand that was holding mine . . .

My breath stalled in my throat as we approached the narrow, curvy section of road that overlooked the rushing creek below.

We turned a sharp bend, and Francine exclaimed, "Oh, me!"

My stomach lurched. There was Toby,

trudging along the outer curve of that narrow road, just steps away from the steep decline, still wearing his teddy-bear pajamas, holding his little fishing rod over one shoulder, his sneakers untied, his shoe laces dragging . . .

And that huge German Shepherd named Killer just a step behind him.

Panic slapped me hard at the sight of that dog so close to my boy. My world went hot and cold and still. But before terror could rush to my head and wash away all good sense, I realized Killer wasn't tracking him like some bloodthirsty predator, as I'd first thought. He was keeping even pace, wedging himself between Toby and the drop-off, nudging up against him now and then . . . *forcing him back from the danger zone.* And when Toby heard our car approach and turned to look, Killer grabbed hold of those teddy-bear pajamas — a big mouthful of cotton britches — and tugged him back off the road.

I'll never forget the sight, as long as I live, that dog holding my boy in the slim safety zone between the dangerous roadway and the deadly drop-off.

I'm not sure when I started crying, but as we climbed out of the car, I noticed Francine blinking back tears of her own.

Talk about an alien dimension from some video game. That ride back to my house couldn't have been any stranger. There I was, with my boy on my lap, a Mossy Cracker on either side, and a big ol' panting beast of a dog breathing down my neck from the back seat. The strangeness didn't end with that ride. When we reached my house where the passle of intruders awaited us, a mighty cheer went up all around. We were hugged and kissed and fussed over, and someone set me down with a blessedly hot cup of coffee and a warm piece of pecan pie. Francine gave a lively account of how we found Toby, and everyone talked at once.

By the time I'd finished my pie, Rainey had asked if I still sang and invited me to stand up with her band, the Screaming Meemies, at O'Day's Pub some Friday night.

Her mention of the pub brought up the annual All-County Mossy Creek Labor Day Dart Competition, and Mutt suggested I throw for the Mossy Creek team. That suggestion started a debate on whether they could claim me for their side.

"She might've been born a Bigelow, but she's living in *our* town now," my next-door neighbor Professor Egbert said.

"And her husband is kin to Miss Winnie,"

Sandy Crane added.

"And her mama is second cousin to Ellie Brady's niece by marriage," put in Adele Clearwater, surprising me with this bit of information I'd forgotten — or purposely blocked out, seeing as how it had always linked me to the lowly Mossy Crackers.

They continued rationalizing my switch to their side, and I couldn't help but gaze around in wonder. This was *my* house, with neighbors gathered, chatting and laughing and sipping coffee. These were *my* sons, throwing a football around the front yard with other kids, and that big killer dog scampering between them. That was *my* husband, his hospital bed now parked in the living room and surrounded by men who were watching the baseball game on television and asking Bunkin which team he was pulling for. He answered by means of his finger movement: one crook for the Braves, two for those suck-egg Yankees. At least, this was the choice posed by our neighbors.

In the midst of all this light-hearted commotion, I stood up, strode to my kitchen telephone and called Bigelow Security Systems. "I've decided I don't want the fence," I told the clerk who answered. "Cancel the installation."

My Bigelow cousin, who owned the company, promptly got on the phone and informed me it was too late to cancel the order. "We delivered it, Tammy Jo. You own that fence now, whether you have it put up or not."

If that isn't just like an ornery, low-down Bigelowan!

Mayor Ida Hamilton Walker herself took the phone and made it very clear that if my cousin didn't take back that fence and refund my money, she'd have her daughter-in-law Teresa represent me in a lawsuit against him. She also informed him, right then and there, that I'd be throwing darts this year for the Mossy Creekites. "She's one of us now."

A curious heat rose to my eyes, and a tightness gripped my throat. I looked across the room at Bunkin. As if I'd called his name aloud, he met my gaze. The worry lines were gone from his forehead, I noticed, and his mouth was turned up at the ends — as much as it *could* turn up with all those wires clamping his jaw shut. The message in his eyes couldn't have been clearer.

We're home, Tammy Jo. Home.

That wondrous realization sent the sun rising in my chest, warming me with happiness. And pride: pride in my husband for his quiet wisdom, pride in my boys for their loving natures, pride in my community for being the kind that stands staunchly behind its own.

I realize I'm getting prideful again, but suddenly I'm not afraid.

For the first time in my life, *I'm not afraid.*

Oh, I reckon that sooner or later fate will give me another big ol' shove. But there's just something about being a Mossy Creek-ite that cushions even the hardest fall.

A WMOS COMMUNITY ANNOUNCEMENT

Bert Lyman here, for the Mossy Creek Dramatic Arts Guild. WMOS Radio, The Voice Of Greater Mossy Creek, is a proud sponsor of the production of *A Midsummer's Night Dream* at the Mossy Creek Theater. Tickets are still available for opening night next week. Guild publicity manager Maggie Hart promises some amazing surprises. Our own Anna Rose Lavender is directing and starring as Titantic, Queen of the Fairies. What? What, Honey? Excuse me folks, while I confer with my wife over at the station's engineering control board, which doubles as our kitchen. Huh, Honey? Oh! Sorry. Folks, that's *Titania.* Not *Titanic.* I guess you can say Anna Rose is playing a fairy queen who's not going down with her ship . . . ouch! Honey, you promised not to throw biscuits when I'm on the air. . . .

Anna Rose

BOTTOMS UP

Life's a stage, Shakespeare said. But
some stages of life are more joyful
than others.

"Line!"

I stared at Waylon Sansbury, wondering
how a man could forget lines he'd known
perfectly only the day before. This was our
big love scene. I disengaged myself from his
arms and stepped back. "Waylon, how is it
possible that you can't remember your
lines?"

"You're real intense these days, Anna
Rose. You make me nervous."

"Shakespeare *deserves* intensity, Waylon."
I heard a chuckle and glanced toward my
grinning daughter, Hermia, whom I call
Mia. She was no stranger to my perfection-
ism, but she loved me, anyway. I nodded to
Darva, our assistant stage manager. "Let's
try it, again."

She cued Waylon and waited while he

hesitantly practiced his line several times. Then, as if launching himself off a front loader at a construction site, he threw his arms around me again and nearly knocked me down with an awkward kiss.

I staggered back. Nothing. The stage chemistry that had made us a good romantic pair for *A Midsummer Night's Dream* had simply vanished. I was intimidating him. And we had only one week before opening.

"Okay, let's just take a break," I said and stepped aside. "Please, everybody, let's try to concentrate. Opening night is looming, and the drama critic from the *Atlanta Journal-Constitution* is going to be in the audience for final dress rehearsal. What he says will either give us a boost or kill us. And, believe me folks, we need the ticket money — it's not enough for our own Creek-ites to support us — we know we can count on them — but we need to draw people from the surrounding counties and down in Alanta's northern suburbs, too. It's a long time until we can get more grant money. So relax, prepare, and I'll see you tomorrow night."

"They'll certainly relax after *that* speech, Mom," Mia said, chuckling again, and dropped a kiss on my cheek. "I'm going to spend the night with Darva. We'll work on my lines together."

"Okay. But that working on lines better not include driving down to Atlanta to party at some Buckhead nightclub. You need your rest for the performance."

She smiled. "This isn't Broadway, Mom."

"It is, to me."

"I know." She hugged me, ignored my scowl, and grabbed Darva by the arm. "Let's go party all night! . . . Just kidding."

"Beat it," I growled.

Interesting twist on life, I thought as I watched my beautiful daughter leave. Hermia playing Hermia. My own daughter was playing the part that I'd played nearly twenty years ago when my heart had been permanently wrenched from my chest. I thought I'd die, but then she was born. When I saw her the first time, nothing else mattered. Not much anyway. There was still a vacancy, but Mia and my work usually filled the void.

Usually.

Directing and starring in this play had made me more depressed than I'd felt in years. I knew the reason, but couldn't do anything about it. In fact, I'd chosen *A Midsummer's Night Dream* as Mossy Creek's reunion year production to challenge myself to *forget* the past. So far, it hadn't worked.

I watched my cast members dash off toward the tiny cubbyholes that served as dressing rooms. As usual, they'd head over to The Naked Bean for a cup of coffee and discuss the rehearsal. Waylon lagged behind.

"Is something else wrong, Waylon?"

"I don't know. I've just never acted in a real theater with paying customers before and I'm getting the willies, I reckon."

I smiled, remembering my own stage fright back in my years at Mossy Creek High before I settled confidently into my position as the lead actress in every play and musical the Fighting Rams Theater Club put on. I was only a junior when the school burned, but I'd starred in a dozen productions by then. I patted Waylon on the back. "Don't worry. Opening night is the best cure in the world for the willies."

In his case, I wasn't sure. I'd taken a risk, signing a novice to play Bottom in *A Midsummer Night's Dream.* It was a pivotal role. Waylon, who owned Mossy Creek Heavy Equipment — Sales and Rentals, wasn't my first pick. In fact, there had been no real first pick. Of everybody who'd auditioned, he'd been the most impressive. But Waylon was a lot better with bulldozers than with Shakespeare.

"Maybe I'd feel better if I could wear a

tractor cap for the show," he said.

I smiled. "Get some rest tonight. You'll be fine by tomorrow."

He gave me a thumbs up and wandered off stage. I heard him mumbling his lines as he headed for the dressing rooms. He got them wrong. My confidence evaporated, and I groaned. Replacing Waylon at this late date would be disastrous. Impossible.

Well, more disastrous than letting him continue in the role. I sat down on the edge of the stage's lovingly scuffed wooden floor, then froze. I had an inkling I was being watched. It had happened several times recently.

I squinted into the darkness. It was almost impossible to see anything beyond the first couple of rows. I felt a sharp sense of life out there. Except for that presence, I was alone in the theater. I could almost feel someone breathing in concert with me. Strangely enough, it wasn't frightening.

"You're losing your mind," I whispered aloud. "It's the reunion year. And the play. And the memories." I leapt up and hurried backstage to my dressing room, changed quickly, and headed out the side door.

Maybe I was being haunted by the Mossy Creek Theater ghost. The Phantom of the Mossy, we jokingly called him. Some folks said it was the ghost of Noah Widdington, the builder of the theater. He'd been a man ahead of his time, according to everything I'd heard. In 1922 he'd built the small, beautiful theater on the south end of the square, organized a theatrical society, and directed everything from the classics to vaudeville to the current Broadway shows. The theater had been a marvel of its time. And still was.

My usual encounters with Noah's ghost, if it *was* him, were confined to a sense of movement or a misplaced prop. Usually, finding that item or the search for it brought me to a better understanding of the play in production at the time. Noah was still directing.

But this time the visitor didn't *feel* like Noah. This presence was very much alive.

As I stepped into the sweet, hot summer night, I inhaled deeply. Mountain air can be intoxicating sometimes. I turned on the sidewalk to stare back at the darkened Theater. From outside, nothing seemed strange or out of the ordinary.

I suddenly felt a strong urge to sit by the creek and think. I strode down a knoll behind the theater and headed into a small park lit only by a gentle street lamp. I'd loved the little park behind the theater as a child; it was a place where the outside world couldn't intrude. A place where my father's drinking couldn't hurt me. It was my refuge and, for some strange reason, I desperately needed that refuge now.

Yes, I had a lot on my mind. For one thing, my very best friend in all the world, Maggie Hart, had become increasingly secretive lately, and I couldn't understand why. Every time I visited her shop, she seemed to draw up in a knot. At first, I thought she was still adjusting to her mother moving out and just didn't want to talk about it. But we'd always talked about our family problems, before. So what was up?

Sighing, I watched a fat moon rise golden over the mountains as I picked my way carefully down the bank to my favorite spot along Mossy Creek. The roots of a mammoth oak cradled me as I sank down into fragrant, wild thyme. I kicked off my shoes and dangled my feet in the water, as I had done so often in the past. The cool water rushing over my toes soothed me, and some of the tension floated away with the gurgling of the creek as it tumbled over time-worn stones.

Again, I sensed a presence. But as before there was a familiarity about it, as if to comfort and protect me. As I leaned against the old tree trunk, I closed my eyes and dozed as if I were a child, again. I'd dreamed I'd seen fairies once when I'd run away from home. Hundreds of them. All flitting about, soft and pastel, translucent living beings that had come to me when I needed a friend.

I dreamed now, as an adult. What was that twinkle just past the gnarled cedar? It pulsed with life, and a strong sense of magic enfolded me. The pulsing light grew stronger and was soon joined by others. Dozens of them hovering just out of sight, as if they were suddenly shy. I hardly breathed for fear of frightening them away. Ever since I'd seen them, that sultry summer night so long ago, I'd wondered about them. Was it just another dream?

I let myself drift back twenty years to the 1981 production of *A Midsummer Night's Dream.* I was just a teenager then, eager and naïve and crazy in love with the best-looking troublemaker in the county, a hellraiser with a good heart and a wrong-side-of-the-tracks charisma that stunned people even then. When I coaxed him into taking a part in the play, everyone said it was either a miracle or a big mistake. He'd never acted before in his life, but when people saw him on stage with me they knew they'd never forget him.

Beau Belmont.

Those few weeks were the best and worst times of my life. The critical acclaim we received was unheard of. Every little newspaper in North Georgia reviewed the play and lauded our performances as 'the most passionate performance of Lysander and Hermia ever witnessed.' After the last performance, Beau and I slipped away to another county, got married, and plotted our future in the world outside Mossy Creek. There was only one problem — he was eighteen, and I was only sixteen, still legally under my father's control.

When Dad discovered what we'd done, he threatened to kill Beau. He had the marriage annulled and locked me in my room. He swore I'd stay there for the rest of my so-called childhood. Very few Creekites liked my father, but they didn't disagree with his reaction in my case — after all, Beau was considered nothing but bad news around the local girls. Dad even stirred up such righteous wrath that Battle Royden ordered Beau out of the county for his own safety and — not unkindly, but firmly — escorted Beau down to Bigelow and put him on a bus headed west.

"Come back in two years when she's legal," the old chief told Beau. "And I swear to you I'll walk her down the aisle to you, myself. But come back before then, and I'll throw you under the jail."

So Beau didn't have much choice, and neither did I. Being young and stupid, I was terribly hurt when he left town and felt deserted. Especially when I realized a couple of months later that I was pregnant. Yes, that's an old saw of a predicament, and it went about the way you'd expect. I slipped away from home with nothing but one suitcase and Maggie's help. She took care of me until Mia was born and helped me get an office job with a theater company out of state. I wrote to Beau and told him I never wanted to see him, again. And being so young, so stupid, and so wounded, I also told him I'd had a baby by another man.

It was years before I came back home to Mossy Creek. My dad was dead by then, and I wanted Mia to have a real hometown. Her mother's hometown, and her father's. She didn't know her father was Beau. I'd made up a name and said he died in a motorcycle accident. God help me.

Beau began to show up as a supporting actor in action-adventure films. Those dangerous good looks of his combined with an expression in his eyes that said he'd never let himself love anyone again eventually made him a star. He hit the big time a few years ago with a film called Top Force that broke all box office records.

Since then, his name had been connected with every starlet in Hollywood at one time or another. When he never married any of his leading ladies, some of the tabloids speculated that he must be gay. I knew better. And I knew that Beau wasn't the heartless ladies' man everyone believed him to be. Even when we were young, I understood the difference between love and lust. We had both, but the love meant much more.

So here I was, twenty years later — dreaming of midsummer night fairies and loving Beau, again.

When I opened my eyes, dawn sunlight was filtering through the leaves, sending sparkles of silver dancing over the creek. Appalled, I sat up and looked around wildly. What must Mia think? That her mother had been kidnapped by ghosts and fairies? That I'd lost my mind?

The fresh scent of thyme blended with cedar greeted me. A pathway of cedar branches led from the creek back up the worn track I'd followed the night before. There'd been no wind, so I couldn't understand what happened to place the tiny branches in the path. My feet padded softly over the trail as I slowly entered reality again, sort of a soft green tunnel from the ethereal to the commonplace.

Suddenly, I had to see Maggie. Folks say confession is good for the soul. I needed to confess. Or, at least, talk about what had happened last night and all those years ago. Maybe she could offer some insight. At least she would listen and be non-judgmental.

I hurried through the woods, across the square and through the park. I realized it was too early for a social call but decided to take a chance. When I reached her flower-and-vine draped house, I took the porch steps two at the time and then rapped on the door. "Maggie, open up!"

A healthy dose of her tea and common sense would make my life seem much better.

"Anna Rose?" The door flew open and Maggie, dressed in a cozy nightshirt, stared past me briefly before hugging me. "Where have you been? I called last night after rehearsal and wanted to —"

"I've been at the creek all night. I fell asleep. I dreamed of fairies and Beau. Maggie, what's happening to me? Why did I pick that damned play to do in the reunion year? *Reunions.* What do reunions mean to *me?*

Heartbreak and loss and missed chances and lies and —"

"Fairies? You saw fairies down at the creek?"

"Don't look at me that way. It's not the first time."

"Let's have a cup of strong tea. Are you drunk?"

"Maggie, you know I don't drink and —"

"Just an expression." She grabbed a cup, measured some loose tea into a tea ball, and poured some boiling water over it. "Give that a minute. It's good for you, especially when you're overwrought. Now, start at the beginning. Slowly."

We sat down on the plush sofa. I heard a noise upstairs. I groaned. "Oh, Maggie, I shouldn't have come by. Tag's upstairs, and he must think I'm the rudest person —"

Tag pulled up in Maggie's driveway at that moment. I stared out a window as he climbed from his car carrying a take-out bag from Mama's All You Can Eat Café. Maggie leapt up as he bounded up the porch steps then shoved her front door open with his shoulder. Maggie made little shushing motions with her hands. "Ham and biscuits and hot buttered grits, Magster, as promised —"

He saw me and stopped. Maggie pressed

her lips together. I stared at their sneaky expressions. Something or someone made another noise upstairs.

"Maggie, did your mother move back home?" I asked.

"No. It's . . . It's somebody you . . . you don't know."

For the first time in our friendship, I knew she was lying to me. "Okay, Maggie. Tag, you too. Confess. What's going on?"

"Going on? Nothing. Why do you ask?"

"Because you've both got that funny little pinched look over your eyes. What gives?"

"I'm getting ready to do a massage. That's it. A massage. For somebody you don't know."

"At dawn?"

"He wanted the earlybird special. Look, Anna Rose, it's not what you think. You'll see. Soon. I promise. Now, I need to go and change clothes for my . . . appointment."

She waved goodbye, then rushed upstairs. I heard the thump as she knocked hard on the door of Millicent's old bedroom. "Sir, I'm ready to give you that massage! Hope you're dressed! My friend, Anna Rose, is downstairs, and I wouldn't want to scream and upset her! Anna Rose, that is!"

Someone opened the door, and Maggie disappeared inside. Tag and I stood downstairs gaping at each other. Me, shrewd but astonished. Him, awkward.

He held out the bag from Mama's and cleared his throat. "Ham biscuit?"

I paced back and forth, waiting on Maggie to arrive at rehearsal. Evidently, she didn't want to talk to me alone because she came in at the last minute, dressed quickly, and took the stage. My interrogation would have to wait until later. Because of a hectic schedule, we were doing technical checks and the final dress rehearsal all in the same day.

"Okay, people, listen up, please," I called, hoping to get through this without strangling Waylon, Maggie, and myself. I was in no mood for Waylon's bumbling, mumbling, ski-jumping portrayal of *Bottom* today. "I know this is tedious, but we've got to do it. We have an audience tomorrow, and they'll be expecting magic on the stage. Let's give it to them, shall we? Mr. Stage Manager," I said to Hank Blackshear, who stage-managed four-footed dramas over at his vet clinic when he wasn't involved in the theatrical kind. "We're all yours."

Hank stepped onto the stage and waited for quiet. "Okay, folks, we're working cue to cue. Anna Rose is right. It's tedious, but if we all cooperate, we can get through it without shedding blood. Places, everyone."

A chuckle rippled through the cast as we all moved offstage to assume our places. There is nothing more boring than tech rehearsal. Working from one light cue or sound cue to the next, stopping, and starting over again, is the worst part of live theater. After weeks of rehearsal, incorporating the magical elements of sound and light cause a certain amount of tension after a while. But we managed to get through — as Hank said — without bloodshed.

"Okay, thanks everybody. Be back in an hour for final dress. I expect everybody at places, and we'll run without stopping." I turned to leave the stage, hoping to catch up with Maggie, but she was already gone. More than a little hurt, I turned out all the lights and sat alone on the stage, hoping for the magic, the ghost, the fairies, or the *someone* from the night before to help me make sense of it all.

But I was all alone.

I had a case of opening night jitters like none I'd ever experienced before. There was something in the air, something different. I sometimes got premonitions, and now I was in the middle of a very strange one. I felt sure something earth-shattering was about to happen, something I would have no control over, and it would change my life forever. I'd had this premonition before — on the night Beau and I eloped.

"Places, everyone," Hank said, as he passed through the backstage area.

"Where's Waylon?" I asked, pacing.

"Still putting his donkey head into place."

"He should be out of the dressing room by now!" I began to panic. Where was Waylon? Oh, God, he wouldn't do this to me! What would I do if stage fright got the best of him and he bolted?

I'd have his ass, if he did.

The house lights dimmed, held at half, and then went out. I held my breath and prayed.

And the play began.

Suddenly, Theseus was on stage, yearning for the moment of his marriage to Hippolyta, Queen of the Amazons. Enter Egeus. Just like my father forbidding me to see Beau, Egeus had brought his daughter to King Theseus, who would order her to marry Demetrius instead of Lysander.

Instead of playing Hermia, as I had all those years ago, I was now Titania, Queen of the Fairies. And, I was destined, due to a trick played by my husband, Oberon, to fall in love with Nick Bottom — a man with the head of an ass. But, true love it would be — until Oberon discovered what Puck had done.

True love. Hah!

Somewhere in the audience, Tag was watching Maggie onstage. He adored her. Somewhere nearby, Mayor Walker and her studly retired Lt.Colonel, Del Jackson, were no doubt holding hands. Hank's wife, Casey, sat in her wheelchair lovingly watching the results of Hank's behind-the-scenes stage-managing. Rob and Teresa Walker leaned close together in their seats with their little girl, Little Ida, grinning between them. True love was out there for everyone else, but not for me.

The path of true love never runs smooth, according to William Shakespeare. Mine never ran, period.

I made my entrance, praying Waylon — Bottom, that is — would be on stage waiting. He was. But I stopped and stared. *Waylon?* I said under my breath. *My God!* No. One look at the way Bottom filled out the rest of his costume and I couldn't believe Waylon was under the donkey head. I squinted at him. The long floppy ears were the same, but the eyes peering out from the mask weren't. And, the voice. Bottom was

. . . acting. Orating. Speaking in a deep, melodic, breathtaking voice that lived in my heart and memory, in my blood and soul.

A sensation flowed over me like a soft mist of kisses.

I calmly let Bottom take me in his arms and kiss me. The passion that shimmered through that embrace made my knees weak. I looked up into his eyes, murmured my lines and swayed.

"Beau," I whispered.

The audience stood up and cheered.

Somehow we finished the play without too much ado and took our bows to thundering applause. I was far too stunned to appreciate or not to appreciate it. My mind was numb; my body was numb. I had to get away. Somehow, Beau and I had to get away from everybody and talk.

Maggie caught my hand and whispered, "He's been upstairs at my place. Planning this surprise."

Instead of removing my costume when we left the stage, I dashed out the side door and ran toward the same haven I'd sought before, with Beau following me. I reached the creek and snuggled into the cradle of the tree trunk. For the first time, I related the wild thyme in my sheltered bower to the bed of thyme in the play. The scent of it reached me as I inhaled and exhaled steadily to calm myself.

Before I could slow my hammering heart, I heard a noise. "Damn. Briars and vines tripping me up." I heard the splash of Beau's feet hitting the creek. "Still cold!" he said. "I'm freezing my butt off." He made his way to me and dropped Bottom's empty head beside me.

I started laughing. It was so dark I could barely see the white shirt he'd worn in the play. The moonlight glanced off his face and his wonderful, mesmerizing eyes caught mine.

"Here, let me help." I stood and tried to stop laughing, but couldn't. Extending my hand, I braced myself to keep from falling in. "The least you could have done was to take off that ass's head before following me."

"I think it fits." He grabbed my hand and tried to step up on the bank. His hand slid from mine and he fell backwards, splashing water all over me. I began to laugh again.

"Funny, is it?" He slung his hair so that a string of jeweled droplets of water caught the moonlight, spun off and disappeared into the forest. He reached up, pulled me down into the creek with him and kissed me. "Sorry I'm a little late," he whispered.

"No. Right on time."

We both took a deep breath. "I know the truth about Hermia," he said gruffly. "Maggie told me last week."

I bowed my head against his. "I'm sorry I lied to you."

"I'm sorry I left you."

"Forgive me."

"Forgive *me*."

"Stop, Beau. It's too late."

"It's not too late." He rose to a sitting position, stood, and lifted me into his arms. He made his way to my secret bower, as if he'd been there many times before. Had he? "It's never too late. I'm moving back here. I love you, Anna Rose. I always have, and I always will. We'll find a way to explain everything to Hermia. About me. About us. From what Maggie tells me, she's a smart girl. A strong girl. She'll understand."

I nodded, but a tear slid down my cheek, dropping onto my filmy, wet costume. Beau brushed back my hair and stared at me for a long moment. "It's never too late, little Anna Rose. Never too late for us." He leaned down and kissed me again.

The world stood still. I looked up at him. "We would have been married twenty years, today."

"As far as I'm concerned, we've just said

our vows, again." Suddenly, a light flickered in the distance. And then another. And another. Ordinary fireflies.

No. Fairies. But I had to believe.

"Looks like the fairies are giving us their blessing," I whispered.

He looked at me tenderly. "Whatever you say."

I was at home in his arms. Explanations could come later. Beau and I were together. On our anniversary.

The dream had come true.

MICHAEL
AND HANNAH

KATIE BELL NABS TWO MORE VICTIMS
FOR HER SURVEY

Librarians and bartenders both know what
it means to get drunk with joy over ideas.

What do reunions mean to me, Michael
Conners, aka "Father Michael" and owner
of O'Day's, the notorious Mossy Creek pub,
scene of the annual rowdy dart tournament
between Mossy Creek and Bigelow?

Ahhh. Reunions are in an Irishman's
blood, even when he was born and raised in
America, like me. Nothing better than gettin' together with the far flung arms of the
family for a few pints, some merry old
stories and, when opinions — usually political or sports related — get crossed, a punch
or two. The stories are the best part, if you
ask me. Reunions seem to bring out the liar
in us all, and there's nothing better than a
grand tale that everyone knows is a crock of
. . . well, you know what I mean. If the truth
were to be found at the bottom of a glass,
pubs like mine would be empty, and there

would be reformed Irishmen all over the world.

What is the one thing that happened to me in high school that made me the person I am today?

You know, then, that high school is a very important time in a man's life. I'm sure it's the same for the women as well, but we men have a bit more hormone overload and, at that age, a tad less maturity to handle the crush. Anyway, mostly we think about the opposite sex, and then sometimes when the opposite sex isn't around, we bash our heads together in one form or another of manly recreation. Basketball was my game, and I spent most of high school perfecting my chops, hoping to gain fame and fortune — or at least a girlfriend. But then, as usual I've gotten off the subject. Let's see, the one thing that happened in high school?

Well, besides my sophomore English teacher who threatened to fail me for flirting with my female classmates by reciting risque poetry instead of Tennyson, I would have to admit it was meeting my first love — Laura Riley. She was a senior, an older woman you might say, and as pretty as my Irish-American eyes could withstand.

As to how it changed me, just let me say this . . . she taught me more about what it means to be a man than basketball, or any teacher before or since.

And that's enough said about *that*.

What do reunions mean to me, Hannah Longstreet?

As a librarian, I see the best reunions in the Mossy Creek Library every day. People bring their children in and find themselves bonding over *The Secret Garden* or *The Black Stallion,* or introducing their kids to funny new stories such as *Bunnicula.* A personal favorite of mine, I think, because I love the idea that something as harmless as a bunny — or a small town librarian — could have a wild fantasy life. Watching from behind my staid desk I see people smile when their chldren reverently reach for *Little House On the Prarie* or *The Hobbit.*

As for Mossy Creek High, I remember being so sad for the wonderful library the librarian had built. The books that didn't burn were ruined by the fire hoses. All those old friends. I spent a lot of time in the library my freshman year — right before the school burned down. Actually, I *hid* in the library.

I wasn't really old enough to be in high school, but my mother and my grade school teachers had pushed me up to that level fast. Too fast. I was only twelve when we moved to Mossy Creek from Tennessee, and I entered Mossy Creek High looking like someone's kid sister who'd made a wrong turn at the playground. So I was new to town, the youngest student at the high school, with no friends and no training bra. Mother wouldn't let me wear one — a decision that became the bane of my existence when I found out that in high school girls have to dress-out for gym.

A lady coach showed us a horrible room of little gym lockers, sinks, and shower stalls with no doors. I'm guessing they just built the girl's locker room to the same plans as the boy's. Coach seemed oblivious to the fact that girls of high school age have enough problems with body image without having to parade around an open room while trying to dress and undress. There isn't a woman in America who can honestly say she's perfectly happy with her shape. Hips, thighs, butt, tummy, chest, feet, cheeks, nose . . . you name an area, and there's a woman who bemoans the sorry state of her genetic material.

Being twelve, I was the poster child for Stick Figures of America.

After the fire, we all transferred down to Bigalow High. I hate to say it, but I was so happy. The gym facilities over there were made for shy girls like me, and the library had a little nook in the back that no one used. In fact most of the books looked like they'd never been read. It was a very lonely library. You could almost feel it perk up when I started haunting it.

Mother never has understood why I became a librarian. She wanted a rocket scientist. I'd have made a lousy rocket scientist. She doesn't understand that it's lovely to be the woman who can unlock the world for people. She doesn't see the patrons faces light up when they find the research they want or get the new bestseller before anyone else. She doesn't see me light up when my library's full of people wanting to talk to me. She has no idea how much I know about the people in Mossy Creek or how many people send me Christmas cards.

Katie, don't print all of this. I'm getting too sentimental and the last thing the world needs is more sentimental librarians. I'd rewrite it, but I have a ton of new fiction to catalogue and get out to the shelves. So, just print about the books burning and me being sad that we lost those books. Thanks.

P.S. That book on the secret language of

symbols is finally here. What did you want that for, anyway?

Rob, Rainey, and Hank
I HEARD THE ELEPHANT CALL MY NAME

The offices and boardroom of Hamilton's Department Store are in a lower level just above the basement, where the old furnaces still roar and grumble. Not only that, but the hundred-year-old joists, handcut stone, curlicue plaster cornices, and fancy pink-marble tile of the whole three-floor building creak and groan and shush and tremble. It's like the building has twitchy memories in its bones. As owner and president of Hamilton's, Inc., Rob planned to renovate as soon as he got the old store back into black ink. In the meantime, I squirmed in an upholstered conference chair, listening to the store's whispers.

"We all know why we're here tonight," Rob said quietly.

Across from me, Hank nodded. His wife, Casey, looked up at Hank gently but clutched the armrest of her wheelchair.

Rob's wife, Teresa, seated next to him at

the head of the long, handsome conference table, sighed with a lawyer's sympathy for justice and looked at Rob with real love. I'd never been able to hate perky, brunette Teresa for being a sophisticated college woman and winning his sophisticated love.

Lor', I'd tried.

I looked at the empty conference chair next to me. *Where are you when I need you?* I asked of the husband I didn't have. Rob and Hank had told their dearly beloved mates the whole truth — at least, as much as we knew and remembered — about the night of the fire. But I had *no* one to tell. My dearly beloved sat at the head of the table, unaware, with his wife.

"We all know why we're here," Rob said again. "It's time to tell the whole town what we did."

Hank nodded wearily. "All these years, I've tried to convince myself it wasn't our fault. But we'll never really be certain." He looked at Casey and her wheelchair tenderly. "I've learned a lot about personal courage since then. I'm willing to risk the consequences."

"Oh?" I squawked. "Everybody will *hate* us. All our old friends and neighbors will call us cowards and deceivers for keeping quiet so long. It won't matter that we were just kids twenty years ago and we didn't mean to cut the elephant loose. People will just purely *hate* us. I don't mind confessing the truth, but I sure don't want to be an outcast and lose all my customers and all my friends. I don't want to have to move my salon down to Bigelow or even way down to Atlanta, somewhere. What good am I going to be down in the flat-land suburbs? I do *mountain* hair. *Big* hair. Hair designed to survive cold winters and high winds and hard, mineralized well water. I'll be nobody outside my styling market."

Casey made a soothing sound. She was good with animals, kids, and upset hairdressers. "Rainey, no one is going to blame you and Hank and Rob for an *accident*. Don't forget, you three didn't kidnap the ram and set him on fire. *That's* what spooked the elephant and caused the trouble. Obviously, *someone* knows who kidnapped that ram."

Teresa nodded. "That's right. Whoever kidnapped Samson is the primary suspect, here. That someone *wants* to be caught. That someone *has* to be the person who sent the Ten-Cent Gypsy back to Mossy Creek as a taunt. He or she is returning symbolically to the scene of the crime. It's a classic example of guilt syndrome. Guilt by association."

"Guilt by association?" I muttered. "With a plastic carnival hoochie? I don't think so."

Rob shook his head. "Regardless of the Ten-Cent Gypsy, what it means, who sent it, and who kidnapped Samson that night, I've decided to tell what part I played in causing the fire. That doesn't mean I expect you, Rainey, or you, Hank, to break your silence. I don't want either of you blamed. I was the oldest. I was the leader. You both trusted me, and I got you in trouble. So I'm the one who has to take responsibility."

My heart broke with appreciation and lost dreams.

"No." I stood. "Rob Walker, you just forget about sacrificing yourself alone. I said this twenty years ago, and I'll say it now, it's all for one and one for all."

Hank stood, too. "I agree with Rainey. We'll all confess together. I say we do it at the reunion ceremonies in November. Wait until then. Tell the whole town, all at once, what we did on the night of the fire. Take the consequences." He looked down at his wife. "Casey, it may mean the end of my vet practice here. We may have to move if people won't forgive me."

She nodded. "You're doing the right thing. That's all that matters."

After a long, intense silence in which tearful looks were traded by all of us, Rob's shoulders sagged. "I love you two as if you were my sister and brother," he said quietly, looking at Hank and me. "You're the most stubborn people I know."

"That's right," Hank said and smiled sadly.

"I love you and Hank," I told Rob with tears in my throat and *sister* settling hard in my stomach.

Rob Walker. How I loved him — and not as a brother. He was tall and dark-haired and handsome and noble. He dressed in gray suits only a banker or young businessman would wear. He looked like that actor, Dylan McDermott, on *The Practice.* Teresa even resembled Dylan's wife on the show. Their daughter, Little Ida, was one of the prettiest, most level-headed girls in town. Rob had everything a Creekite could want. He was sophisticated, rich, kind, and perfect.

But I, Rainey Ann Cecil, of the "po' but proud" Cecils, looked like Dolly Parton's pink-jeaned, red-headed baby sister from a bad country-western song. Tacky Rainey Ann Cecil. And I had nothing I wanted.

Except my principles. I wouldn't back down. Neither would Hank. Come November and reunion time, we'd spill the setting lotion of our permanent misery. Curl everyone's hair with the facts about us, Rose the elephant, and the night that would live in blazing infamy, in Mossy Creek.

"We're agreed, then," I said. "November. All for one and one for all."

Rob and Hank nodded.

A little while later Rob, Hank, Casey, Teresa and I walked out a dark lower door of the old department store, our footsteps muted and somber on the carefully tended bricks of a Mossy Creek sidewalk. I told everyone good night then wandered alone up an old alley toward my salon and the little apartment I lived in, above it. I felt like the only soul on the face of the earth.

Out of the summer darkness came a scratchy female drawl. "Hey, Rainey, were y'all just having a little social visit at Hamilton's, tonight?"

I jumped. Sandy Crane loitered near the gas lamp on Main Street, looking little but official in her dispatcher's shirt and A-line skirt. Her eyes narrowed shrewdly in the glowing light. She plucked at her curly blonde hair as if calculating how long before she could corner me in my own salon during her six-month body-wave job.

I puffed myself up. "Can't a person visit

with friends and take a walk without bein' eyeballed? Especially by a woman who refuses my advice to use smoky smoke eye shadow color instead of that gunslinger silver. That silver washes out your whole inner lid crease."

"My crease is just fine, thank you. I'm just here *observin'*. An officer of the law can't let her guard down, not with such a big mystery in town this year and *some* folks acting secretive."

My skin chilled. "Nothing secretive about a *walk*." I breezed past her onto Main Street in a flash of pink jeans and knock-off Oscar de la Renta perfume. "Nighty nite, Sandy. Your hair's looking real good with the new cut I gave you. See you soon for a trim?"

"Oh, yeah, I'll be seein' ya," she said. "You know, I still do some house cleanin' on the side from my duties as a law officer. You want me to spruce up your apartment for you? You know, it's always good to *come clean*." Soft, sly tone. Those shrewd Bambi eyes. She twirled a piece of her hair around one super-efficient little finger. It was like being stalked by a Cabbage Patch Doll with a badge.

"I like my dirt," I said.

I hurried upstairs to my tiny apartment, locked my door, and sat in the dusty dark.

SANDY

ON THE TRAIL

I knew something was going on with Rainey, Rob, and Hank — I just couldn't put my finger on what, yet. Besides, I had bigger fish to fry in Mossy Creek. Somebody left a note on Jess's and my doorstep the morning after I had my conversation with Rainey. "Hon," my husband said as he carried the envelope inside, "either the raccoons have started writing thank-you's for the seed they're stealing from your bird feeder, or you have a secret pen pal."

"Gimme that. It's probably from my boyfriend," I deadpanned, then gasped when I opened it. The envelope contained an anonymous computer print-out note. I read it five times, then rushed to the police station.

"I've been tipped off to a new clue, Chief," I told Amos as I ran into his office. I bent over his desk and repeated that real loud. "I got some *great* clues about one part of the school mystery!"

He looked at me over a copy of the *Gazette*, like he usually did, trying to hide. "I operate on a need-to-know basis."

"It's about the elephant."

He lowered the paper. There's nothing like a twenty-year-old unsolved crime to get the attention of the son of the police chief who couldn't solve it. Family pride and father-son competition would raise the hairs on the back of Amos's neck every time.

"Tell me," he ordered.

"I'll tell you on the way. We've got to drive to Memphis, Tennessee. Right now, Chief. It'll take all day."

He studied me for a second, decided to risk not asking for more details, then stood. "Get my car."

I grinned. "I'm on it, Chief."

Then I was out the door.

Memphis is a damp old city. Smells like rich dirt, barbecue, and the Mississippi River. Lots of fancy old buildings and fine old homes. Lots of good blues music. Lots of Elvis knicknacks.

And lots of elephant bones.

Lord have mercy, who'd have believed it? By late afternoon, Amos and I drove down a sandy lane through a pine thicket then stopped where the woods opened up into mowed pasture and the weirdest cemetery on the face of the Southern planet. I sat there beside him in the patrol car with my jaw hanging to my collar and just stared. So did Amos. We were only a mile inland from the river and only a few miles outside the Memphis suburbs, but we might as well have been in Strangeville, USA. If Elvis had stepped out of the woods, it wouldn't have surprised me a bit. Stranger legends than the King's had come to rest there.

"Big Top Memorial Garden," I read from a circus billboard at an entrance which was just a pair of steel livestock gates. Kind of appropriate, I guess. Inside, in the "garden," bizarre tombstones marked gravesites big enough to fit my truck. My jaw still hanging open, I wandered around with a throwaway camera in one hand and my eyeballs hanging out on stems of amazement.

Amos shoved his hands in the pockets of his khaki trousers and read the tombstones aloud in his driest *ThankYouGladToBeHere* tone of voice. "Bertha The Lioness, R.I.P. Hannibal The Camel, May He Hump It To The Pearly Gates. Twinkle The Tap-Prancing Pony, We Hope He's Tap Prancing In A Three Ring Heaven."

"Interesting poetry," I said.

Amos looked at me as if I wasn't serious. I shrugged.

We walked on, reading more tombstones. Chimpanzees and cheetahs. Ostriches, one water buffalo, and a boa constrictor. Lions and tigers and bears. Oh, my. And every other kind of formerly performing, now decomposing, circus critter. We reached a white wooden archway and stood gaping up at the words *Pachyderm Paradise,* when an old man drove up in a rusty sedan and walked out to meet us.

"Chief Royden, Officer Crane?" he called.

Okay, I'd lied and told the caretaker I was a real law officer, not just a dispatcher. Amos eyed me for a second, and I puffed up like a little hen trying to look bigger to a snake.

He looked away and sighed. "Are you Mr. Thornton?"

"Yessir."

"I'm a little stunned by what you have here."

"Most people are, the first time they see this place." He swept an arm at the grave makers. "We've got deceased performers from just about every circus and big carnival there ever was. It's an honor to have an animal perfomer buried here at Big Top Memorial Garden. Why, just last week a theme park out on the west coast shipped the remains of Danny The Dolphin here." He pointed to a backhoe sitting next to a big open hole. "Services are next week."

I just stood there praying Danny The Dolphin was on ice somewhere. A lot of ice. I held up my mysterious note. "Mr. Thornton, about this information I got . . ."

"She's here." He put a hand to his heart. "Follow me."

Amos and I walked beside him into the elephant section. All of the tombstones were carved in the shape of rearing elephants with their trunks curled like S's over their heads.

"Some granite company in Memphis has a monopoly on the rearing-elephant-headstone market," Amos said.

Mr. Thronton pointed. "There's your gal."

We looked at a rearing elephant marker and frowned.

Lucy. A Perfect Lady.
Beloved by the Sumter Sweet
Traveling Circus.
Sumter, Iowa
Died 1997

Amos shook his head. "We're seeking an

elephant named Rose, not Lucy."

The old man nodded. "This is her. I checked with the Sumter Sweet people. They bought her from her first owner in 1982. Her name was Rose, then. Came from somewhere down south of here. No other notes on her." He paused. "Except she was scared of fire. Nearly trampled the Sumter Sweet's Tahitian Fire Twirler when he got too close, one time."

I gasped. "Then it can only be Rose!"

So now we knew. Obviously, Rose had been sold under a new name only one year after Mossy Creek High School burned down. Somehow, someone had spirited her out of the mountains around Mossy Creek without a soul knowing.

"I smell a big cover-up," I muttered under my breath.

"Usually is, where elephants are concerned," the old man said.

From: Katie Bell
To: Lady Victoria Salter Stanhope

Dear Vick:

I just happened to be at Mama's All You Can Eat Café the other day along with Louise Sawyer. We were having iced tea and apple pie with some elderly ex-patriot Creekites who'd come back for a pre-reunion visit. Everyone was talking about the discovery of Rose's grave up in Tennessee. Sandy Bottoms Crane wandered in. They say curiosity kills a cat — well, if Sandy was a cat she'd be on her ninth life — and I say that as a professional curiosity seeker, myself. She's taken on the job of cracking the case of the high school fire as a way of proving herself to Amos. Her dearest dream is to be promoted from police department dispatcher to a full-fledged officer, like her brother, Mutt.

"Sandy, you look distracted," Louise said. "Anything wrong?"

"Just pondering the case of our dead, disguised elephant. You know, Ms. Sawyer, I've never forgotten the pet rooster your Cousin Minn used to have. What was his name?"

"Henry."

"Hmmm. There were a lot of animal lovers around here way back when. A lot of kindly people who would have fed an elephant and hidden her in their barn out of the fear that she might get blamed for causing the fire. But whoever shipped Rose out-of-state to the Iowa circus had the kind of money it takes to pay trucking costs for an elephant. That leaves out most Creekites and most Bigelowans, too."

Louise nodded. "But it also means that somewhere, in the dusty files of some local trucking company, there may be a record of the shipment."

Sandy stared at her like a frozen blonde squirrel while that idea sank in and took root. Then she yelped with glee. So did I. Before I could get a word in edgewise, Sandy paid for a bag of fried chicken and yeast rolls and rushed out.

I leapt up to follow. Louise gave me an odd look. "You and Sandy have spent too much time thinking up wild theories on this case," she ventured.

"A wild theory is better than no theory at all, I say."

Louise just laughed. "At least I'm glad she remembers Henry and Cousin Minn. Speaking of which, let me tell you all the story I told my guests the other day . . ."

Katie

LOUISE

COUSIN MINN AND THE BANTY ROOSTER

Often, the sweetest reunions are with our memories of childhood adventures we weren't supposed to have.

"Louise Sawyer, why in the world do you keep that old gun in your nice living room?" Marge McCracken asked. She'd graduated and moved away from Mossy Creek to Atlanta long before the fire. Although she'd only come home for the high school reunion, she had told several people she might move back now that she was retired.

I took the gun down carefully from the two iron pegs that held it. "It's an old shotgun my granddaddy carried in France during the First World War and smuggled home in his kit afterwards. I inherited it from my Cousin Minn about thirty years ago."

The noise of a reunion party eddied around Marge and me. I, too, had graduated from the old Mossy Creek High School before it burned. I felt duty-bound to 'have a little something' to honor the returning alums. I'd wanted to have champagne punch, but had been advised to stick to what my mama used to call *rinso* — lime sherbet and gingerale. The table looked lovely covered with Mama's antique Irish linen cloth. I prayed it wouldn't wind up pale green from spilled punch.

I patted the scratched wooden stock of the gun gently. "Can't say I keep Cousin Minn's gun on display for its artistic value, now can I?"

I sat down in a pale blue silk wing chair beside the ornate fireplace with the shotgun across my knees. All my old friends gathered around.

"No, I keep it for its moral value. It's a constant reminder to me not to think I know all there is to know about anybody."

Especially my Cousin Minn.

"Louise!" The whisper came out of the darkness. "Wake up, Louise."

"Ma'am?" I rolled over and opened my eyes. It was still dark. School was out for the summer. I was twelve years old, had no cares, and could sleep until noon. I groaned and turned over again only to have my shoulder roughly shaken.

"Louise, get up! I can't find Henry."

I blinked a couple of times and struggled to a sitting position. I could see Cousin Minn's aging, pale face in the pale light of the false dawn that was beginning to show through the sheer lace curtains. Her hair, wavy and streaked with gray, was wildly ruffled. "He's probably roosting in the fig tree."

"No. I've called, I've looked, I've spread chicken feed all the way to the alley gate. He's not in the yard. You've got to help me find him."

I glanced at the old wind-up alarm clock on the bedside table. The big numbers still retained enough radium so that I could read them. "It's five o'clock in the morning. If he's not home by eight, we can look for him."

She stood and clasped her small hands in front of her. "*Now,* Louise." Without another word, she turned and walked out of the small bedroom I used when I stayed with Cousin Minn during the summer.

I flopped back on the sad old feather pillow that was damp from the sweat on my neck, but after a second I got up and tried to find the shorts I'd worn yesterday. I had heard something in her voice I had never heard before. There was fear, but there was also a firmness that surprised and kind of bothered me.

My Cousin Minn was only in her mid-fifties at that time, but to me she seemed ancient. She weighed maybe eighty-five pounds dripping wet and wore neat Liberty print dresses with hand-made Belgian lace collars, winter and summer. She was still slim and erect, and swore the scissors had never touched her hair. I could believe it. It was heavily streaked with gray, but the plait she did it up in every night was as thick as my wrist. She wore lisle stockings and sensible shoes whenever she went out. The only jewelry I ever saw her wear was an antique cameo brooch she said her mother had left her. I still wear it, although I'm hardly the cameo type.

I was more a not always benevolent despot to her than a child, and like most tyrants, I was sometimes bad-tempered about it. She never complained, not even when we stood in line two hours in the blazing sun outside the Mossy Creek picture show on Saturday afternoon to buy ten pieces of bubble gum for a dime. Bubble gum had been rationed because of the war. Then she had to put up with my tantrums when I couldn't blow a bubble.

I have no idea what actual kin we were —

all that once-and-twice-removed stuff went over my head. The sister with whom she shared a house was called Aunt Bertie. If she was an aunt, then how could Cousin Minn be a cousin? An elderly female relative of mine, always called "Daughta" — not daughter — by everyone in the family, including the children, attempted to explain the relationship to me one snowy afternoon, but I couldn't grasp it, so I simply accepted it. Even my friends called her Cousin Minn.

I had heard that she and Aunt Bertie had a younger brother who died before I was born, but there weren't any pictures of him in their house. My mother said that Cousin Minn had been engaged to a young man who had died in the First World War. I couldn't picture her as a young woman going on dates, dancing, laughing, and dressing up. I saw her only as she was now, an indulgent and doting elderly relative. Whatever existence she'd had when she wasn't spoiling me was irrelevant. Children are selfish monsters.

That morning, I thought she was crazy to go hunting for a darned old banty rooster before dawn in the middle of August, but I figured I owed her. I hated Henry and the feeling was mutual. He adored Cousin Minn but figured any other creature in her proximity was either an enemy or a rival. While Cousin Minn worked on her hands and knees in her garden, Henry strutted back and forth behind her like a member of the Praetorian Guard. Maybe he thought of her as his prize hen, although he had a harem of half a dozen Rhode Island Reds that Cousin Minn kept in a cage on the back porch.

He greeted each dawn raucously. Nobody in the neighborhood complained or seemed to mind, which shows you how much nastier people are than they used to be. Now some lawyer or stockbroker would probably sue her for noise violations and keeping poultry in a residential area.

That morning, however, the still, sodden air was silent. I ran barefoot down the back porch steps into the yard and felt the damp Bermuda grass between my toes.

"Henry!" Cousin Minn yodeled. "Ooohooh, Henry, time for breakfast."

No response. Although I considered myself fully grown at twelve, I didn't want to have to explain to Cousin Minn that Henry had been a step slower than some possum or raccoon. I just hoped we wouldn't find his bloody body under one of the trees. It would be much better if he simply disappeared.

We searched her back and front yards, the neighbors' yards, and even the alley that ran behind the house where we put out the trash twice a week for the garbage men.

"He never went into the alley, Louise," Cousin Minn said as she slammed the solid wooden gate shut. The fence was made of six-foot wood slats that leaned slightly but still stood so close together that not even a grown cat could slip between them.

We walked up the long stretch of the back yard, checking the fig tree and the pear tree for the twentieth time without success. Henry could probably flutter over a six-foot fence, but I saw no reason he would try. He was too fat to enjoy fluttering. He preferred a stately meander.

Cousin Minn collapsed on the bottom step of the back porch and burst into tears. I was horrified. I couldn't count the hours I had spent slumped against her meager bosom while I sobbed my heart out about everything from the loss of my favorite doll to my grandfather's heart attack. She had comforted *me.*

I had no idea how to comfort *her.*

I sat beside her and patted her hand. The skin felt like fine silk stretched over tooth-picks. I looked up at her tear-stained face and realized that she was *old.* And with that came the realization that I could lose her the way she had lost Henry. I could not bear it. I put my arms around her, and we clung together on the back steps wailing like a Greek chorus.

I have no idea how long we stayed that way before the screen door to the porch opened and banged shut above us. A moment later, I heard Aunt Bertie's voice. "Minn, Louise, have y'all lost your minds? Get up from there this minute. What's wrong?"

I sniffled, "It's Henry, Aunt Bertie. He's missing."

"Huh. All this wailing over a tomfool banty rooster? Get up this minute and come in the house, Minn. Do you realize you are still wearing your nightdress? You're half naked, and your hair looks like the rats have taken up permanent residence."

Minn continued to cry. I was left to do the talking.

"But he's gone," I wailed, bemoaning not so much the loss of the rooster as the terrible sense of loss that seemed to pervade my soul.

"He'll either come back in his own time, or he won't. If he doesn't, we'll get another one. Minn, he is just a bird."

On that note, Cousin Minn was up and

facing Aunt Bertie so fast she almost tipped me off the step. I had never seen her so mad. "He is not just a bird. He is a hero, and if he is still alive, I intend to find him." She stalked up the stairs and shoved past her sister and into the house. "And you can fix your own breakfast."

The screen door slammed behind her.

Aunt Bertie and I simply gaped at one another before she turned on her heel and went back inside to get ready to go to work. She did some kind of accounting-bookkeeping thing that brought in what money they had, which wasn't much. She tolerated me, but then she seemed barely to tolerate the whole world. I was scared of her, but I tried never to let her know it.

At the top of the stairs, she turned back and gave me that look — the one that makes kids feel about two inches tall and rotten to the core. "Your feet are dirty, Louise, and I doubt that you have brushed your teeth. Please go and do so."

We didn't go in for 'ma'am' and 'sir' much in my family, but I always ma'amed Aunt Bertie. I did so now.

While I ate my cereal, I could hear Cousin Minn on the telephone to the neighbors asking whether anyone knew the whereabouts of Henry. From her replies, no one did, but they all seemed sympathetic.

Aunt Bertie left to meet her ride at the end of the street without speaking to her sister. They had an old Hudson that Cousin Minn drove occasionally, but Aunt Bertie's friends drove her to her job down to Bigelow, and someone always picked her up for church on Sunday, so the Hudson didn't get much use.

Cousin Minn did not go to church. I was six or seven before I realized that, and when I asked her why she didn't, she said she'd discuss religion with me when I was older. Period.

Now, my family are all big Baptists and have been since we got to Georgia sometime in the eighteenth century. I thought the fact that nobody tried to save Cousin Minn's immortal soul and get her to accept Jesus as her personal savior was odd. One day, I asked my mother if Cousin Minn was going to hell because she wasn't a Christian.

She didn't smack me, but she came close. Then she explained to me in no uncertain terms that Cousin Minn was a very good Christian even if she didn't go to church and never to mention the subject again to anyone. So I didn't. But I kept worrying nonetheless.

I suggested now that it might help if we prayed for Henry's safe return. That brought on more tears. Cousin Minn hugged me and said she'd been praying hard ever since she realized he hadn't crowed at five-thirty.

Despite my personal aversion to Henry, I prayed as well. I knew how much he meant to her, and I hated to see how miserable she was not knowing what had happened.

I spent the morning hand-printing signs that said, "Reward for Return of Missing Rooster." Then gave a description of Henry, who really was a handsome bird with his long russet tail and his brown plumage.

Cousin Minn and I tacked the signs to at least a dozen telephone poles — which pretty much meant *all* the poles in Mossy Creek. By the time we got back to the house, we were both faint from the heat. Since there were no answering machines, we had no way of knowing whether anyone had called about Henry or not. While I gobbled down a homemade pimento cheese sandwich made with Worcestershire sauce just the way I liked it, Cousin Minn fidgeted. She never ate much anyway, but so far as I could tell, she hadn't had a mouthful all day.

And she was tired. I could see that in her eyes.

After lunch, I took my current *Nancy Drew* mystery out on the front porch and stretched out in the glider to try to read and catch some breeze. A few minutes later, Cousin Minn came out with her hat on her head and her purse in her hand.

"Louise, you are old enough to stay by yourself for a few minutes. I am going to the crossroads store to put up one of those signs you made."

The crossroads store was a couple of miles down South Bigelow outside of town. Surely she planned to drive, and if so, I intended to go along. Signs were one thing. Ice cream was quite another.

We drove to the small grocery, put the sign on their bulletin board, and bought me an ice cream cone and half a watermelon for dinner.

As we were crossing the dirt parking lot to get back into the old Hudson, Albert Whit sidled up to us. The Whits were about the only black family in Mossy Creek back then, and Mr. Albert had a reputation as a good farmer who minded his own business. He wore an old Panama straw hat that had once been very fine, overalls that were patched but clean and ironed, and a pair of fine leather shoes that had been cut along the inside to accommodate his bunions.

"Ma'am," he said quietly.

Cousin Minn turned to him and smiled. "Yes?"

"You needs to give up looking for your bird." His voice was nearly a whisper, and he kept looking over his shoulder as he spoke. "You ain't gonna find him. Not in this world."

Cousin Minn's face froze. "Are you saying that you know he's dead?"

The man shook his head. "Good as. You get you another." He started to walk away.

Cousin Minn followed him around the corner of the building and under a shed where firewood was sold in the wintertime. "Just a minute, Mr. Whit. Please, wait!" She put her hand on his arm. He frowned. To have a white woman touch him worried him, and with some justification in those days.

She dropped her hand. "Please, if you know anything about Henry, help me find him. He is very precious to me."

The old man shook his head, but his voice was gentle. "He good as gone. Come nightfall, he'll be out of this world for sho'."

She huffed. "You are speaking in riddles. Who took my bird? Do you know where he is?"

"Shouldn't 'a said nothin'."

"But you did." She pulled out her change purse and extracted a five-dollar bill — a huge sum for a reward. "Tell me where I can find my rooster and this is yours."

"You keep your money, ma'am. If you're that determined, then all right. They's some old boys comes through here looking through the trash, looking for things to take."

"Burglars?"

"No'm. Just takes what they can see. I heard 'em talking 'bout your bird. What a fine cock he was. Saying how they'd like to try him, see how he'd do."

"I do not know what you're talking about."

"I didn't think they'd steal no bird, but when I heard you in there, I knowed they must 'a done it."

"For what, for pity's sake?"

"Fighting, ma'am. That's a fighting cock you got there, and a fine one at that. I seen him in your yard a time or two."

"Henry? Fight? Don't be ridiculous."

"He's a fighter all right. And them ole boys, they runs a fight a couple of nights a month down in the bushes behind the switchin' yards down in Bigelow. They got a fight tonight. To my mind, that's where your bird'll end up."

Cousin Minn was too stunned to hang

onto it. As he scuttled away, she called after him, "Where behind the switching yards?"

He stopped. "Don't you even be thinking of going there or sending anybody. Po-lice leaves those boys alone. Me too."

"Are they white or colored?"

He whispered, "They white men. Now you go on home, and don't tell nobody I talked to you."

He disappeared into the shadows around the back of the store.

I put my arm around Cousin Minn's waist and leaned my head against her shoulder. "I'm so sorry."

She shook me off. "It is too soon to be sorry. Come along, Louise, we have work to do."

Cousin Minn drove to the rail yards in that old Hudson, bouncing over the rutted gravel paths along the far side where the locust trees and the wild roses and the honeysuckle grew in profusion.

We turned up every track and path. Finally, we found a rutted space where the gravel showed that several cars had recently parked. A narrow path led off through the underbrush.

"Stay here, Louise," Cousin Minn said as she climbed down from the Hudson. "I am going to investigate."

She hadn't taken a dozen steps when I plastered myself to her back and grabbed her arm. "Come back. You can't go down there. Lord only knows what would happen if there's somebody down there."

She shook off my arm and kept walking. I was scared to death as I followed. She was acting like a total lunatic who belonged in a home, and all over a cursed chicken!

Ahead we could see the dying sunlight on an open patch. She did have sense enough to creep, although I don't see how an Indian scout could be silent walking through that mess. I kept whispering, "Go 'way, snake," and trying to stamp my feet — but silently.

We smelled it before we saw it. I had never seen a cockpit before. This one was only a bunch of rough plywood pieces nailed up around a dusty area to form a sort of amphitheater. Old lawn chairs and broken down sofas with the stuffing coming out sat around the edges of the pit. Behind the far side were stacked wire cages. Empty wire cages.

Nobody was there, thank God.

But there weren't any birds there either.

"Pee-eeew," I whispered. The place smelled of drunken male sweat, the dregs of old liquor, and chicken droppings. Over everything lay a metallic odor like an old copper pot left too long on the stove. Blood, but whether chicken or human or a mixture of the two I couldn't tell.

The fear and the scent and the place made my stomach turn. I began to retch and the remains of that ice cream cone erupted.

"Lean over, Louise," Cousin Minn pushed my head over toward the honeysuckle.

When I had finished, she grabbed my hand. "Come on, child. Lord, what am I thinking bringing you to a place like this?"

I flew back to that Hudson and hung my head out the car window like a dog all the way home.

"You gonna call Chief Cochran?" I asked as we pulled up in the driveway. Before the Royden dynasty began, Nocturne Cochran was Mossy Creek's answer to Andy Griffith.

"You heard that old man. The police know to avoid this place. Calling them would do little good. Obviously, the fights start at night after dark."

"So I guess that's it." I climbed out of the car. I felt God-awful. I itched from the mosquitoes, the chiggers, and my own sweat. My stomach kept giving little after-shocks. Somehow that watermelon didn't sound nearly so appetizing as it had.

As we climbed out of the Hudson, Aunt Bertie appeared on the front porch in an apron. She was holding a big soup spoon. "Minn, where on earth have you been? I was worried sick . . ."

I saw her eyes light on the Hudson, which was covered in muddy splotches from the puddles we'd driven through and caked with dust from the dry spots. "My land, what have you been doing?"

"We went to the grocery, then because it was so hot, I took Louise for a little drive to cool off." She sailed into the house while I stood dumbfounded behind her. I had never heard her utter even the smallest falsehood, yet that was a flat lie, and we both knew it. She didn't so much as look back over her shoulder at me, so sure was she that I'd back her up.

And I did. I managed an "Uh-huh," followed by a swift "Yes, ma'am," before I scuttled by Aunt Bertie who was wielding that spoon like a weapon.

Cousin Minn shut her bedroom door, and I heard the slide go home. She had locked the door! This was an entirely different woman from the Cousin Minn with whom I had spent almost every weekend and half the summer since I was big enough to walk.

I crept out the front door and down the driveway to the backyard so that I could avoid Aunt Bertie and whatever she had concocted for dinner — black-eyed peas, probably, and sliced tomatoes from the garden. The watermelon still sat on the back seat of the Hudson. It was much too hot to eat before tomorrow evening.

I spent twenty minutes calling for Henry and feeding his 'ladies,' then went in to dinner. I must admit I ate like a field hand, chigger bites and all.

Aunt Bertie tried to commiserate with Cousin Minn, but she merely dropped her head meekly and moved her food around with her fork.

Despair.

I felt sorry for her, but there wasn't anything we could do we hadn't done. I didn't want to think about Henry being torn apart by another fighting cock, but at least he'd die doing what he had apparently been bred for.

After dinner, I cleaned up the kitchen and took a bath without being told to. I heard Cousin Minn gargling and brushing her teeth, and watched her come out of the bathroom in her nightdress with her hair neatly braided. She and Aunt Bertie slept in separate bedrooms on opposite sides of the small bungalow, while I slept just down the hall from Cousin Minn. She stopped in to say goodnight, and I told her again how sorry I was.

She thanked me and turned away. But there was something about the set of her shoulders that did not speak of misery. I knew as clearly as though someone had spoken the words in my head that she was up to something.

Surely she didn't plan to go back and accost those rowdies at their game! Even Cousin Minn could not be that naïve. Why, she'd get herself cut to pieces or thrown into the pit with the roosters or God knew what all.

I put my clothes back on and found the old flashlight I kept to read under the covers after I was supposed to be asleep.

Then I unhooked the screen from the open front window of my bedroom and crawled out. I'd done it a million times. I knew precisely how far away I had to land to avoid winding up in the hydrangeas. I slipped around to the far side of the Hudson and slid in, hoping the dome light wouldn't alert anyone to what I was doing.

Miraculously, it didn't go on. I checked and saw that someone — obviously Cousin Minn — had unscrewed it. So I was right. She was planning to slip out.

I climbed into the space between the back and front seats and hunkered down. The carpet smelled musty like old dirt and prickled where it touched my skin. I was sure I was going to have a full blown sneezing attack. I stuck my finger under my nose where the nerves are and kept it there.

It seemed like hours before I saw the front door open and shut. Cousin Minn came down the stairs with her purse. But she was carrying something else. Something long that she held straight up like a spear. Please God, I thought, let her not put that thing on the back seat. She'll see me for sure.

I had no idea how to stop her. I just figured she was better off with me than without me. That I was giving her the added responsibility of protecting a twelve-year-old girl as well as getting herself and Henry out of that cockpit did not occur to me.

She backed out of the drive with no lights. Aunt Bertie slept at the far back of the house. With luck she wouldn't hear us leave.

Cousin Minn's driving was erratic in full daylight after a good night's sleep. At night with nothing but the moon to guide us away from the house, she was a positive horror. I prayed that there were no other cars on the road and Chief Cochran or his deputy wouldn't spot us.

Finally, the glow told me that she'd turned the headlights on. She had also sped up and was taking corners like a race car driver. I braced myself fairly well until we went over some railroad tracks and became airborne for an instant before the car slammed down on the far side.

My shoulder hit the metal support for the front seat. I yelped.

Cousin Minn screamed.

And slammed on the brakes. I hit the front seat again.

I looked up into her stunned face. "Louise, what on earth are you doing back there?"

I struggled to a sitting position and climbed over the seat to the front.

"Trying to keep you from getting blown straight to Kingdom Come." I barked my shin on the long thing that lay beside the door. "Ow!"

"Don't touch that, Louise! Lordy, I'll have to take you home. We'll never make it in time now."

"No, ma'am. I am not going home unless you are." Then I realized I was staring down into the double barrels of a shotgun.

"Get back in the back seat."

"That's a gun!"

"And it is occupying the front seat. Get in the back, Louise."

"You don't have a gun." I retreated over

the back seat while keeping one eye on the twin barrels.

"Indeed I do, although Bertie would have a conniption if she knew I took care of it all these years." She drove on without checking to see whether there was anyone coming up behind her. Luckily, there wasn't.

"Is it some kind of antique?" Probably didn't have a chance in Hades of firing.

"A very fine one and in perfect condition. Did you know that when I was a girl I was a crack shot at skeet and trap?"

My tiny little old Cousin Minn?

"I gave it up after . . . after the First World War."

Maybe if I got her reminiscing about old times, I could get around to talking her out of this crazy thing we were doing. "Did you lose somebody in the war?"

"Louise, after every big war in which a great many men are killed there is always a generation of women who never marry because there aren't enough men left. It happened after the Revolution, the War of Northern Aggression, the First World War, and it's happening now after the Second. Yes, I lost somebody. I had other chances to marry, but they all seemed like settling for somebody less. So I didn't."

"Was the gun . . . his?"

"No. It was my brother Sam's. He died holding it."

I froze. "Did somebody — you know — shoot him?"

Since time for a kid is relative, I had visions of something like the shootout at the OK Corral, or maybe a duel of honor. Something very grand and romantic, at any rate.

"No. He wasn't shot. He lived with Bertie and me. He'd been too young for the war, and I suppose that bothered him some because he never seemed like the type to take up hunting. But after my granddaddy left him that shotgun, he took to hunting ducks and geese and I don't know what all."

"Was he any good at it?"

"My lands, yes! Except for one thing. He longed, no Pure-D lusted, to bag us a wild turkey to have for Thanksgiving dinner." She began to laugh softly and shook her head.

Reminiscing hadn't turned the Hudson for home, but it had certainly slowed her down. She was driving sanely now. That was something, at least.

"Wild turkeys aren't easy to shoot, Cousin Minn. Even I know that."

"So did he. He was a wonderful wood carver — that mirror over my dresser is one he carved for me. Every year, he'd swear the new turkey caller he'd carved would be 'the one.' He'd cluck on that thing until Bertie'd send him to the basement to practice."

I could see her head shake in the reflection from the headlights, and I could see she was smiling — a secret smile that I had no part of. I suddenly felt as alone as I had ever felt.

"Year after year, he'd go out in the woods all by himself just before Thanksgiving, and year after year he'd come back at night worn out, filthy dirty and empty-handed, and we'd have to go get us a turkey to serve for Thanksgiving. Everybody in the family laughed about it."

We turned off the road onto the gravel track we'd followed that afternoon. At night, it was like turning into the mouth of hell, dark and steamy and full of creatures that flitted or scurried away. Cousin Minn had to slow down or wreck the car.

"The last time he went turkey shooting," she continued, "he didn't come home at dark the way he usually did. By ten o'clock we were worried sick. He was almost like Bert's son — she's twelve years older than I am, and sixteen older than Sam. The weather had turned dreadful — cold and spitting sleet. We organized a search party come dawn. Took until nearly dark to find him."

"Were you there?"

"Heaven's no, child! You think those men would have let a woman tag along in the woods? It's not as though I hadn't grown up in them and knew them better than my backyard." She shook her head. "Men!" We bumped along much slower than we had earlier. The branches brushed the open windows like arms reaching in to snatch us.

I had stopped noticing where we were. "Was he hurt? Did the gun go off or something?"

She closed her eyes. "I didn't see him, of course, but the sheriff said he was sitting propped against a big pin oak with that old shotgun across his knees and the biggest gobbler they'd ever seen lying dead beside him."

"But what happened to him?"

"Heart attack, they said. He was only thirty-three, but they say when the heart goes early, it goes hard. I like to think his burst with pure joy after he shot that turkey." She sniffled.

"I've never even seen a picture of him."

"Bertie destroyed all she could find, she

was so angry at him — but I hid a few she doesn't know about."

"Like the gun?"

"In the very back of my chifforobe where nobody could find it."

We pulled to a stop, and Cousin Minn began to back and turn the Hudson around in a space barely big enough for it. I could see her hands straining on the wheel. This was long before power steering and she was a very small woman.

When at last she got the car positioned so that it faced the road, she let out a big sigh, turned off the ignition and shifted around so she could look into my face.

"My brother Sam was the dearest, sweetest, kindest boy. Everybody loved him. Always a smile. And funny! He could keep us in stitches. He's the one that played the piano in the living room. Kept it tuned perfectly." She cut the lights, and we sat in the sudden darkness while around us the katydids racketed and the night birds called. "Your mother says you're worried about my immortal soul because I don't go to church," she said.

Oh, fine. My mother always did have a big mouth. I started to answer, but she stopped me.

"Maybe this isn't the time to tell you all

this, but could be it's the only time we'll have."

As her words sunk in, I began to shiver.

"Back at the house after Sam's funeral, the preacher found me on the back porch and told me he was real sorry about Sam. He said God 'visited' his heart attack on him because he'd gone hunting on Sunday instead of coming to church like a good Christian. He said Sam was no doubt burning in hell."

"But that's awful!"

In the faint glimmer of moonlight that came in through the windshield, I could see that her eyes were hard and dry.

"I told him my brother was as fine a Christian as ever lived, and that he was a good deal closer to God out in His woods than he was listening to one of that preacher's mean-spirited sermons. I refuse to believe in a God who would condemn his child for something any human father would forgive. Then I did something terrible, Louise. I slapped him. I've never been back to church since. Remember this, Louise, whatever happens tonight. God does not turn his back on his children."

She opened the car door. "Stay here now. I mean it." She walked around to the passenger side of the car, opened the door and pulled out the shotgun. She checked to see that it was fully loaded, then reached into the glove compartment, pulled out a box of shells and dropped half a dozen into the pocket of her house dress. "Louise, can you drive a car?"

"You know I can. I been driving my daddy's old truck on the farm since I was nine and he had to hold me on the seat in front of him."

"I am leaving the keys in the ignition. If you should hear the sound of gunfire, I want you to drive this car out of here, find the nearest policeman and bring him back."

"No ma'am. I'm coming too."

"Louise, you are not." She turned around and walked off with the shotgun in the crook of her arm. She was a little old lady walking into a nest of God knew what sort of men, like Daniel into the lion's den, and with about as much fear.

I was scared enough for both of us. I had learned too much about my Cousin Minn tonight to let her go now just when I was truly coming to value her as a real person. Besides, I was terrified in that car by myself. I climbed out and followed her at a discreet distance so she wouldn't hear me.

I could see the lights dancing in that clearing and hear the drunken shouts of the men fifty yards before we reached the area around the cockpit. Cousin Minn stood quietly behind a clump of wild laurel, and I stood behind another while I prayed that the copperheads were asleep tonight.

There were only four men lounging around the pit in the old beat up chairs. The headlights of half a dozen automobiles that were lined up around the edge lighted the pit itself. The woods on the other side had looked impenetrable, but there obviously was some way through.

Two men were down on their hands and knees in the pit itself. One was holding a rooster while the other fitted long steel spikes onto his legs. I couldn't tell whether we were looking at Henry or not.

Apparently Cousin Minn had no doubts. She stepped from the shelter of her tree and racked a shell into the chamber of her shotgun. If you've ever heard that sound once in your life you'll never mistake it again. Obviously these men had more than a nodding acquaintance with the sound. All six froze, then two of the men in the chairs shaded their eyes to try to see into the shadows.

"What the hell?"

"I have come to reclaim my property," Cousin Minn said in a voice that might sound steady to the men in that pit but came across as pretty shaky to me.

"Your property?" The largest man who had taken up most of the sofa began to stand.

"Sit still, please. And keep your hands where I can see them. Preferably locked behind your head."

"Hell, it's some little old lady. Lady, you shoot that thing, you gonna be flat on your tee-hinie in the bushes."

The gun boomed. I jumped a good six feet straight up.

When I opened my eyes, Cousin Minn still stood at the edge of the circle, but now the gun rested against her shoulder and was aimed straight down into that pit.

"I cannot prevent your continuing this abominable fight another night in another location," Cousin Minn said. "But not here and not now. Bring me the property you stole from my yard this morning, and I will leave you in peace, though I think you all deserve to be strung up for what you are doing."

I could see things were about to turn mean. From the clink of bottles we'd heard, they'd been drinking, and here was this little old person threatening to string them up.

And all for a stupid bird.

"This gun is fully loaded with buckshot and on full choke. I doubt that I'll hit Henry if I fire at you, but I would prefer he die an honorable death at my hands than in your ring torn to bits."

"Hey, lady," the man holding Henry said, "This here's a bird born to fight. We just giving him what he needs. He ain't no panty-waist chicken for no old lady's pet." He spat into the dirt.

"I am well aware of his fighting capabilities," she said.

I looked at her in surprise.

"He tore apart a large copperhead that was poised to strike at my knee when I was gardening. He is a hero and deserves to be treated as one. Now, please bring him carefully and gently to me. Louise, you pick him up and carry him to the car."

I had no idea when she'd realized I was there. I didn't think she would have fired the gun if she'd known, but I'd apparently given myself away somehow.

"Hell I will," the man said.

With the second shot, however, he moved.

He put Henry down some six feet from Cousin Minn and backed up while I ran down, snatched up the traumatized bird, and lit out for the car.

By the time Cousin Minn reached the car,

I had it running and the lights on. Henry sat like a lord on the back seat.

Cousin Minn tossed the shotgun in the back seat beside Henry, shoved me over to the passenger side and floored the poor Hudson.

"I don't think they'll come after us, Louise, but you never know."

Actually, I suspected they were having a good laugh at our expense. Laughing was the only way they could get their manhood back intact. Even I knew that much about men. By the time they told this tale a dozen times, they'd have taken pity on the poor little soul who just wanted her stupid old chicken back.

Fine with me. I didn't want them plotting vengeance.

The minute we got back to the safe streets of Mossy Creek we both broke out in gales of laughter. Henry even essayed a weak crow, although it was a long way from daybreak.

We snuck Henry onto the back porch, moved a grumpy hen from her nesting box to share with one of her sisters for the night, and installed Henry in her place with fresh water and grain. He went to sleep at once while Cousin Minn stroked his feathers.

Sneaking ourselves in wasn't nearly as

easy, but somehow we managed. Cousin Minn locked the shotgun in the Hudson's trunk. She would move it back to her chifforobe after Aunt Bertie left for work in the morning.

The clock on my bedside table said twelve-thirty. I crawled into bed with no thought for chiggers, mosquitoes, or brushing my teeth. I knew I was filthy, but it didn't seem to matter.

As I snuggled down under the single sheet, Cousin Minn scratched at my door and opened it. She wore her dimity night-dress, and her long braid hung over her shoulder.

She sat on the edge of my bed and hugged me. "What you did tonight was foolish, Louise. You might have been hurt."

"Me, foolish? Cousin Minn, you could have gotten us *killed.*"

"Oh, no. Those men wouldn't hurt an old lady like me." I saw her grin. Downright wicked. I shook my head.

"But, Louise, this must stay between us. You must never, ever, ever tell anyone, not a single living soul, not even your mother and father, about all this. Do you promise?"

"Cross my heart and hope to die."

"Good. I love you, Louise." She kissed my forehead.

I felt the tears spill. "I love you too, Cousin Minn. I didn't know Henry saved you from a copperhead."

"Oh, yes. A big one." She stood and walked to the door.

"Cousin Minn?" I whispered. She stopped with her hand on the knob and turned to look at me. "What happened to the turkey?"

She grinned. "Bertie said we ought to throw the awful thing away, but I wouldn't have it. If Sam died for that turkey, the least we could do was to eat it. So we did. For Thanksgiving. Best I ever had. Go to sleep now."

"Cousin Minn left me the shotgun in her will," I said many decades later at the reunion party, "and when I went to get it out of her chifforobe, I found beside it a brown paper bag, and inside, carefully wrapped in yellowing tissue paper, were half a dozen turkey feathers. I still have those, too. Just not on the mantelpiece."

"Did you ever tell anybody?" Martha asked.

"My husband, of course. He wanted to know why I had that old shotgun. Nobody else knew about it as long as Cousin Minn, Aunt Bertie, and Henry were alive. Of course, they're long dead now. But in my dreams, sometimes I see Cousin Minn digging in the heavenly pansies while her brother Sam sits whittling near her." I raised moist eyes to a framed photograph of a rooster among the fine portraits on my living room wall.

Reunions, as some people say, are times of tearful joy. Not to mention faithful roosters. "And beside her Henry keeps watch, in case a celestial copperhead should manage to slither under the pearly gates."

From: Katie Bell
To: Lady Victoria Salter Stanhope

Dear Vick:

The big news in town this week is the arrival of a new cook. His name's Win Allen, and he's setting up his catering business in time for the fall reunion. My sources who've sampled his food tell me he'll give Mama's a run for her money.

But there's room for a lot of new restaurants in Mossy Creek. Creekites love to eat. They eat home cooking, they eat soul food, they eat fancy food. They wash their meals down with iced tea and hot coffee, cold beer and good wine, brand liquor and homemade moonshine, and the clearest, coldest, purest water from Mossy Creek. And then they eat some more. If we could just get Michael Conners to serve cornbeef and cabbage or shepherd pie at the pub, we'd have international cuisine.

In the meantime, we've taken a liking to Win Allen. After all, a stranger bearing good food isn't a stranger for long in Mossy Creek.

Katie

Win Allen
AND HIS ALTER EGO, BUBBA RICE

Katie, I'm not sure you really want my thoughts on reunions. You see, planning and attending the big Allen Reunion is a blood sport in my family. It's a one-day gauntlet of memory, manners and masochism. God help you if you run out of food. The buffet is the only thing keeping the Allen clan from killing each other because it gives us something to do with our hands.

I've never seen a more diverse group of folks from the same basic genetic pool in my life. Why we torture ourselves with this show-and-tell of our lives each year is beyond me.

Oh! And if you sample Aunt Minnie's fried chicken, you'd better grab a leg from Aunt Tilly as well. They keep score. I'm not lying. There are generally more than seventy assorted relatives at our reunion each year. Those ladies keep track of every single food selection. At reunions, I think of myself as

Switzerland and do my best to stay out of the war.

Pies and cakes are in competition with the cookies and the brownies. The various leftover vegetable casseroles are carefully inspected as to quantity remaining so that a crowd favorite can be declared. I wouldn't be surprised if they weighed them. I've seen men receive stern looks from their wives and valiantly attempt yet another helping of their spouse's offering.

Some of the younger women in the family have resorted to bringing obviously store-bought, boxed food as an expression of submission. Either they don't have a prayer of winning this trophyless contest, or they know it would be political suicide to 'win' at their age.

There's a female pecking order inherent in any gathering of family women. New brides know better than to come swooping in with a fabulous recipe. It's much better to be patted on the hand and taken under the wing of one of the grand dames.

The smart men bring bathing suits and volunteer to supervise the little kids in the pool. The smartest among us grab four plates of food and wedge our backs into the corners of the room. As long as you're busy eating, you don't have to explain what happened to the girl who came with you last year. It takes a long time to eat four plates of food if you do it right.

As soon as they find out about my new restaurant and catering business, I'm dead meat. Those women will be insulted if I don't bring food, and they'll be hostile if I do. Switzerland has unwittingly joined the skirmish.

Why do you think I moved to Mossy Creek and changed my name?

Winfield Jefferson Allen. A perfectly reasonable name. If you don't mind being beaten up in school.

I did.

When the first day of third grade rolled around, I made the decision that changed my life. I asked the teacher to call me Bubba.

The Bubba's of the world have a certain swagger of confidence. They're the elder sons, the big brothers; they rescue damsels in distress . . . usually from other Bubba's.

However, in the third grade I wasn't thinking much about damsels. I was just concerned with making it through recess in one piece. I became Bubba. With the stroke of a pen on a roll-call sheet, I changed my life.

Thus began my life-long pattern of becoming someone else. Anytime I didn't like my life, I picked a different part of my name and started over. Like in college. I "walked on" to the community college basketball team. Went right up to the coach and said, "Hello. I'm Win Allen. You need someone like me on your team." He asked me why. I told him my name said it all. He laughed and asked me to prove it. I played point guard at that tiny college for two of the best years of my life. I had no illusions about taking my game to another level. I just wanted to play.

My whole life has been about getting in the game.

Someone once told me that people fall into two categories: producers and achievers. A producer is someone who finds his satisfaction from amassing a body of work. An achiever is someone who finds his satisfaction in mastering the next challenge.

I think that may be why women tend to get a little skittish when I get serious. They put me in that achiever category. I'm not sure they trust me to be a one-and-only kind of guy. The funny thing is, they don't realize achievers need a solid base. We need a heart to come home to after risking failure. Because that's what achievers do. We fail as often as we succeed. Being an achiever is a scary proposition.

Like my new business — Bubba Rice Lunch and Catering.

This time I think I've lost my mind.

It all began when I sold a piece of computer software I had developed to some nice folks in the air freight industry for an indecent amount of money. Let's just say that I've got twenty years to retirement age, and I don't ever have to work again. At least not at anything I hate. So I asked myself what I liked and discovered that real men do cook. Puttering around the kitchen is a necessity if you're single. I'm talking good solid southern favorites here. Nothing fancy.

My little hole in the wall behind Mossy Creek Drugs and Sundries is only open for lunch . . . two days a week. There is no fixed menu with the exception of my trademark specialty — good ol' boy fried rice or 'Bubba Rice.' Nice marketing hook, huh?

I'm talking to Bert Lyman at WMOS Multi-Media — he owns the town radio station and just set up a TV studio in his barn — about producing a local access cable show called Cooking with Bubba Rice. I figure if Emeril, Bobby Flay and the Iron Chef can do it, so can I.

On the tables at the restaurant, I've got these great laminated placemats that offer colorful advice to get the ball rolling on my new career as a "character." The idea is a take-off on the posters proclaiming all people need to know in life they learned in kindergarten.

"All I ever need to know, I learned from cooking with Bubba Rice."

1. Starch is the glue that holds a family reunion together.
2. Measuring takes all the fun out of cooking.
3. Always write down Mama's recipes so you can sell them later.
4. A pinch of this and a pinch of that will get your face slapped.
5. Barbeque is pork. Always. Beef is a steak.
6. Never insult the people who handle your food.
7. Never be afraid to eat the last piece of cake.
8. Don't plant a garden unless you have lots of friends who'll take tomatoes.
9. If you need friends, plant a garden. Everyone wants fresh tomatoes.
10. A slow, promising simmer never hurt any relationship.

The door opens tomorrow. The menu's

eclectic to say the least. But that's half the fun. For me, anyway. Don't know about the customers. Guess Bubba and I will find out soon enough.

From: Katie Bell
To: Lady Victoria Salter Stanhope

Dear Vick:

I'm still on the trail of answers about the fire and the Ten-Cent Gypsy. Sandy Crane and I are sharing notes and getting closer to pointing a finger or two in the right direction. Honestly, I'm a little afraid we'll find out that one or more of our own Creekites were involved. Remember what I've said about Rainey, Millicent, Dwight, and some of the others? But I don't want any of my friends and neighbors to be guilty.

However, there are *some* Creekites I find so backward and annoying I can't help but wonder what kind of stunts they're capable of pulling.

Orville Gene Simple's little brother, high school dropout Roy Gene Simple, was caught the night of the high school fire making homemade stink bombs behind the Mossy Creek Fill-U-Up gas station owned by Phillip Donlevy. Which made it Phillip's Fill-U-Up, a hard mouthful to spit out — especially for old people with false teeth — but that's another story. Roy Gene, who doused himself in cheap cologne purchased at the Woolworth's store down in Bigelow, smelled worse than his stink bombs and could not have been in the vicinity of the school without being smelled, so Battle Royden said he wasn't a suspect. But, in my opinion, there's been an odd scent around the Simples ever since.

Sometimes, fate wins. Sometimes, the beaver does.

Katie

ORVILLE GENE
UP THE 'DAMMED' CREEK

My name is Orville Gene Simple, and I hesitate to tell this story, but it's hardly a secret, anymore. Especially since the whole town of Mossy Creek has witnessed my humiliation. I thought, what with the upcoming reunion and the reappearance of the Ten-Cent Gypsy that my early defeats would go unnoticed, and I think they might have, if it hadn't been for my old friend Derbert Koomer, who runs the I / Probably / Got / It store, and Sue Ora Salter Bigelow, owner of the *Mossy Creek Gazette.* It was bad luck all around that Sue Ora would have been the first to witness the beginning of what I like to call . . . my situation.

It all started in early September after Sue Ora brought her boy, Will, to fish in the pond down below my house. She'd been pestering me for weeks about how Will wanted to fish in my pond. I thought maybe she was hinting for me to bring her some catfish, but I never was real fond of anything involving water and told her to bring Will and catch some for herself.

She and Will arrived just after daybreak. I saw her through the kitchen window as I was making coffee and waved at her as she and the boy hoofed it past the house down to the pond. The woman wore fancy jeans and a mail-order canvas vest. Like the catfish had an eye for fashion and she didn't want to be embarrassed.

Later, I was outside feeding my dog, Duke, when I saw her and her son coming up from the pasture with fishing poles over their shoulders and a big smile on their faces. I knew then they'd had some luck.

Better than me, as it turned out.

"Hey, Sue Ora. Hey, Will. Looks like you caught yourself a fine mess of cats."

Will held up his stringer, eyeballing it proudly.

Sue Ora nodded elegantly. "We certainly did, Orville Gene, and I thank you for letting us fish in your pond. I'll be serving these with a nice lemon-rosemary sauce for Will, Great Aunt Livvy, and myself tonight. And I promised John a plate, if he stopped by."

John Bigelow was her husband, Will's

daddy, though she and John didn't live together and pretended not to be in love.

I saw her eyeing the old commode I had setting beneath the shady elm to the south of my porch, but I refused to comment. It was my house and my yard, and that old toilet was a right comfortable seat. Besides that, it was weatherproof, what with it being porcelain and all. She got this look on her face.

Thinking back, if I had been quick-witted enough to change the conversation, she might have gone on her way without saying what was on her mind. But I hesitated and she spoke again, and it was too late to stop the inevitable. "You know that the Mossy Creek reunion isn't too far away," she said.

"Yeah, I know. Seems like that's all any-one's talking about these days."

"Everyone coming into Mossy Creek from the west has to drive right past your place," she said.

I failed to see the point, but felt obligated to point out the obvious. "That's because about eighty years or so ago, the state of Georgia decided to build a road straight through Great-Granddaddy's land."

Sue Ora shifted her stringer of fish to the other hand, obviously unwilling to give up until she'd had her say. "What I was trying to say is, you might want to think about cleaning up your place a bit. You know . . . making the scenery more appealing, so to speak. Everyone in town is fixing up and cleaning up."

I felt myself glare and didn't bother to hide it. "My scenery suits me just fine. That's why I don't live in town."

She shrugged. "Well, it's your place. It's your reputation. But it does color people's opinions a bit if toilet seats in the front yard are the first thing they see when driving in on West Mossy Creek Road."

Then, before I could think of a smart comeback, she added. "By the way, you've got a couple of big fallen trees down at your pond. I'd think you would at least chop them into firewood instead of letting them go to rot."

"What trees? I don't know about no trees down at my pond."

"Really? Well, I apologize. I didn't realize the destruction was recent."

Now I was really getting nervous. "Destruction? What destruction?"

She shrugged again, which was beginning to get on my nerves. When women shrug, it usually means they know more than you do, but they'd rather watch you make a fool of yourself before you find out. "I have no idea. I just saw two big willow trees that had been cut down. You know how limby a willow tree can be. They're all over the place."

I wasn't familiar with the term, *limby,* but I was guessing it had to do with the number of limbs a willow tree might have, and I did have to admit that there was usually a good number of them on an average size tree. While I was still thinking about willow limbs, she smiled at me, as if the smile would fix all her criticisms. Some women just take the cake, and Sue Ora was one of them. She beat all, trying to tell me how to run my business — and after I'd let her fish in my pond and everything.

"I'd better get on home and get these fish in the refrigerator. I'll ask Will to clean my catch so I can change clothes and get to the office. I'm already late as it is."

"Your son looks nearly grown these days," I commented, hoping it would get her off the subject of the condition of my property and that danged reunion. I was wrong.

She nodded as she eyed the toilet bowl one last time. "Just think about what I said. It would be a boon to Mossy Creek to have a town beautification project before the reunion."

"I don't live in the town, and I didn't

graduate from Mossy Creek High, Sue Ora. I am a bonafide high school drop-out, which some folks insist explains the presence of the commode underneath my shady elm and the hubcaps lining my driveway."

She gave me another shrug-look. You know the one I mean. The one that women give you when they're remembering that you used to pick your nose as a kid.

I sidestepped her. "I think I will go down to the pond and see what's happened to my trees. Drive safe now, and I'll be in soon to renew my subscription to the *Gazette*."

That satisfied her enough to get her into her car with her fine catch of catfish. I stood there a bit, pretending to study the late summer weed problem in my mama's old daylily bed next to the porch, but in truth, I was just making sure that Sue Ora was good and gone. Nothing makes me more nervous than a woman on a mission.

I thought about going back into the house and having a third cup of coffee, just to let my breakfast settle, then decided to walk on down to the pond and take a look at the felled trees — just out of curiosity, you understand. Not because I thought there was anything to Sue Ora's concern.

As I walked through the pasture, my curiosity turned to a bit of pique. I couldn't remember a time when them willow trees hadn't shaded my great-granddaddy's pond, although I knew things don't live forever. Great-Granddaddy sure hadn't. He was thrown from a horse and died on his thirty-second birthday, leaving Great-Grandma with five kids and no money to raise them. It's a testament to Great-Grandma's fortitude that she didn't lose the farm.

Of course, I suppose it helped that she turned around and married the local undertaker, who was pretty well-off. That's one business that never goes out of style. People are always dying, no matter how hard they try not to.

As I walked, I remembered we'd had that hard wind a few nights ago and decided that the willows had probably blown down. And that's what I thought all the way up to the moment I reached the pond and saw that mound of limbs and twigs in the water about twelve feet off the shore. From where I was standing, the top of the mound looked like a giant chocolate cupcake floating three or four feet above the water line.

My heart sank. It was no wind that had felled my willows.

A beaver had taken residence in my pond.

As I stared in disbelief, I saw sudden movement in the water and then lo and behold, out pops the danged beaver as brazen as you please. He lumbered up onto the bank where he proceeded to chew off another limb of my poor willow. At that point I didn't think, I just started running.

"Dad blame it, you pesky critter! You have crossed the line of peaceful co-existence. One of us has got to go, and it ain't gonna be *me.*"

The beaver took the limb into his mouth and headed for the water, moving like a kid with a stolen lollipop making for the grocery store door. He hit the water with a splash, dragging the limb behind him. Just before the beaver reached the lodge, he slapped the water with that big old flat tail, then, along with the limb, disappeared beneath the water.

I took it as the insult it was meant to be and headed for the house. Something had to be done before that damned furry water bug ruined the rest of the trees.

If he was sprucing up for the reunion like everyone else in Mossy Creek, he was in for a surprise.

It was seven minutes after eleven when I pulled up in front of the I / Probably / Got / It and bolted from my truck. Derbert Koomer, the owner and sole resident of the establishment, had just settled down on the stool behind the counter with a salami and red onion sandwich and an RC Cola, anxious to watch *Days of Our Lives*. It was his favorite show.

Although he was addicted to soap operas, he violently denied it. I saw him through the store's windows. The minute he saw me driving up, he grabbed the remote and changed the channel to WMOS's new cable-access cooking show featuring Bubba Rice, some kind of caterer who'd just moved to town.

"Hey, Orville Gene! How's it hangin'?" Derbert asked, as I entered the store.

"I'm fine. Just tell me where you keep your shotgun shells."

Derbert pointed toward the back of the store. "Goin' huntin'?"

Knowing it was bad manners, I tried not to roll my eyes. Derbert Koomer was a good man and all, but he didn't have a lot going for him between the ears.

"No, I'm making a new set of wind chimes," I said.

"Really?" Derbert asked and took a bite of his sandwich.

"No, not really. Good lord, Derbert, you've watched so damned many of those girly shows that your brain has done turned to mush."

"I don't watch nothin' of the kind," Derbert muttered and pointed to the little black and white set on the wall behind the counter. "Looky there, it's a manly cooking show. You can't call Bubba Rice *girly*. He's liable to whip your butt with his mixing spoon."

As much as I enjoyed Derbert's company, I didn't have time to swap lies with him.

"The shells, Derbert. Where do you keep the shells?"

"Back yonder, past the chicken feed and the brown blocks of cow salt." Then curiosity got the best of him. "Whatcha' huntin'?"

"I need some 30 aught 30 shells. I got me a beaver."

Derbert took a big swig of RC Cola to wash down the salami and onion then felt compelled to point out the obvious. "If you done got the beaver, how come you need the shells?"

"I don't actually have it in hand. It's in my pond, but by God, it's not gonna be there long."

Derbert nodded, as if he completely understood the situation, although the story was still a little vague for his liking. He took another bite of sandwich, then slid off the stool and walked to the rack where an assortment of chips were on display to be sold, chose a bag of corn chips and sauntered back to the stool just as I came from the back of the store.

"I found them. Put 'em on the ticket."

Derbert nodded, frowning slightly as he added the cost of the box of shells to the growing list of charges that I was always making.

As soon as I began backing out of the drive, I just know Derbert grabbed the remote and switched channels back to *Days of Our Lives.*

"Okay, you flat-assed little varmint, stick your nose out of the water again, and you're gonna wind up plucking buckshot out of your tail."

It was a fine promise, and one I had every intention of carrying out, but the day was getting hot and laying flat on my belly on the pond dam was starting to get uncomfortable as hell. Besides that, I could feel ants crawling up my pant legs and across the back of my neck. Convinced that I might come to a certain amount of harm from the ants and the heat of the sun, I decided to make a move and headed for a tall grove of laurel near the edge of the pond. There was plenty of shade, and I could prop the barrel of my gun in the big shrubs to steady my aim. I slipped the barrel of the shotgun in a comfortable position, took careful aim toward the beaver lodge, and settled down to wait.

And wait.

And wait.

And wait.

I waited so long that my feet were numb and my knees were about to give out. I kept thinking how I'd been meaning to take off that extra thirty pounds I'd been carrying for close to ten years. Then I thought of the old commode under the tree in my front yard and wished I had it right now. It would make a real fine chair to sit in while I waited for the beaver to show.

By the time four o'clock came around, sweat was coming out from under my John Deere 'gimme' cap and running into my eyes. I was as miserable as a man could be. Early September in the Appalachian mountains of Georgia can be hotter than high Hell.

"I know you're there. Come on, you little water skunk. Show yourself."

No sooner had the words come out of my mouth than that beaver's head popped up like a cork float on a fishing line. At last, I thought, and steadied my aim.

The beaver swam out from under the woody dome and then crawled on top of the lodge like a big brown tick readying for a nice afternoon nap.

Like shooting sitting ducks.

My finger curled around the trigger of my daddy's old shotgun as I lined him up in my sites. And that was when I made my first mistake.

In my eagerness, I leaned forward and as I did, impaled my belly on the sharp stob of a broken laurel branch. It was the pain, coupled with the shock, that caused my shot to go wild, which of course pushed the stob in a little deeper.

"Ohmigod! Christallmighty!"

I jerked backward in reflex, which caused me to stumble into a clutch of briars. Thorns pierced my back and butt. I was caught just as tight in that laurel and briars as the tar baby had been caught in Brer' Rabbit's briar patch. I stood there bleeding and cussing while the beaver slipped into the water and disappeared from view.

With no small amount of patience, I set to freeing myself, then limped slowly toward the house, dragging Daddy's gun behind me. I needed some antiseptic and a good pair of tweezers and knew I had neither. This meant another trip to Derbert at the I

Probably Got It.

Derbert was stacking cans of motor oil onto a shelf when he heard the bell over the door jingle. He turned just in time to see me coming inside. The front of my shirt was dotted with droplets of what appeared to be drying blood, and when I ambled past where Derbert was standing, he could see that my backside looked about the same.

I looked like a man who'd been buckshot, both coming and going.

"Lord a' mercy, Orville Gene, what happened to you?"

I didn't want to go into details, so I shrugged it off. "Nothin' much. Got any Mercurochrome?"

Derbert scooted behind the counter and lifted a small bottle of the reddish-pink medicine from a shelf.

"And some tweezers?"

Derbert frowned and then rummaged through a drawer beneath the counter.

"I ain't got any for sale, but I'll loan you these," he said.

I didn't want to let on that it was paining me to reach for the stuff, so I waited until he bagged up the items and put the bag in my hand.

"Put it on the ticket, old buddy."

Derbert nodded an okay, then watched me as I limped back toward the truck. He couldn't figure out what was going on at my place. If I'd been shooting at that beaver as I'd claimed I was going to do, then how in blazes had I managed to shoot myself in the belly and the butt, and all at the same time?

Derbert, being the busybody that he was, couldn't keep the news to himself. He picked up the phone. He had just enough time to tell his neighbor, Foxer Atlas, about what he'd just seen. Foxer was a right good hand with woodworking and such. Maybe he'd get a notion to carve out a laughing beaver in my honor and sell it for a fine penny on reunion day.

Or maybe Derbert just couldn't resist talking.

I was stark naked and standing in front of the full-length mirror in my bedroom, trying to pick thorns out of my chest and back, but with little success. Finally, I tossed the tweezers aside and then stood and stared at myself, wondering how I'd come to this. It wasn't so much that I minded turning forty last year, or that my fine, hard physique had gone to jelly-soft flesh. And I didn't mind that these days I had more skin on my head than I had hair, or that I was probably never going to find a woman who suited me enough to get married. But it did gall me no end that I'd failed to dislodge that danged beaver from his pond.

If I'd known what Derbert was about, I would have been even more distressed.

The next morning, I was careful as I crawled out of bed. The thorns that I hadn't been able to get out were red and sore. I staggered to the mirror, scratching at the hair circling my belly button. I frowned at my image.

"Well, I look like crap."

Having stated the obvious, I swabbed the thorn punctures with some more Mercurochrome and said a few choice curse words as I put on some clean clothes. I knew enough about beavers to know that once you shoot at them, you'll never be able to get a good second shot again. Beavers aren't all that good to look at and even less tasty to eat, but they're smart. However, I had options. Plenty of options.

The trap I'd borrowed from Smokey Lincoln last night was certain to do the job. With him being a forest ranger and all, I figured he knew most of what there was to know about the woods and wood critters. I also thought that Smokey would volunteer to set the trap for me, but all he did was show me how to do it myself. It was one of those new kinds that only catches the beaver and doesn't hurt him. What was the world coming to?

After a hearty breakfast, I called old Duke, and we made our way to the pond. I was still a bit sore, but moving around fine under the pain and pretty optimistic about what I was about to do.

When we reached the pond, Duke took to barking at the beaver lodge, as if he'd just noticed it was there, and to make matters worse, he wouldn't stop. I knew for a fact that he'd been swimming in the pond on a regular basis, 'cause he always came back to the house wet, so I wasn't too impressed with his attitude. Sort of a "too little, too late" guard dog stunt.

I chunked a stick at him and told him to shut up. Duke took the hint and wandered off into the trees. Later, I heard him thundering through the brush and figured some rabbit had seen its last sunrise.

I waded into the water and began going about the business of securing the cage with some bait. I fastened the long end of the chain to a big stake just like Smokey told me to do, then drove the stake deep into the mud. The next step was to set the trap on a little hummock of debris so I waded out about eight feet from the lodge. I set the cage up and positioned the trap door. I was just about to move back when the water behind me commenced to a fierce churning, coupled with a series of excited barks.

I knew it was Duke. Without turning around, I started to give him what for when I looked up and found myself eyeball to eyeball with the beaver, hisself.

It was hard to say who got the most excited, Duke, the beaver, or me. There was this moment where everything sort of slid into slow motion. I thought of the trap and reached for old Duke as the beaver hit the water with his tail.

A huge plume of water splashed in my face as Duke jumped in the middle of my back. I staggered forward, flailed wildly, grabbed the trap for balance, then staggered backward to steady myself, and fell down, the cage going with me. I felt a crunch. The sound of the trap door was slightly muffled by the water, but there was nothing quiet about the pain radiating up my ankle and toward my knee.

"Christ all mighty! Oh Lordy. Oh no!"

I was chin deep in water, sitting in mud, with my ankle caught fast in Smokey Lincoln's trap. Duke seemed to think it was all a big game and commenced to licking me in the face. I grabbed at the chain, but I'd done too good a job fastening it down and it wouldn't come loose. I wished it had been a mite longer — at least long enough to strangle old Duke. He took a big drink of water then bounded out of the pond, pausing only long enough to shake himself dry before giving chase at something else in the woods. As I watched him disappear, I thought of Lassie.

Lassie always went for help in situations like this.

Something told me old Duke wasn't geared quite that way.

It set me to wondering how long it took to die from a beaver trap and decided I'd rather not have the title of my obituary read *Stupid Is As Stupid Does.*

I managed to drag myself upright and tried to get my foot out of the trap while keeping an eye out for the beaver, which by the way, was a lot bigger up close than he appeared to be from across the pond.

After ten minutes of sweating profusely — which I didn't know a man could do while soaking wet — and cursing at the top of my lungs to keep from crying — because a grown man shouldn't cry — I managed to drag myself and the big cage out of the pond. Using one of the willow branches the beaver had chewed off as a pry bar, I did get my boot out of the trap's door, then proceeded to beat the piss out of said trap for a good five minutes with that branch, just because I needed to hit something, and it was the closest thing within reach.

I thought about tossing the trap in the pond, but since it belonged to Smokey Lincoln, I threw the cage over my shoulder instead and hobbled my way up the hill.

By the time I got to the house, Duke was asleep beside the commode and my ankle was so swollen that I had to cut the boot off my foot. I sat on the porch step, contemplating the loss of a good pair of boots and knew that my troubles were only beginning. I needed to doctor my ankle, and there wasn't a drop of liniment in the house. This meant another trip to the I Probably Got It.

Too weary to bother changing clothes, I hobbled into the house to get a bedroom slipper, got my daddy's old cane out of the hall closet, and headed back out the door, wishing I'd taken a snort of corn liquor before I set about making the short drive to the four-corner crossroad where Derbert had his store. It was between me and Mossy Creek, and unless I was in need of a lot of groceries, I rarely drove all the way into town.

Especially when I expected to be laughed at.

Derbert was watching *The Young and the Restless* when my pickup turned off the road in front of his store. I glimpsed him grab the remote and turn off the TV.

"Dadgumit," Derbert muttered as I walked in. "You, again."

When he saw the condition of my clothes and the fact that I was walking with a cane, he came off the stool and headed for the door, holding it wide as I hobbled in. "Have mercy, boy! What happened to you?"

I just shook my head, unwilling to go into details. "That beaver is meaner than he looked."

Derbert's eyes bugged. "You mean to tell me that beaver did this to you?"

I chose not to mention that I'd done most of it to myself. "Hey, Derbert, you got any liniment left over from last Fourth of July when the Fiesty Felines from Bigelow ran that marathon past here?"

Derbert thought for a moment, smiling. "God bless sports bras," he said, as he headed for the back of the store. He must have been remembering the very buxom females from Bigelow's Aerobic Center for Mature Women, who'd thundered past his store that day.

I followed him because sitting was still uncomfortable, although I thought the remaining thorns in my butt had probably benefited from the dunking I'd just taken. The way I figured it, they'd eventually fester up and pop out, or take root. Either way, I wasn't asking anybody to pick stickers out of my behind.

"Yep, here's that liniment," Derbert said. "How much you want?"

"The biggest you got."

Derbert handed it over. "That must be some beaver. He's drawed blood on you and has now got you so crippled you can't even walk. You're liable to run up quite a bill before you get rid of that pest."

I ignored the hint about paying any on his bill, and Derbert was forced to "put it on the ticket" with all the other charges I'd been making.

However, as soon as I left, Derbert apparently couldn't let the latest news pass without sharing it, and must have been back on the phone to Foxer Atlas, who then passed the information on to Eleanor Abercrombie when she came to pick up her *Don't Pick The Flowers* sign that she'd hired him to paint. She was sick and tired of everyone messing up her fine display of annuals in the town square and figured if people didn't have enough upbringing not to mess in the flower beds with the reunion festivities coming up, then what they needed was a sign.

By the time Eleanor was through telling the story to Sue Ora and Katie Bell down at *The Mossy Creek Gazette,* the scratches from the thorns had become real wounds, and the cane I had been using had turned into a pair of crutches, and the beaver's presence had taken on a threat that could even spill over into the town itself. One never could be too careful about beavers.

Katie Bell knew what the headline for her weekly column would be as she gathered up her camera and headed out to my place. As my mother used to say, "A picture was worth a thousand words." The way Katie must have figured it, getting a picture of the monster's lodge would be a fine accompaniment for the gossipy piece she was going to write. Maybe she could even get me to stand on the shore with my bandages and crutches, if I wasn't too crippled up. I could see it all now.

ORVILLE GENE SIMPLE OUTWITTED
BY DENIZEN OF THE DEEP

432

Maybe the story would even get picked up by the Associated Press.

Fortunately, I was not at home when Katie Bell drove up, and she had to settle for a shot of the pond with the two felled trees and the beaver lodge, minus the beaver, of course. She left in a hurry, anxious to get the film developed and unaware that I was still over at Smokey Lincoln's place, returning the trap.

"How did the trap work?" Smokey asked.

I didn't want to let on too much about what had happened, although I knew he was staring at my foot.

"Not so good. The durned thing didn't work right. New fangled junk. Humane trap, my fanny. What it did to my foot wasn't humane."

Smokey nodded like he wasn't going to argue the point, especially with a man who looked like he'd come out on the bad side of an angry bobcat.

"So, what are you going to do now?" Smokey asked.

"I don't know. I'm thinkin' of blasting him out. Might get me some dynamite. I don't plan to kill him, just make his ears ring."

Smokey frowned. "Before you get too violent, I heard tell of something else you might want to try. Can't say how well it works, but there's more than one old-timer I've heard swear by it."

By now, I was desperate. I was willing to try anything, especially if it didn't hurt.

"What's that?" I asked, then wondered why Smokey gave me such a funny look.

Suddenly, he leaned forward in a confidential manner. "They say that if you put your scent all over his lodge, it will insult him enough that he'll get up and move."

I snorted before I thought and then took out my hanky and pretended to be blowing my nose. It wasn't nice to be disdainful of a man who was just trying to help, even if the suggestion — and the man — were sort of dumb. I mean, last year Smokey Lincoln had been stupid enough to let Tag Garner steal Maggie Hart's affections from under Smokey's nose. And Tag had a blue streak in his hair.

"Scent? How is a fella supposed to put scent on a lodge?" I asked. "Bury his underwear on it or somethin'?"

Smokey shook his head. "Nope, but you're on the right track. What you do is . . . the next time you got to make a trip to the outhouse, do it on top of his lodge instead."

I heard my voice rising a couple of octaves, even as I was trying to stop it, but it was too late. "You mean I'm supposed to do my

. . . my . . . business . . . on top of the beaver lodge . . . out in the water . . . in front of God and ever'body? No way! Anyone heard I did somethin' like that, and they'd have me committed."

Smokey shrugged. "Well, don't say I never told you. Anyway, thanks for bringing back my trap. Sorry it didn't work."

I got in my car and drove away, but I couldn't get his advice out of my mind. It sounded stupid, but a little poop on the lodge was a lot cheaper than dynamite. And, considering the luck I'd been having, probably safer, as well. Considering the fact that I've always been regular as clockwork, the business of doing my business on the beaver lodge didn't pose any kind of a problem that I could see.

So, on my way back home, I pulled in to the I Probably Got It.

"Hey, Derbert. Gimme about six rolls of toilet paper and put 'em on the ticket, will ya?"

"What's the matter, Orville Gene? You eat too much late-summer sweet corn?"

"Naw, but I'm gonna catch the beaver for sure, this time," I said, as Derbert sacked up the toilet paper and marked it on my bill.

"With toilet paper?"

435

I smiled. "In a manner of speaking."

I headed home with renewed hope, unaware that Derbert was already spreading the news that I was losing my grip on reality.

The next morning dawned with a promise of a real nice day. I made my coffee and had a whole cup before I grabbed me a fresh roll of T.P. and headed out the back door at a fine clip, figuring that I should reach the pond just in time. Duke started to follow, but I sent him back to the porch. I didn't need a replay of yesterday's folly.

My belly was in a fine grumble by the time the pond came in view. I stopped at the edge of the water and was reaching for the buckle on my overalls when I heard someone calling my name.

"Good morning, Orville Gene!"

I was gawking and all the while remembering that my mama had taught me it wasn't polite to stare, but seeing Mayor Ida and ancient little Adele Clearwater sitting in their lawn chairs on the pond dam with binoculars in their laps took me aback a great deal. And if that wasn't enough, Maggie Hart had spread a blanket on the ground and was smearing jelly on a slice of bread.

"Ladies," I muttered and wondered how long I could hold my need to poop. "Is there something I can do for you?"

"Oh no," Adele chirped. "We just read about your ordeal in the paper this morning and thought we'd come and see for ourselves." She waved one of those little throwaway cameras in the air. "See. I brought my own camera, just in case that monster shows his face."

"Monster? What monster?" Then I zeroed in on the rest of what she'd said and heard the whine setting into my voice as I asked. "What ordeal in what paper?"

"Why, the *Gazette,* of course. You made the headlines, Orville Gene! It's all everyone's talking about."

I made a silent vow to kill Derbert Koomer first chance that I got, then waved goodbye at the women, and made a run for the house just as Maggie passed Adele a grape jelly sandwich.

Mayor Ida got a sassy, smile-biting look on her face. "Problem, Orville Gene?" I will say that I didn't have to change my britches, but it was close. Real close.

That, however, wasn't the extent of the *problem* I now faced. I wasn't the kind of man who went more than once a day. If I was going to follow through on the plan, I'd have to wait until tomorrow for another try. Only thanks to Katie Bell's yen for news, I might never have the privacy I needed to follow through.

All morning, I sat on the porch watching first one set of sight-seers and then another making their way toward my pond. Everyone wanted to see the denizen of the deep and the man who'd survived it. Rosie Montgomery, who cooks at Mama's All You Can Eat Café, even brought me one of her famous chocolate meringue pies, and Nona McPherson, who subs at Mossy Creek Elementary when she's not in training for her next body-building contest, stopped by after that with a plate of deviled eggs.

Personally, I wanted to wring Katie Bell's neck, but what was done was done. I did make a vow never to wonder again if I'd made a mistake by not marrying. Women were nothing but trouble, even the ones who could cook. Of course, Derbert had done his part in starting all the hoo-haw, but I figured it was because he watched too much TV.

It wasn't until mid-afternoon that an idea struck me, and I knew when it hit, I had the answer I needed. I hobbled into the house and headed for the refrigerator. It was all jumbled up and full of cartons and cans that I'd been meaning to throw away. But I distinctly remembered the juice I'd bought after the pre-dart tournament party at O'Day's Pub the week before. I'd had way too much beer and way too much cheese. If you've never had a combination of a constipation and hangover, you don't know what sick is. Anyway, I was plugged up for two days until I thought to get me some prune juice. I knew there was bound to be some still left.

It wasn't until I moved the jug of buttermilk on the bottom shelf that I saw it. *Madeira Prune.* Thick and sweet and the best natural laxative on earth.

I pulled it out and took a big swig, thinking to myself that it was thicker than I remembered, but I figured age had something to do with it, and it went down just fine. I checked my watch against the amount of remaining sun and then decided to hurry things up and took a big glass out of the cupboard, filled it full to the top and downed it in three gulps. The way I figured, by the time it got dark, the gawkers would all have gone home, and I could do what I had to do under the shelter of night. By morning, that danged beaver would be gone and I could rest easy, knowing that man was the ultimate animal after all.

Sundown came. The sight-seers went. Duke settled down under the porch while I had fried potatoes and greens for supper, along with a small brick of cornbread, slathered in butter. Along about nine, I felt the first signs that the juice had been working and grabbed my flashlight and a roll of toilet paper.

Halfway to the pond, I realized my timing was going to be off and stopped beside a bush. A couple of minutes later, I was buckling up my overalls and regretting the fact that I'd had such a big glass of juice, when I realized there was life in me yet. Hopeful that I still might make it to the pond after all, I started off at a fast clip.

I won't bore you with the grisly details except to say that I stopped four more times before I made it to the pond, and by then, I was getting nervous. The roll of toilet paper was getting smaller by the hour while the grumbles in my belly showed no signs of letting up.

It wasn't until I was standing at the edge of the pond and shining the flashlight into the water that I realized I was not only going to have to wade back in the dang-blasted water, but I was also going to have to crawl up on the lodge, and it was growing wider and taller by the day.

However, I hadn't come this far to quit. I stepped into the water. It didn't take as long to get to the beaver lodge as I thought. Partly because I'd forgotten about the possibility of water moccasins, and partly because I didn't want to go in my pants. I crawled up on that lodge, clawing and grabbing at sticks until I was standing smack dab in the middle.

"I've got you now, you over-grown rat."

It was a fine moment and one I'll never forget, right up to the place where I reached for the toilet paper and watched it roll into the water.

"No."

Even as I said it, I knew I was beating a dead horse. The paper was a thick, sodden mess and sinking fast, and I wasn't much better. However, I still had my flashlight, and I wasn't about to give up. I shined the light around the lodge, then began grabbing at some of the willow leaves and greenery that were still clinging to the limbs. It wasn't the first time I'd depended on Mother Nature for help, and I wasn't averse to doing it again.

A short while later, I was striding up the hill toward the house, about five pounds lighter, but a satisfied man, confident that by morning, my troubles would be over.

Again, I had counted my chickens before they'd hatched.

By morning, the itch on my butt that had started around midnight had turned into a full-fledged disaster. And with daylight, I was able to diagnose my problem. My only conclusion was that there must have been poison ivy tangled up in the leaves that I'd used in lieu of paper. Everyone had laughed over Amos Royden's bout with poison ivy back in the spring. Now it would be my turn. I couldn't bear to wear clothes, let alone stand or sit, and by daylight, I was also out of calamine lotion. I knew what I had to do, even if it meant lowering myself even more. I reached for the phone.

Derbert was watching *Regis & Kelly.* I heard it in the background just before he hit the mute button on the remote. "I Probably Got It, Derbert speaking."

"Derbert, it's me, Orville Gene."

"Hey, Orville Gene. You've gone and become a real celebrity since I saw you last."

"No thanks to you," I muttered, then held my tongue. No sense antagonizing the one man I needed to help me. "I need you to do me a favor."

Probably feeling guilty that he'd been found out, Derbert quickly said, "Anything for you, little buddy. What do you need?"

"I need you to bring me some calamine

lotion. I'm kind of laid up and can't drive until . . . uh . . . things heal a bit."

"Sure thing, Orville Gene!" Then Derbert must have realized what I had just said. "Say, you don't mean that beaver done put you in bed?"

"In a manner of speaking, I guess he did just that. Oh . . . and about that lotion. . . ."

"Yeah, yeah, I know. Put it on the ticket."

"Right."

Wondering how long it would take Derbert to get there and making a mental note to pay some on my bill real soon before my credit was cut off, I grimaced and scratched as he hung up the phone. To my relief, Derbert arrived within fifteen minutes, expressing his condolences while trying to figure out exactly what awful thing had befallen me that I couldn't bear to tell. All Derbert knew was that I was lying in bed and covered up to my chin, and there was toilet paper hanging from trees and bushes all over the back pasture.

He left the calamine lotion with a promise to bring more if needed and headed back to the store. I didn't doubt he was wondering exactly how to tell Foxer Atlas what was going on now without committing an out and out lie.

■ ■ ■ ■

By nightfall, I had gotten some relief and was lying in bed, feeling sorry for myself as I listened to the rain pounding down on the roof. If my trip to the beaver lodge hadn't worked before the nightfall, it was too late to worry about it now. I was getting so desperate that I even thought about going into town the next morning and putting my money into that gypsy fortune-teller machine and seeing if she had any new ideas.

Along about midnight, the storm had increased in intensity, and I was wondering if I dared make a run for the storm cellar. But the longer I stood at the window watching the rain lashing against the panes, the more convinced I became that I'd rather die in bed. The way my luck was running, I'd probably die from a lightning strike before I ever reached the cellar door.

No sooner had I thought about the lightning, than one big old sucker hit the ground and lit up the night. I caught myself flinching as the windows rattled.

"All right, all right, Lord. I get the message. You're the one in charge. I'm going back to bed and that's a fact. If I was meant to share quarters with a beaver, then so be it."

It was way past sunrise when I got out of bed. I doctored myself good with the lotion again, then put on my oldest and loosest pair of overalls and headed for the pond. I had to check things out, if for nothing more than peace of mind.

Duke whined as I stepped off of the porch.

"All right. You can come," I told him. "But no sneak attacks, now . . . you hear?"

Duke barked once to show his appreciation, sniffed the backside of my coveralls, then sneezed before bounding out in front of me.

A little indignant that man's best friend was passing judgment on my doctored behind, I refused to throw him a stick to fetch.

"Yeah, you think that smells bad. You need to be in my shoes, old boy. You'd be too danged sore to sneeze."

My mood stayed sour all the way to the pond. Partly because I realized the toilet paper I'd used that night in the dark was not only visible from the house, but also from the road. I could only imagine what Sue Ora would make out of it on top of my commode. And added to that, the rain had pounded the paper into the bushes and the grass until it looked vaguely like some vast paper mache project gone horribly wrong.

I stomped and I fumed all the way to the pond where my disposition took a quick turn to the good. I stared at the place where the beaver lodge was supposed to be and started to grin. There was nothing left of it but a floating pile of limbs and sticks, drifting to and fro upon the surface of the pond as the run-off from last night's rain continued to flow.

Duke's occasional yap suddenly turned into a vigorous bark as he bounded past me and plowed into the water. Before I could stop him, he was swimming toward the middle of the pond, then through the floating debris with some purpose in mind that I couldn't see.

It wasn't until I saw him clamp onto a brown, sodden mass that I realized he had captured my beaver. That it was obviously dead didn't matter a whit. What counted was that the war was over.

Duke swam toward the shore with it held in his mouth, as proudly as any fine Retriever might do. That Duke was a hound with a suspicious pedigree was, at the moment, beside the point.

"Here, boy! Come here."

Duke dropped that sucker at my feet and

then shook himself dry.

"Good boy," I praised and patted him hard on the back — just behind the shoulders — the way he liked it best. "Let's go to the house!"

Duke took one last look at the beaver, whined once to let me know I owed him big, and headed away from the pond at a lope, his big ears flopping as he ran.

I picked up the beaver by the tail and as I did, saw a large, jagged stripe of black down the middle of its back. Curious, I twisted a bit of the hair between my fingers and was more than surprised when they came off in my hand. It felt stiff and dry, unlike the rest of the pelt, and when I lifted it to my nose, it smelled of smoke.

Immediately, I thought of the lightning I'd seen hit the ground, then looked back at what was left of that lodge. My mouth fell open.

Lightning.

It was the only explanation.

As sure as I was standing there, I knew that the lodge and that beaver had been struck by that lightning. I looked up at the bright and shining blue of heaven and right then and there made a promise to myself to attend church more regular.

"Well, Lord, I'm right beholden, and

considering the issue Katie Bell would make of this . . . like probably calling it a miracle and designating Great-Granddaddy's farm as some holy shrine . . . I won't tell if you won't."

I took my beaver to the barn, and even though I was feeling the need for more calamine lotion, I skinned him right then and there and tacked his big, burn-striped hide to the barn door for everyone to see.

And that's the truth of it all, and I'm only confessing it now because I got saved last Sunday in church and don't see as how it seems right to let people keep on thinking I felled the beast alone. Besides, I don't want the animal lovers to sic the Bigelow County Humane Society on me. I tried my best to keep that beaver alive. I doubt he could say the same for his intentions toward *me*.

And I've also been thinking that when the time arrives, I just might attend the Mossy Creek reunion after all. Just because I didn't graduate from the high school don't make me any less of a hero.

I am, after all, the man who survived the Creekite Denizen of the Deep.

IDA

READING FROM THE HEART

It's an old Southern tradition, keeping up the graves of loved ones. But even in Mossy Creek — where traditions are lovingly set in stone and even the most peculiar rituals are accepted with a wink — my son Rob and I are said to have gotten a little carried away.

Rob reads books to his dead father. And so do I.

People regularly spot one or the other of us sitting on a handsome bench under a canopy of oak trees at the cemetery. A book in hand, we read to Jeb Walker, our voices begging to turn back time with the soft recitation of stories Jeb loved. In summertime, birds flit around us, filching berries off a fat Mahonia shrub beside the dark-gray stone over Jeb's grave, as if they knew he had always been a tough but forgiving man.

Rob showed up one Saturday afternoon while I was reading from a ruffled, spine-broken paperback of Jeb's favorite John D. McDonald novel. "This guy writes about real life," Jeb liked to say. "Morals and mayhem, sloe-eyed women with no shy ideas, men who'll risk their own hide to defend what they believe in, and cigar-smoke philosophy. Perfect." Yes, that description had fit Jeb's own life — and our life together. I had been his sloe-eyed woman.

"I need to talk to you, Mother," our son said, sitting down next to me with his shoulders hunched inside his father's old leather bomber jacket. Rob laid his big, competent hands on the knees of nice gray slacks, and once again I wondered why he wanted to spend twelve hours a day under the fluorescent lights of our tame department store. My son, the president of Hamilton's. Selling home goods and goods for the heart. Such an honorable but conservative life to lead.

"You have some kind of trouble at the store to discuss?" I asked.

He frowned. "You think I'm always consumed by work. I'm not."

"What *are* you consumed by, then?" I closed the novel and laid it flat on the lap of my pale wool slacks, then pulled a large cashmere scarf closer around my shoulders, like a shawl against a slight chill in the October air.

Rob looked into a distance only he could see. "If Dad had lived — if he'd been there when the high school burned down, he'd have been ashamed of me."

After a long, stunned silence, I finally managed, "Your dad loved you like his own life. He was always proud of you —"

"Not if he'd known what I did that night."

My breath caught in my throat. I laid a hand on his arm — on the softly burnished leather of the same jacket that had kept Jeb Walker's strong arms warm and safely around us. I had long suspected that our son harbored something deep and painful, but nothing to do with the fire at the high school.

"All right. Then tell the truth to your dad and me," I said. "Read to him from your conscience."

Rob bowed his head and told me what he'd done the night of the fire at Mossy Creek High.

From: Katie Bell
To: Lady Victoria Salter Stanhope

Dear Vick:

Autumn is here in full-blown color under crisp, bright skies, now. Normally, it's my favorite time of year, but this year the whole town seems edgy and excited and weird. Everyone seems distracted. Ida worries me. She's got this dangerous look — as if she's ready to get the guns out and go hunting. Sandy and Amos confer behind the closed door of his office so often that people whisper about them — not the rumor of any romantic shenanigans, but what are they up to?

Rainey paces the floor behind the curtains of her shop and keeps to herself. Rob Walker looks haunted. And the other day, up at a farm in the Bailey Mill community, Dr. Hank Blackshear yelled at an ornery calf he was treating for a barbed-wire cut. Hank Blackshear yelled at an animal.

You *know* something's worrying him if he loses his temper with one of God's creatures.

Then, on top of it all, one of my favorite people, Eula Mae Whit, decided to die. Or pretended to. Just to draw attention, I think.

Like Millicent Hart, Miss Eula Mae swears she knows what really happened the night of the high school fire. "But that's between me, the culprits, and God," Miss Eula Mae insists. Once you get to know Miss Eula Mae the way I do, you'll see why she's lived so long. She never caters to anybody's rules but her own. Not even God's.

Or Willard Scott's.

Katie

EULA MAE

WHERE I BELONG

Sometimes it's good to look back on what might have been because what "might have been" might still be possible. But you have to take the chance by looking, first. And that's the hard part.

My name is Eula Mae Whit, and I'm the oldest living native and resident of Mossy Creek. The reason I know this is because when I was a little girl, my great-grandma showed me the tree she'd planted the day I was born. It's big now. The only living symbol of my one hundred years of life on this earth. Besides me, of course.

Might become the one and only, I thought the other day. 'Cause I'd been taking short, shallow breaths since midnight.

The light of my life, my great-great-granddaughter Estelle, stood by the window of my private room at Magnolia Manor, looking disgusted. She probably didn't like the fact that my granddaughter, Clara, was sitting by my side, holding my hand, making it all sweaty in her rush to see me dead.

Clara had gone down to Bigelow and brought back a minister from a church who was now into the second verse of *Bringing in the Sheaves* and singing it right in my ear. It sounded like *Bringing in the Sheep* to me, maybe because one of my cousins' granddaughters, Carmel, had done nothing for months but talk about the old high school and how somebody set Samson the sheep on fire and how the truth was going to come out, you bet.

So I heard 'sheep,' not 'sheaves.'

"Sing, Miss Eula Mae," the minister kept urging. "Rise up out of your coma and let your soul sing as a lamb of God."

Last I checked, I was less a warbling lamb than a dried-up raisin. Frankly, I prefer to be referred to as a fruit because fruit keeps me regular, whereas meat got me uninvited to the pinochle tournament at Magnolia Manor five years ago. I still carried a grudge about that. Gas was just a part of life, and those old fools better start to understand you didn't get to be my age by keepin' your innards all blocked up!

Anyway, so there I was, checked into a hospice bed at Magnolia Manor on my one-hundredth birthday, waiting to die. Partly because I was tired of hearing about sheep, but also because Willard Scott had said my name and showed my picture on national television that morning.

I have to say I looked right nice on TV with my last real tooth so handsome next to my pearly white dentures. I began bettin' I'd die by midnight because tradition and Willard Scott have never let a Whit down. All the women in my family die on their hundredth birthday.

Except Cousin Chicken.

Chicken only missed it on a technicality, though Willard spoke her name on his Peacock Station. I really do believe Chicken caught Willard's eye the way no other Mossy Creek woman has. Willard said Chicken was pretty as a picture! Now that's high praise from a white man, as we Whits like to say with one eyebrow raised.

Anyway, Chicken drove her chicken-legged self to the baptismal pond behind Mossy Creek First Baptist to make a request on her future living arrangements. Frankly, I didn't think God was going to grant it because there were saints more deserving than Chicken. But what I thought didn't stop her. She went right on and asked that her eternal home be right next door to Jesus' house.

The rest was pure speculation, but we thought she got so caught up in the Holy Ghost dance that she slipped, fell in the water and drowned. Chicken wasn't found until the next day, but because she made sweet potato pie so good it would make you call on the Lord, I let her in what I call *The Dead Hundred Club.*

I used to think once Willard Scott mentioned your name, your number was up no matter where you lived in the country. But then I heard through the Whit family gossip and information line that Willard was sweet on Southern women. Especially if they were from Mossy Creek. I watched the Peacock Station everyday to see if he was going to be on because Mossy Creek women always got that cute little jelly label.

I was ninety-five when Clara told me Willard was married. For that bad news, I mixed a little concoction in with her soup, and she sat on the toilet for the rest of her stay. She left on the first bus heading north. You couldn't trust a Whit who lived above the Virginia state line.

After Willard announced my birthday, I called the ambulance and got myself over to Magnolia Manor because, well, dying while standing at the mailbox could have made me sound like a show off on the Bereavement Report, and anybody that knew me knew I didn't do things in a show-offy kind of way.

I was just bold. Straight as an arrow. Honest in a righteous way. Dignified to a fault. Truth be told, I scared the daylights out of people. And I was glad about it. I'm the oldest black person in this area. And in a hundred years, I'd seen just about everything. So people didn't mess with me.

Only, I couldn't say the same for my relatives, like Clara, from up North.

They had no respect for Southerners. No respect for people about to die. Clara's sixty-five. Wore elastic in her pants and a two-inch heel on her shoe. She was just a little too sassy for my taste.

Personally, I didn't like pants. I preferred the floral dresses from the Bigelow Wal-Mart. Breezy and easy to whip up if you had to go in a hurry. But not dignified if you were lying on the floor dead and your hem was hiked a little too high.

Clara didn't used to be so unbearably Northern, but after she moved up to New Jersey she lost all the 'country' we tried to instill in her here in Mossy Creek. Why, by now she couldn't kill a chicken if her family was starving. Worse than that, she'd forgotten the importance of land and home and heritage. She'd forgotten what being buried on family land in Mossy Creek meant to a Whit. To me.

All my family was here. Mama. Daddy. Gran. Poppy and all the greats before them. True, the first few came because they didn't have a choice. But I chose to stay.

Clara thought my last day on earth was my hundredth birthday, and she was "struck with a sense of nostalgia," so she said. Hence her visit. But what she wanted was to take my bony body back up North to be buried in the cold, hard ground next to people I didn't even know!

"They ain't my kin," I told her. "Besides, I heard they don't respect the dead up North. When you're being paraded through town to your final restin' place, none of them bow their heads or cover their hearts with their hats. They just stand in the street drinkin' soda pop and planning how they gonna get your furniture out the back door. Heathens. That's what I heard."

"That's just not so, Grandmama," Clara insisted. But she couldn't fool an old lady like me. She used to be a true Whit. Now she's Clara The Heathen.

So I was lying there at Magnolia Manor, and Clara gripped my hand, and I parted my eyes just enough to squint and see what she was doing. Sneaking to take my pulse, that's what. The heifer. All she wanted was my land. She'd probably already got my flower bed dug up, my furniture on the side of the road, lemonade on the window sill, and the deed in her beefeater-sized hand!

My land was worth a ton of money. Bigelow Realty must have wooed her from New Jersey because they've been wantin' to steal Mossy Creek land from true Mossy Creekites for generations, and they would take every slimy chance they got. But they wouldn't get Whit land. Not as long as I was still here taking slow, shallow breaths.

Clara's sweating hand was a terrible trigger for my bladder, and I couldn't bear many more verses of *Bringing in the Sheep.* I was beginning to fear I had to give up my ruse of dying. I wasn't in a coma, but the minister's sheep song *had* given me a headache bad enough to make me *wish* I were.

I was a little disappointed not to die. I had hoped to see Josephine Baker dance with Sammy Davis Jr. my first day up in the great beyond, but I wouldn't disrespect God's enrollment policy by being anxious.

I had only about another minute on the bladder, so I sat up and grabbed the hymnal from the minister.

Clara screamed so loud she gave me a nice

soprano note, and I started singing, *"Bringing in the sheaves, bringing in the sheaves, hi ho the d-a-r-i-o, bringing in the sheaves."* They oughta have been glad I didn't sing *sheep.*

I swung my legs over the side of the bed just as the minister fainted to the floor.

As I scuttled to the bathroom and got ready to shut the door, the look on Clara's face was worth me wetting my *Depends* diaper. Her chubby cheeks were so puckered up she looked like a fallen chocolate cake.

I felt real joy in my heart.

Over by the window, Estelle was laughing so hard she nearly sat down on the floor. I smiled at my great-great-granddaughter, closed the bathroom door, and locked it. You never know when them Bigelowans were going to launch a sneak attack. They liked to catch you when you were vulnerable. Right then, my *Depends* were around my ankles.

I got put out of Magnolia Manor.

On the drive home, Clara had me so hemmed up in a coat, I thought I'd suffocate or melt to death. We were in Clara's car, a Chevy of some sort, and we drove through the streets of Mossy Creek I'd known since I was a little girl. Clara just wouldn't give up and leave me alone, dead or alive.

"I don't want to go to New Jersey, Clara. You can just take me home and let me die there."

"Grandmama, you'd like New Jersey if you tried it. We have a big house."

"So do I."

"A nice yard."

"Me too."

"We have cabs."

"What's that?" I asked, 'cause I suspected she was trying to pull a fast one on me.

"That's when you call someone on the phone to take you where you have to go."

I sat there blinking. "Why wouldn't I just go across the road and ask Henry Louis's retarded boy Al to take me? Or call Amos Royden over at the police station? Y'all don't have slow folks or policemen up there that don't mind carryin' an old lady to the store?"

"Grandmama —"

"Just as I suspected, them city folk ain't nothing but a bunch of uncharitable triflin' heathens!" My short shallow breaths returned, so I closed my eyes. "Take me the long way home. Estelle?"

My great-great-granddaughter leaned over the back seat and lowered her voice. She knew I was old, but my ears were as keen as a bird dog's. "Yes, Great Gran?"

"Write down the time. I left Magnolia Manor at two-forty three in the afternoon."

"Great Gran, why do you want me to record what time we left? You're just fine."

"Everybody in this town knows Whit women die on their one hundredth birthday. Today is *still* my day. Just because I wasn't one clogged artery from dropping dead, they threw me out, triflin' hussies. Used to be, you could stay in the hospital until you decided to go home. Now they throw old ladies in the street. And I heard, about three years ago, they stopped circumcising boys."

I shuddered at the thought.

Something happened to Estelle's nose, so she sat back with her hand over it. I didn't mind. Snot happens.

"Grandmama —" Clara patted my hand, "You're getting excited for nothing. Aren't the trees pretty? It's leaf season."

My granddaughter had that tone her mother Alma, God rest her soul, used to take when she was tired of me making my point. But the thing was, I knew what I was talking about. I decided to change the subject. "Over there, Estelle, that's where I went the first time women were allowed to vote. I was young, then."

The old Mossy Creek post office had been torn down years ago, but I could still see everything as if it were happening right then.

"My Mama and I were working as maids for the Hamilton's," I said to my only living relatives. "We got done in a hurry and planned to leave on time for the two-mile walk from Hamilton Farm into town. I was too young to vote, but I wanted to accompany Mama.

"Lots of hell was going on in the world, but Mama was proud to go vote. I remember us leaving, and Mrs. Hamilton stood on her veranda. Mayor Ida's grandmama, the one everybody called Big Miss Ida. As we started off, Mrs. Hamilton called us back. 'Girls,' she said. 'Y'all going to vote?'

"We just nodded. We didn't know what she would say. She came down the steps and stood in front of us. 'Watch your mother's back,' she said. Then she pressed a cold piece of steel in my hand. 'Put it up.' I quickly hid the little pistol in the pocket of my skirt.

"I was scared and Mama's bony knees were waving in the wind. 'Don't take that gun out unless you have to use it', Mrs. Hamilton said, 'but if you do have to use it, they'll have to lock me up with you.' "

I'd been so scared, I couldn't speak.

"What did she mean, Great Gran?"

"She meant for us to come back in one piece, and if we had to shoot somebody, then —" I merely shrugged.

"Did you?"

I was quiet for a while, one because talking so much was wearing me out, but also because I could still feel the fear in my body.

"There were protesters on the sides of the street and police everywhere. Women of every age and race were walking into town. Black and white, it didn't matter. For a few hours, we'd become a sisterhood. Granted, we got in our line and they in theirs, but we was all there for the same reason. Women had finally been granted the right to vote."

"I had family then," I said in a stronger voice. "Family who remembered the old family. We knew when to laugh at each other and when to cry. We were close-knit. Wasn't nobody trying to make somebody do something she didn't want to do. We didn't move away. We stayed in Mossy Creek and died in Mossy Creek."

"Now, Grandmama, be reasonable," Clara put in. "The old days were all well and good — at least to your way of thinking — but you can't live here alone anymore."

"I been fine here for one hundred years, Clara. When I die, there won't be much to do except plant me."

We all sat quiet.

"Great Gran, are you all right?" Estelle asked me.

"Yes, chil'."

"So did you shoot anyone?"

"Estelle, you'd think you were fourteen instead of thirty-five."

"You're so interesting. I never knew how much."

"Your great-great-grandmother can share all her stories after she's settled at my house," Clara said.

"Yes, Estelle, we shot the gun."

"What!" Both of them looked like they'd seen a ghost.

"At who?" Clara screeched.

"That's between me and Mama and ol' Chief Cochran, rest his white policeman's soul. I got a lot of secrets in me."

I looked out the window. On the town square, a big blue monstrosity of plastic was reaching for the sky. Some kind of tent. "What's going on over there?"

"Grandmama, you know what that is. Mossy Creek's getting ready for the school reunion next month. I think they're planning fun things for kids and a parade."

"That's why this is the best town to live in. At least we entertain each other better than them Bigelowans. You shoulda' seen that Casey Blackshear with a softball bat in her hand and those braces on her legs going for home base last Fourth of July. That was a proud day for Mossy Creek."

We headed around the square, driving slow because it was crowded with Saturday shoppers. "My Uncle Eldon's church was up that sidestreet over there," I said. "Didn't have a name until I was about twenty-five. Everybody just knew where Eldon Whit's church was. He farmed all week, then preached on Sunday."

"I don't suppose you want to explain blaspheming the Lord's song this morning."

"No, I don't, Clara. I'm a bit closer to God than you, if only by age. Next time you want to have people sing at me, make sure they strong enough not to fall over when I sit up! You sent a boy to do a man's job. That's what you get for bringing a preacher from Bigelow."

"Why do you hate those people down there so much?"

"Bigelow wasn't much bigger than us at one time and suddenly they *got* big. Overnight, they snubbed us. The same maids we used to know didn't speak no more. They deserted Uncle Albert's little church and started taking their tithes to the fancy

Presbyterian Church in Bigelow! Deserted the one all-colored church in Bigelow County and just about closed its doors! That was the talk amongst us for years. How could they? I mourned for every time I had to snag a splinter from the back of my mama's thighs. Uncle Albert's church went dirt poor. We could have used new church pews and would have gotten 'em, too, if those Bigelow folks hadn't got too big for they britches. Those Bigelowans got they moonshine out the mountains just like the rest of us."

Clara just glared at me and nearly ran off the road. Typical. "Moonshine?"

I ignored her. "They *still* too stuck up for my taste. Keep your eyes on the road, Miss Missy Clara. I'm gonna die today, but I don't want to be killed in this car before I go."

Estelle sighed real hard. I completely understood. Clara was getting on my nerves too. I took a few short shallow breaths and mentally took my pulse, 'cause my hands were pinned to my sides. Still tickin'. "Estelle, when I do finally go, sue those Presbyterian Bigelowans for every nickel they worth. When you get the money, honey, come and dance on my grave. Pin a few dollars to your bra strap for savings, though." I winked even though she was sitting behind me and couldn't see anything but the back of my head. I heard her laugh, though.

"Go around to the other side of the square here," I told Clara. "There's a coffee shop that got the word *nekked* in it. I like that Jayne. Can't have her coffee, though. Old womens like me don't need to be up past eight o'clock."

"Grandmama, it's barely three o'clock," Clara chided. "Why don't I take you to your house so you can watch the TV I bought you."

"Clara, that's another thing. I know you brought that thing all the way from New Jersey, but I think that's why it don't work right down here in Mossy Creek." I ignored the fact that she rolled her eyes. "Something's wrong with it. My boyfriend doesn't come on anymore."

Clara snorted. "Grandmama, you know you don't have any boyfriend."

But Estelle clapped her hands. "Great Gran, you have a boyfriend?"

"Sure do," I said firmly. They both sounded like an old woman like me couldn't have some men friends. They just didn't know the power a one-hundred-year-old great-great-grandmama used to have and still had. I was some doll.

"People used to compare me to Lena Horne," I told Estelle. " 'Cept I was darker. Thicker, too. She didn't eat much, I think. My hair was kinkier than hers, and I couldn't sing. My smile was brighter. And I was taller. All in all, I think I was cuter than her!" I smiled real big at this realization. Because Lena Horne was a real lady. Me, too.

Estelle leaned over the seat again and looked at me, smiling. "So who's your boyfriend?"

"George Jefferson. You know, on the TV show. He caught my eye, even though your great-great-granddaddy will always have my heart."

Clara huffed. "George Jefferson."

Estelle covered her nose again and sat back. I heard her chuckling, though.

I bared my teeth in my biggest denture-bright smile. "Drive up that side street yonder."

Clara did. I was silent for a few minutes as the newer houses gave way to old ones.

"Clara! Stop!" I shouted.

She hit the brakes, and for once I was glad to be strapped in by a seatbelt. Else I would have flown straight out the windshield, and my dress would have poofed up, and then I would have been a sight for Jesus. I closed my eyes and took a few short shallow breaths.

Then I opened them, and the memories returned. My eyes teared.

I pointed to a wide oak tree covered in green moss. A one-room house leaned to one side in front of it, protected by the tree. The one-lane dirt drive that led to the house had been overgrown with weeds, but I was close enough to see. "Roll down my window. Can you see all the folks? Can you smell the good smells of this place?"

Clara didn't fuss like she usually did. My window slowly went down, and I could see myself and Chicken, Mama and Daddy, and Uncle Albert, and everybody.

"Smell what?"

"Dinner. Breakfast. Work. Love. Boy, do I miss that smell." I sighed. "All our houses were real close by, and the kids used to run between them to play or work. There were more trees, but I guess they went the same way as the houses and the people. Back to the earth. But the big oak is still here. My birthday tree." I wiped my eyes. "Little baby has surely grown up."

Estelle said softly, "Tell me what you see, Great Gran."

Clara said nothing but made a sniffling sound.

I looked at her. "Remember that tree, Clara?"

Clara left Mossy Creek when her daddy died and her mama, Alma, found work up North. I begged her mama to stay here — school teachers was needed everywhere, and our baby cousin Carmel had already proved that we Whits had a calling to teach in Bigelow County. But Alma packed up and took her precious baby, my granddaughter, Clara, with her. Clara had been ten at the time. And how she'd loved Mossy Creek.

I brought my shaking hand to my lap. "Clara, that house right there is your birth place."

"I thought I was born in the hospital down in Bigelow." Clara sounded disappointed, but facts was facts.

"You were born into the hospital of love. You was fine."

We sat real quiet for a while.

"Whose house is that now?"

"That's my house."

"Grandmama, I think you're confused. Your house is on the other end of town. You have a nice garden that you get your tomatoes from, and you have a pear tree."

"Well." I don't know what to say. For a minute, I'm confused. That house looked like my house. But yesterday I dreamed I was listening to James Baldwin recite a poem at the Golden Palace. I was tired. It'd been a long day.

But I'd wanted Clara to see her home, my home. "This was my home with my mama and daddy. But you're right. *My* home is across town. Take me, Clara. And watch your speed. Thirty-four is a mite fast for Mossy Creek."

As we headed along, we passed a brand spankin' new sign welcoming folks to Mossy Creek for the reunion. "That's right nice of you," I said to it. "Thanks for having me."

Estelle read the whole thing from the back, even though Clara acted like they were selling dinners at the church for a quarter, the way she was speeding.

"Ain't goin' nowhere . . . and don't want to?"

I took short shallow breaths, waiting for Estelle to say something else about the town's snazzy sign. Estelle didn't grow up here either, so I had to make allowances.

"It's charming," she said softly. "I like it."

Clara groaned, and I peered out the window, smiling. Estelle was my favorite for a reason. "Pretty soon I'm not goin' see these leaves change again. Guess I'd better get one last good look."

I watched my town go by for a while, but

the speedometer was tipping thirty-nine, and I started to get dizzy, so I turned to look at Clara, instead. "Clara, don't you have *any* good memories of Mossy Creek?"

Her mouth worked for a minute, and she took in a big breath.

"It's not the same, Grandmama. I left when I was a little girl."

"But you was happy when you was here. Have you been happy since?"

"Of course. I had Ella, and she had Estelle. What couldn't I be happy about?"

I looked at my time-worked hands. "You got married, had a baby, your husband ran out, your baby grew up and had a baby, and now you're here driving me extra fast to my freezing-cold grave up North. Besides Ella and Estelle, I don't see much for you to hurry home about."

"Aren't you getting sleepy, yet?" Clara said. "Isn't it time for your nap?"

I fixed her with the old-lady eye that used to send her mama runnin' for cover. "Clara, sixty-five ain't too old to take one right across the mouth. I'm still your elder."

Estelle snorted and rolled down the window.

I watched her from the rearview. Her face was stuck out like how dogs do. Hair flappin', eyes closed, a smile on her face. I wasn't gonna say nothin' else, but I decided I didn't want to see Jesus yet and couldn't hug him right then, anyway, because my shoulder had a touch of arthritis.

"Estelle, baby, can you roll the window up? My shoulder ain't ever gonna be right for Jesus."

I figured she caught a bug, 'cause she started coughing.

I turned to Clara, again. "Clara, you remind me of the Bigelowans. Black, white, and every other kind of Bigelowan."

"Grandmama, please. Can we ride in quiet?"

"I suppose we can, but when you a hundred and it's your special day, you should be allowed to speak your piece."

Her speed picked up to forty-one. The trees a-whizzing by as we zoomed past Beechum's Bakery, and I swear I saw Bob the Chihuahua lift off in our wind. I decided I was just remembering when the hawk grabbed him last year, and I closed my eye that had the cataract. Much better. Bob had all fours on the sidewalk.

"You always wanted more," I told Clara. "You ain't never satisfied, never was. Them Bigelowans are the same. They wanted a big city, and now Ham Bigelow is running for President. Do you really think the country is ready for his big-headed self? If I was going to be here in a year, I'd run for President just to give him a scare. I'd call all the AARP's around the country and have that flabby Bigelowan outvoted in no time flat!"

Clara clamped her mouth tight and said nothing.

I sat there picturing myself in an Abe Lincoln hat holding a *Eula Mae for President* sign. The hat would need a little dressing up for my taste. Some fruit and flowers and maybe a ribbon made a nice pick-me-up for any hat.

"Your mother had that same wanderlust," I went on, "and I suppose she was happy, but only you know the truth. Was she, Clara?"

"My mother was very happy, Grandmama." But Clara looked sad. 'Cause she knew if that was happiness, she should give it a good knock with her straw broom. As we approached my house, the house my husband Daniel and his family built, but which folks now call the Whit Place in my honor, calmness settled over me. There were cars parked on the grass, and the door stood wide open.

Estelle gasped. "Great Gran, somebody's in your house without your permission!"

City folk. Estelle can't help herself.

"I know. They come to see me. Clara, get close to the door. Estelle, hand me my purse. Check my hair. Yessiree, I got visitors."

I flipped down the fancy lighted mirror on the sun visor and checked my face. I showed myself my teeth.

"Grandmama? What are you doing?"

"Clara, when a woman sees that she's got company, she's got to be prepared. Estelle, let me out this car door. I've got people to see before I go and meet Jesus."

Inside my house were many friends I'd made over the years. Old and young. Black and white. And even some foes. The governor himself, Ham Bigelow, was there, probably sucking up to any excuse to campaign early, but still. I noticed Mayor Ida giving him looks that would have killed a gopher at twenty feet, and I said to myself, *She's onto the scent, and that reunion is going to be mighty interesting next month.* But I kept my mouth shut.

Everybody applauded when I walked through. I scooted to the bathroom and changed my *Depends.* Then Estelle got me settled in my chair so I could receive my guests.

The first one over was Ida and her granddaughter, Little Ida. Ida sat next to me and took my hand. "General," she called me.

"Colonel," I said back.

"I'm glad you're still here."

"For just a little while longer," I assured her.

I pointed to Clara, who was over in the dining room trying to tell country women how to lay food out on a table. Ida and I shared a resigned look.

"Don't worry," I said. "You can't hurt city folks' feelings. They gonna kick her out in a minute. I miss your grandmama, Colonel. Was thinking of her today when I went by the old voting hall. She loaned me something that day. I guess I'll return it to you."

I looked for Estelle. "Estelle, reach inside that drawer and give me that package wrapped in white."

She did my bidding as the Colonel looked on. Little Ida's eyes were as smart as her grandma's.

I winked at Little Ida, and she winked back at me. I liked that.

Estelle gingerly handed me the item. I leaned into Ida because Bigelowans are present. "Your grandmama gave this to me so many years ago I can't remember how many. It's time it found its way home." I stopped her from unwrapping it. "At home. Just you. You'll know what to do with it."

The Colonel pressed a kiss to my cheek. "I love you, Miss Eula Mae Whit."

"I love you too, Miss Ida Hamilton Walker."

"Kiss my grandmama for me," she added, her eyes bright.

"I surely will."

"But not this year." She rose, and her grandbaby slid beside me. Little Ida looked me in the eye. "May I have a kiss on the cheek, too?"

I leaned over and kissed her, then touched both her shoulders. "From this day on, you'll be Captain Ida."

"Thank you very much, General."

"You're surely welcome, Captain."

The Colonel and Ham passed without a word, and Ida gave me a look I'll remember forever. We both remember the past, and now there's *no* doubt in my mind she's caught a certain secret by its elephant's tail. I smiled to let her know all would be well.

At eight o'clock, I tucked myself in my bed, my pulse still racing along as it had been for the past one hundred years.

God only had four hours left in my birthday, and frankly I didn't know why he was waiting. Estelle shooed Clara out of my room, and I felt relieved. As much as I loved her, sixty-five-year-olds have energy like small children. Clara was so hyper, she caused my heart to race one extra beat a minute. She was lonely. I could tell that's why she wanted me to come live in New Jersey with her.

But talking to a headstone wasn't gonna cure her troubles. I lay there thinking I might have to stick around. The longer I stayed alive, the longer she'd stay in Mossy Creek, and the longer Whit land would stay with Whits.

I'd never considered what I'd do if I didn't go home to glory on my hundredth birthday. Whit women have always been timely.

I thought about if there was anything God needed for me to do that I hadn't. I'd been a good citizen. Gone to church on Sundays. Married. Raised my daughter the right way. Shot a man — oops — violation of that Commandment.

I needed to talk to God in person about that. He'd understand my side . . . once I explained.

So I lay in my bed, listening to my heart-beat.

Estelle peeked in my door. "Great Gran, you still awake?"

"Yes, baby. Come on in. What can I do for you?"

She cut on the light, and I was struck by

how much she favored my daughter Alma, God rest her soul.

Estelle sat on the side of my bed. "Great Gran, I like Mossy Creek. I feel connected here."

Joy ran through me as if my legs were ten years old.

"Me too. That's what our town sign means. 'Ain't goin' nowhere . . . and don't want to.' "

"I was wondering . . . if you were thinking about delaying your trip into eternity, I'd like to stay with you. Get to know Cousin Carmel and the other relatives around here."

My heart was racing now. I realized I was not ready to die.

"What does your grandmama have to say about that?"

"I was thinking of coming home, too."

Clara stood in the doorway. This had me stunned and a little dizzy. "Why, Clara?"

"Because you're here. My roots are here."

"So no selling of my land?"

"No, ma'am."

"And no burying me up North?"

"No burying you up North."

"Ain't goin' nowhere . . . and don't want to?"

"Yes, ma'am."

I ran my tongue over my last real tooth and smiled. "Then welcome back to Mossy Creek, baby."

It was a good day to be alive.

RAINEY

HOMECOMING DAY, 1981, PART TWO: THE FIRE

Sometimes, losing a symbol of the community is like losing pieces of our own hearts. Can we ever fill that empty spot?

"Hey, Rainey Ann, did you hear about the fortune-teller?"

I turned from tossing softballs at wooden cutouts of ducks. "What fortune-teller?"

Smug Amy Champion stood there outside the carnival booth, lugging her blond toddler-cousin, Casey, in her arms. "The gypsy fortune-teller that's predicting bad things about tonight's football game."

"What gypsy?"

Now Hank and Robbie were close beside me, staring at Amy. Amy fluffed her hair and hoisted Casey, higher on her hip. The toddler gazed at Hank with wide blue eyes. Hank, who could never resist petting any critter smaller than himself, brushed Casey's pink nose with the tip of his finger. She watched him like a kitten hoping to catch a junebug. Then she smiled. Casey Champion fell in love with Hank Blackshear that day. I was there. I saw it.

Amy sighed at our ignorance. "The gypsy's a machine."

"Like a computer?" Computers were like elephants, to me. I had to see one in person, so I'd believe they existed.

Amy rolled her eyes. "No, it's like a wind-up doll, or something. It's over next to the spin-the-wheel booth." She pointed. "You put in a dime, and you get a card with your fortune on it. Only instead of real fortunes, it's handing out cards that say bad stuff. Look. I got one." She dug a little card from her jeans' pocket. We scrutinized it. In big, black typewriter type it said:

TONIGHT THE RAM SAYS GOOD-BAH.

I frowned. "What's that mean?"

"I dunno. But Jewel Abercrombie got a card that says, WE'RE GOING TO COOK THE RAM'S GOOSE. And Dr. Thorogood's wife got one that says, SAMSON GOES UP IN FLAMES TONIGHT."

Samson. The Pep Club was in charge of washing Samson and brushing him and tying a big, green-and-white MOSSY CREEK

RAMS sash around his middle. During half-time, the cheerleaders would lead Samson onto the field. Every year, he escorted the Homecoming Court down to the fifty-yard line then stood there, chewing his cud, while everybody cheered.

"I bet the Fang and Claw Society is going to try to kidnap Samson," Robbie said grimly.

I shook my head. "I thought that club didn't exist anymore."

"So people say. I think it still does. And I think the Fang and Clawers are going to get Samson tonight."

"And kill him and roast him," Amy added helpfully.

Hank screeched, then took off at a run. Casey started crying.

I rapped Amy on the side of the head. "Troublemaker. Did your mama raise you to be a lank-haired doofus?"

"Who are you calling a doofus, you little pink poodle!"

I rapped her, again. It was a day for insulting neighbors.

"Come on," Robbie ordered.

Robbie and I rushed after Hank.

We got Hank calmed down, then sidled up to the edge of a crowd watching Chief Royden and Mossy Creek Mayor Zeke Abercrombie — Miss Ida began her stretch as mayor in the next election — pry a back panel off the strangest contraption I'd ever seen in my life, even compared to Rose the elephant.

If you've ever seen one of those old carnival fortune-telling booths, you know what the fortune-teller looked like. She was supposed to make you think of a gypsy woman sitting inside a booth. The booth was made of painted metal. It had a curlicued top panel on the front and was decorated with a lot of gold flourishes and elaborate words in old-timey script.

YOUR FUTURE, TOLD HERE, one side of the booth said in words as tall as my hand. On the other side, the words read, ARE YOU BRAVE ENOUGH TO ASK THE GYPSY FOR YOUR FORTUNE? But most dramatic of all, across the curlicued top panel on the very front was written in big, scrolling letters like something on an old movie poster:

BEWARE THE TRUTH TOLD BY THE TEN CENT GYPSY.

"There's the card mechanism," Mayor Abercrombie said. He pushed a switch.

The whole booth whirred and clicked, and suddenly the gypsy's left hand began to rise. I got goose bumps all over me. The gypsy's stiff arm went up and up until the hand's forefinger pointed right at us. A card popped out of her palm.

Chief Royden plucked it from the mannequin's hand and read it. "Yep," he said, because nothing rattled him. "Here's another one that says Samson's a goner."

People gasped.

Mayor Abercrombie pulled a wad of cards from the booth's innards. He and the chief and several citizens sorted through them. "All fake cards like the first one," the mayor reported. "Somebody rigged this machine to stir up trouble."

"Chief Royden, do you think Samson's in danger of being stolen and, uh, turned into lamb chops?" a woman asked.

The crowd looked worried. Over behind the chief, I saw his son, Amos, who was about seventeen then and a second-stringer on the Mossy Creek Rams. Amos and some of the other football players looked as though they were ready to head down to Bigelow and start a fight.

Chief Royden knew that, I'm sure. "Everybody calm down. I'll just lock Samson in a jail cell until game time."

People just stared at him. We were all struck speechless. I know Robbie and Hank and me stood there with our tongues glued to our gullets in amazement.

The chief was goin' to lock up a sheep.

That was a first, even for Mossy Creek, where people love to be strange.

About fifty Creekites traipsed behind Chief Royden, Mayor Abercrombie, and Principal Doolittle as they walked into the parking lot behind the high school. On one end of the building was a loading ramp where the cafeteria staff carried supplies into the school. Nearby, the shop class had built a nice pen of wide boards and hog wire.

Samson, the fattest boy sheep in all of north Georgia, gazed out nervously from a bed of wood shavings inside his home-away-from-home. Two of the Pep Club girls were trying to fluff his coat with a blow dryer. Samson crawfished and let out a loud *Baaaah.* The girls shrieked.

Chief Royden reached over into the pen, took the blow dryer away from them, and shut it off. Biting back a smile, he looked over at a beady-eyed, big-eared, pinched-nose young man in a sweater, bow tie, and khaki pants. The man had been sitting morosely in a lawn chair until he saw

Principal Doolittle. Now he smiled and marched right up to the chief, the mayor, and Principal Doolittle.

He was Dwight Truman. Uggh. Mama hated him. "Wants to change everything," she said. "A stupid young rooster like him can ruin a good town. He's all crow and no scratch. Unfortunately, he's all we've got."

"I've got everything under control here, Sir," Dwight said to Principal Doolittle. "Samson is as happy as can be."

"Thank you, Dwight, but I'm a little worried."

"I'd be worried too, Sir, if I weren't in charge. But I am, and Samson's safe."

Dwight Truman was running for state senate from our district, and everyone intended to vote for him. The other candidate was Ham Bigelow.

"He's worse than Dwight," Mama always said. "He's a Bigelowan."

"Dwight," Chief Royden said with just enough spin on the name to show he thought Dwight was a pismire, "Stand back. I'm takin' the sheep into custody for his own safety."

"No," Dwight said loudly. "Principal Doolittle, I give you my word that this fine sheep will be safe in my care. I am a citizen of this community who means what he says and will do whatever it takes to promote Mossy Creek's best interests. As our candidate for state senate —"

"Spare me the campaign speech, Dwight," Principal Doolittle said, "I really think the chief ought to put Samson under protective custody —"

"Sir, do you and Mayor Abercrombie want word to get out that Creekites can't take care of their own trouble? That we're a bunch of nervous Nellies? *That we have to lock up our sheep?*"

The principal turned a little red. "No, Dwight, but —"

"The future of our town and our children's trust rests with me, Sir. And I promise you, I'm a match for the future." Dwight pressed a hand to his heart. "As our candidate for state senate, I won't let the future down."

Principal Doolittle glanced at Mayor Abercrombie, who shrugged, and Chief Royden, who looked from Samson to Dwight as if trying to decide which was the bigger dumb wooly animal.

"All right, Dwight," the principal said finally, with a sigh. "But keep my Samson safe from harm."

"No one will touch so much as a curly hair on his curly head, Sir."

Late that afternoon, Dwight and about half the Pep Club got ahold of some bad barbecue. Nobody else at the carnival got sick from that barbecue, so it looked like an inside job. Anyway, they made a major run on the portable toilets, with the upshot being that Dwight and the Pep Club left Samson alone for maybe five minutes, tops. When they came back, the pen's gate stood open, and Samson was gone.

There wasn't so much as a *baaah* of evidence, either.

Principal Doolittle went into an uproar, and we knew Dwight's career as a suck-up teacher and future state senator was over, too.

Samson had been kidnapped.

The Bigelowans had gotten our goat.

This was war. Creekites spent the rest of the day searching for Samson.

Robbie, Hank, and I did our part, scouring every nook and cranny until we straggled to a halt outside Mama's salon doors around sunset. We sat down on the sidewalk, too tired to do much more than breathe. I had to get home and put on warmer clothes and pretend to eat some dinner with Mama, Grandma, and Daddy before we headed out to the game. Hank's mama had cleared the way for Hank to eat with us. And of course Robbie was invited. But he looked angry and said he couldn't eat a thing.

"I hate the whole world," he announced.

"What are you talkin' about, Robbie Walker?"

"It's crazy and mean and makes no sense. Bad things happen for no good reason. And there's nothing anybody can do about it."

"We helped look for Samson. What else can we do?"

"My dad always said you've got to have the courage to fight back even when you know the odds are against you."

"We don't know *who* to fight."

"Bigelowans, that's who."

"All of them?" We were outnumbered.

"Their attitude. Their whole way of doing things."

"Huh?"

"We'll start with the ones who rigged the Ten-Cent Gypsy and stole Samson. They've got to be guys from Bigelow High. I think the Fang and Claw Society really does still exist. I bet they did this."

I shivered. My granddaddy had been knocked in the head by some Fang and Claw boys back when he was a kid in the 1930s.

"I'm not afraid of the Fang and Claw

jerks," I lied.

"Whether it's them or not, somebody has to do something to stand up for Mossy Creek."

I clamped my mouth shut and stared at Robbie. So did Hank, making little mewling noises under his breath. We got nervous when Robbie's ideas wandered down peculiar roads. He had so much misery in him that he just had to let it lead him somewhere he'd never been, before.

"The Bigelow Wildcats don't have a wildcat mascot we could kidnap," I pointed out. "Not even a kitty cat who *looks* wild. So what are we —"

"We'll tie the elephant to Mrs. Goodwin's car."

I gasped. Mrs. Bamalynn Goodwin, principal of Bigelow High School, was a very large, blonde lady who drove a vintage white Cadillac. "We'll be found out and killed! I hear she's mean when anybody messes with her car!"

"We won't get caught. We'll tie the elephant to her car tonight and make it pull the Cadillac out of the parking lot. We'll lead Rose and the Cadillac into downtown Mossy Creek and leave her and the car right in the middle of square. The Bigelowans kidnapped our sheep. So we'll kidnap their principal's *car*."

Hank clutched my hand. We both looked up at Robbie in excited horror. I could have talked Robbie out of the plan. But the little devil who sat on my shoulder whispered that I'd do anything for the pride of Mossy Creek, and anything Robbie Walker asked me to do.

"Let's get the elephant," I said.

The night sky was sprinkled with bright, cold stars, and the stadium at Mossy Creek High glowed with lights. Cheers went up from the Creekites or the Bigelowans every few minutes. The Mossy Creek Rams Marching Band whomped their big bass drum like a tom-tom. The football game was still in the first quarter, tied at six-six.

Mossy Creek High had fielded the best team since 1972, when Buck Looney was a star tackle who went on to play for the Green Bay Packers. For once, the Rams had a good shot at a district title, maybe even the state playoffs. Beating the Bigelow Wildcats at our own homecoming game would take us a long way toward that goal.

Robbie, Hank and I crept into the carnival area and crouched behind some laurels. We toted a heavy canvas bag stuffed with some old wigs, a dozen feet of garden twine, and a large plastic duck from Hank's Easter basket the spring before. Principal Goodwin wore wigs and collected duck figurines. We'd decided to dress up the elephant with cheap wigs and a necklace made of twine, dangling a plastic duck.

"We'll make her look like Miz Goodwin," I said fiendishly, using some convoluted line of reasoning that said Mrs. Goodwin collected duck figurines so we'd make fun of that, too. I figured when the Bigelowans found Rose tied to the principal's car in the Mossy Creek town square it would be a double insult to see how she'd been decorated.

The carnival had shut down for the night and looked like a creepy set from a horror movie. The only light came from the campers and little house trailers of the carnie workers. We snuck through the shadows down an alley of booths and concessions, then crouched on Robbie's signal. He peered around a corner, checking out our next move. My teeth chattered with nerves.

Hank made a low sound of worry, poked me on the shoulder, then pointed. I looked up. We were hunkered down across from the Ten-Cent Gypsy. A streak of light from a camper window touched her face, lighting it up in weird angles.

Lor', I swear, that painted plastic hoochie was staring down at us like she knew what we intended. My innards turned to pudding, but I refused to act scared. I opened my paper sack, took out a squirt bottle of perm solution I'd brought in case I needed a weapon and wobbled to a stand. I edged toward the Ten-Cent Gypsy, holding the perm bottle in front of me with the business end pointed at her head. "You're just a hollow dimestore doll," I said aloud. "You don't even have legs. You're just a machine with phony Bigelowan cards up your butt. One squirt and I'll frizz that fake hair of yours forever-and-ever-Amen." I advanced, lifting the bottle.

The beam of a flashlight skittered over our heads. One of Chief Royden's officers was on patrol. Hank yipped. Robbie grabbed Hank and me, pulling us down to a squat with him. *"What are you doing?"*

"She's putting the evil eye on us! I'm gonna perm her to a fare-thee-well!"

"Sssh!"

He waved for us to follow him, and we crept through the carnival until we reached Rose. The elephant dozed peacefully. We glimpsed her owner through his camper window as he staggered around inside. He had a beer can in one hand.

"He's drunk as a skunk and not paying any attention to Rose at all," Robbie confirmed. "Let's go."

We tiptoed up to the elephant. She opened her big, beady, elephant eyes and looked down at us without much reaction, but when Hank stroked her trunk she curled it around his head and made a happy, snuffling sound.

"Hank, you keep petting her," Robbie whispered. "Rainey, climb up. I'll hand you the wigs."

I gulped and latched a hand in Rose's harness. Robbie gave me a foot up, but he hoisted me a little too hard. I sailed a good ways and flopped across Rose's shoulders, grabbing for a handhold. Rose shifted a little and switched her tail.

"Pet her some more," Robbie told Hank.

Hank did, and Rose got quiet again. I righted myself and caught my breath. "Lordawmighty, Robbie. Throw me into outer space, next time."

"Sorry, Pink." That was his nickname for me, and whenever he used it, I melted like fresh butter.

"No harm done. I got ahold of the harness. I'm okay."

Robbie pulled the wigs out of the bag. They were cast-offs from a trade show

Mama had attended, and she'd given them to me long ago. I'd permed and colored those wigs a hundred times. They looked appropriately ratty. Robbie, Hank, and I had bound them together with twine so they formed a patchwork wig big enough to fit an elephant.

"Here goes," Robbie said. He tossed the armful of hair to me. Rose stood quietly while I arranged it on her knobby head.

Robbie tied lengths of twine under her neck. "Done," he announced.

Rose peered at us from beneath bangs of long spit curls.

"Now for the plastic duck," Robbie said.

Hank quacked when we maneuvered his Easter toy into place. We hung it on Rose from a twine necklace, so the duck bobbled just below her chin. It was good-sized duck, and on its plastic side we had scribbled a message with a fat, black poster pen: BRING SAMSON BACK OR ELSE.

We didn't have any suggestions for what *else* might be, but it made a good, vague threat. After all, it was attached to an elephant, and the elephant would be attached to Bigelow Principal Bamalynn Goodwin's Cadillac.

"Ready?" Robbie asked.

"Yep." Hank nodded as he scratched

Rose's trunk.

Robbie helped me down. He pulled a pair of bolt cutters from the canvas bag, and we squatted by the long chain that anchored Rose's left front foot to her owner's camper.

Robbie clamped the cutters on a link in the chain, and began to squeeze. About that time, we heard the stadium announcer call out over his loud speakers, "Welcome to the Mossy Creek Rams' Homecoming!"

We froze. The marching band began playing the Rams' fight song, and people cheered. Halftime had arrived. We'd been so busy and so scared we hadn't realized.

Robbie pulled the bolt cutters away from the chain and sat back. "Too many people'll be moving around the parking lot during halftime. We have to wait until third quarter starts."

I forced a shrug. "Okay. So we'll just stay right here and keep hidden. I'm not worried."

"How's your pet pack-a-perm doing, Hankster?"

Hank smiled and chirped. Rose had wrapped her trunk all the way around his shoulders. It looked like she was hugging him, and he liked it.

"Okay, then," Robbie said. "We'll wait."

We sat there a few minutes listening to

the muffled blare of the band. We heard the announcer call out, "And here's the 1981 Homecoming Court, Ladies and Gentlemen! And the 1981 Mossy Creek Homecoming Queen is —"

His microphone died exactly then, and so did the stadium lights. Blam. Just like that. Pitch darkness. Then we heard the crowd yelling. Even screaming. Something terrible had happened, but we had no idea what.

"Head for the bushes," Robbie ordered. We stumbled through the dark and dived under some laurel along the high school's front wall.

A big fireball galloped into the carnival parking lot, headed straight our way at a dead run. Smoke and sparkles shrouded the thing, until suddenly, when it was no more than a half-dozen yards from us, it let out a sound.

"BAAAAAH!"

"Samson!" I yelled.

Sure enough, it was our lost sheep. The kidnappers had stuck sparklers all over his wooly pelt, then set every one of them afire. Sparks shot from Samson in all directions. Including ours.

Robbie gasped. "Oh, no, he's headed for Rose!"

Rose the elephant might have been tamer

than a wad of old gum under most circumstances, but with a hysterical sheep coming at her like a wooly shooting star, she panicked. She jerked her tethered leg, and we heard a metallic screech as her chain snapped. Samson ran under her, then began crawfishing and baaahing and droppin' sparklers all over her straw bed. Little fires began to spring up in the straw.

Rose bolted under the awning at the school entrance, made a right turn, lurched up the stone steps, and butted the school's big, fancy double doors with her head. The doors gave way, and Rose disappeared inside. Samson, still sparkling, raced blindly after her. I guess he thought he was going into a nice, safe barn.

But it was Mossy Creek High School.

Hank crawled out from under the laurel and ran into the school. Rob and I charged after him.

We halted inside the dark front hall and pressed ourselves to the wall. Rose and Samson charged up and down. Samson dropped sparklers as he ran, igniting a teepee of cornstalks from an autumn display. Rose trailed flaming paper streamers from a Pep Club banner. The plastic duck swung wildly from her neck.

"Get out," Robbie yelled. "I'll try to shoo

Rose and Samson back toward the front doors. But y'all go on outside! *Now!*"

"No way!"

Hank's throat worked. Words finally spewed out. "I've got to save Fluffy and Booger!" he yelled. Then he took off down an opposite hall. His daddy, Dr. Blackshear, had loaned a pair of pet rabbits to Mrs. Almira Olsen, the biology teacher. Mrs. Olsen was hoping the bunnies would make bunny love in public so she could avoid teaching the new eighth-grade sex education class. She figured a little bunnie-show-and-tell would pretty much explain everything eighth-graders needed to know.

We tore after Hank. By the time we found our way in the dark to Mrs. Olsen's classroom, the smell of smoke was everywhere. Robbie popped the door on Fluffy and Booger's cage. Hank took Fluffy, and I grabbed Booger.

"We can't go back that way," Robbie said. He ran to one of the room's tall windows, unlocked it, and shoved the bottom half up.

Hank and I scrambled out, clutching the rabbits, and tumbled in the laurel shrubs. I looked back up at the window. "You come out right now *too,* Robbie Walker!"

He hung over the sill for a minute, looking down at us somberly. "If my dad were here, he'd try to save the elephant and the sheep. That's what I have to do." He disappeared back into the smoky darkness.

I yelled like a banshee. Hank and I ran to the front entrance. By then, Chief Royden was on the scene with a big crowd of people. Everyone was shouting and turning their car headlights on the front of the school. Smoke had begun seeping from the windows and the open doorway. In the distance, we heard the sirens of the Mossy Creek Volunteer Fire Department.

Tears slid down my face. Hank was crying, too.

"Come out, Robbie, come out," I whispered.

Rose's owner wobbled around the entrance, drunk, yelling, "Rosie? Oh, Rosie, com'ere, Rosie, where ya hiding?"

As if she heard him, Rose came thundering out the school's front doors, followed by Samson. Who was still sparkling. Chief Royden dodged Rose and Samson with only an inch or two to spare.

Rose charged down the steps, made a right turn, ran through the parking lot, and evaporated into the pitch-black forest. Samson halted on the school's lawn, uttered one long, plaintive baaah, then hid behind the ram statue. He looked like a toasted cotton ball with legs.

Everyone was so busy gaping at Rose and Samson they didn't notice when Robbie staggered out of the doors and into the shadows. Hank and I snuck over to him. The three of us huddled in the woods — dirty, sweaty, smoky, and holding traumatized rabbits.

Hank tearfully peered into the darkness where Rose had vanished. "Poor pack-a-perm," he whispered. "Poor sheep." That was one of the few good things that came out of that night. Shy Hank Blackshear took up talking.

But fire leapt from the roof of Mossy Creek High.

"I did it," Rob groaned.

"What?"

"I cut Rose's chain — part of the way, at least. That must be why she was able to break it so easy and escape. It's my fault."

"No, we were all in on it," I corrected, crying. Hank nodded and began crying, too. Robbie just sat there in dry silence, looking as if he wanted to tear his heart out.

We watched Mossy Creek High burn to the ground.

What followed was one of the darkest times in the history of the town. People mourned like the high school had been living kin to them. Rose was spotted once out in the hollows along Trailhead Road, still wearing the wig and duck. Chief Royden made it his business to find her — after all, what police chief wants people to snicker that he can't even find an elephant? But the man hunt — well, the elephant hunt — went on for weeks, with no luck.

Rose the elephant was never found. Nothing was ever proved one way or the other as to who kidnapped Samson and set him afire with dozens of sparklers. The school was never rebuilt, and from then on, Creekite kids were sent down to Bigelow High.

All because we'd cut Rose's chain. Or thought we had.

We began to do penance in ways no one but the three of us would recognize. Hank devoted himself to animals. Robbie went to work at his family's failing department store, Hamilton's, as if saving one of the town's landmarks would help make up for destroying another. And I hid myself under layers of makeup and hair dye.

Twenty years later, I was still hiding.

Until the reunion.

SANDY

THE MASK

"Miz Hart? Miz Whit?" I whispered loudly.

Beside me, Katie Bell whispered just as loudly, "Ladies? Are you *there?*"

A piping, crackly little voice snapped back, "You're standing just around the corner of the statue, so you *know* we're here."

"Tell Sandy to get a move on," another old-lady voice intoned. "We're not gettin' any younger. Oughta be glad I decided to live."

"Just hold on, Eula Mae."

"Don't you 'hold on,' me, Millicent. I got better things to do than play cops-and-robbers out here in the broad daylight with a crazy old woman like you."

"Who are you calling crazy, you dried-up piece of bacon? I'll. . . ."

"Ladies," I interrupted.

Millicent Hart was eighty-something years old going on a twinkle, and Eula Mae Whit was an even one century young. Both of them liked to give people headaches.

Katie Bell and I peered around the weathered edge of the statue of General Hamilton in Mossy Creek's square. Millicent, a shrewd-eyed little oldster wearing a Britney Spears's t-shirt — probably stolen from Hamilton's Department Store — peered back at us defiantly. Beside her, ancient Eula Mae scowled in a flowered housecoat. Old white lady and old black lady. Both of them glared like we were the dumb-gray color of dishwater.

"Who are you callin' *Ladies?*" Eula Mae demanded, as if I'd insulted them.

I shook my head. "All I'm sayin' is let's hurry. What have y'all got for us?" I looked around furtive-like, since it was high noon, and we weren't exactly the only people in the park. This meeting place sure wasn't *my* choice.

Millicent and Eula Mae had made it clear they wanted our rendezvous kept secret, but they were the ones who picked this spot and this time.

"They like to live on the razor edge of public curiosity," Katie Bell told me.

Well, their idea of 'secret' made my back itch.

"Here." Millicent thrust a dusty, battered, twenty-years-out-of-date Hamilton Department Store shopping bag into my hand. "He was wearing this, that night. We saw him. He dropped it outside his car as he drove off."

"Tell us his name."

"You are two of the stupidest white girls in the county." Eula Mae said. "We didn't see *him*. We saw *him*."

"Ma'am?"

"We saw what's in the bag, not what was behind it," Millicent explained.

"But I thought —"

"I got to go," Eula Mae said. "There's my niece, Carmel, and she's nosier than a squirrel in a bag of nuts."

"There's Maggie and Tag," Millicent yelped. "Why don't they stay in bed and quit spying on me?"

Millicent and Eula Mae left us standing there without another word.

Holding the bag, so to speak.

"Let's get out of here." Katie Bell dragged me across Main Street into the alley between Rainey's salon and Dan McNeil's Fixit Shop. Once in the shadows, I pulled the wrinkled paper sack open, and we looked inside.

President Nixon looked up at us without any eyes. A plastic Halloween mask, that is.

Regardless, I nearly wet on myself.

Katie Bell said a couple of bad words and dug out the dusty, bent, Halloween mask. Turning it in her hands, she sighed with defeat. All our detective work, for this. We had a dead elephant and a Nixon mask.

I moped around the police station for the next few days. All this work, but no good leads. For weeks I'd talked to shipping companies all over Georgia, begging them to search their files for any record of transporting an elephant away from Mossy Creek twenty years ago.

One morning the phone rang on my dispatcher's desk. The call was from the elderly, retired owner of a little trucking company in Atlanta.

"Miz Crane," he said, "I think I moved your pachyderm."

"Red Skelton," I said to Amos. "That's who shipped Rose the elephant out of Mossy Creek without anybody knowing."

The chief looked at me over his *Gazette,* as if afraid to lower the paper. "Red Skelton."

"Red Skelton."

"The old comedian? TV. Movies. The Red Skelton Show. That Red Skelton?"

I nodded, then held up a fax of a twenty-year-old shipping invoice. "Magnolia States'

Shipping delivered one Rose the elephant to the Sumter Sweet Circus in Iowa. Right here is a copy of the invoice from Magnolia States' files. The perpetrator who contracted with them to ship Rose from Georgia out west to Iowa signed his name *Red Skelton*."

Amos dropped the newspaper, took the fax from me, and scowled at it. "This is just a hunch, Sandy, but I'd say your perp used a fake name."

I grinned. "That's why I've sent a copy of the signature to the state crime lab for handwriting analysis. I used to clean house for the sister-in-law of the mother of the head of the lab. I got us some premium attention from the state lab folks. It's a longshot, but they say they'll run this Red Skelton against every signature in their files. Chief, they've got a new computer database with samples of every criminal's handwriting from here to forever and then some. They've got handwriting samples from all sorts of government officials and celebrities in the database, too — to check out cases where some so-and-so tries to fake a famous signature."

"Maybe we'll get lucky," the chief deadpanned. "Maybe it really *was* Red Skelton."

I huffed loudly and pursed my lips. "You know what, Chief? You're not many years older than me, and you're a good-looking man — not as good-looking as my Jess, but not hard on the ol' eyeballs, either. I'm gonna find more clues in this Rose case just to startle you into putting your paper down. So I can enjoy the sight of you lookin' impressed."

Amos arched a brow. "I *am* impressed. I'd love to see this case resolved. My father couldn't crack it, and he worked on the mystery for years."

I waved the invoice. "But *he* didn't have Red Skelton."

After a moment, Amos squinted one eye just a little. He was either having an allergy attack or fighting one of his little anti-hero smiles. The kind that put the *iron* in *irony.* "Do me one favor," he said. "Don't tell anyone else we're going down to the state crime lab to investigate Red Skelton."

I gave him a thumbs up and whooped. "We're on it, Chief."

Amos and I sat in a dark office cubicle peering at a big computer screen next to a preppy little black guy named Ronell Sommersby. Ronell put the *gee* in geek.

"Gee, baby," he said to his computer as he typed in codes and commands that split the screen in half. "Gee, baby. Gee. Come on."

The Red Skelton signature had been scanned into the system and suddenly appeared on one side of the screen.

Ronell said, "Gee, baby," then punched one last key and sat back. "Watch this. All likely handwriting matches will zip-zap-zing through the system. The closest matches should pop up within a few seconds. This baby has a ninety-eight-percent accuracy rate."

"Gee," I said politely, and hunched forward with Ronell.

Amos stood behind us, leaning over our heads and staring at the computer intently.

On the screen, thousands of signatures flashed by in a blur as the computer sorted them. The speed made me a little dizzy. I looked away, sipped a Coke from a glass bottle — the only way to drink the best elixir ever made — and asked myself if I hadn't dragged my chief and myself down to the crime lab for nothing.

"Look at all those names going by," I muttered. "How can I expect the computer to match up some stranger's handwriting style with my one puny offering of loops and squiggles?" I sighed. "A longshot? Hah! An *impossible* shot."

"No," Amos said, his eyes never leaving the screen. "There it is."

"Gee!" Ronell yelled, then shoved his chair back so hard its rolling feet squealed.

I whipped toward the computer screen and stared. There, side by side with Red Skelton, was the signature of the real perp. The hider of fire-bug elephants. The face behind the Nixon mask. The villain who'd masterminded the burning down of Mossy Creek High School.

Amos went stone-silent. Then, "Battle would have eaten his heart out over this."

Ronell, who looked as if he'd just discovered a good reason to polish up his resume for a new job, said something a lot worse than *Gee*.

And I took a hard gulp of air. "It's reunion time," I whispered.

From: Lady Victoria Salter Stanhope
To: Katie Bell

Dearest Katie:

My dear mum used to say, "Be careful what you wish for, my darling, else you might receive it." Though you may have believed everyone in town would begin confessing as soon as your surveys provoked them into lowering their guards, have you considered the fact that the fire was a serious crime and the criminal mastermind behind your Nixon mask might be a dangerous person? I'm most certain you and Mrs. Crane enjoy playing sleuths, but please, my brave stateside Miss Marple, be careful. And do tell me everything that happens next.

Vick, wishing she were
on the case with you

From: Katie Bell
To: Lady Victoria Salter Stanhope

Dear Vick:

Not to worry. I think the lid's about to blow on our twenty-year-old mystery. Just the other day, I looked at an old red brick flecked with gold specks on my fireplace mantel. The bricks of Mossy Creek High School were made at a kiln in a mining area of northern Georgia and bore bits of real gold ore inside them. After the fire, the gold-speckled bricks were sold to locals and raffled off to raise money for local groups. It was said the school was the foundation of Mossy Creek, and so it was only fitting that it support good causes.

In my mind, a father and child ought to serve the same purpose. One builds the next, but they hold each other up. The same way a town can hold its heart together if its people build more than they tear down and keep that foundation in their hands.

Speaking of which, I have some sad news to report about Ed Brady and his son. They've been estranged for a long time, but Ed, Junior, has come back home. The reason why is the sad part.

Vick, remember me telling you last year about Mr. Brady and his beloved wife? I'm so sorry to report this to you, but Ellie Brady has died.

Katie

ED, JUNIOR
COMING HOME

Sometimes the past and present come together like a sweet, old-fashioned puzzle, and pieces that seemed so hard to find begin to fit perfectly.

I stood in the cemetery of Mossy Creek Presbyterian Church along with everyone else in town that fall, watching my father, Ed Brady, bury my mother, Ellie. Pop looked like what he was — an old, tired farmer, wearing an outdated sports coat and a tie knotted loosely beneath a white shirt too large for his neck. I remembered how big I once thought he was. He didn't look that way any more. I felt out of place, standing there in my expensive pinstriped suit, a middle-aged businessman who'd left Mossy Creek almost thirty years ago and had only come back periodically since.

After the graveside service, the minister and every oldtimer in the church congregation came up to me. I shook the men's hands and hugged the women, while my father went through the motions. Every person who spoke to me said the same thing, *Good to see you, Boy.*

I was still Ed Brady's *boy,* who'd come to say goodbye to his mother and give his father support, not that the old man seemed to need me. He'd never needed me — only my mother. Throughout the service, he stood stony faced and erect, holding all his emotions inside as he'd always done.

Now, as I drove him home in a car I'd rented at the airport down in Atlanta, he grumbled softly. "Ought to be in the truck. It got me back and forth to see Ellie in the nursing home. Should have got her running for Ellie's funeral."

I started to say something soothing, but my throat closed. As we headed out of town, I saw a banner over the door of the town hall: MOSSY CREEK SCHOOL RE-UNION, NOVEMBER 2.

Pop spoke again. "Don't reckon you'll go." It wasn't a question.

I hadn't made up my mind until then. "I thought I would," I answered. "I haven't been to a reunion since I graduated from high school."

"No, you haven't. Always figured it had something to do with what happened that night at Ida's silo."

"No," I said. I'd thought about that often. I didn't have anything to do with burning the high school down in 1981. I was long gone by then. But ten years before, on the night he was referring to, I'd been part of something that people swore led straight to the fire, a decade later. I think Pop had never forgiven me. Ed Brady's boy should have stopped the prank before it got out of hand. I hadn't.

People ought to have their own name. I was christened Edward Alton Brady, Junior, then shortened it to Eddie. I spent the first seventeen years of my life in the shadow of my father, as if he'd moved in a photograph and I was the blur behind him. If Mossy Creekites had been asked to describe me, all they would have come up with was something like, "Well, he's Big Ed's and Miss Ellie's boy."

Growing up, I never quite felt at home in Mossy Creek. Everyone else was trying to keep the town just like it was, particularly Pop, who thought that his service during World War II gave him the right to expect the whole country, including Mossy Creek, to stay the same as when he'd defended it. My father didn't enlist until late in the war. Before that he was exempted as a farmer.

He said it was time he did his part and turned over the running of the farm to a veteran who'd already been wounded and sent home. Once Pop made up his mind, there was no changing it. When the war ended, he came back — wounded but proud — and married my mother, Ellie Whitaker, the old maid of the community. He said they were both surprised when I was born eight years later.

They loved me, but mostly they loved each other. They laughed and talked, often in some kind of brief shorthand that went over my head. I always felt like I intruded in their lives. I think that's why I never married. I wanted my parents' kind of completeness, and so far I hadn't found a woman who offered it.

My father was a good man, but stubborn. Everything in his world was black or white. That made it simple for him.

It was never simple for me. My life evolved in shades of gray until the night ten years before the fire. The night of the 1971 Mossy Creek High School Homecoming Game. The Mossy Creek Rams were playing the Bigelow Wildcats; we always played Bigelow at Homecoming. Traditionally, the boys from Bigelow tried to capture our ram mascot. At that time, the mascot was a big wooly ram named Ulysses from a herd Pop kept. In return for the Bigelowans' effort to kidnap Ulysses, we Creekites painted the big rock in front of their high school. It was supposed to all be in fun, but even then, it was serious business.

That was the night I became Ed Brady in my own right. It was my job to defend Ulysses. I didn't. Let's just say it was my first experience with a blond decoy named Buffy who was wearing *Charlie* cologne and a mini-skirt.

While I helped her change her tire out on North Bigelow Road and accepted her thanks in the form of a kiss hot enough to peel the paint off the fender of her blue Mustang, the boys from Bigelow stole Ulysses from his stall in the parking lot at the high school. To my credit, I tried to do the right thing, later. Didn't matter that the world never found that out. I knew.

I couldn't tell Pop and Mama what really happened; I'd sworn to keep it secret. Pop didn't ask much but didn't forgive much, either. Maybe he thought when I was ready to admit my weaknesses, I'd explain. I never did.

When I won a scholarship in track to a small college out West, I left home and didn't look back. It took me a while to get myself together, realize I had a talent for computer programming, and get a real job. To begin with, I was happy to be a ski bum, but eventually I partnered with some fellow computer gurus and found my calling. Brady, Inc. developed computer games. Our business grew by bits and bytes. Then by leaps and bounds. I had money. I had women.

But I had no family.

Once Mama's health started to fail, Pop stopped farming to stay close to her and protect her. At first, even her friends in Mossy Creek didn't realize her mind was going. Pop feared she'd wander away from home and get hurt. I didn't know just how sick she was until I came for a visit.

"Who are you?" she would ask me, wringing her hands. "What are you doing in my house?"

She still knew my father, but she'd become so anxious at the sight of anyone else that I stayed away. That was hard.

Then Mama had a stroke, and she had to go into the Mossy Creek nursing home, Magnolia Manor. I called and offered my help, but Daddy said he could handle it. I knew he couldn't afford her care. Sending the nursing home money so that he wouldn't know how much it cost was something I could do.

Snow Halfacre, the administrator at Magnolia Manor, had been in my class at the high school. We'd had a little romance between us in the tenth grade, and a friendship survived it all those years. She handled my secret payments to Magnolia Manor and kept me informed about Pop and Mama. When Pop had his cataracts removed, she told me the surgery helped his sight but the life just went out of him. He got himself back and forth to the nursing home to see my mother and played Santa for the town, as usual, but other than that no one could get him out of his house, much.

Then Mama died.

It was as if fate had meant for her to leave and me to go back to Mossy Creek. My partners and I had just sold our company to an international media conglomerate, leaving me a reasonably wealthy man with plenty of time and money to do whatever I wanted.

Including go home.

So I came to bury my mother and take care of my father.

"I don't think he should be living alone, anymore," Snow told me. "Why don't you consider moving him to our assisted living apartments?"

"Could he bring Possum?" I asked. "Possum is living with the Blackshears at their vet clinic, for now. But I think Pop really wants him back."

She sighed and shook her head. "No dogs."

"No Pop, then," I said.

So I was right back where I started. Maybe the town motto ought to be, "Ain't going no where, and even if you leave, you can't help but come back." I decided I'd get the farm spruced up, stick around for the reunion events in November, and — with any luck — by the first of the year, I'd get Pop settled in some apartment that allowed old hound dogs, too, and I'd move on.

Whoever it was that said, *The best laid plans of mice and men oft go astray,* obviously had me, Pop, and Mossy Creek in mind, beginning with the sales agent at Mossy Creek Mountain Real Estate, Inc.

Farm Land, Log Homes and Mountain Retreats For Sale.

The sign outside the office said nothing about selling memories, too.

"I'm interested in farm land," I told the good-looking brunette sitting behind a fake mahogany desk. Both she and the elegant desk looked out of place among the dried corn stalks and pumpkins decorating the fake cedar cabin interior.

She held out her hand and gave me a welcoming smile. "I'm Julie Honeycut, and I'm sure we can find what you want."

I hated to disappoint her. "You misunderstand. I'm not buying. I'd just like to know what land is selling for up here in the north end of Bigelow County these days."

She frowned. "Oh. Mr. Brady, I'd heard you were *staying.*"

"You heard the wrong gossip, then."

Her mouth flattened, and she turned to her computer without another word. Thirty minutes later, I learned that my father's rolling two hundred acres with its mountain views was one of the most valuable pieces of land in Mossy Creek. "You do know that the Bank of Bigelow County threatened to foreclose on his land last year," Julia said, scowling at me as if I'd willingly let my family farm go to bankers.

My blood froze. "No, I *didn't* know that."

She smiled.

I headed for the Mossy Creek branch of the Bank of Bigelow County, where I deposited money to pay two years' worth of back taxes. On the way out, I was intercepted by Amos Roydon. Amos was nine years younger than me. He'd been just a lanky kid when I left town. Now he was in his mid-thirties and the police chief. He'd come back from a career as a cop down in Atlanta. He'd learned to fit in, again. I envied him.

"You planning to stick around for a while, Ed?"

"I don't know yet."

"You know your father needs you. He's just too stubborn to admit it."

"He's always been that way."

We talked a few minutes, and I started to move on.

"I suppose you've heard," Amos said. "Ham Bigelow is planning to run for President in two years."

I stopped cold. "Bribing half the state to elect him governor wasn't enough?"

Amos smiled and left me standing there in a state of shock.

Ham Bigelow. I had bad memories of him. And that was an understatement.

I drove down to Bigelow in a foul mood. At the County Tax office, I learned an even more surprising truth; Ham's cousin, John Bigelow — husband of *Mossy Creek Gazette* publisher Sue Ora Salter Bigelow — had loaned Pop money with the farm as collateral. Although John was a lawyer, he had taken over management of the bank as a favor to Ham, who was busy governing the state. Pop had missed the last few months of payments, but John hadn't foreclosed. I headed straight for the Bank of Bigelow County's main office.

"Good to have you back, Eddie," John said. "Your dad needs you."

"Call me Ed," I said.

"Sorry. Ed. Are you going to stay?"

"Hadn't planned on it, but now, I don't know. Why haven't you foreclosed on the farm, John? Excuse me for putting it this way, but Bigelowans in general, and the family's banking presidents in particular, aren't known for being kind-hearted. Your cousin's still running this bank behind the scenes, even though he's governor. And there's no love lost between him and my father. Or me."

John looked out his office window, made a show of straightening some papers on his desk, then brushed an invisible bit of dust off a framed desk portrait of Sue Ora and their teenage son, Will. John was a prominent Bigelowan married to a prominent Creekite, with a mixed-blood son to bind them. Maybe he had a conscience. "I talked with Ham. I told him I intended to let the mortgage ride while your father took care of your mother in her final days." John smiled without using his eyes. "Ham is happy to help out an old friend. He just hopes you'll . . . return the favor."

"Ham and I were never friends, and you know it. Look, I appreciate your concern for my father, and I appreciate Ham's, well . . . I'll call it *self-serving kindness,* but I'll take care of Pop's debts myself. Today." I pulled out my cell phone. With one call, I'd have my bank transfer the entire amount of the loan.

John nodded. "Good. I hoped you'd be back for homecoming, and I planned to talk to you about your father's options. I would have called you, but I knew your father would reject anyone's help. Even yours."

I thanked him, paid off the loan, then headed back up to Mossy Creek with more questions than I started with. I didn't know John well, but I knew Ham.

And Ham was running scared.

Governor Ham Bigelow and I were about the same age. Mid-forties. Thirty years ago he'd been a senior at Bigelow High when I was a junior at Mossy Creek. My own carelessness had involved me in a dark event that year at homecoming, and I'd lived with a guilty conscience ever since. I doubted Ham felt any guilt for his part — he wasn't exactly a model of ethics — but he certainly didn't want anyone to know the truth, either. So Governor Ham Bigelow had made certain the Bank of Bigelow County ignored my dad's missed loan payments. Ham owed me. He was trying to keep me quiet.

"Do you know you forgot to pay last year's taxes?" I asked Pop.

"Taxes? Got no children in school and don't farm anymore. The government'll have to give me a discount before I'm gonna pay taxes." He paused. "Besides, I was takin' care of your mama. That's more important than taxes."

"If you don't pay the taxes, the government can take the farm."

"Take my farm?" He snorted. "Bradys have been on this land since 1850, and I'll be damned if the government will tell us to leave before we're ready." He stared at me. " 'Course, if there ain't no heir willing to stay on here after I'm gone, I guess Ham Bigelow and his kind will get the land, anyhow." He continued to look straight at me for one of the few times since I'd been home. Then he shook his head and went to feed Possum, as if he'd answered his own question.

I followed him through the house. "Pop, I don't know a thing about farming."

"Pop? Sounds like breakfast cereal."

He was right. I had a hard time being comfortable with what I called him, even in my thoughts. Away from home, he'd been Father. As a boy in the south, he was Daddy. Never Dad. Addressing him as Pop was too casual, and the look he gave me said plain enough that he wasn't pleased. Maybe *Ed* fit better.

"All right, Ed," I deadpanned.

He snorted, again.

Later, I watched as he sat on the back porch in his old rocking chair and looked off across the pasture behind the barn. Suddenly, I realized how hunched and thin he looked, his big body curved like an old bow. A stubble of white beard emphasized his sunken cheeks. I reached out to touch his shoulder, then stopped myself. Together, we looked at the Brady view of the world.

With the mountains behind, most of our land spread out to the southwest of the house toward Bigelow. To the north, there was a wedge of cedar trees and a wire fence heavy with trumpet vines between our property and Ida Hamilton Walker's well-kept dairy pastures. The famous silo of Hamilton Farm peeked over our trees.

Our house was a typical seventy-five-year-old frame house with a tin roof and fading white paint. Across the front was a porch made of aging tongue-and-groove flooring. Nobody ever came in the front door, so it didn't matter that they could have fallen through a rotten spot here and there. Visitors drove up the lane that circled around behind the house. They knocked on the back porch door and entered through the kitchen. The original long, open porch had been shortened by half when Pop added indoor plumbing and built a bathroom. But Pop, true to his traditions, hadn't closed the well at the other end of the porch, near the kitchen. The galvanized bucket and tin dipper still hung on a hook on the post beside it. I could drink sweet, ice-cold Creekite water from the same well as my grandparents and great-grandparents and great-great grandparents.

My great-great-grandfather had built the house on a slight rise. "So he could hide up in the trees," my mother had liked to tell me. What she called our "grand driveway" snaked through maples and oaks to South Bigelow Road. As a boy, when the leaves fell in the fall I'd climb onto the roof outside my window then down a hundred-year-old oak tree with limbs that made it easy for me to escape into the night.

Now I debated sitting on the roof, but

decided I was a grown man and couldn't. I went inside and cooked Pop some dinner.

"What's this?" he asked, staring at one of Mama's old blue willow plates filled with something besides pork chops, turnip greens, and cornbread.

"Pasta covered with cheese and sun-dried tomato sauce." One of my ex-girlfriends had been a chef. She'd taught me to cook. There was a lot Pop didn't know about his middle-aged son.

"Humph! What's wrong with plain old macaroni and cheese?"

"That's what this is," I assured him. "Just with fancy ketchup on it."

He sat down and ate a few bites, looked impressed, refused to say so, and refused a second helping. The next night I served him some fish and chips from Fish Stix, a take-out place down in Bigelow. "Not near as good as fried trout caught from Mossy Creek," he said, while cleaning his plate.

"Sorry to see you could barely stomach the food, Ed," I said.

"Pop, there's something I've been wondering about. You used to watch all the University of Georgia football games on TV. Never missed one. When your TV died you could have afforded a new one. Why not get a TV?

Don't you like sports anymore?"

Pop stared at me over the breakfast table. "I still got my radio. Don't have to see it to listen."

"Tell you what, I'll buy you one of those big-screen televisions, so we can watch the Bulldogs and the Yellow Jackets in style."

"My antenna got blown down two or three years ago."

"I'll pay to have you hooked up to Big-elow Cable."

"I appreciate the offer, son, but I don't want you to spend all your money on me. I can get along without a TV, just like I have been."

"Don't worry, Pop, I can afford it. Another thing — you know I'm driving a rental car. I'd like to get your truck fixed and turn the rental car back in."

He looked surprised. "You want to drive my old ugly truck?"

"Sure."

"Suit yourself. Craziness." And he shuffled off into his bedroom and shut the door.

"This is war, Ed," I said under my breath.

The next day I ordered cable, bought the big screen TV, and arranged for it to be delivered, then drove Pop over to the Black-shear Veterinary Clinic. It was a rare fall morning, warm with a crisp taste to the air.

I felt curiously content, and that surprised me.

Hank Blackshear had made a lot of improvements to the place since the years when his father was the town vet. The house sparkled with fresh white paint. Ramps connected the office and the clinic so Casey could roll her wheelchair everywhere.

I parked at the side of the clinic, cut the truck's engine, and opened the door slowly. A frantic barking came from the office. Casey opened the office door, and Possom nearly fell all over himself in his frantic rush to get to Pop. The old hound jumped into the truck and climbed onto Pop's lap, slobbering all over Pop's face.

"Fool dog!" Pop snapped. "Sit down here like you got good sense."

But Possum was having no part of any sense that didn't allow him to show his joy in being reunited with his owner.

Casey rolled herself outside. "Hello, Mr. Brady. And you must be Eddie," she said in a voice that sounded like sunshine. Strange. She was in her early twenties, too young to have known me at all when I lived in Mossy Creek. I felt old, suddenly.

"Ed," I corrected and gently shook her hand.

"I kept telling Possum that Mr. Brady

would be back for him, but he was beginning to doubt me."

"Thank you for looking after Pop and for taking care of Possum."

"That's what we do in Mossy Creek — look after each other, whether we want to be looked after or not. Would you like to come in for coffee? Hank's performing a minor surgery on Zeke Abercrombie's cat right now. I'm manning the office."

"Pop and I have a date with the Georgia-Georgia Tech football game on television this afternoon. Dad's a dyed-in-the-wood Georgia fan. Me? Well, I'm a Tech man."

Casey smiled. "Are you going to stick around Mossy Creek for a while?"

"Looks like it. At least for now."

"Good." She waved to Pop, reached up one hand, and Possum clambered to the truck's open door and licked her fingers. "Mr. Brady, I've never seen a happier dog. And you're looking pretty happy yourself."

Pop grunted. His face turned red. Possum flopped across his knees and snuffled the front of his overalls lovingly. "Fool dog," Pop whispered, then turned his face away and looked out his window.

Later, back at the farm, Pop had nothing good to say about the new TV. "Too big. Nobody needs a thing this big. And new recliners, too. Where's my old lounger?"

"You mean the one with the broken springs and the split leather? They hauled it off when they delivered the new ones. Which one do you want, the green leather one or the tan leather one?"

Possum, who'd come running in, promptly choose the green one by jumping into it and barking at Pop.

"You're a turncoat!" he growled and edged Possum over so he could sit down. "All right, son, turn that monster TV on. Your mother would say it's 'tacky,' just like that aluminum Christmas tree you bought for her one year."

"I heard you decorated one more tree for her last Christmas," I said quietly.

He looked away. "She needed her Ugly Tree."

The Ugly Tree. She'd always send my father out into the woods to cut down the ugliest tree he could find for Christmas. To her, making it beautiful with decorations was loving it to life. I took my place in the beige chair beside him, hit the button on the remote, and found the ball game.

"By the way, Pop, I ran into Mayor Ida when I was arranging for the television. She asked me if I'd play Santa Claus this year in the Christmas parade. What do you think?"

"I don't know why anybody would want to. I always nearly froze to death up on that fire truck. Then when you come down, the brats will pull your whiskers and the babies spit up on you."

"So you think I ought to tell her no."

"I don't know about that. You're a Brady. And being Santa is a Brady tradition. That is if you're into that sort of thing. I never was."

Tradition. Home. Mossy Creek. There was something to be said for all of that. "Maybe I'll give it a try. And maybe we'll cut down and decorate an Ugly Tree for Christmas. What do you say?"

He stared hard at the giant television set, his jaw working and his eyes wet. He scrubbed a hand over them. "I say you talk too much. You're just like Ellie used to be, always interfering with me watching the game. I'm betting on Georgia. Guess you'll take Tech."

"That's right, Ed."

He snorted.

I let up the footrest on my recliner and stretched out. Some things never changed. And maybe that's what tradition was, making the past a bridge to the future.

Over the next few days, I cooked safe,

ordinary food and talked about safe, ordinary subjects. Pop ate and grumbled. I cleaned the house, rebuilt the floor of the front porch, and even hung new living room curtains to replace a dingy pair of bath towels Pop had thrown over the curtain rod after mice chewed holes in the old drapes.

Pop pretended not to notice anything I did until two days before Halloween, when I decided to crank the tractor. I planned to clear the sagebrush and frostbitten weeds choking the ditches on either side of Mama's grand driveway. I didn't think any kids would come trick-or-treating so far out of town — when I was a kid we all gathered up on the square and got our candy from the shop owners — but if any kids did venture up our driveway, I'd at least make sure they didn't hurry back down to South Bigelow Road brushing beggar lice off their Star Wars Jedi robes and pulling blackberry briars from their Batman capes.

The tractor refused to make a sound. I went into town, bought a new battery and new spark plugs, installed them, and cleaned the tractor's carburetor. Nothing helped. Pop sat on the porch watching me all morning before he finally roused himself and, using a stick for a cane, made his way to the barn.

"What are you doing?" he asked.

"I thought I'd clear the driveway and mow the pasture."

He looked surprised. "Why?"

"Well, it's almost Halloween. We might have some kids."

"Doubt that. I'm the crazy old man of South Bigelow Road."

Right. He played Santa Claus every year at Christmas, and the kids loved him. Pop was just being ornery. I shrugged. "I'm still going to get this tractor running."

"Didn't think you'd even remember how." He poked the rusting John Deere symbol on the engine cover. "Ain't got no computer for you to use."

"Maybe I'll add one."

He stared at me until he realized I was joking. "She'll run, but she's a mite touchy," he said.

"That she is," I agreed. "Any suggestions on how I can get the engine to crank?"

"Been a while," he said, running his knotted fingers across the tractor's fender as if they were communicating through the metal. "The last time I drove her it was to see Ellie. Then I broke my leg, and Chief Amos wouldn't let me back on the highway. She might need a little toddy to grease up her innards."

"Toddy? Don't tell me you still claim to pour liquor into the gas tank."

He laughed. I hadn't heard him laugh in a very long time. "Moonshine's good for what ails a body. Even a tractor likes it."

I called his bluff. "Let's go get some, then."

He eyed me, smiling. "Aw, just pour a little diesel fuel in her gas tank and let it set a spell. That ought to do it."

It did. The tractor started the next day. And so did Pop. It was as if he needed some job to grease his own innards. In fact, he insisted on mowing the sides of the driveway himself. I started to say no, then took a look at his face and just opened the front gate to let him through. I sat on the porch and watched my father clear his road. Pop knew every inch. As the brush got mowed down, I realized he was leaving one scrawny pine tree in the corner where the road ran close to a pasture fence.

Our Ugly Tree, for Christmas.

Two hours later, he drove the tractor into the barn and climbed down. There was a lightness in his shuffle as he headed for the porch with his stick-cane perched on one shoulder like a fishing pole. He pulled up the bucket from the well and plunged the tin dipper into the cold water. "Nothing like a good cold drink of water after working hard." He sat down on the porch and wiped the perspiration and flecks of grass from his face. "Been a while."

"Why'd you let everything grow up like that?" I asked.

"Didn't seem to matter. Couldn't see it from the porch anyway. All the livestock's gone. And old Possum even quit chasing the rabbits out of the brush."

I stroked the old hound's head. He lay devotedly by Pop's feet. "Your hunting dogs were the only friends you ever needed — other than Mama."

A frown wrinkled his forehead, and he stared at me. "There was you, boy."

"Me? I don't know. I didn't seem to fit into your scheme of things. Farming, tractors, livestock. The only animals I liked were the chickens, and then we ate them. I was out of place. But you and Mama had each other. I thought about it a lot. You didn't seem to need me."

"No need to think on families. We don't have to be alike. Thinking like that makes a person crazy. What is just is. Ellie was my wife. You're my boy. That's all you have to be. I always thought you leaving home had something to do with them Bigelow boys stealing the ram. Wish you hadn't left home, but you did, and you made a life for yourself. It didn't have to be my kind of life."

In his mind it was that simple. Family. We connect with each other in whatever way we can. We don't have to be the other person. We just have to be ourselves. "I'm sorry I didn't want to be a farmer when I was growing up. What I loved in high school — running track, playing tennis — all that was nonsense to you. You told me so."

"I thought you ought to be learning to make a living instead of playing," he said.

"That 'playing' got me an athletic scholarship to college. It got me an education." He wouldn't have understood that my education led me to another kind of play. Computer games. "I was lucky to be in the right place at the right time."

"And now you've come home. Ellie said you would. I wish it had been sooner. While she still knew who you were."

"So do I," I said gruffly.

"Son, I don't know what's in your mind, but you don't have to do all this."

"Like you always told me when I was a kid, 'Brady's don't do anything they don't want to, but when they do, they don't talk much.' "

"Guess I never did too much of that, did I? Talking."

"Neither did I. Think we can change that?"

"Maybe. There is something that's been bothering me. Don't you think it's time you tell me the truth about that homecoming night and the ram?"

"Does it really matter now?"

"Considering all the talk about the old high school these days, I think it does."

"What happened to me was ten years before the fire."

"Then it's so long in the past you ought to just tell me. But if you can't tell me, I'll respect your decision."

I sat there another long time, the past rising up inside me like the cold, clear Creek water that fed the well of our Brady heritage. And then I began to talk.

1971.

Punky Hartwell and I were stationed by a makeshift pen filled with hay in the graveled parking lot behind Mossy Creek High. There stood Ulysses the ram, the school mascot who preceded Samson. Two Creekite boys were elected to watch over the mascot every year before homecoming, (this was before teachers like Dwight Truman took over the job,) and that year Punky and I won the honor of being Ulysses' royal guardsmen. All we had to do was keep him safe until he was led onto the football field during the homecoming halftime show.

A pretty girl from our rival, Bigelow High, called to me from beside her little blue Mustang. She was crying. I left Punky with Ulysses and went off into the darkness to change a tire for her. She thanked me with a kiss. Several kisses. When I got back to the pen, Punky and Ulysses were gone. I'd been set up by the Bigelow boys.

I jumped into a friend's car and went after them. Tracked them south of Mossy Creek and out to Hamilton Farm.

When I drove up, I saw a truck tearing out of Ida Hamilton Walker's front pasture. I heard somebody yelling from the Hamilton grain silo. Then I heard a terrified 'baaaah' that could only be Ulysses. Both cries for help came from forty feet above my head. I tilted my head back and stared at the dark silhouette of the Hamilton silo against a moonlit sky.

Punky and the ram were up there.

The Bigelowans had stranded Punky and Ulysses forty feet high on a narrow, hand-cranked elevator platform that was used to lift sacks of grain up to a hatch on the silo's curving metal roof, where the grain was dumped inside for storage. The platform, which had no safety rails of any kind, was barely big enough for Ulysses, let alone the terrified Punky.

"Help me, Eddie!" Punky screamed. He pressed himself as flat against the silo's side as possible. Beside him, Ulysses danced from foot to foot and baaahed wildly.

"I'll let you and Ulysses down slowly — just hold on!"

I grabbed the hand crank and tried to inch the platform down smoothly. It dropped several inches with a screech of gears and the metallic clank of chain jerking hard. Punky screamed. Ulysses butted Punky in the stomach, and, since the platform had no safety railings, suddenly Punky Hartwell fell past me and hit the ground, hard. Punky lay there moaning, and I stared at him in horror. His right leg was broken. But worse than that, he'd landed face down on a small tree branch. Blood dripped from the corner of his left eye socket. The eye looked mushy. My stomach rolled.

"Don't tell anyone how it happened," Punky begged. "Those Bigelow boys are with the Fang and Claw Club. If we get them in trouble, they'll kill us."

"I'm not letting them get away with this."

He moaned. "The leader was Ham Bigelow!"

"You saw him? Good. Then you can tell Chief Royden." Battle Royden wouldn't hesitate a second about arresting the rich son of the richest family in the county.

"No! I'll never tell! I'll swear I don't know who did it! And you can't tell either, Eddie! If you do, the Bigelowans will protect Ham and hurt you! Your daddy has farm loans with their bank, Eddie! They'll call in the loans and take everything him and your mama own! Give me your word! You won't tell!"

I groaned low under my breath. "I give you my word." Then I ran up to Miss Ida's big house with a weight inside me like a stone.

In the aftermath of Punky's accident, he and I were accused of playing some kind of stupid joke — that is, "kidnapping" our own school's mascot — and I was blamed for hoisting Punky and Ulysses up the grain elevator.

Punky lost his left eye.

I lost the power to tell the truth.

Pop and Mama were humiliated and could only believe the worst about me.

One afternoon, I cornered Ham Bigelow behind a bank of laurel shrubs outside his parents' country club, down in Bigelow. I slugged him in the mouth, broke two of his front teeth, then stood over him as he lay on the ground, moaning and bleeding.

"I know you set Punky up as an initiation prank for your damned Fang and Claw Society," I told him. "You sneaking coward. I swore I wouldn't tell anyone what you did, but *I'll* always know the truth. Don't show your face at another Mossy Creek home-coming game. Ever. Or I'll knock out the rest of your teeth."

Ham's head lolled.

He was never seen at a homecoming game, again.

Thirty years later, Pop and I sat in silence on the porch.

"All I could think about," I said gruffly, "was that Ed Brady's son let the ram get stolen and let Punky get hurt. I'm sorry I didn't tell you the truth. It seemed impor-tant to keep quiet, back then. I gave Punky my word."

"A man's word is always important, son. I'm proud of you."

I hadn't expected him to understand. I swallowed hard. My eyes blurred with tears. Naturally, I changed the subject. "Now, you want to tell me why you didn't cut down that last ugly pine tree in the pasture, Daddy?"

"*Daddy?* Don't get soft on me, son. That ugly tree is a story for another day. Too much confession at a time gives a man a heartache." He smiled at me. And suddenly, after all those years, we shared a peaceful moment, just the two of us.

Father and son.

Halloween night was a bust, as far as trick-or-treaters went. I'd bought a couple of bags of bubblegum and chocolate bars, just in case, but by ten o'clock Pop went to bed, so I turned out the porch lights and took the candy upstairs to my room. I opened the window and climbed out. The window had seemed larger when I was sixteen. I lay on the roof, planting my heels against a two-by-four I'd nailed along the edge to keep myself from falling off.

Now, almost thirty years later, I had to bend my knees to fit into the space. Looking up at a full moon and the stars in the night sky, I thought about my father and how he had respected my promise.

The sound of a car roaring up the driveway broke into my thoughts. I heard young voices, laughter and a couple of spirited "Go, Bigelow Wildcats!" Then the car backed out and screeched down the road toward Bigelow.

With a spidery feeling zippering up my spine, I climbed down the oak tree for the first time in thirty years. Quietly, I headed along the long gravel drive in the dark, ready to surprise anyone planning to give us a trick instead of a treat. I needn't have bothered. Our visitor began making enough noise to drown out my movements. The intruder stumbled into a patch of moonlight.

"Agggh. Why'd I do this-ss?" a youthful male voice slurred. "Initiation-smitiation. Agggh." The sounds that followed were unmistakable; he was throwing up. Moans followed. "Fang and Claw. Fang and Claw. Agggh. Should call it the Hurl and Vomit Society, 'stead."

The Fang and Claw Society.

Bigelow High's notorious secret prank club had gone completely underground after Punky lost his eye. Now it was supposed to be just legend. Or maybe not.

I swore and started toward the victim in the moon-streaked darkness. I could see him hunched over the top rail of Pop's pasture fence.

"Hold onto the rail," I called drily. "And don't turn your face upwind."

The boy whirled around and tried to run. His feet got tangled in a clump of newly mowed brush, and he fell with a thud. "Aggh."

"Are you all right?" I knelt beside him.

"Yes, sir," he managed, trying unsuccessfully to sit up.

"I'll give you a hand. Ed Brady, here. Who're you?"

"You're not Mr. Brady."

"Mr. Brady's my father. What's your name?"

He hesitated, then groaned in defeat. "Will Bigelow, sir. Just kill me and get it over with, please. Before my parents get the chance."

Will Bigelow. John and Sue Ora's teenage son. "Sorry, Will, but I've got to call them." I took him by one arm and helped him stagger to his feet. "Let's get you to the house and clean you up. At least your mother won't have to cover her nose when she gets here."

Will groaned. "Just call my mom. She'll kill me, but she won't *Bigelow* me to death like my dad does."

"Bigelow you to death?"

"You know. It's like you hear a drum roll, and you're told, 'You're a Bigelow, Boy. There are standards for people who bear the Bigelow name.' "

I smothered a laugh. "Been there, done

that, Will. I'm Ed Brady's boy. You're John Bigelow's son. Fathers always have expectations."

The kid moaned.

"Come on. Tell you what. I'll help you wash up with the garden hose, then drive you over to your mother's house. Give you some time to get your story straight."

"I just hope Dad's not there. Agggh. For once, I'd be glad they don't live together all the time. He'll never understand this. Never."

I led the kid up to the house and reached for the garden hose by the front porch. "So I gather the Fang and Claw Society still exists?"

Will stiffened, halted, and wavered in place as if trying to come to attention. "I'm forbidden to talk on penalty of . . . of something . . . can't recall right now," he slurred, then clamped a fist over his heart. "I know *nothing.*"

I nodded. "Same Fang and Claw ritual crap, just like thirty years ago."

He groaned.

I pushed his head under the garden hose and turned the ice-cold water on.

John, looking rumpled in khakis and a sweatshirt, was waiting on the porch of Sue

Ora's handsome little house just outside town. He pulled his son out of my car, hugged him grimly, and helped him to the house, with me following.

His mother, wrapped tightly in a long terrycloth robe, glared at him from the front door. "Is this a new kind of trick or treating? You sneaked out of this house after lying to me that you were going to bed early? What were you doing? You could have been killed by alcohol poisoning. Haven't we taught you better?"

"Aw, Mama, I didn't have that much to drink. Just a couple of beers." He paused. "And some bourbon. And a little tequila. And . . ." He clamped his fist to his chest and swayed. "Sworn to silence." He hiccupped.

John guided him into the living room. "Will, dammit . . ." John swallowed the rest of those words and said instead, "Let's get you in the shower and wash off the smell. Sue, will you make some coffee?"

"I don't drink coffee," Will said. "It's unnatural. I drink healthy herbal tea."

Sue Ora snorted. "Sure, and I didn't think you drank liquor, either."

She left to make the coffee while John pushed Will down a back hall.

"Don't go, Ed," John called over his

shoulder. "I want to talk to you."

"I'll be waiting," I said, then found the nearest bathroom and washed Will's vomit scent off my hands. My own stomach twisted. For a second, I went back thirty years to the dark shadows of another autumn night, when I stood over Punky trying not to throw up when I saw what the stick had done to his eye.

When John and Will returned, Will wore jeans and a Bigelow Wildcats sweatshirt. He looked scrubbed and his dark Bigelow hair stood up in damp spears. Slumping on a couch, he leaned back and took a deep breath. "I apologize," he said.

"Tell us what happened," John ordered.

Will squirmed. "There's a code of honor and silence —"

"Not where the Fang and Claw Society is concerned," John said in a tone that made his son sit up straight.

"Dad, you don't understand. You couldn't understand. You were never —"

"Don't make assumptions," Sue Ora said as she set steaming coffee mugs on a bar between the living room and kitchen. "We're going to find out one way or the other."

"Start by telling us why you were out at the Brady farm," John said.

Will slumped. It was clear he didn't want

to confess. History was definitely repeating itself.

"Maybe I'd better leave," I said.

"No, please don't, Mr. Brady," Will said, his face sunk in misery. "I need a witness when Dad and Mama kill me."

"Trust me, Will. Tell the truth. Trust your parents."

Sue Ora sat beside her son and took his hand. "Why were you in the Brady driveway?"

"I was looking for something." He winced.

"Something?" she coaxed.

"A girl's bra. It was a kind of initiation. I had to bring it back."

John's face went hard. "I thought so. Dammit. The Fang and Claw Society."

"You don't understand, Dad."

"I thought you were smart enough to stay away from those idiots."

"Dad, the Fang and Claw doesn't hurt anybody. I'm a Bigelowan. I have to keep up the tradition. I'll look like a wimp if I don't join. Besides, nothing bad happened."

John sat down in a chair across from his son and jabbed a finger at him. "You have no idea what the Fang and Claw is all about. Or what kind of stunts the members have pulled over the years."

"Dad, that's just talk. Look, just because

you weren't part of it when you were in high school twenty years ago doesn't mean —"

"I *was* part of it."

That brought Will to the edge of the couch. He stared at his father. So did I.

Righteous, conservative John Bigelow?

In the meantime, Sue Ora retrieved something from the pocket of her robe. "As you said, Will, the Bigelows follow tradition." She held out two small pendants on her palm. "I believe the way it works is that all the Society pledges get a fang pendant. When they've been accepted, they get the claw pendant, too. Both are worn secretly on a chain around the member's neck. Is that still the way it's done?"

Will nodded and gulped. "Are those Dad's?"

"Yes. Your dad and I were dating, then. He gave me these. He said he was too ashamed to keep them but wanted me to have them, so I could always remind him of what he'd done."

"What'd you do, Dad?"

John ignored the question for a moment as he studied the wife he obviously still loved but didn't live with.

"You belonged to the Fang and Claw?" Will persisted. "Why didn't you ever tell me?"

John continued to look at Sue Ora. Her face filled with sympathy. She touched his arm. "You were going to sit down with him and admit everything before the reunion festivities next month. This is just an opportunity to do what you intended — a little early."

John laid his hand over hers, his face tightened, and he nodded. Then he turned to their son, and to me, and said very simply, "Twenty years ago, I burned down Mossy Creek High School."

Rainey

REUNION DAY

When it's time to pay the piper, don't procrastinate to beat the band.

It wasn't just Reunion Day. It was Judgment Day.

There were a good five thousand people in town that sunny November weekend — more than twice the permanent population of Mossy Creek. Almost all of them crowded into the old high school site along with me for the fun, the tears, and the speeches. Cars and trucks were parked ten-rows deep on the school's former football field, and more vehicles lined the road out of town on both sides. The fat yellow buses of Mossy Creek Elementary shuttled people back and forth from the town square, where the Mossy Creek Kiwanis had set up a big tent to sell barbecue. The merchants propped their doors wide open and set out their prettiest welcome signs for business. The reunion was the biggest single-most-attended-one-

557

day event of the last twenty years in Mossy Creek. The record holder had been Homecoming, 1981. The day of the carnival.

The night of the fire.

Music whirled around me from a bluegrass band playing some old, toe-tapping local tune called *Bailey Mill Breakdown.* Heavy on the fiddle, with a washtub bass thumping like a fast heartbeat. It made me so nervous I couldn't listen. I angled between Creekites I'd known all my life, former Creekites I'd only heard about, and friends of Creekites who'd just come along for the festivities — and not a single soul caught the whiff of my misery. In fact, I was so good at hiding my true feelings behind my petite pink wall that I was cheerfullly put upon by my unsuspecting clientele and their reunion guests.

A professional stylist is like a doctor out in public. Always being asked for free diagnoses and ad-lib advice. So I listened solemnly, checked the tightness of aging perms, calculated the next-cut-needed-when? status of growing hair-do's, peered at split ends, and upended acrylic nails to study the tips for consistency. I noticed my new unofficial competition, Jasmine Beleau, handing out cards for her beauty and fashion consulting service, but we nodded to each other with professional friendship, and I let it go at that.

Tents from the Mossy Creek Funeral Home lined the perimeters of the old high school site, sheltering foods and crafts, smiles and memories. *Funeral tents.* Appropriate. To me, the day was a memorial service for my, Rob, and Hank's reputations as Creekites of good conscience. We had kept an ugly secret that hurt our whole town for twenty years. A person can expect sympathy for making a childhood mistake, but not for being an out-and-out adult coward.

In the middle of the broad, empty field where Mossy Creek High had stood in all its handsome glory now there was only a speakers' platform, about fifty-feet long, draped in green-and-white bunting, the colors of the old school. A web of cables and electrical cords snaked off the platform's back end, connecting a large podium to huge speakers, which Bert Lyman of WMOS Media had loaned for the event. When Rob, Hank, and I got up to confess, our voices would carry to the farthest ends of Mossy Creek and all its outlying communities, reflect off Colchik and all her sister mountains, and echo the revelation of our cowardly shame back to us, the truth coming home to nest like a vulture of the spirit. I cringed.

About two dozen speakers had already taken to the stage to commemorate and celebrate Mossy Creek High School, reunions in general, and the faithfulness of Creekites in the world in particular.

"God's own special tribe," Carmel Whit called us. To hear her and the others talk, the Israelites had wandered in the desert looking not for the Promised Land, but for Mossy Creek.

Still, I knew exactly what Miss Carmel and the other speakers meant. I'd never loved our funny little town more than I did that day, with my own public ruin right around the corner. Epic emotion and biblical doom began to settle on me. *I will lift up mine eyes to the hills from whence comes my strength.* I gazed up at Colchik for inspiration.

"See somebody with bad hair to be fixed up there, Rainey?" someone called and laughed. The world was full of jokes and laughter and friendship, except for me.

Tammy Jo Bigelow walked by in deep ex-beauty queen conversation with Josie Mc-Clure and Josie's big, hulking, sweet fiancé, Harry. I blinked back tears and shook my head. Harry had come down from hiding on the mountain. After today, me, Hank and Rob might have to live up there instead.

I wandered among my friends and neighbors, pretending to browse the booths as if I saw anything but loneliness in front of me. Rob and Hank sat with their wives somberly marking time, like me. They'd secluded themselves on a picnic blanket beneath one of the umbrella-like oaks near the old ram statue. The statue had been sandblasted and painted a clean, bright white for the day, and it made a proud sight. I couldn't bear to look at such a symbol of pure Mossy Creek loyalty. Rob and Hank were torturing themselves.

"Come sit with us until it's time," both of them urged, and Teresa and Casey dogged me to come and sit, too, but I said, *"No, I can't wait in the valley of the shadow of the stone sheep."*

They stared at me sympathetically. Yes, I was speaking melodramatic gibberish. I was one curler short of a set, in terms of clear-minded thinking.

"Seeds, Rainey?" one of the women of the Mossy Creek Garden Club asked. I found myself standing at the club's booth without quite realizing how I'd gotten there. The new club member, Miss Peggy, they called her, smiled and held out a plastic sandwich bag filled with seeds. "Zinnias," Miss Peggy explained. "Plant them next spring and you can sit by the blooms sipping a cold margarita all summer. I gathered these seeds from my own flowers. You might call it a special harvest."

I thanked her and tucked the seeds in my tote bag. Margaritas in the summer by the zinnias? The garden clubbers had a reputation for partying, and it was clear this Miss Peggy fit in fine. Nice to be wanted by a group of friends. I had gotten used to being wanted by *my* friends. I better get unused to it. I wandered on. *As ye sow, so shall ye reap.* And it wouldn't be zinnias.

Eula Mae Whit and Millicent Hart sat in folding chairs beneath a canopy attached to the Magnolia Manor booth, talking in low voices, their grizzled heads bent close together. Miss Millicent's boyfriend, Tyrone Lavender, dozed in a lawn chair nearby. Across the way, Win Allen had debuted his Bubba Rice Catering Company — a success, judging by the crowd who were eating his stew, potato salad, and namesake fried rice at picnic tables scattered in the warm autumn sun. Michael Conners was selling beer in Reunion Day plastic mugs, which I think his waitress, Regina Regina, ordered without him knowing, because Michael is not a cute-beer-mug sort of man.

At the forestry service booth, Orville Simple was giving away hand-whittled wooden whistles he swore would scare off bothersome yard critters. "Made from the wood of a former beaver dam," Orville proclaimed.

"Don't work on the beavers, though," Derbert Koomer said real loud, then guffawed. Orville scowled and held up a whistle in a way that said if Derbert didn't shut up he'd be carrying a tune where nobody would want to hear it.

Ed Brady and his son sat in the booth for the volunteer fire department. Mr. Brady, Senior, was a charter member. The department had had two men injured fighting the school fire. So it was a matter of pride for Mr. Brady and the other volunteer firemen to be there handing out candy to the kids on reunion day. They'd invited our paramedics, which included Sandy and Mutt's brother, Boo Bottoms.

Boo was demonstrating CPR on a plastic CPR dummy stretched out on the grass, but this one kid took candy from Mr. Brady then, when Boo turned his back, secretly stuck the candy inside the dummy's plastic lips. So when Boo squatted down and began his demonstration on how to pump the dummy's bosom, a Tootsie Roll popped five feet high and hit Adele Clearwater right between the eyes.

Miss Adele squealed and jumped back faster than you'd think a scrawny old lady in a corset could move. Nearly dropped her custom made purse with the hand-embossed insignia of the Mossy Creek Social Society on the leather. Miss Adele was rarely startled by anything other than the degree of people's inferiority to herself.

"Seeing Adele hop like a frog was worth the trip into town," Mr. Brady said to Ed, Junior, a middle-aged man who smiled like a boy at his daddy's joke. Ed, Senior and Ed, Junior had already held their own reunion — a good one, I could tell. I stood there watching them wistfully, with my fists shoved inside the pockets of my long pink sweater. I couldn't stop thinking about the firemen who'd been injured twenty years ago at Mossy Creek High — not badly injured, Lor', but still . . . what would those men think of me and Hank and Rob after we admitted we set the elephant free and caused the fire?

"He's here," Ed, Junior said in a low voice to his daddy. "Looking rough around the edges, but he came to do what he said he'd do. There he is, over there."

"He won't back out." Old Mr. Brady squinted at someone behind me. "He's had twenty years to chew on hisself over this. He's started talking, and he won't run scared, now. Not after what he told you the other night."

What in the world? I looked around quickly to see who they meant, but all I saw was John Bigelow walking up from the parking area. Sue Ora and Will walked with him, all three of them close together, John and Sue Ora holding hands and looking somber. Will stuck his chin out as if he expected to fight somebody. He slung an arm around his father's shoulders and looked even more defensive.

A strange tingle went up my spine. What was going on with pillar-of-the-community John Bigelow? I turned to just flat-out ask old Mr. Brady, but before I could, everyone craned their heads to watch the governor arrive.

Ham Bigelow didn't drive himself up to Mossy Creek like a regular potentate, anymore — Mossy Creek is the hometown of his mama, Ardaleen Hamilton Bigelow, remember — no, now he *paraded* into town with an entourage. His motorcade included one state patrol car in the lead and another bringing up the rear. Ham rode in a long black limo in the middle, and behind Ham's limo came a big, dark sedan full of Ham's aides — Creekites called his two top flunkies Mayo and Mustard — and then a *second* big sedan carried his press secretary, campaign manager, and personal photographer.

As Ham and his gang got out of their cars, I noticed the strangest thing. Sandy pulled up in a Mossy Creek patrol car and blocked the governor's limo. Ham's state troopers headed over to tell her to move — you just don't block the governor's car. Amos was on the scene supervising, walking the perimeter of the festivities, watching his officers and his townsfolk just as you'd expect on the day of a big event, but suddenly Amos put his hands in his pockets and looked the other way.

For Amos Royden to *look the other way* when his feisty little glorified secretary-dispatcher-compulsive cleaning woman deliberately blocked the governor's motorcade — well, I was flabbergasted.

Sandy waved her arms and called out to the troopers, "I got engine trouble, boys. Can't move another inch. We'll have to call a tow truck." She looked around dramatically for help, as if she couldn't see her own chief fifty feet away.

Ham scowled at his blocked limo. His aides and his local toady, Dwight Truman, gathered around him, and I could tell from the way they huddled and patted his back they were smoothing his feathers. With an air of impatient disgust, Ham waved his troopers away from Sandy and her *stalled* patrol car. He and his entourage headed for the speakers' platform. The big after-lunch ceremonies were about to begin.

My shoulders slumped. I forgot everything but the misery ahead.

"Rainey, what's wrong?" Mayor Ida had walked up while I was lost in my thoughts. She was a sight, as always, dressed in sleek black jeans and a cashmere sweater that showed off a body a woman half her age would envy. Her red-brown hair, piled up on her head, gave her more than the usual regal sexiness. Of course, she wouldn't look like her usual sexy, confident self if she knew her son was about to confess, along with Hank and me, to burning down the high school.

"What's wrong?" she repeated, and her motherly tone did a terrible thing to me. Without warning, tears seeped through my mascara. "I have to tell you something, Miss

Ida." I gulped down a hard breath. I had to help Rob any way that I could.

"What, Rainey?" She put an arm around my shoulders.

"Rob's a wonderful man. *I love him and I always have and I always will.*"

She said nothing. Just studied me.

I went on blindly, "See, I've loved Rob since I was a little nothing-and-nobody girl, and I'll love him today and every day after this for the rest of my *life,* even though I know he'll never love me that way back." I pressed a hand to my mouth and turned away from her shrewd maternal eyes. I fumbled with my tote bag of cosmetics and tissues, determined to hide the tears, the truth, the whole awful moment beneath a fresh coat of pink color. Otherwise, I'd be soggy when I got up to confess, and nobody liked a weepy coward. "I don't mean I'd ever flirt with him or try to cause trouble in his marriage. He worships the ground Teresa walks on. I don't mean I'd ever even *think* about trying to be a homewrecker. But I just . . . I just can't stop loving him from afar."

Miss Ida put her hands on my shoulders and gently forced me to turn around. She was tall; I was a munchkin. I looked up at her and nearly sobbed. But she only nodded. "I've always known you love Rob."

I groaned. "It's that obvious?"

"Only to me. I make it my business to observe the people who care about my loved ones."

"Miss Ida, this whole town is your 'loved one.' "

She nodded, again. "But some people in it are special. And you're one of those people."

"No, I'm not. But Rob is. I've tried to find someone to love besides him. Lor', you know I like men. I've dated. I've gotten close to picking out Mr. Permanent a time or two, but in the end I always pull back and say *No.* Miss Ida, I don't want to spend the rest of my life grieving over Rob. What am I going to do?"

"First of all, never stop believing that there's someone special out there for you. Someone who is meant to be loved by you even more than you love Rob. Someone who will love you back the same way. Someone who will take the hurt away. Keep looking. And always believe. Then you'll be open and ready when your own special person finds you — and you find him."

"I'll never tell Rob I love him. He'll *never* hear it. I swear. I won't embarrass him that way. But I just had to tell *you.* In case you ever need to remember how wonderful he is, how brave and noble and — if you ever need to hear somebody say how wonderful your son is, I'll be right here to say it — oh, Lor', I'm just babbling, and I know none of this makes any sense right now but it will pretty soon, and oh, I'm just trying . . . Miss Ida . . . whatever happens today, please don't forget he's a wonderful person."

I clamped my lips together so tightly I tasted the raspberry flavor of my lipstick on the tip of my tongue. I'd said too much, or not enough. Miss Ida studied me the way a mother cat studies a wayward kitten — for a second, I didn't know if she would nuzzle me or cuff my ear. Then she reached out one strong, graceful hand, stroked the side of my face with just her fingertips, and whispered, "Don't worry. I know everything."

I know everything?

I gaped at her and took a step back. She nodded, but didn't say another word. She knew everything — everything. "Everything?" I asked sickly.

She nodded. "Everything."

She knew what Rob had done, about what we planned to say, and maybe more than that. I was so addled my imagination took off. Maybe she knew *everything* that happened in Mossy Creek behind closed doors or outside them. Maybe she knew the past, present and future. Maybe even what people thought without saying it. What people did without doing anything.

Maybe she was the gypsy fortune-teller come to life.

And then, it hit me. She *was.* "*You* sent the old gypsy fortune telling machine to the party on New Year's Eve." My voice shook.

She nodded. "I found it in an Atlanta antique store last year. I sent it to the town in the hope it would scare the truth out of everyone. So far, it has."

My mouth popped open. I stared at her. "But . . . but you acted so surprised. You made us all think —"

"If people suspected I was the one who sent the gypsy, it would have ruined the sinister effect."

"But . . . what now?"

Her expression turned sly and proud. "Let's just say the rest of the truth is in the gypsy's cards." She nodded to someone behind me. "Take it up on stage, boys. We're ready to start."

I whirled as several men carried the mechanical gypsy up on the speakers' platform. The crowd saw it and went quiet. People stopped whatever they were doing and began to gather before the platform.

They looked from the carnival machine to Mayor Ida and back to the fortune-teller.

On the sidelines, Ham Bigelow began to frown. He looked back over his shoulder at his blocked limo. Sandy waved at him merrily from beside the Mossy Creek patrol car.

Five thousand Creekites, past and present, waited for the future to be told.

I clutched my chest. My heart thudded against my hands. "Miss Ida, what're you planning to do?"

"Nothing. Just watch."

"But —"

"Good afternoon, friends and neighbors and family." Rob's voice. I whirled back toward the stage. Carrying a microphone, he walked up to the podium with Hank behind him, both of them as solemn as preachers. Rob beckoned me with a regretful but resigned look.

I hurried through the crowd.

"I've asked the mayor, my mother," Rob went on, "to let me have the podium this afternoon. There's something I need to tell you all about the night of the fire that burned down Mossy Creek High. I wish I were up here to tell this story alone and take full responsibility, but Dr. Blackshear and Rainey Ann Cecil won't let me do that. So here they are, too."

I bounded up the platform steps. Rob and Hank made a place for me between them. I stood there with as much dignity as I could muster, feeling an invisible noose go around my neck and theirs. The Ten-Cent Gypsy sat next to us in her rusty metal booth, looking weird and stern. Down in the crowd, people traded bewildered glances.

Rob began, "Twenty years ago, with the best intentions but the worst common sense, my friends and I burned down Mossy Creek High School."

Five thousand hearts stopped. The silence of that many people, all staring at us, seemed a wall of rejection, to me.

Then a strong male voice rang out. "No, you didn't."

John Bigelow stepped forward. You could have knocked me over with a feather. He looked up at the three of us sadly, then climbed the platform steps and stood beside us. Even Rob looked speechless. John took the microphone out of his hand. "You and Hank and Rainey couldn't have burned down the high school." He paused. "Because I did it."

Shouts of dismay and cries of misery went up from the crowd. People were finally beginning to find their voices. A wave of whispers rose and fell.

Rob shook his head. "John, I put bolt cutters to the elephant's chain. I can't be sure, but I tried to cut it, and I must have. That's the reason Rose was able to *break* her chain when the ram spooked her. Hank, Rainey, and I didn't intend to set her loose to do any damage, and the last thing we expected was for her to head inside the front doors of the school —"

"She got loose because someone jimmied the padlock that held her chain around the bumper of her owner's camper. I know." He paused. "Because I'm the one who did that. Would you like to hear the whole story?"

Rob nodded.

John Bigelow took the podium and faced the crowd.

Twenty years ago, when John Bigelow was a senior at Bigelow High School, he'd been elected president of the Fang and Claw Society. The society was only a dangerous, whispered legend by then — which made the boys at Bigelow High want to be part of it even more. Most of them never stood a chance.

The Fang and Claw members came from wealthy, namesake Bigelow clans. Hamilton Bigelow himself had been the last official president of the Fang and Claw before it was drummed out of sight, and every boy wanted to mimic Ham. He was rich, he was good-looking, he did whatever he wanted and always had. By 1981, he was running for his first term as a state senator — only 26 years old and already planning his political dynasty. When he wasn't getting his handsome Bigelowan face in the news, he was off skiing in the Rockies or snorkling in the Caribbean or chasing various Southern beauty queens — Miss Lawson County Laurel Princess and Miss Greater Delmar Foxfire Queen before he married Miss Blue Ridge. Though nearly ten years out of high school, he was still the Big Man On Campus to wannabe Fang and Clawsters.

And he was John Bigelow's first cousin.

"I was told that I had big shoes to fill, and it would take a big demonstration of courage and loyalty on my part to raise my name to the level of honor all the past presidents had achieved," John told the reunion crowd. "A group of alumni blindfolded me in the middle of the night and took me into the woods to meet someone they called The Trouble Master. I never saw his face. He stood in the shadows. Wearing a Nixon mask. I didn't recognize his voice, either. I think he disguised it.

"He told me I had to win back the honor

Bigelow High had lost over the years to Mossy Creek. He said he wanted the Creek-ites to never forget their homecoming game with Bigelow that year. He told me it was my job to single-handedly kidnap the Mossy Creek mascot and bring that mascot to him before the game started. He said I'd get further instructions when I did.

"It wasn't easy, but I managed to get Samson out of his pen at Mossy Creek High and hide him in a truck on a street near the school. During the first quarter of the homecoming game, The Trouble Master showed up at the truck. It was dark, and he was still wearing the Nixon mask, and he didn't let me get too close. He said, 'I'll take over from here. You only have to perform two more duties: Go unchain the carnival elephant, wait in the bushes until halftime, and when you see Samson run out of the stadium, shoo him toward the elephant.'

"None of that sounded wise to me — someone could get hurt — and I nearly told The Trouble Master I wouldn't do it, but I didn't. *I didn't have the courage to tell him no.* So I left Samson with him and slipped into the parking lot of Mossy Creek High, where the carnival was set up. I managed to break the lock on the elephant's chain but left the chain looped so no one would notice. Then I hid in the bushes and waited for halftime.

"I never dreamed The Trouble Master would do what he did. Cover Samson in sparklers and set him on fire. When Samson came running through the darkness, I think I was more scared of *him* than he was of *me.* I stepped out of the bushes and just stood there, but it was enough to make Samson charge the other way — straight for the elephant. The elephant panicked, pulled its chain free, and ran for the nearest hiding place. Which happened to be right through the front doors of the high school.

"When I saw the first flames inside the windows I wanted to die. I was still just standing there in shock when the first people ran up from the stadium. I joined in. No one ever wondered why I was already there. No one asked what a student from Bigelow was doing lurking right outside Mossy Creek High when the fire started that night. Because I was a good guy who would never have risked hurting anyone or deliberately setting a fire. Because I was John Bigelow. Because I was crying as I helped fight the fire.

"And no one thought a Bigelow could cry if he was guilty. Only if he was caught."

John cleared his throat then took a moment to swallow hard and wipe a hand over his eyes. He wasn't the only one. Half the crowd was in tears, and the other half weren't sure whether they were mad or just grateful to finally know the truth. "Last winter, when the Ten-Cent Gypsy showed up in Mossy Creek, I knew someone was determined to find the truth, and I decided I had to help expose that truth — even if it included me. I've lived with a lot of guilt for the past two decades, but I've told myself I was only doing what I was instructed to do that night, and so I convinced myself it wasn't my duty to take all the blame. So I . . . attempted to keep my cover but help the investigation." He looked down at Sandy Crane. "I sent you the anonymous note about Rose's burial place. I hired private investigators to check with small circuses all over the country for evidence that she'd been sold somewhere. I had a feeling that she'd been disguised. I was right."

He stood silent for another long moment, clearing his throat, obviously struggling with emotion. Sue Ora and Will held hands and cried. He looked down at them with a heartbreaking return of their love. "I can't be a father and a husband," he said gruffly, "unless I'm willing to take responsibility for the fire like a man. So now I plan to walk over to the Mossy Creek jail and turn myself in," he said. "Amos? I'm sorry your father didn't get the honor of arresting me and booking me for arson, but —"

"Now just hold on, John." Ham strode up on stage, red-faced and a little antsy but very much in command. He clapped a hand on his younger cousin's shoulder the way a minister lays a healing palm on a sinner. In a way, he subtly sealed John's guilt by focusing everyone's blame on John as a pitiful sinner. "As head of the Bigelow family, and your elder cousin, I have to suggest that you're under tremendous stress and not thinking clearly. I see no need — and I'm sure these kindly Creekites, my own mother's beloved people — will agree — I see no need for a member of the Bigelow family to publicly throw himself into the arms of the law over a twenty-year-old mistake. Come down from here, Cousin John. I'll escort you and your family to my mother's house in Bigelow, and we'll get you calmed down and decide whether you've condemned yourself unfairly, and from a legal standpoint, not in an appropriate —"

"Oh, no you don't. Because we know who Nixon was."

Ham froze. The crackly little lady voice

came from the sidelines. Miss Millicent and Miss Eula Mae stood by their lawnchairs.

"I stole the mask from its owner that night," Miss Millicent added.

"I saw her," Miss Eula Mae put in. "And I saw *him*, too. Me and Millicent been sitting on what we know like hens on eggs. Now my butt hurts, and I'm tired of sitting. Tired of worrying about the trouble it'll cause to tell the truth, too. Show everybody the mask, Sandy."

"Yes, ma'am." Grinning, Sandy bounded up on the platform with a paper bag. "Your Trouble Master wore this very one," she said to John. With a flourish, she pulled out a dusty, bedraggled Nixon Halloween mask.

"Now, see here, this is a ridiculous bit of so-called evidence against some poor soul —" Ham began.

"Let's see if the gypsy fortune-teller agrees with you, Ham," Mayor Ida said. During the distraction she'd sidled up on the stage — *prowled* up, might be the better word. And so had Amos.

Silence. Five thousand people stared at the machine, at Mayor Ida, at John and Sandy and Amos and Millicent and Eula Mae and Rob and Hank and me. And at the governor, who stood there with an expression that said his eyes wouldn't quite focus and he might need one of Eula Mae's *Depends* at any second.

"Through the concerted efforts of this dedicated group of Creekites," Mayor Ida said, "we now know who was behind the plot that caused the fire. One person, and one person only, deserves to be blamed. The Trouble Master. That person's real name is on the next card in the fortune-teller's hand. Governor, would you do the honors?"

Ham twitched like someone had just plugged a high-power electrical line to his tender parts. "Mayor . . . Aunt Ida . . . I certainly want to *expose* this criminal as much as any of you, but as a servant of the people and a servant of the *laws* of the people, I have to say we can't risk vigilante justice. Americans —" he intoned loudly and dramatically — "are innocent until proven guilty."

"Proving his guilt shouldn't be a problem," Mayor Ida said, smiling. "We have amassed considerable other evidence, Governor." Ham's eyes went even glassier. He stared at her. She kept smiling. "But why don't you just take a look at the name on the card and then . . . well, we'll abide by your decision whether to announce that name or not. Amos? Will you start the process?"

"My pleasure," the chief said. Amos walked over, flipping a silver dime in his hand, his eyes never leaving the governor's face. If a coin flip can demonstrate cold, calm menace, Amos managed to do that. "I brought a dime from my father's coin collection," he said. "I think Battle would appreciate the symbolism of dropping his own dime on the person who burned down the high school."

Amos smiled thinly as he deposited the coin in the fortune-teller.

The machine whirred, the machine clicked, and slowly, the plastic, painted hoochie raised her damaged plastic hand with its accusing fist. A crisp white card popped out of the slot in her palm.

"Governor?" Mayor Ida said and handed the card to Ham. "Your choice."

He held the little card by his fingertips. I saw his Adam's apple bob above the white collar of his expensive shirt and the knot of his silk tie. He slowly looked down at the card. A fine tremor shivered his hands. His face turned redder than it already was. Beads of sweat broke on his forehead.

We all waited with held breath.

"The name is . . . the name is. . . ." He swayed in place, then suddenly, as if some idea suddenly rooted him to solid earth, again, he went very still. His head snapped up. He looked out over the crowd with stately indignation.

"The name is too evil to speak!" He jabbed the card inside the breast pocket of his sleek gray suit and planted his hand over it for safe-keeping. "But I promise you all, my fellow Creekites, my fellow Georgians, my fellow Americans, that justice *will* be done!"

Mayor Ida leaned close, her smile so catty and so hungry he might as well have been a small, squeaking mouse. "But how will we stand it if you don't share the name, Governor? What could you possibly say to us that will calm us down?"

"The name," people called. "The name, Governor! Tell us whose name is on the card! Tell us who was behind the burning of our school!"

Ham gulped. "Now, now, that kind of impulsive announcement would not serve justice. No, I have a *duty* to see that this matter is handled fairly and properly — and I have a *duty* to see that these festivities are not ruined by a public . . . well, a public . . ."

"Ass whupping?" Mayor Ida inserted helpfully.

"A public *display* of unseemly anger."

Ham waved his free hand dramatically, never taking the other one off the card in his breast pocket. "And so I think it's time for me to take the high road —"

"That road's blocked," Amos put in dryly. "And so's your limo."

"The positive road, that is," Ham went on, his eyes shifting wildly, "meaning I'm offering a message of unity and forgiveness and forward-thinking progress and traditional peacemaking and —" his voice rising, he clutched at thin air in a gesture so filled with Shakespearean drama that down in the crowd, Anna Rose and Beau turned to each other and whispered *Macbeth*, "— And so, my fellow Creekites, my good, fair, forgiving Creekites, I am here to announce that on this very site, next spring, *Mossy Creek High School will rise from the ashes! You're getting a new high school!*"

The collective gasp that went up from five thousand people nearly sucked Ham off the stage. A new high school. We were going to have our own high school in Mossy Creek, again. People began cheering. Cheering and whooping and applauding and hugging one another. John Bigelow stared at his cousin with something hard I can't describe in his eyes, then turned away. Sue Ora and Will raced up on the stage and threw their arms around John.

Mayor Ida laughed and stroked Ham's shoulder in a way that said, *I let you live. This time.* She knew that some fights are won punch by punch, and on that day she'd scored a knock-out for Mossy Creek — and for her son, who bowed his head to her for the soft caress of a benediction.

In the meantime, Amos opened the gypsy's coin box, retrieved his father's dime, and pocketed it. Then he turned to Sandy, who beamed at him. "We did it, Chief."

"No, you did it. Dispatcher Crane," Amos said. "In honor of your work, you're now promoted to *Officer* Crane."

Her eyes widened. Her mouth fell open. She clutched her heart, began to cry, and then, like a little, curly-blonde boxer at the end of the first Rocky movie, she searched the crowd tearfully and began bellowing, "Jeeeesssss! Jeesss!"

As her husband galloped to the stage she whirled back to the chief and threw her arms around him. "I'm on it, Chief, I'm on it!" She buried her face in Amos's shirt and boo-hooed loudly.

Amos awkwardly patted the top of her head. "Thankyagladtobehere."

Hank, Rob, and I traded stunned looks. Then the weight from twenty years of uncertain guilt slid fully off our shoulders, and we grabbed each other in hugs.

Rob Walker held me in his arms that day, in front of his wife and his mother and his daughter and all of Mossy Creek, and though to him it was the gesture of a loving friend, to me it was a sweet, sad, but contented goodbye, as an old door closed between us, forever.

I held him tight, then let him go.

A cool autumn evening settled gently on the empty field where our high school had stood — and would stand, again. A harvest moon rose handsome and bright orange over Mount Colchik. The lights of downtown Mossy Creek winked happily in the growing darkness. A scattering of litter and the vacant speakers' platform were all that marked the scene of perhaps the greatest surprise and greatest victory in Mossy Creek history. And a victory of the heart, for me.

Sandy, Katie Bell, and I sat on the dewy grass in the shadow of the ram statue.

"What you and Rob and Hank tried to do today took real spunk, Rainey," Sandy said. "I know you've been aggravated with me over the past months — my investigation and all — but I'm here to tell you I never really thought y'all were serious suspects. I'm glad I was right."

I eyed her drolly, then leaned close to Katie Bell. "Write that down and tell everybody she apologized."

Katie Bell laughed but gave us a shrewd look. "I've got bigger fish to fry."

"What?" we asked in unison.

"We know whose name was on that card. We *know.* Any doubts?" Sandy and I grimly shook our heads. Katie Bell smiled wickedly. "Did you notice Dwight Truman staring up at the governor with his mouth hanging open?"

We chortled.

"Like a trout who's just been hooked."

"Like somebody goosed him with a cattle prod."

"Like his whole life just flashed before his eyes — with Ham in his place at the White House."

"Dwight *had* to be standing there remembering how he lost the state senate seat to Ham twenty years ago and *why* he lost and how *convenient* it was for all hell to break loose at homecoming the year that he, Dwight, was in charge of the ram, *only a few weeks before the election.* It all adds up, doesn't it?"

"One thing's for sure," Katie Bell said,

nodding for emphasis. "Dwight's not going to be Ham's Creekite 'yes man' any more. Not that Dwight will level any accusations at Ham. Because Dwight wants our school rebuilt as much as anybody."

"Maybe there's some hope for Dwight, yet."

"Maybe there's some hope for us all," Katie Bell amended. "This whole town, I mean. Getting our school back. Forgetting the past. Moving forward."

"Nope. Ain't going no where," Sandy chimed.

"And don't want to," I added.

We all chuckled.

The moon rose higher, the breeze sweetened with the pleasure of memories that had been restored to their original shine, and when we squinted just right, a moonlit ghost of the old school shimmered in the field, like a new promise.

Good night, Mossy Creek.

From: Katie Bell
To: Lady Victoria Salter Stanhope

Dear Vick:

So that's the story of the reunion. The governor promised to rebuild Mossy Creek High School, then left town as fast as his unblocked limo could take him. Ida admitted she sent the Ten-Cent Gypsy to town to scare the truth out of everyone with a guilty conscience. She says we'll put the gypsy on display and charge tourists to try their luck. The money will go towards buying a new truck for the volunteer fire department. We're not taking any chances with fires at the new school. We've decided the next ram who's appointed mascot will have his wool sprayed with flame repellant.

To recap the big reunion surprises: The Fang and Claw Society was held up to public ridicule once and for all. Rainey, Rob and Hank tried to confess to the prank that caused the fire, but John Bigelow stepped in and said it wasn't them, but him. Then Eula Mae Whit and Millicent Hart announced the real culprit was Richard Nixon. As a reporter, I'm sworn to tell the truth, but sometimes the truth is stranger than fiction. Aren't you glad I'm not making any of this up?

In other news: Everyone is happy that Beau Belmont and Ed Brady, Junior, have returned to Mossy Creek for good. Sue Ora and John are holding hands in public, and Ida and Del — well, who knows about those two? Del's a military man who says he's retired, but you know how that kind of man wanders, and Ida is a frisky babe with a young police chief who just naturally draws her attention . . . but I better stop right there if I don't want to be plucking buckshot out of my reporter's notepad. Let's just say I'm going to keep a close watch on Ida and Amos.

From what my sources tell me, we can expect at least two weddings in the near future — Josie and her Bigfoot, and Anna Rose and Beau. I understand the Mossy Creek Garden Club has decided that Peggy's poison garden is the perfect setting for both weddings. Millicent Hart has booked the garden for Maggie and Tag's nuptials, even though they're not even engaged. Millicent likes to plan ahead. And so do I.

See, Sue Ora has promoted me to assistant editor of the *Gazette.* I'm thinking that I'll give myself a little more column space now, so I can run more surveys and publish more titillating Creekite answers. I believe I'll start next spring with an innocent-sounding survey to collect Creekites' thoughts on something less threatening than reunions. *Friendship* sounds like a nice, tame subject, doesn't it? *Who is your best friend in Mossy Creek, and why?* Yes. Such a pleasant subject. Such a . . . boring one.

Okay, I've got a better idea: *Who's your best friend, and what's the biggest secret you can never tell about the two of you?*

Yes!

Watch out, Creekites, here I come.

That'll do until I win the Pulitzer.

Love to you and yours until next time, Vick. Remember, keep your toes in Mossy Creek and just go with the flow.

Katie Bell

ROSE

NOT AN EPILOGUE, BUT RATHER AN "ELEPHANT-LOGUE"

What do reunions mean to you?

Work, work, work, work, work. Any time humans got together in large numbers, I was taken away from my nice bed of hay and dressed up like a circus pony. I was gawked at, rode on, poked and prodded — all for their amusement.

When you look at the empty spot where Mossy Creek High School stood, what person comes to mind, and why?

How could just one person come to mind? There were thousands, weren't there? And all of them were hunting for me in the woods around Mossy Creek like the villagers in a Frankenstein movie. That night was a blur of panic and mayhem and the scent of my singed hair. Yes, elephants have some hair. The fire changed my life forever. Before, I had plenty of peanuts and a nice warm trailer between gigs. Afterward, just the thought of crowds of people sent me into such a panic I couldn't work for months. No one likes it when an elephant gets jittery.

What is the most hurtful and publicly humiliating thing that ever happened to you in high school?

Setting a high school on fire is the only thing that's happened to me in a high school. I don't know how it happened, exactly, but there was an awful lot of crashing and obnoxious smells in something called a chemistry lab. I could have been hurt, but did anyone think about that? No. No one *ever* worries about the *elephant's* feelings.

What is the one thing that happened to you in high school that made you the person you are today?

First of all, let me say that I'm not a person . . . and I don't want to be. As for what happened that made me the *elephant* I am today, see the answer to the second question, above.

Besides, I'm dead.

On that note, I have to also say I'm glad the mystery is resolved, so I can rest in peace up in Memphis. I heard the Creekites are going to put a plaque by the front doors of the new high school, in my honor.

No Elephants Beyond This Point.
Fine by me.

■ ■ ■ ■

Reunion Day Recipes

COURTESY OF
THE BUBBA RICE CATERING COMPANY

■ ■ ■ ■

BUBBA RICE'S 'BUBBA RICE'

A Southern guy's version of fried rice.

Ingredients:
1 1/3 cups white rice
2 eggs
6 slices of bacon
2 boneless, skinless chicken breasts
1/2 cup celery, chopped
1/2 cup green pepper, chopped
1/2 cup green onions, chopped
Soy sauce
1 tbsp butter
4 tbsp extra virgin oil

Prepare the rice according to the maker's directions, should yield about 4 cups of rice. Fry the bacon, drain, and crumble. Brown the chicken breasts in 2 tbsp of olive oil and cut into small cubes (approx. 1/2 inch pcs.). Scramble the eggs in 1 tbsp of butter and chop.

Heat the remaining olive oil in a large griddle or electric skillet at about 425 degrees. On one side, add the celery, green pepper and green onions and sauté for about 3 minutes, then add the eggs, bacon, diced chicken. On the other side of the griddle, add the rice. Using a mixing method similar to tossing a salad, combine all the ingredients quickly to keep the rice from sticking. Add soy sauce to taste. In about 5 minutes, you've got Bubba Rice.

Serves 4–6

BUBBA'S CHOCOLATE CHIP COOKIES

Ingredients:
2 1/4 cups all-purpose flour
1 tsp salt
1 tsp baking soda
16 oz. semi-sweet chocolate chips
1 cup butter, softened
3/4 cup sugar
3/4 cup + 2 tbsp brown sugar
1 tsp real vanilla extract
2 eggs

Pre-heat oven to 350 degrees. Sift the flour, salt, and baking soda together and set aside. In a large mixing bowl, add the butter, sugars, and vanilla extract, and beat until smooth. Add the eggs and beat again until smooth. Add in about 1/2 of the flour mix and beat, then add the rest of the flour and finish beating until completely blended and smooth. One of the secrets to this recipe is a very smooth mixture; unblended clumps of brown sugar or flour are a *bad* thing. Once this is done, remove about 2 tbsp into a small bowl and deliver along with a glass of cold milk to your "salmonella-be-damned, I want cookie dough" significant other. Then, using a large spoon, stir in the chocolate chips. Put teaspoon-sized lumps of dough onto an ungreased cookie sheet and bake until the tops start to turn golden brown, approx. 10 minutes. Makes about 4 dozen.

POTATO SALAD
FOR FOLKS WHO DON'T LIKE
POTATO SALAD

Ingredients:
Red potatoes
Eggs
Yellow mustard
Mayonnaise
Salt
Pepper

OK, here's the deal . . . use 2 eggs for every pound of potatoes. For a large group, I usually use 5 pounds of potatoes and 10 eggs. Peel and dice the potatoes (try for 1/2 - 1 inch cubes, mix it up, uniformity is boring). Boil until fork tender and drain. Hard boil the eggs and remove the shells. In a large bowl, use a potato masher to crumble the eggs as finely as possible. Add mayonnaise and mustard in an even mix, one tbsp at a time, blending with the eggs. Usually, 2 tbsp each per one pound of potatoes will give the right consistency. Add salt and pepper to taste and blend. When the potatoes have completely drained, stir them into the mix until evenly coated.

DEVILED EGGS

A very simple crowd pleaser. It's another recipe that is definitely *not* an exact science. It's one of those "until it looks right" things.

Ingredients:
Eggs
Mayonnaise
Olives (1 per egg), finely chopped
Salt
Pepper

Hard boil the eggs, allow to cool slightly, then remove the shells. Cut the eggs in half (length-wise . . . yes, some people *do* have to be told), remove the yolks and put them in a mixing bowl. Use a potato masher to mash the egg yolks as finely as possible, then start to add mayonnaise, one tbsp. at a time, and blend. You're looking for paste-like consistency. About 1/2 tbsp. per egg seems to be a good starting point. Once you have the right consistency, add the chopped olives. Salt and pepper to taste. Fill the egg halves with the mixture and refrigerate.

AUNTIE'S BEEF STEW

I got this recipe from my great aunt. Of course, she NEVER measured anything, "unless add until it looks right" counts as measuring. A warning, this thing takes time (minimum 3 hours cooking time, but 4 is better). Don't cut corners by using any canned/frozen vegetables. The flavor just won't be the same.

Ingredients:
2–2 1/2 pound roast. Use either a chuck roast or a rump roast.
4 cups of diced potatoes (about 1/2 inch)
2 cups chopped celery
2 cups sliced carrots
1 large onion, diced (about 1 inch)
4 cloves garlic, finely chopped
3 tbsp canola oil
1 1/2 cup water
1 tsp. salt
1 tsp. pepper

Start by searing the roast. In a large stock-pot over medium high heat, heat the canola oil and then sear the roast about 2 minutes per side. Add the garlic, cover and lower the heat to a simmer. Cook the roast for 2 hours, turning it once. After 2 hours, the roast should be tender enough to shred in the pot with a fork. Be sure to remove any large pieces of fat that remain.

Add the remaining ingredients, stirring thoroughly. Add salt & pepper. Raise the heat to bring to a low boil, then cover and lower the heat to simmer again. Simmer for 1 hour, stir at least once every 20 minutes. Check the "gravy" at about 45 minutes. If it appears too thin or watery (you'll get a lot of moisture out of the celery and onions), here's a trick that I learned from that "Bam!!!" guy on TV . . . remove about 2 cups of the stew (be sure to get a little of all the ingredients), put it in a blender or food processor, and puree it. Stir it back in to the stew.

Serves 4–6

THE VOICES OF REUNION AT MOSSY CREEK (THE MOSSY CREEK STORYTELLING CLUB)

Amos Royden and Win Allen — Debra Dixon

Ed Brady, Sr., Ed Brady, Jr. and Katie Bell — Sandra Chastain

Jasmine Beleau — Virginia Ellis

Josie McClure — Martha Shields

Maggie Hart and Anna Rose Lavender — Nancy Knight

Rainey Ann Cecil, Ida Walker, and Sandy Crane — Deborah Smith

Orville Simple — Sharon Sala

Eula Mae Whit — Carmen Green

Peggy Caldwell and Louise Sawyer — Carolyn McSparren

Tammy Jo Bigelow — Dee Sterling

The employees of Thorndike Press hope you have enjoyed this Large Print book. All our Thorndike and Wheeler Large Print titles are designed for easy reading, and all our books are made to last. Other Thorndike Press Large Print books are available at your library, through selected bookstores, or directly from us.

For information about titles, please call:
    (800) 223-1244

or visit our Web site at:
    www.gale.com/thorndike
    www.gale.com/wheeler

To share your comments, please write:
    Publisher
    Thorndike Press
    295 Kennedy Memorial Drive
    Waterville, ME 04901